Conscript's C

Conscript's Call

Book 1 in the Rifleman Series

By

Griff Hosker

Conscript's Call

Published by Griff Hosker 2025
Copyright ©Griff Hosker

The author has asserted their moral right under the Copyright, Designs and Patents Act, 1988, to be identified as the author of this work.
All Rights reserved. No part of this publication may be reproduced, copied, stored in a retrieval system, or transmitted, in any form or by any means, without the prior written consent of the copyright holder, nor be otherwise circulated in any form of binding or cover other than that in which it is published and without a similar condition being imposed on the subsequent purchaser.

A CIP catalogue record for this title is available from the British Library.

No generative artificial intelligence (AI) was used in the writing of this work. The author expressly prohibits any entity from using this publication for purposes of training AI technologies to generate text, including without limitation technologies that are capable of generating works in the same style or genre as this publication. The author reserves all rights to license use of this work for generative AI training and development of machine learning language models.

Dedication

To one of my oldest friends who fought a long fight against cancer but died this year. I shall miss you, Pam. You had a warrior's spirit and you always had my back. True friends are hard to find and you were mine for 52 years.

Conscript's Call

About the Author

Griff Hosker was born in St Helens, Lancashire in 1950. A former teacher, an avid historian and a passionate writer, Griff has penned around 200 novels, which span over 2000 years of history and almost 20 million words, all meticulously researched. Walk with legendary kings, queens and generals across battlefields; picture kingdoms as they rise and fall and experience history as it comes alive. Welcome to an adventure through time with Griff.

For more information, please head over to Griff's website and sign up for his mailing list. Griff loves to engage with his readers and welcomes you to get in touch.

www.griffhosker.com
X: @HoskerGriff
Facebook: Griff Hosker at Sword Books

Thank you for reading, we hope you enjoy the journey.

Contents

Conscript's Call..i
Contents 5
Prologue 7
Chapter 1...17
Chapter 2...29
Chapter 3...41
Chapter 4...54
Chapter 5...67
Chapter 6...81
Chapter 7...92
Chapter 8..102
Chapter 9..113
Chapter 10...125
Chapter 11...141
Chapter 12...153
Chapter 13...164
Chapter 14...174
Chapter 15...188
Chapter 16...201
Chapter 17...212
Chapter 18...224
Chapter 19...238
Epilogue 252
Glossary 254
Historical Note 255
Other books by Griff Hosker 258

The section

Corporal Jack Williams
Private Geoff Vane
Private Wally Salter
Private Ray Jennings
Private John Sharratt
Private Harry Cunningham
Private Bert Dixon
Private Dave Proud
Private Norman Thomas
Private Roland Poulter
Private Sandy Brown
Private Charlie Topp
Private Steve Smith
Private Fred Pratt

Prologue

My name is John Sharratt and what you are reading is the story of my life in the Second World War. It is little different from thousands of others who fought in that Second World War. Perhaps the only remarkable thing about it is that it is written at all for it tells you that I survived. Of course survival does not mean I did so without any hurts but that will come later. My story begins before the war began. Growing up in Northern England we all knew that war would come. We lived close enough to Liverpool to be kept up to date with the wider world. The knowledge that war was imminent however, came from within our home and little community. My father, Jack, had been a soldier in the Great War and although he knew that wars did not always solve things and that it was the, as he put it, '*poor bloody infantryman who carries the can in the end*', he believed that Neville Chamberlain's appeasement policy would not work either. He also hated the Germans with a passion. Some of his friends had been gassed and died a most horrible death. Such men never forgot nor did they forgive. His friends who had survived the war concurred with his views.

Even though we knew that war was coming we just carried on with our lives. What else could we do? Life was hard enough without sitting at night and fretting about what might happen. There were six of us in our family: my mother was Alice. She was related, in the dim and distant past, to the Blundells who were the landowners in Ince Blundell, which was the village where we lived. That vague connection did us little good. We farmed a smallholding squatting on a marshy piece of land. The nearest neighbour was a hundred yards away. Most of the land hereabouts was either riven with streams and bogs or sandy. We were just over a mile from the sea and the dunes. We raised vegetables that we sold at Ormskirk market. Any that were not sold we ate. Our diet consisted largely of what we grew and augmented by the animals that I hunted. I should say poached for we were not supposed to hunt without the permission of the Blundell family. The rabbits I shot were, perhaps, legal. I would

Conscript's Call

trek over the dunes beyond Hightown, and I could normally bag a few bunnies. The dunes, it seemed, belonged to no one, although in the pub someone said that the foreshore belonged to the crown. It may have been that I was poaching from the king. My sisters, Sarah and Kath, along with my younger brother, Tom, would go cockling on the beaches when the tide went out. We had a varied diet but none of us were what you might call well fleshed. We lived a life that was as far removed from that of our distant relatives, the Blundells, as was possible. It was little different from the others in the village. The difference between us was that while we ate similar food and lived in homes that had much in common, generally others had coins in their pockets and we had few.

The gun I used to hunt was not a shotgun but the Lee Enfield my father had brought back from the war. He should not have had one, that was clear, but he had always been a resourceful man and we had the rifle. The ammunition he took from the Territorial Force he had been in after he left the army. That unit became the Territorial Army. We still had clips of bullets but we used them sparingly. The limited supply of ammunition meant I learned to be accurate for I could not be profligate with bullets. My dad taught me to shoot and I had a good eye. His eyesight worsened after the war. He blamed the gas attack his platoon had endured and so I was the one who went hunting. To minimise the risk of being caught I learned to wrap an old piece of cloth around the end of the barrel. It dampened the noise and hid the flash. I became better as a hunter when we had a bad late frost that killed the young plants we had just transplanted.

I remember the day I was sent, not to see what I could get, but told that I had to get something and bring it back to feed the family. I would have to find food for the family for at least three weeks. By then we might have been able to grow more. I went out at night. I darkened my face and my hands and passed through the herbs mother grew close to the house. Brushing against my clothes they would disguise my smell. I had discovered how to spot the signs of rabbits and I knew that there was a warren in the pine forests that lay between the dunes and the farmland. I would lie in the forest and be hidden by the trees and the undergrowth. There I would see the rabbits as they came

Conscript's Call

to forage on the land that bordered Old Joe's. I gauged the wind and approached it so that the air was in my face. Then I moved watching each step as I did so. The closer I came to the entrance, I stepped so slowly that I barely moved. Such was my gait that an owl swooped not far from my head to take a mouse. I was part of the forest and unseen by the other hunters. It was a good one hundred paces from my encounter with the owl that I saw the single sentry bunny and I lay down very slowly. I tried to do so imperceptibly. I picked somewhere close enough to see them but where I would be hidden by the undergrowth. I pulled my dad's cape from the war over me. I was patient. I had to be. This time I would not just take a single rabbit. I needed to take as many as I could. This would be my best chance and I let them leave the warren and wander to graze. I chambered a round and sighted the sentry. Eventually the sentry became satisfied that the owl had gone and the rest of the rabbits appeared. I was patient and waited. There were twenty of them. Some were too young to shoot. I wanted the bigger ones. We would stew the meat and that would tenderise even old animals. The animals began to spread out. I aimed at the one closest to the main entrance. I wanted to panic the others. I would have more chance of success if they tried to crowd through the main entrance. I took a deep breath. I had not just identified the first one I would shoot but the others. I fired and reloaded, fired and reloaded. I moved steadily down the line. I was aiming for the head for not only would that kill the animal quickly it would also ensure that little of the meat was damaged. I stopped firing when the movement ceased. I looked at the entrance and five rabbits lay there. I rose and went to examine my bag. I had killed five and only one of them was not a head shot. I was pleased. I put them in my dad's old pack and headed home. Old Joe, one of my dad's friends, lived the closest to where I had hunted. He would say nothing even though he knew it would be me who hunted. He was an old soldier and even a muffled Lee Enfield would be recognised. Those in the manor house might have heard the sounds and thought that it was a poacher and the next night or two would see the gamekeeper more vigilant. He would seek me in vain. I would stay at home for a couple of days before finding a different warren. I became a skilled hunter who was both still and watchful. I did not know I was preparing myself for a future life. I managed to shoot enough animals to keep us fed during the time we waited for new crops to grow. I had to cut down my hunting for we were running out of bullets. One thing my hunting did was to teach me not to waste ammunition.

I remember when the Prime Minister came back from Munich and I was sat with my dad and the other veterans in the bar of the Weld Blundell public house. I was too young to drink but the constable who patrolled our village did not work on Sundays and besides, there was a tacit agreement that so long as those like me who were too young to drink did not abuse the privilege, then a blind eye would be turned. I only ever had a pint of best mild. I enjoyed the dominoes and the banter as the four men from the village who had survived the nightmare of the trenches drank and gambled for pennies. It was as they talked that I learned about war. It was not about shooting and fighting for survival but how they had existed in the trenches. I learned how they made the food more palatable. Things like bully beef, corned beef cooked with water and whatever was to hand, could seem like the finest food cooked in an expensive restaurant. They made it clear that simply existing was their main aim but it always came back to the Germans and the threat that they represented.

"It will never work, appeasing the Boche." My father's views were well known. He hated the Germans and when they had begun to rearm had warned everyone who would listen that it might lead to war.

"You are right but do you want to send lads like my Peter to fight in trenches?"

My father shook his head as he put double nine on the table, "Different war these days, Harry. We have tanks and aeroplanes. Remember those tanks we saw at Cambrai? They crossed trenches as though they weren't even there and the ones they have these days are even better. When the war comes it will be over quicker."

"Aye, Jack, but in April they passed the conscription bill." The quiet one, Old Joe, the one who had never married and lived alone nodded over to me, "Lads like John here could still be called up. I have no family but I wouldn't want lads like John to

Conscript's Call

have to fight for the Belgians, like we did. Mark my words that is what it will come to."

The others looked at me and I found myself squirming under the scrutiny.

My dad said, "Are you going, John, or are you knocking?" I put a nine and one down. My father studied the dominoes as though they were the most important thing in the world, "If he is called up then he will go. My family have always fought for England and this Hitler needs putting in his place. He wants an Empire."

The conversation then drifted on to the ambitions of the new enemy, the Third Reich. Having fought in the Somme they had an idea of the geography of the land and the nature of the people. They were scornful of the ability of the French and Belgians to stop the Germans. My father hated the Germans but he knew that they were good soldiers. I was still wondering if I would be called up. I was not yet eighteen and so it couldn't happen yet but it might. I thought I might like the army. If they let me shoot a rifle and put money in my pockets then I would be happy. The only money I had was from the rabbit skins. I was also skilled at skinning and cleaning them before taking them to Ormskirk market to sell. They ended up being made into coats that purported to be expensive fur, bought by gullible women who wanted to emulate the stars they saw at the cinema. I rarely had even half a crown in my pocket. It was another reason I didn't smoke. Most of the other lads in the village did. They liked to look like tough men. I could not afford it despite how cheap Woodbines were. My one pint a week was a pleasure for me and a reward from my father for my hard work. I worked, as we all did, for the family and without pay.

The other young men in the village all worked on the estate of Lord Blundell. The cottages in the village belonged to the Blundell family and were tied cottages. The young men were not paid well but they were paid and regularly. Some of them even went into Liverpool on Saturday night and enjoyed the dances and cinema there. That was where they saw, on the screen, cowboys and gangsters. Saturday night always saw me cleaning the rifle and dreaming of a better life and wondering at a normal life like the others.

November 1940

The letter that told me I was conscripted arrived one Wednesday morning. We rarely had letters and I had never had one. My mum and dad stood nearby as I opened it. I think Dad knew what it contained but Mum did not. To her it was just a plain brown envelope.

I read it and then handed it to my dad. He read it aloud for the benefit of my three siblings, "John Sharratt is to present himself at Seaforth Barracks on the 10th of November 1940." My dad frowned and looked at the calendar. "That is four days from now." He looked at the date on the letter and shook his head. "This has been sat on some desk waiting to be sent."

Mum's eyes welled up, "You are too young! This is a mistake."

My dad handed the letter back to me and then put his arm around Mum's shoulders, "Now then, Alice, you know as well as I do that conscription means he has to go. He is a good lad and has a sound head on his shoulders. He will do alright."

I clutched the letter and said, "What will I need to take?" We were ordinary people and when an official letter came we obeyed its commands. It was as though I was to leave immediately.

Dad smiled, "Nowt, Son. The army will give you everything you need. Anybody who turns up with a suitcase will have to work out what to do with it afterwards. Don't worry, there will be training first and lots of marching. We have already lost the Low Countries and France. It will take time to build up the army until it is ready to take on the Boche." He shook his head, "I knew that Maginot line would not hold the Germans. We lost a lot of good lads at Dunkirk and for no good reason. Thank God the RAF stopped the Luftwaffe."

I was excited and disappointed too. I had seen a girl in Hightown the last time I had returned from market. She had worn lipstick and smiled at me. I had never spoken a word to her but I hoped that I would have my first kiss with this unnamed girl. I had planned on finding a way to meet her and ask her for a date. I had two shillings and sixpence I had saved up and I wanted to take her to the dance they held at the Locarno in Liverpool. It cost eight pence to go in and I thought I would

Conscript's Call

impress her by offering to buy her ticket and pay for the train ride from Hightown to Bootle.

I had just a few days and so that night I dressed as smartly as my limited wardrobe would allow. I put on my decent trousers, shirt and tie. I polished my shoes and donned my only jacket. I said, "I think I will go and see some of the lads for a pint."

My dad grinned, "Aye, you are the first to be called up. They won't be far behind you."

It was a lie, of course, I planned on going to Hightown and watching for her. I would wait close to where the young people gathered. Once I spotted her I would casually walk by and smile at her. When she smiled back…I had not worked out the rest but as with my hunting expeditions, often improvisation gave an answer. I was confident that if she did smile at me I would know what to do and say.

As I walked down the country lane that led, eventually, to Hightown, I worked out a story that I might use. I had my dad's old army greatcoat. It was warm and I could use it to make an improvised seat if I managed to find this unnamed girl and somehow find a way to talk to her. Even as I began to work out what to say I found myself thinking about what my dad had said about training and equipment. It was all very well my dad saying there would be training. What if I was sent to serve abroad and the ship I was on torpedoed? We had heard of submarines hunting convoys. Training would not avail me at sea. The thoughts brought me back to the girl with the red lipstick. I wanted to kiss her before I died.

I could just see the shadows of the houses in Hightown when I heard the sound of aeroplane engines in the dark skies. I looked up and saw ominous winged shadows above me. What were the RAF doing over the sand dunes? I made out the shapes as they turned and headed down the coast. When the guns around the docks began to open up I knew that they were not the RAF but the Luftwaffe. The flashes of the anti-aircraft shells exploding confirmed that they were Germans. I saw the black crosses on the side of the aeroplanes. When the bombs exploded the sound reached me after I saw the flashes as bombs struck the ground. Liverpool was being bombed. We had heard that London had been attacked but Liverpool! It was not that far away from our home but we had always thought that we were safe here. Suddenly the kiss seemed irrelevant. I turned and headed back to my home. It was then I heard the sound of a single aeroplane. The engines seemed to be labouring and I saw it in the skies ahead, lit by the flashes from the south. It was lower than the others had been. I saw something fall from it and then it rose as it managed to climb higher and head east. The explosions I saw and heard were much closer. My ears hurt from the sound and the wall of flame that rose in the sky seemed close enough to touch. It was then I realised where the bombs had fallen. It was our farm. I ran.

By the time I reached it the fires were still burning but there was a hole where our farm had been. I saw Peter, Bill and Joe there with other men from the village. They were hurling buckets of water onto the flames. It was like spitting in the wind. The fire had consumed everything. We had more wood than brick in the outbuildings and they were on fire. I ran and discarded the greatcoat when I neared them. I joined with them to make a chain to throw the water. The smoke was choking and the heat almost unbearable. More men arrived to help and someone brought a stirrup pump and a hose. They used the water from the stream to add to the buckets. It worked and within an hour the flames had died down and there was just a column of smoke rising in the dark.

The constable, without his uniform, had arrived. He said, when I tried to run to find my family, "Hold on, young John. Let me have a look first." He gave me a sad smile, "It is my job. If anyone is going to get hurt it should be me."

Bill and Joe held me so that I was forced to obey. The women who had come to help were quietly crying. They knew what I knew, what we all knew, that my family were dead every one of them. I was hoping that they were not. In my mind I created stories that would explain why they were not in the house. They had heard the bombers and run from the house. They had decided to visit a neighbour. Mum and Dad had gone to the pub. Every one of the ideas seemed plausible for a heartbeat and then I knew they were fantasies. If they had been outside the house we would have found them. The neighbours were all outside. Mum never went to a pub and would not dream of leaving my

Conscript's Call

three siblings alone. They had been in the house. If it had been Sunday lunchtime then my dad would have been in the pub. He would never be out at night in the middle of the week.

The constable had a torch and I saw its weak beam as he searched the rubble that had been our home. It had never been a palace but it had been comfortable and we had been happy there. I had enjoyed a room with my brother, Tom, and I knew that others, in the village, had up to six in a room. We might not have had money but we had space and now we had nothing. I had nothing. I had just the clothes I wore.

When Constable Wilson headed back to us his face told us the news before he uttered a word. I felt Bill and Joe put their arms around my back as we waited, like men waiting for a judge to pass sentence, "They are all dead, John." He made his voice as gentle as he could.

"All of them?" I knew in my heart that none had survived but I wanted one to be alive. I did not want to be alone.

"If it is any consolation I don't think they knew anything. They were all sat in the living room. I think they were listening to the radio."

Bill said, "Lucky you weren't there with them, John."

"All dead? Even…"

The constable nodded, "All of them." He looked at Joe, "Do you have room?"

Joe nodded. When he spoke I knew that he was on the verge of tears. "Aye, of course. John, you can stay with me until…"

The letter was still in my pocket and I took it out, "Until I have to join the army." My voice was flat. All the excitement of joining up had evaporated. Now there was nothing in my future.

Bill's wife said, "Noooooo!"

Bill said, as he put his arm around his wife, "It will be for the best. It will give the lad something to focus on."

The constable said, "I will see Lord Blundell. We will have the funeral sooner rather than later."

"Come on, son, let us get you to my house."

Joe tried to lead me away but I tore myself from his grasp. "We can't leave them there!"

Bill's voice was suddenly firm, "And we won't but this is a job for your dad's mates. We will take them to the church and keep watch until…You go with Joe." He had been my dad's best friend and had been the platoon sergeant. His voice took on the authority that had carried him through four grisly years in the Great War, "That is an order. You had best get used to obeying them."

Constable Wilson nodded, "We will do right by them."

I was numb and I let Joe take me to this cottage. My life, as I knew it, had ended. What did the future hold for me?

Chapter 1

Seaforth Barracks.

Dad had said I would not need to take anything with me. He was right but it was not by choice. I had nothing. Joe and the others had made sure I had a few bob in my pocket. They had a whip round amongst Dad's friends, the ones who had served with him in the Great War. Joe had given me a spare razor to carry in my jacket pocket and that was it. The clothes I wore were now not only my best ones but until I was given a uniform, my only ones. There was nothing else that I owned. The bomb had destroyed everything. Dad had rented the smallholding. Lord Blundell would rent the land to another. There might not even be a building there. My past might simply disappear as crops were grown or animals reared on land that would be cleared of the burnt-out building. As I approached the barracks I reflected that there was no reason ever to return to Ince Blundell. Joe had said there would always be a room for me but the village would just have memories I could do without. The army had to be my future. I had nothing else and the bombing raid had brought the war home to me. My fingers clenched into fists. I wanted revenge. I would never be able to find the airman who dropped his bombs because he thought he was going to crash. He had not intended to kill my family but he had. I would make it my mission to kill as many Germans as I could. They had started this war and I would finish it or die trying.

It was noon by the time I reached the barracks. I had until 1700 to report. Dad had told me how the army liked to use such numbers. I stood outside the gate staring at the khaki sentries standing guard. I hesitated. I was not afraid of entering for I had nothing left, except for the army, but I knew this was a moment to remember. A handful of other conscripts, clearly from somewhere that was local, all came past me. Smoking cigarettes and with flat caps cockily slanted over their heads they were full of banter. They each had a small suitcase or valise. It highlighted the fact that I was alone for I was different from them. Not only were my family gone but no one else from Ince Blundell had

Conscript's Call

been called up. We all knew that they would, eventually, but at that moment I was the solitary conscript. I could almost hear my father's voice, '*Go on, you daft bugger, stop worrying and get on wi' it.*'

I forced a smile and followed the group. They were the ones who had to endure the challenge of the corporal of the guard, who said, "Where do you think you are going?"

One of them, the cigarette hanging from the side of his mouth, said, in a broad Scouse accent, "We have been called up, pal."

The corporal smiled but it was not a pleasant smile. It looked like the sort of smile a crocodile might give. He had not liked the tone and the use of the word, '*pal*', "Where is your letter?"

The young man shrugged, "Dunno. Lost it."

I saw the anger come into the corporal's eyes. Before he could explode one of the others proffered his letter, "Here's mine." The others all followed his action.

The corporal saw me, "And you?"

I do not know why I said it but I said, "I am not with them, Corporal, but here is my letter."

The cocky young man turned and glared at me.

The corporal nodded, "Private Atkinson, take them to the office." He jabbed a finger at the cocky young man, "You, what is your name?"

"Kenny McGuire."

The corporal sniffed, "A Mick as well as a Scouser, I might have known. You go over there and wait until I can verify your identity." He grinned, "Who knows you may be a German spy." It was clear he knew that was not the case but the young man was being punished for his attitude. The look on his face as I passed confirmed my suspicions. It was a lesson. I would say '*yes sir, no sir, three bags full, sir*' to any question or order that was given.

I followed the others, just a step or two behind, as Private Atkinson led them to a temporary hut. It was made of wood and contrasted with the brick buildings of the older barracks. The private said, "Line up here. Put out those cigarettes and take off your hats." He looked at me. I was the only one not smoking and I wore no hat. My hat had been burned by the bombs. He poked his head inside and shouted, "A bunch of new conscripts, Sergeant."

A disembodied voice said, "Send them in."

"Right, in you go."

Inside there were two desks and some filing cabinets. A sergeant, sporting a fine moustache that reminded me of Lord Kitchener's, was seated behind the desk and he had a clip board which he was scrutinising. Two privates were at the other desk and they were examining us as though we each had three heads.

The sergeant looked up, "I am Sergeant Jones and my job is to see that you are who you say you are. When I call your name show me the letter you received and your identity card. When I point then go to one of the clerks who will fill out the paperwork."

He began to call out the names. He did so in alphabetical order. I worked out that Sharratt would be towards the rear and I was proved correct. There was just one youth left after me when I was called. The sergeant looked at the letter and the identity card. He looked up and studied me. He had not done so with the others. What was wrong? He nodded to the clerks. "Go over there and answer his question, son." I saw that there was just one clerk left and half of the group, like the first clerk had disappeared. The rest were waiting. I did as I was told. I was questioned and the clerk wrote down my answers. They were about religion, disease, injuries and the like. The other youth followed me and I waited while he answered the questions.

The clerk stood, "Right, let's go and get your kit then. Follow me."

Sergeant Jones said, "Hall, take the rest. Sharratt, you wait behind." The rest of the group and the clerk stared at me. Sergeant Jones barked, "Shift yourselves! There is a war on!"

As they hurried out I wondered what I had done wrong. I just wanted to fit in.

The sergeant lit a pipe and tapped the letter I had given him, "Are you Jack Sharratt's lad? I believe he lived in Ince Blundell and it is an unusual name."

"Yes, Sergeant, it is."

"And how is Jack? We served together in the last war under Sergeant Hogarth."

Conscript's Call

"Bill Hogarth lives in Ince Blundell too but my dad is dead."

I saw genuine concern on the sergeant's face, "How?"

I told him the story and he shook his head. He put his hand on my shoulder, "You poor bugger. You could have asked for a deferment you know." He reached for a piece of paper. "I will get you some compassionate leave."

I shook my head, "There is nothing outside the army for me, Sergeant Jones. I have no home and no family. If I went back to stay with old Joe…"

"Joe Walsh? He is still alive?" I heard the wonder in his voice.

"He is but if I went back to stay with him I would just dwell on what happened. It is better if I am occupied and doing something. Besides, I want to get back at the Germans."

He shook his head as he relit the pipe that had gone out, "You won't be facing Germans for a long time, son. We took a beating in the Low Countries and France. There's no getting around that. We left all our equipment at Dunkirk and we are starting from scratch."

Just then Private Atkinson came in the hut with Kenny McGuire, "Here is the last of them, Sergeant."

I saw the flash of anger on the sergeant's face. There was clearly more he wanted to say and this intrusion had stopped him. He put the pipe down, "Right, Atkinson, you run along back to the gate. You wait there, Sharratt." He sat and said to the cocky young man, "Your identity card and your letter."

He snorted, "I told the other bloke I forgot my letter. He checked and they confirmed who I was. Isn't that enough?" His voice was not respectful. It was angry and I could see the sergeant, already cross, did not like it.

I saw the sergeant redden, "I will decide if it is enough. Identity Card!" The young man handed it over, some of the cockiness already evaporating. As the sergeant wrote down the information I saw the youth studying me. I did not like his scrutiny. "Sharratt, pass me the clipboard please." The change in tone did not go unnoticed by McGuire. I picked up the clipboard and handed it to the sergeant. He asked all the same questions I had been asked. The difference was that the cocky youth answered them, somehow, a little more insolently and it was

Conscript's Call

noticed. When the sergeant had finished, he stood. I saw that he towered over the young man and he put his face close to him, "Listen to me, Sonny Jim. You have been conscripted. If not then there is no way on God's Earth that we would have had rubbish like you in the British Army. Get this clear, once you have taken the oath, you are in the army and that means when any superior says jump you ask, how high. Do I make myself clear?"

I saw the young man's hands clench into fists. I wondered what would happen if he struck the sergeant. The sergeant held his gaze. I am sure he was well aware of the threat but a thin smile appeared on his face as though he was willing the man to take a swing. McGuire nodded, "Understood," there was the slightest of pauses and then he said, "Sergeant."

"Good, now you two follow me."

I tried to keep in step with the sergeant, I am not sure why. The sergeant was marching smartly. McGuire tried to walk jauntily as another act of defiance but he found he could not keep up and he had to run. He looked ridiculous but I kept a stoic expression on my face. I think I had already annoyed my fellow conscript. We reached the quartermaster's store. Sergeant Jones said, "The last two are here, Jim. I will wait until they have their kit and then take them to the adjutant to be sworn in."

"Righto." The quartermaster pointed a finger and said, "When you have your kit put it on the floor and go next door." He smiled, "Time for a short back and sides, eh?"

My hair had been recently cut by my mother but I saw that the others had a variety of hairstyles. They would lose their style soon and become brown, anonymous soldiers. I was happy at the thought but from what I had seen of Kenny McGuire, he would not.

I was given my battle dress, trousers, shirts, greatcoat, and underwear. I had been expecting that but then I was presented with my pack and webbing. The orderly said, "Waistbelt, bayonet frog, pouches, two, braces, two, haversack, one, trenching tool carrier, one, water bottle carrier, one, large pack, one, shoulder straps, two, support straps, two." The next orderly gave us our water bottles, trenching tools, as well as the little housewife kit. I was laden.

Conscript's Call

We were the last two to be kitted out and therefore the last two for the haircuts. I saw the shocked look on McGuire's face when he saw the savage haircuts the others had been given. We sat in the chair and I was given the fastest haircut I had ever experienced. It was mainly done with what were called dubbers. It was a closer haircut than I was used to and my ears felt cold as well as my neck.

"Right, next door and get changed. Put all your old clothes in the bags provided."

McGuire looked around the chilly and bare quartermaster's stores, "Here?"

The quartermaster had lit a cigarette and after taking a puff said, "Don't worry, son, you have nowt down there we haven't seen before."

McGuire and his fellows were not happy but I resigned myself to the indignity and did so quickly. My father had told me that was what the army did. It was like a Lee Enfield. They stripped you down and then rebuilt you.

Once in the uniform we all looked the same. We donned our field service caps. Some of the others tried to put them at a jaunty angle but Sergeant Jones jammed them on correctly. "Now follow me and keep in step. We are going to meet an officer." He said it as though we were meeting someone like Lord Blundell.

The swearing in, for me, was a serious event. The white-haired officer, clearly a man close to retirement, perhaps kept on because of the war, was slow and serious in his delivery. The Scousers, as I had come to term the others in our small group, appeared to be almost amused by the process. Sergeant Jones did not like it.

The sergeant's anger manifested itself once we were outside the office. The wind was blowing and it was freezing. We wore just our Battle Dress blouses and trousers. The greatcoats were still rolled in our packs at our feet. Sergeant Jones seemed oblivious to the cold. "Attention!" The sergeant strode along the line glowering at each man as he passed. I was at the end. "That was a shambles for," he reached me, "most of you. Private Hall, go and find Company Sergeant Major Hutton."

Conscript's Call

"Sarge." He hurried off. Private Hall would be briefly warm when he found the sergeant major and then he would have to endure the Atlantic chill of the parade ground once more.

I noticed then that Sergeant Jones had a swagger stick and he was slapping it rhythmically into his left palm. "You are all in the army now and that means orders and discipline. You do not smile when in the presence of an officer and the swearing of an oath to the king is not a joke." He shook his head and looked McGuire up and down, "When I think of the good chaps we left on the beaches in Dunkirk..." he glanced at me, "and the ones who died in the trenches in the Great War...and you shower are the ones supposed to save England again. We might as well run the white flag up now."

I heard boots marching across the parade ground. I did not turn but a couple of the Scousers did and it gave Sergeant Jones the chance to snap, "Eyes front!" and give the two men a sharp rap from his swagger stick.

Private Hall, a sergeant major, and another sergeant hove into view. I studied the men and saw the differences in rank. I knew it would be important to know to whom I was speaking and give them the correct title. The three sergeants conferred while Private Hall stood to attention, his expression never changing. Sergeant Jones took the clipboard from Hall and gave it to the other sergeant. When the two new sergeants had studied the list and Sergeant Jones had jabbed his finger now and then at the list they all turned. Sergeant Jones saluted and said, "Right, Private Hall, time for us to get back to work."

The two of them left us and silence reigned. I say silence but the empty parade ground appeared to act as a sort of echoing chamber for the wind which started to howl a little. The wailing noise seemed to make it colder. I could hear one of the others as his teeth chattered. The sergeant major and the sergeant said nothing. They were studying each of us. They walked to my end of the line and the two of them looked at me and the list, "Sharratt."

"Yes, Sergeant Major."

He raised his voice. I assumed it was for the benefit of the others in the line, "I am Company Sergeant Major Hutton of B Company the 2nd Queen's Rifles and this is Sergeant Jackson who is your platoon sergeant." I did not know what the response should be and I kept silent. "From what Sergeant Jones has told us you are the only one from this batch who seems to have what it takes to make a soldier." He leaned in, "Don't worry, son, the rest of the intake are more like you and not this shower." They moved to the next man, "Private Millican."

"Yes, Sergeant."

"The rank is Sergeant Major."

"Yes, Sergeant Major."

He moved on. Most responded properly until he came to Private Harrison who said, "Yes, Sergeant Major. Can we get out of the cold? I am bleeding freezing."

It was the wrong thing to say. Yet he was not reprimanded, not at first. McGuire also gave a polite response.

Sergeant Jackson said, "Pick up your gear and sling it over your shoulders."

Company Sergeant Major Hutton said, "Not you, Harrison. You and I will have a little word and then we will see if we can make your delicate little fingers a little warmer."

It was then that McGuire made another mistake, "Come on, Sergeant Major, he did nowt wrong."

"And you, McGuire, can stay with him. I have your little card marked already."

Sergeant Jackson said, "Left turn. March,"

I was at the front and I turned and marched, I had no idea where to but I knew that if I was going to survive I had to obey every order. The sergeant marched to the right of us. I found that swinging my left arm helped me to balance the bag on my right shoulder. I also noticed that the sergeant swung his left arm too while his right grasped his swagger stick.

We came to a building and at the end the sergeant said, "Left turn." I turned. One of the others must not have been paying attention for I heard the sergeant shout, "Flynn, have you two left feet? Just follow Golightly!" We marched towards a barracks building and outside a soldier was having a cigarette. When he saw us he stubbed it out and went back inside. We reached the door and the sergeant said, "Halt!" We stopped. "About face!" I turned as did most of the others. "The other way, Marsden!" The sergeant moved and stood before us, his hands and stick behind

Conscript's Call

his back. A corporal hurried out of the building, jamming his field service cap on as he did so. He scurried to the side of the sergeant and adopted the same pose. "This is Corporal Williams. He is your corporal. Do everything that he tells you and you might have the chance to become soldiers. Corporal Williams began this war as a private but showed that he can lead." The sergeant caught my eye. Was he telling me something? "That is the way forward." He turned, "Corporal."

The corporal was Welsh. I suppose his name should have given me a clue but his accent had the slight twang of Liverpool about it, "There are eight bunks inside for you. You are the last of our intake. All the rest of the platoon are conscripts and you should fit in. You have missed the lunchtime meal but the good news is you have the afternoon off."

Sergeant Jackson interrupted, "Do not waste the time. You have been given new kit. Find out what every piece is for. Corporal Williams will be on hand if you have any questions. Better to ask them now than later." He nodded to the corporal.

"Your evening meal will begin at 1700 in the Mess Hall. You will hear the bugle. Lights out at 2200." He smiled, "We do not have to stand stag yet so you will get a good night's sleep before 0500 when your training really begins." He stood to attention, "Pick up your gear and follow me."

We entered the barracks and I saw that it was packed with the other conscripts. There was a fug of smoke as most of them appeared to be smokers. The beds were mostly occupied. We followed the corporal; the sergeant came behind. I was keenly aware that we were being scrutinised by the rest of the platoon. The empty beds were identified by the fact that the bedding was folded neatly at the foot.

"Choose your own beds."

By the nature of the fact that I was at the front I naturally chose the first bed that was empty. It meant the Scousers would all occupy the next seven beds.

The corporal pointed to the bed at the end, "That is my bed."

I heard a groan from the Scousers. They would be under the eagle eye of the corporal.

I deposited my bag on the bed and saw that there was a small cabinet next to each bed. I wondered which one was mine. The

Conscript's Call

soldier lying on the next bed was reading a comic and when he saw my look he patted the one to his left, "This one is yours, chum." From his accent he came from one of the places to the east of us, Bolton, Wigan or St Helens. They were bigger than Ince Blundell and the people there tended to work in factories.

I smiled, "Thanks." Dad had often told me stories about his time in the army. He had never spoken about the fighting or the trenches but he had told me about the camaraderie of the platoon he was in. I had seen evidence of that from Sergeant Jones already and I wanted to fit in. I held out my hand, "John Sharratt from Ince Blundell."

The man smiled and held out his hand, "Walter Salter from Wigan." He shook his head, "I always get that out of the way first. My dad had a wicked sense of humour. Call me Wally."

I returned the smile with a nod, "I will, Wally. Wigan, that is where they like their pies."

He grinned, "The best pies in the world and the best Rugby League team in the Northern Union."

The man in the next bunk snorted, "Don't listen to Pie Face. That is rubbish, we all know that St Helens has the best pies and the Saints are the best team."

Wally pointed to the side of his head, "Take no notice of Glass Man. He took too many knocks to the head when he was younger."

I said, "Glass Man?"

Private Jennings nodded, "Not only does St Helens have the best pies and the best rugby league team, they also make the finest glass, Pilkington Brothers." The two were clearly friends. They bantered the way my dad's mates had done. Private Jennings stood to shake my hand, "Ray, pleased to meet you." He nodded to the others who had come in with me. "Are they mates of yours?"

I shook my head as I unpacked the newly acquired equipment, "Never saw them before today." I lowered my voice, "They all seem to be from Liverpool and know each other."

Wally shook his head, "Then it is time to lock up the silverware. Here let me help you with that. Ray and I arrived last week so I suppose that makes us old hands."

Conscript's Call

He took me through the equipment explaining the function of everything and giving me the slang for it all.

By the time McGuire and Harrison entered the barracks I had everything stowed away. The faces of the two looked blue and both of them had an angry look on their faces. Company Sergeant Major Hutton stood in the doorway.

"This platoon is now at full strength. Tomorrow you will be issued with your rifles and training will begin in earnest. Get a good night's sleep tonight because by this time tomorrow you will not know if you are coming or going." He turned and left. Sergeant Jackson followed him.

Ray said, "Do you play dominoes, John?"

I nodded, "Double nines?"

Wally snorted as he took the wooden box from his locker, "It's only southerners who play double sixes!"

I smiled. Dad and his other old comrades in arms had said much the same thing. I began to think I might fit in. As we played I was able to study some of the others. I now saw men who might be comrades in arms and with whom I would form bonds. I hoped so.

I was starving by the time we were called to the mess. I was lucky. Ray and Wally took me under their wing and I did not have to ask anything. I saw the Scousers struggling for no one from our platoon seemed keen to offer them advice. In the barracks it was as though I was some sort of invisible barrier between the seven of them and the rest of the platoon. Ray and Wally had talked to me and the Scousers conspired together. The incident with Sergeant Jones had clearly upset them and they chuntered and grumbled all afternoon as I played dominoes and won four pence.

That evening the food in the mess was bland but filling. There was plenty of bread. It was not the bread I was used to. My mum had made bread every day and I was spoiled. There was a pudding: spotted dick and custard. There was also plenty of tea so I was satisfied. Back in the barracks I found myself yawning. It had been a long day but the next one promised to be even longer. I desperately wanted to go to bed but knew that there would be too much noise and I did not want to be mocked by the Scousers. I knew that they would. Instead, I played more dominoes and ended up losing tuppence. Guided by Ray and Wally I went to the washrooms just before the rush. It ensured that we had first choice of toilets and sinks. When the corporal called for lights out I was already in the crisp white sheets and the Army Issue pyjamas. Before I went to sleep I said a silent prayer. The bombing was still a raw scar and each night since they had died I prayed for my family. I think I wanted some sign that they were in heaven. It worried me that no sign came.

Chapter 2

I woke early and I didn't, at first, know why. It took me a moment or two to realise where I was. My bladder then told me that I needed the toilet and so, grabbing my towel and wash gear I hurried to the washroom. Ray and Wally had told me to keep my wash gear close to hand and it paid off. I stood to allow my eyes to become accustomed to the dark. There was a variety of noises from the platoon, everything from gentle snuffling to snoring. There were the occasional blasts from someone breaking wind and some men mumbled in their sleep. I suppose they must have been going on all night but I had been so weary that I had not even noticed. I saw one empty bunk and when I reached the washroom saw someone having a shave already. It was a very big man. I remembered him from the night before, he had not played dominoes but lay on his bed reading a Zane Grey Western novel.

He glanced at me through the mirror, "Morning, sunshine. Do you like a bit of peace while you shave?"

I shrugged, "I just woke early." I went to the urinal and said, smiling, "But I do like it peaceful." When I had finished I went back to the sinks and filled the sink with water. I was unused to an indoor bathroom. We had a toilet in the yard and the sink we used for washing was the same one my mother had used to wash dishes in. I said, "John Sharratt, Ince Blundell."

He nodded as he scraped the last of the soap from his face, "Geoff Vane from Billinge."

I said, "Billinge Bump."

"Aye, that's right." Just then another two men came in and Geoff grinned as he wiped his face with his towel. "And now it begins."

It was at that moment that the strident notes of the bugle sounded. It was reveille. By the time I was drying my face the washroom was already full and three men were waiting for my sink. As I entered the sleeping quarters I heard Corporal Williams bellow, "Wakey, wakey, rise and shine. Hands off cocks and onto socks!"

I knew even without looking that it was McGuire and his grumblers who were still abed. I laid out my uniform and by that time the last to rise were up and stumbling towards the washroom.

McGuire jabbed a finger in my direction, "You lickspittle! I can see that you will be the teacher's pet. We have our eye on you!" He flicked his towel at my face but I managed to move back.

I had not deliberately done anything but I now had seven enemies. It seemed I was fated to have bad luck.

Wally shook his head, "Don't worry about them, John. They are all mouth and trousers. Ray and I have your back."

I turned, "Thanks, Wally, but I don't know what I have done wrong."

"You have done nowt wrong, chum. They are a bad bunch but the sergeants will sort them out."

Wally, Ray and I were dressed before the grumblers returned and we were already heading to the mess hall. While there were people already in the mess hall, the queue was not as bad as it would get later on. Anticipating a long and hard day we filled our plates. I was full by the time we left. It had been plain fare but a full belly always helped. We had time, back in the barracks, to make our beds and arrange our lockers before Corporal Williams shouted for us to parade. I learned that he was really trying to help us. The bugle sounded a few moments later but those who had heard his words were already heading out to the parade ground.

Even though it was less than twenty-four hours since I had arrived a pattern was emerging. McGuire and his gang were the last to arrive and, as the officers were all assembled and the company sergeant major was on parade, they were in for trouble.

We were addressed by Captain Whittle, the company commander. He looked to be in his thirties. Once we were at attention he addressed us all. "Now that we have our full intake this company, and the battalion will begin to train harder. Today will see not only marching drill," he smiled, "something I know you will all come to love, but also the beginning of rifle training. The rifle is the weapon that you will all need to use. There will be other weapons you will be taught to handle but baby steps, eh?" I learned that the captain had an easy manner mainly because, in civilian life, he had been a teacher and had been in the territorial army. He knew how to talk. "You may not see much of me over the next days but your officers and sergeants will be giving me constant reports." He paused and scanned the faces. "There will be rumours about postings and you may read in the newspapers of offensives. What I want you all to know is that as soon as I am told where we will be sent and when, then you will know. Until then disregard any gossip. However, what I can tell you is that there will be no leave. We may well be confined to the barracks until we are posted. Your letters will be censored by the lieutenant. What was learned in France is that the enemy uses what we might consider inconsequential information as intelligence that can be used against us. Loose lips cost lives." I had seen the poster but hearing it from the captain brought home its seriousness. "Sergeant Major."

CSM Hutton roared, "Company, Attention!"

I would say we all snapped our heels to attention at the same time. I know I did as did Ray and Wally who flanked me but the ripple of sounds that followed told me that some were tardy.

What followed was three hours of what I learned was called squad bashing. Without rifles it seemed to me easy. In the days before the bombing dad had drilled me with the Lee Enfield. Without the nine pounds of rifle I found it easy. Not everyone did. The sergeants barked at and harangued all those who failed but by the time the bugle sounded for mess we were, generally, all in step. The ones who had endured problems marching from the quartermasters to the barracks seemed to have no concept of right, left and about face.

As we headed into the mess hall, however, I heard the carping begin. There had been no opportunity to talk on the parade ground but now there was a buzz of conversation as though a swarm of bees or wasps had entered the hall. The strident, high-pitched voices of the grumblers from Liverpool were the ones I heard.

"No leave! That is a liberty. They are not allowed to do that."

The flatter vowels from further north gave an immediate answer, "You are in the army now, Scouser. We are fighting a war or hadn't you heard?"

I did not see who spoke but I saw McGuire's angry face as he turned, "We have rights, you know."

Wally shook his head, "Aye, son, and responsibilities to our country, one outweighs the other."

McGuire's eyes flicked from Ray to me and back, "I am not your son and I don't give a bugger about responsibilities."

Wally laughed, "Well, there's no surprise. I have never met a Scouser yet who had a backbone!"

The laughs from all around us told McGuire that he was in the minority. The little worm ridden part of the apple that was McGuire and his cronies huddled closer together and conspired.

As we ate Wally said, "My dad told me that there would always be a couple of bad 'uns in every regiment but we seem to have collected more than our fair share."

Ray nodded, "I think Sergeant Jackson and the CSM have their measure." We nodded our agreement.

I asked, "It doesn't bother me but why no leave?"

Ray leaned forward, "I heard a rumour that there are soldiers being sent to Greece. The Eyeties have invaded and they are allies of the Germans."

"Greece? That is a long way away. It is further than France."

"We lost France, John, remember. We now have a new Prime Minister and he is nothing like Chamberlain. He won't sit on his backside and wait for the Germans to make a move. Winston Churchill wants us to have victories."

That night I was one of the first in bed and I heard McGuire and his cronies as they talked. They were just talking about their girlfriends but I did not like their tone. They called them '*Judies*', I think it was as in Punch and Judy. My father and his mates had always treated women with respect. Since I had first met him I had disliked McGuire and his like. Now I found myself wondering if we ought to be in the same army. He and his fellows seemed as far from my family and friends as it was possible to be. How could I fight alongside someone like that? They were in direct contrast to the ones on the other side of me. When they spoke of women it was mothers, sisters and sweethearts and respect oozed from their voices.

I was excited at the prospect of using a rifle. The whole intake of new soldiers, all eighty of us, were addressed by the armourer,

Conscript's Call

Sergeant Daley. As he held up the rifle and described it I saw that it looked slightly different from the one my father had brought back from the war. For one thing the barrel protruded from the end of the fore stock a little more than the one I had used. I could see that there was also a new sight. My heart sank. I had been looking forward to showing off my prowess with the weapon and it looked as though I would be in the same boat as the others. I paid close attention to the demonstration. There were mutterings and grumblings from some of the others who were less interested.

"Right, you have seen how it works and now you need to line up at the armoury to receive your weapon." He held up his hand, "The first thing you will need to do is to clean off the grease!"

CSM Hutton made us line up in platoon and alphabetical order. Once more I was at the back but close to Wally. "When you have your weapon take it back to your barracks and clean off the grease. You have one hour to do so and then we head to the range."

By the time Wally and I reached the barracks the rest of the platoon were cleaning their weapons. Some were doing it more diligently than others. I ignored everyone. I knew how to clean the weapon and despite the fact that it was not exactly the same as the one I had used it fitted together in roughly the same way. I disassembled it as I knew I could clean it quicker and put it back together.

Wally whistled, "I hope you know how to put it back together."

I nodded and grinned, "I used to do this with the old gun. It is quite easy once you know how."

By the time I reassembled the now degreased rifle there were still others getting rid of the grease. I flicked up the ladder aperture sight. Frowning I wondered how to calibrate it. I would ask the armourer or the sergeant. I realised, as I held the stock to my shoulder, that this was heavier than the old gun. It was not much but it would make a difference. The length, despite the protruding barrel, was still the same. I examined the charger magazine. It was no longer rounded. All in all I was pleased with the weapon. I could not wait to fire it. The last thing I did was to alter the sling to make it fit over my shoulder.

Sergeant Jackson re-entered, "Right, pick up your weapons and follow me."

I saw Corporal Williams slip his rifle over his shoulder and become tail-end Charlie. We marched over to the shooting range. The armourer was there with two of his men. As each group of men arrived they had their weapons examined before they were allowed to move on. All those who had not been as diligent as they should were channelled to a hut and ordered to clean their weapons. I saw that the bulk of them were the Scousers.

The armourer nodded his approval and handed me my gun back. I asked, "Sergeant, what is the rear sight calibrated to?"

I saw his eyes widen at the question, "Three hundred yards, Private...?"

"Sharratt, Sergeant."

"Have you handled one of these before?"

I said, "Not this model, Sergeant, the short magazine Lee–Enfield Mk III."

I heard Sergeant Jackson's voice behind me, "His dad was in the Great War."

"Ah, well this is a better piece of kit, Private Sharratt. It is a little heavier but more reliable and accurate."

"Right, Sharratt, move along, you are holding up the line." The words were not barked.

Once we had all arrived and every rifle had passed inspection the method of firing was demonstrated. We would be firing from the prone position. The two armourer's assistants handed out two magazines to each of us. The armourer said, "As you may have noticed, there is a war on. Ammunition is valuable. You are not James Cagney in a movie firing at everything you see nor are you Tom Mix whose pistol never runs out of bullets. You choose your target and squeeze the trigger." That done he demonstrated the firing of the rifle. I saw that the targets were three hundred or so yards away. He hit the bull's eye every time.

Sergeant Jackson said, "Section 1."

We fired by section. Each section fired five bullets. Some failed to hit the paper target but most managed to hit the paper somewhere. I suspected that many of them had used a rifle at the travelling fun fairs. When it was my turn I was keenly aware that the sergeant and sergeant armourer were behind me. Had I not

Conscript's Call

seen the others fire I might have been intimidated but I was confident in my own ability. The new sight helped and I aimed at the bull. I was ready for the kick which was not as bad as the old gun. I waited until the smoke cleared. I had hit the target but only at the right-hand edge. I would adjust my aim. My second bullet was closer to the bull but to the lower right. I adjusted again. By the fifth bullet I was happier and it struck the bull dead centre.

"Clear!"

I realised that I was the last to finish as I stood. The armourer was smiling, "You adjusted your shooting, that was good. I think you will find it easier if you calibrate your own sight. You have a marksman here, Sergeant Jackson."

"I know. Makes up for some of the other dead wood." He said the last part a little quieter.

That evening as we ate, the platoon, or those I regarded as the good soldiers, were all discussing the day's training. Wally was impressed, "Where did you learn to shoot like that?"

I nodded to the north, "Just up the coast at the dunes near to Formby and in the trees. I used to shoot rabbits."

Ray said, "You impressed the sergeants that is for sure. Tomorrow will be interesting. We get to use the bayonets we were issued."

And so it went on. Each day we learned something new. As the week passed and then turned into a month I saw the pattern. We practised what we had learned before moving on to the next phase of training. Once we had the basic skills then Lieutenant Hargreaves, our platoon commander, joined us. We learned the formations we would use when we fought. There were commands we had to obey instantly. Although the bugle would rarely be used in battle we had to learn the signals. We were taught to fire the Bren gun and the grenade launcher. We were taught to throw the Mills Bomb. Skills were assessed and more specialist roles assigned. Harry Cunningham showed skill with the Bren gun and he got to use that. Geoff Vane was a big lad and he was given the grenade launcher. Corporal Williams told us that some companies would still be using the Boys Anti-tank rifle but he was dismissive about it. "You, Private Cunningham, can send a grenade three hundred yards. You won't be able to knock out a tank but Jerry likes to send panzer grenadiers with his tanks. You can make a mess of them." Despite his views on the weapon we were shown how to use one.

We were all keen to get to war especially when we heard of troops being sent to Africa to fight the Italians in the desert. When we were sat in the barracks we hounded the sergeant and corporal with questions.

Sergeant Jackson was a good soldier. He understood us and he gave us answers that we could understand, "You lads are doing well." He glanced over to the grumblers, "Most of you, at any rate, but if you went up against the Germans then Lieutenant Hargreaves would get writer's cramp from all the letters he would have to write to your families." He gave me a sudden glance and I saw that he regretted his words. "We have three months of training and then we will see what transpires." He clearly knew more than he was telling us.

I found that I enjoyed the life of a soldier. It was hard work but no harder than the life I had led when my family had been alive. I was well fed and had money in my pockets and I was so tired each night that I fell straight to sleep and did not have time to dwell on the loss of my family. I enjoyed the company of people like Geoff, Wally and Ray. I found the NCOs all to be good chaps in the main. They had discipline and tolerated no insolence. I liked that. The flies in the ointment were McGuire and his gang for that is what they were, an annoyance. Thanks to them the platoon had been ordered to clean the barracks because of the mess that they left. After the punishment some of the platoon, Wally and Ray included, went to have a word with them. I was sat on my bed and I heard the discussion.

"You shower made that mess and we were all punished for it. You have a simple choice, shape up or we will do something about it."

McGuire, a cigarette hanging from his lip did not move from the bed, "What, you four? Don't make me laugh."

Geoff Vane rose from his bed. He was a big man and his voice was deep and resonant. "Don't be daft, lad, they are speaking for the whole platoon." He waved an arm around the rest of the men. "If it comes to sorting out then you deal with all of us. We do not want to be punished because of a bunch of wasters like you."

Conscript's Call

The words had an effect and McGuire swung his legs from the bunk and stubbed out his cigarette. He jabbed a finger at the man from Billinge, "It's you lot who should thank us. What they are doing to us is not right. We have had no leave. We are worked too hard and they have no consideration for our rights!"

Wally laughed, "Rights? Were you dropped on the head when you were a baby, soft lad? We are in a war and if we lose it then there will be swastikas all over this land and then you will learn about rights."

McGuire then made a cardinal error. He defended the Nazis, "Some of their ideas are alright. They get rid of those who ought to be got rid of and…"

He got no further. Wally grabbed the sheet and pulled it up. McGuire crashed to the floor. "I didn't have much time for you before, sunshine, and now I have even less." He pointed a finger at the others, "And you lot…stop listening to this idiot and start thinking for yourselves."

Ray added, "Aye, and this country too. The black shirts never had any support and neither does Adolf McGuire here."

The rest of the barracks laughed. We had won but there was now a clear division in the barracks and I was on the front line. I was a friend of the three men who had challenged McGuire and my bunk was the closest to them. Even though I had said nothing I would be seen as an enemy. That night I found it harder to get to sleep but then I reflected that I had to side with my friends for they were in the right and that was what we were doing in England. We were standing up to a bully because it was the right thing to do.

It was a few days before Christmas that matters came to a head. At the gunnery practice I had managed to get five bulls. It had impressed everyone and, after we had returned to the barracks, Sergeant Jackson took me to the platoon office. "Have I done something wrong, Sergeant?"

"No, son, the lieutenant wanted to have a word that is all."

Lieutenant Hargreaves was young. I took him to be in his twenties and he had a baby face. He had adopted a David Niven moustache or perhaps he was emulating Errol Flynn, I am not sure. We had little to do with him except at parades or when he lectured. When we had done cross country I had seen that he was

37

a good runner and on our five-mile cross country runs he always stretched out before us. I was normally not far behind but that was all that I knew about him. He seemed keen and I guessed he was an officer who would lead from the front. He appeared to me to be a thoughtful officer and he was our leader.

"Well, Sharratt, you are certainly impressing the sergeants and NCOs in the platoon. They seem to think you could be in line for promotion sometime soon."

I didn't know what to say but I smiled and said, "Thank you, Sir, but I just do my job. It's how I was brought up."

I saw a shadow fall across his face, "Yes, Sergeant Jones told me about your father. This war is cruel, Sharratt." He brightened a little, "Anyway, your demonstration today and every time you have been at the range have shown us that you are the best shot. When we go to war and," he tapped the side of his nose, "that will not be far off, we will use you and your skills. The ability to be as accurate as you are means that you will be the scalpel we use when we fight Jerry. When we are at the range in future you will work with Sergeant Armourer Daley. He thinks he can make you an even better shot."

"Thank you, Sir."

"Don't thank me. In this platoon we reward those who make the effort."

Sergeant Jackson said, "Cap on. About face. Quick march." Once outside he said, "Now you cut along and get ready for mess."

I nodded, "I will go and wash up first."

"Good lad."

McGuire and three others were waiting for me in the washroom. I worked out later that they had been watching me. Flynn, Golightly and Millican were his close friends. I wondered where Murphy was; he was the other one who was close to McGuire. Since Wally and Ray had spoken to them Petersen and Harrison had been less chummy with their leader. I was still basking in the praise from Lieutenant Hargreaves and only realised the danger I was in when the door to the washroom slammed behind me and was barred by Flynn's bulk.

Conscript's Call

McGuire grinned, "Now we are going to teach you a lesson. We will show you that it doesn't pay to be a teacher's pet and from now on you are going to be like us."

I knew that whatever I said I was going to get a beating and if I was going to have one then I would have my six pennorth, "What, you mean a spineless jellyfish who sponges off others? No thank you."

I had angered him and instead of having two of them hold me while he beat me and Flynn guarded the door he ran at me. I was ready and my right hand struck his solar plexus so hard that he dropped to his knees, his tobacco-soaked lungs searching for air. Golightly and Millican came in swinging their arms at me and I simply stepped back so that they hit each other. I punched Millican hard in the ribs with my left hand and managed an uppercut to Golightly. When Flynn's gorilla like arms enfolded me then I knew I was going to have to endure a beating. McGuire could not even get enough breath to tell them what to do and when Golightly, his lips bleeding, swung his arm at my stomach, I was ready and tensed the muscle. As he stepped back to take another punch I used the gorilla to my advantage. I pushed back with my feet and he had to step away to keep his balance. As he did so and as he was still holding me, I brought both of my legs up and kicked Millican in the face. Flynn overbalanced and we landed so heavily that the breath was driven from him and he lost his grip. I stood and made the mistake of heading for the door. I pulled it open and then saw stars as Golightly hit me in the side of the head. I managed to keep my balance. Had I fallen then I would have had to endure a good kicking and standing I had a chance, albeit a slight one. I managed to get my back to the wall as the four of them, for McGuire now had his breath back, advanced on me.

McGuire pulled a flick knife from his pocket. He was still gasping for breath, "We were just going to give you a good beating but now we are going to mark your pretty little face."

Once again his actions helped me for when he advanced the other three waited, not wanting to risk being cut or perhaps risk his wrath. He lunged at me with the knife. I managed to grab it with my left hand and then I punched him hard in the ribs, twice in quick succession. Flynn's mighty mitt hit me and this time I began to black out. I felt myself sliding down the wall.

"Kill the bastard!"

The last thing I saw was the door open and then it all went black. I drifted into darkness and I wondered if this was death.

"John, are you alright?"

It was Wally's voice. "What?" I tried to open my eyes but found I could not.

"He is alright, Corp. He is alive, at least."

"Salter and Jennings, take him to the sick bay."

I was slung between their arms. Ray said, "I hope they throw the book at those four. He had a knife!" There was indignity in his voice and despite my pain I found myself smiling. In Ince Blundell there had been fights. There always were but they were settled one on one and with fists. Knives were somehow foreign.

The medical orderly who dealt with me said I might have something called concussion and I would have to spend the night in the sickbay. Wally brought my washbag and before he left he said, "You did well there, young 'un. Those four were all marked by you. You'll do."

I felt a fraud for I didn't think that there was anything wrong with me but I obeyed orders and spent the night in the sickbay.

Chapter 3

I had plenty of visitors while I was recovering. Sergeant Jackson was my most frequent one coming twice each day. He was genuinely concerned about me. He chatted to me about my life before I had joined up. I found him very easy to talk to and I think that the talks helped me not only recover but to get over the loss of my family. I spoke of life on the smallholding. He wanted to know about my dad but in telling him about my father I told him more about myself. He discovered how I had learned to shoot by hunting. I was proud of the fact that I had fed my family and stopped them from starving. He knew the pine forests I described and the warrens that were there. He seemed impressed that I had managed to acquire such a skill on my own. I also found out a little about him. The army was his life. His wife had died in childbirth a year after the Great War had ended and he had simply stayed on. I sensed regret about the death of his wife and child but he seemed to have accepted that the army offered comfort to him. I wondered if it would do the same for me.

I was not allowed to leave the sick bay until the doctor had signed me off. I had broken ribs, a black eye and I had lost a tooth but, after a few days, the doctor said I was fit to return to the ranks. As I went with the medical orderly to the Headquarters, I saw the rest of the company drilling. Captain Whittle, Lieutenant Hargreaves and CSM Hutton were all in the office waiting for me. The two officers were seated and the CSM stood. They all had solicitous looks on their faces.

Captain Whittle said, as he lit his pipe, "Well, Sharratt, we have an account of what happened from the others involved but we would like your version of events."

Fear filled my head. Was I about to be punished? I looked at CSM Hutton who smiled, "Just tell the truth, son, and shame the devil, eh?"

I nodded and gave them my account from the moment I had left the office until Wally and Ray had rescued me. I saw the two officers exchange a look and Captain Whittle smiled, "Your

Conscript's Call

version of events tallies with the statements of Sergeant Jackson and Privates, Vane, Jennings and Salter." He put his pipe down, "You behaved well in all of this, and it should never have happened." His smile left his face as he looked at Lieutenant Hargreaves.

The lieutenant nodded, "Sergeant Jackson and I were aware of the problems McGuire was causing but we thought we could mend their ways, so to speak. I can see now that we were wrong, Sir."

"That strategy clearly failed and this young man almost paid the price." The captain looked at me, "You should know, Sharratt, that McGuire and Golightly are absent without leave. They have run. The other two are in custody and will be facing the glasshouse. The rest of the members of that group...well, they confirmed much of what you and the other three said. They are to be moved into two different platoons. Hopefully, we can put all of this behind us. It means we are seven men short in the platoon but better that than bad apples who might pollute the rest. Are you well enough to continue training?"

"Of course, Sir, and I am sorry for the trouble I caused."

The captain shook his head, "Any trouble was none of your doing and I want you to understand that. We have a duty, officers of this regiment, to the soldiers in our care. If nothing else this incident has shown me that we need to do more. This war means that we cannot pick and choose who serves. You are an example of what we should have as soldiers and McGuire...well, I suspect that young man will come to a sticky end."

The army liked symmetry, and we had seven men moved in to replace the ones who were either in the glasshouse or had been moved. The barracks became a more harmonious place and once we were told that we would soon finish our training then an air of optimism filled the barracks. Without the rancour of the malevolent ones we found we got on better and we learned more about each other. Most of the lads had enjoyed working for a living before they had been called up. None of them had skills that precluded them from service but they had all experienced work. Glass Man had worked in Pilkington Brothers on the furnaces. If we went to a hot country, he would be well prepared. Pie Face had also worked in a factory but one that produced nuts

Conscript's Call

and bolts. As he told us there was little future in it as they had new machines that could do the work of three men. Geoff Vane had been a farm labourer. He and I had the most in common although he had worked on Lord Derby's estate at Burscough and not on a smallholding like me. Harry Cunningham had worked in a factory too producing a new type of insulation for buildings. It had been hot and dirty work, and he told me he was glad to be out of that factory despite the high wages. The only one with a real skill was Bert Dixon. He had been an apprentice mechanic. His call up had come just six months before he would have qualified. He loved anything mechanical. He was one who, like me, could disassemble and assemble a rifle quickly. While Harry was the Bren gunner, Bert was the one who maintained the weapon. I think that he was disappointed not to have been called up to an armoured regiment. There were a couple I did not know that well. Smudger, Steven Smith, and Carrots, along with Fred Pratt were close mates and while they did not shun the rest of us they appeared to prefer their own company.

The platoon was even allowed to go into Liverpool one Saturday night. Despite the urgings of the others, Ray and Wally in particular, I declined the offer. The reason was one which they would not understand. The last time I had planned a night out my home had been bombed and my family killed. It was a totally irrational thought but I could not shake it and so I stayed in and read a book Wally had given to me. I had never been much of a reader, but I had seen the film of the book, the 39 Steps and I wanted to compare the two. I remembered the lieutenant's cryptic comment about going to war soon and I knew that if we were sent abroad then I would need something to occupy my time on the troopship.

Sergeant Jones entered the barracks. I had seen him around, but I had not had the chance to speak to him since my induction. He said, "I saw that you had not gone into town with the others. I thought I would see if you were alright."

I smiled and put the book down on the bed, "No problem, Sergeant. Just fancied a quiet night in."

He scrutinised my face as he asked, "You aren't afraid of running into McGuire and Golightly are you?"

Conscript's Call

I shook my head, "The thought never crossed my mind. Besides, I think he will be lying low. Wally told me that the Redcaps and the bobbies were after him."

"Aye, but rats have a way of hiding from the rat catchers. We had them in the Great War, too. There were conchies, but there were others who stayed at home and made money. It made us angry when we came home and saw that they had big houses, cars and money." He sat on Wally's bed, "Just so long as you aren't hiding here."

I decided on honesty, "In a way I am, Sergeant Jones. There may well be a time when I can go with the lads and have a few beers on a Saturday night but the last time I did that I lost a family. I know it is daft, and it is something I will have to work out for myself but I am quite happy sitting here and reading my book."

"Just so long as you are sure."

"I am." He stood. "Sarge?"

"Yes?"

"Will you be coming with us when we go overseas?"

He laughed, "You are as sharp as your old man. What makes you think we are going overseas?"

"Lieutenant Hargreaves. When he told me I would be working with Sergeant Armourer Daley he implied we would be going to war soon. That means overseas, doesn't it?"

"I can't say but I can answer your question. Yes, I hope I will be going with the regiment if and when they are posted. I am attached to the Headquarters' Platoon. Is that good enough?"

I smiled, "It is."

I was in bed but not asleep when the platoon returned. I had heard the duty sergeant roar at them to be quiet, but even had they been silent I would have known they were coming back from the smell of beer and cigarettes. I had left the light on and Wally and Ray came over both with the silly smiles of men who had drunk too much. Their voices were croaky when they spoke. It was mixture of too much smoke and shouting to make themselves heard in a busy pub.

"You missed a good night, Johnny." Wally had taken to calling me Johnny. When I had asked him why he said he had a little brother called Johnny. I did not mind.

44

Conscript's Call

"Aye, there were some lasses there too. A bit bold and not the sort to take home and meet your mam but a good laugh."

Geoff Vane was stripping off and he said, "Of course they were a good laugh, you were buying them port and lemons weren't you?"

Ray shrugged, "I don't care what the reason, it was nice to have the smell of perfume and have a quick kiss. I can see precious few more moments like that in our future."

The training intensified over the next month. Sergeant Armourer Daley helped me to become an even better shot. As he said to me I had the basic skills and as I had begun shooting at a young age, I had more skills than the others. He told me I was a natural. We were driven in trucks to the dunes at Formby. For me it was like a second home. There we practised mock attacks and defences. We learned how to dig in sand. It did not take a genius to work out that this was as close to fighting in Egypt as we could get. The rumours of a posting to Egypt became firmer when we were issued KD, Khaki Drill, shorts and a tropical KD shirt, as well as other equipment we would never need in England in late January.

When the orders came we had little time to even think for we were given just twenty-four hours before we were told we would embark on a troopship. No leave was given, and the barracks were on high alert. We were all told to write a letter home as there would be little chance to do so for some time. We were told not to mention any rumours of our destination. As the letters would all be read and censored by Lieutenant Hargreaves, only a fool would have done so. I had no family, but I did not want to be the only one not to do so and I wrote one to Joe. I used just one piece of the precious paper we had been issued. As I did not envisage needing the rest I shared it out between Ray and Wally. I signed it, stuck down the envelope and put it in the tray. Mine was the first to be finished.

We were driven in a convoy of lorries, laden down with equipment to the docks. After we disembarked from the lorries we stood. As was usual, so I learned from Sergeant Jackson, there was more waiting around than moving but eventually we filed aboard a ship. It was the *MV Georgic*. I had been to Liverpool docks once with my mum and my siblings. She had

Conscript's Call

taken us as a treat on the New Brighton ferry and we had seen a ship like the *MV Georgic*. They were called liners and only those with money could afford them. I remembered my mum looking enviously at the beautiful ships as we had crossed the Mersey. I was going aboard just such a ship. I wondered what Mum would have made of it all. I could picture her stroking her hand along the teak rail that ran along the decks and gasping at the fine cabins.

The cabins we had been allocated had been intended for two people in peacetime. We were in the ones that, from the signs in the passageways, were Second Class. They were still well apportioned. Four of us would share a cabin. It would be cosy but as the other three were Geoff, Ray and Wally I didn't mind. Once we had dumped our gear we donned our greatcoats, for it was February and the air was icy cold coming as it did from the Atlantic and we went up on deck. There was little opportunity to explore as men were still being boarded and, as we had found, negotiating the passageways with all our gear was not easy. Instead we lined the sides of what would have been the promenade deck. As such it was relatively wide. I remembered the one we had seen all those years ago and imagined this ship in peacetime. The passengers then would have been excited at the prospect of a cruise and a holiday. For us it was different. We were excited but a little fearful too for we were going to war.

It was dark by the time the gangplank was withdrawn and the hawsers that fastened us to the shore, loosed. Unlike peacetime there were no cheering crowds and ships in Liverpool, taking troops abroad were more commonplace. Dunkirk was still a raw memory. We had all seen the pictures in the newspapers of dispirited men disembarking from ships. We left in silence. A few of the dockyard workers waved an arm but that was all. We headed down the dark waters of the Mersey. It was high tide and we headed out to sea where, we had been told, we would rendezvous with other troopships and transports as well as the warships that would escort us.

When darkness enfolded the ship we went to our cabin and took off our greatcoats. The bugle called us to the mess, the Second Class Dining Hall, and we ate our first meal on the ship. The galleys were manned by army cooks and the fare was what we were all used to. This was not the barracks. We could keep the light on all night and so long as we were not rowdy we could chat away. The others were as excited as I was. I said little for that was my way but the other three were like chattering magpies. They were concerned about German pocket battleships like the *Hipper* and the *Admiral Sheer* not to mention the huge battleships, *Bismarck*, *Tirpitz*, *Scharnhorst* and *Gneisenau*. The navy had a whole fleet at Scapa Flow just waiting for a sighting of them. I confess that their conversation sent shivers down my spine. It was one thing to face Germans or Italians on land where we had the chance to defend ourselves but if we were attacked at sea then our liner would be destroyed in moments. The others had heard stories of ships being destroyed at Dunkirk with a huge loss of life. The German ships were said to be waiting for convoys and we might well be a juicy prize.

"Aye, and remember the *Lancastria*. She was sunk by German bombers two weeks after Dunkirk. There were seven thousand people on board and five thousand of them died."

"Not enough life jackets."

I glanced at the shelf above the beds. There were four of them there. That would not be our fate. Perhaps lessons had been learned.

Wally shook his head, "You pair are right misery guts. Wait until we see our escorts before you sink us, eh?"

I asked, "Where do you reckon then, Wally? Egypt or Greece?"

"Doesn't really matter as we will be fighting the Italians. The sergeant seemed confident that we have the beating of the Eyeties."

Geoff nodded, "We need a few victories. I know that everyone talks about the miracle of Dunkirk but we lost and most of our equipment left in France. If we are going to win this war then we need to start having victories." I was learning that Geoff was a thoughtful man. Whenever he could he had his head in a book. He loved Western adventures but any good yarn would do.

I said nothing. My father had been despondent after the fall of France. The Germans had managed to beat the British, French, Dutch and Belgians in a short campaign. The German soldiers

Conscript's Call

had the confidence of victories. We were raw recruits. What chance did we stand?

The bugle summoned us to breakfast. The dining room might have been that of a pre-war liner but the cooks were still army. We also had duties aboard. We would not be working as hard as we did at the barracks but there would be rifle drill and PE every day.

It was as we drilled that I saw the convoy. There were about a dozen liners, freighters and a single tanker as well as a World War 1 cruiser, a destroyer and two corvettes. It did not seem enough. The sea was empty. Wally speculated that we had headed away from England to make it harder for German aeroplanes to bomb us. We were heading not towards the Bay of Biscay and Brest where the German battleships lay but, instead, we headed into the Atlantic where we could not be so easily bombed. Of course all that did was to take us closer to the U Boats. What was clear was that we were heading south. That meant Gibraltar and then either into the Med or south to the Cape. There had been a rumour that we might be sent to the Far East. Corporal Williams had dismissed that particular rumour, "There are Australian, New Zealand and Indian battalions that can get there easier, quicker and a darned sight safer than us. Besides, there is no war in the Far East. It will be Gibraltar."

When we were not working we took advantage of the opportunities for leisure to spend as much time as we could on deck. In my case it was a fear of being torpedoed while enjoying the comfort of the cabin. Being on deck I noticed that the ships sailed in three columns and we appeared to zig zag. The cruiser led one column and the destroyer a second. The middle column was led by a large liner, the name had been painted out, and one of the sailors told me she was the flagship. There was a Royal Navy Commodore in command. The two corvettes were like sheep dogs racing along the lines. It was then that I noticed, right at the rear of the convoy, a sea going tug. I was no sailor but I worked out that they would be there to tow any ship that was damaged.

We were three days out of Liverpool and asleep in our bunks when the klaxons sounded the alarm. One of the first things we had learned was that when it was used we had to don our

Conscript's Call

lifejackets and get on deck as fast as we could. One of the sailors had filled my head with horror when he described watching a sinking ship go down in minutes. I pulled on my shorts and battle dress before donning the lifejacket. We raced out of the door into the maelstrom and relative confusion that awaited us in the corridor. We ran to our muster stations. Even as we ran I heard the sounds of the klaxons on the other ships. As we emerged I saw a corvette racing between the two columns. She looked too tiny to be a threat to anything. We stood in ranks and Sergeant Jackson and Corporal Williams checked our names off. We waited in fearful silence. No order was needed for we were all petrified. It was nighttime and therefore unlikely to be an aerial attack. That meant either a surface raider or submarines. I found myself praying. Since the bombing of our home I had begun to have doubts about the existence of a god who could allow such things to happen but the prospect of joining my family suddenly made me religious.

The explosion, when it came, was from one of the freighters in the column close to us. It was not the tanker. I had heard that when a tanker went up then all the ships around it risked being damaged by the explosion. The column of water and flames came from just level with the bridge. The destroyer, looking far more substantial than the corvettes, suddenly took off. How they knew where to look was a mystery to me. The sea-going tug was hurrying to get to the stricken ship which had stopped. We watched as the ship sank a little lower into the water. Was she going to sink? When we heard the explosions on the other side of the convoy we wondered at first if it was another ship being struck but then it became clear that the destroyer had found the submarine and was dropping depth charges. The flames on the freighter were doused and darkness enveloped the ship. We had no opportunity to see what happened to her.

We stood on the deck all night. No one objected. There could still be submarines out there. When dawn broke a sailor came to speak to the colonel. I saw the RSM, Dan Lawson, summon the officers. After the colonel had spoken to them they were dismissed. Lieutenant Hargreaves joined us, "The threat is over. The navy sank a submarine." He paused, "This is just a foretaste. Keep your life jackets close to hand."

Conscript's Call

We ate breakfast but I kept my lifejacket within easy reach. After breakfast we went to the cabin to dress and then returned to the deck. I saw that the freighter that had been hit was now under tow but appeared to be riding higher in the water than the previous night. I saw that they had hoses and water was being pumped from her. She might not sink.

There were two more attacks before we reached Gibraltar. Perhaps the first one had gingered up the escorts for the U Boats failed to make another hit but, as it was nighttime, we had a couple more nights on deck. When we tied up I was relieved to see many more warships. We might be safer in the Mediterranean.

The weather was warmer and we were able to ditch the greatcoats when we went on deck. We looked at the port of Gibraltar and the rock which housed a garrison. It was reassuringly solid. It gave me hope that we had a chance. The aeroplanes we saw overhead and on the aircraft carrier that was moored were also comforting. There was no chance of them letting us off the ship and so we looked at the bustling port enviously. It was while we were there that I saw Sergeant Jones again. He was smoking his pipe.

He saw me coming and smiled, "Well, John, how are you enjoying the cruise? Your dad and I would have loved this rather than the trenches of Flanders."

I smiled, "It is all so different, Sergeant. You are right, it does feel like a cruise, at least here. When we were attacked by the submarines it felt like war but this is a little unreal."

"That it is. Still, you look to have got over your little incident." He put the beating in a diplomatic fashion.

I nodded. I did not want to talk of it. I had put it from my mind and I wanted them to, too. I changed the subject, "What do you do with the Headquarters Platoon, Sergeant Jones?"

He tapped the ash from his pipe, "Boring but necessary work, son. We make sure that orders are communicated. See that ammunition and supplies are ready. They keep old relics like me far from the fighting. If Headquarters Platoon has to fight then you know we are up against it."

Just then the adjutant approached, "Sergeant Jones, the colonel needs to see you."

Conscript's Call

"Righto, Sir." He winked and said, "Probably needs more paper clips."

We waited for three days while emergency repairs were carried out on the freighter and then, with another four troopships we left. This time we had an aircraft carrier, albeit a small one, another cruiser and four destroyers. It felt more substantial. Yet part of me worried. Why the extra ships? Was there more danger ahead?

The weather was much warmer and the sea calmer. The skies were blue and the ship felt more like a liner. However, as we neared Malta, we realised the truth. The Italian air force could easily reach our route and we were attacked constantly. The first attack came a few days out of Gibraltar. The klaxons sounded and we ran on deck. We had to be on deck, in case we were hit, but, being on the deck exposed us to more dangers.

The aeroplanes were high up at first and looked tiny. To me they appeared to be like a swarm of bluebottles around the midden at home. They became more menacing as they dived down from the sky, machine guns spitting fire. Other aeroplanes, larger ones like the one that had killed my family, did not dive down but dropped their bombs from on high. I saw that they had three engines. Some of the men fired their rifles at the aircraft. I did not, but I understood the need. I had wanted to do the same with the stricken bomber that had taken my family. The ones who did were reprimanded for wasting ammunition. The marine gun crews who manned the anti-aircraft guns on the liner added their firepower to the destroyers, cruisers, corvettes and the rest of the convoy. However it was the Fairey Fulmars from the aircraft carrier which had the greatest success. They bravely darted amongst the aeroplanes and when they downed one we all cheered. While they did not shoot many enemy down they were able to stop the Italian bombers from accurate bombing runs.

The second attack brought some success for the enemy. A high-level bomber managed to send a stick of bombs to hit a troopship. They were not our battalion but we felt an affinity for them. The flames leapt high and I saw men hurled overboard. It did not take much imagination to picture that happening to us. A Fairey Fulmar rose to try to catch the bomber. Like the German that had killed my family its destruction would not bring back

Conscript's Call

the dead soldiers. We were close enough to see hosepipes sending water to douse the fires and soldiers grabbing buckets of water. The air-raid had long gone before the fires were put out. Even worse was when the burials took place. We were able to count the one hundred men who had died. Covered by flags they were consigned to the deep. Some were the ship's crew but the majority were soldiers. They had not even managed to fight before they were killed. I could not wait to be off the ship.

We endured daylight attacks right up until the time we entered Greek waters and then we had protection from British bases there. We lost no more ships. The bulk of the warships and the damaged troopship left us before we reached Piraeus. The warships had their own war to fight and the troopship was heading...? Its destination provided speculation as we navigated the islands and channels that surrounded Greece.

When they left, that was when we knew where we were bound, it was not Africa but Greece.

Conscript's Call

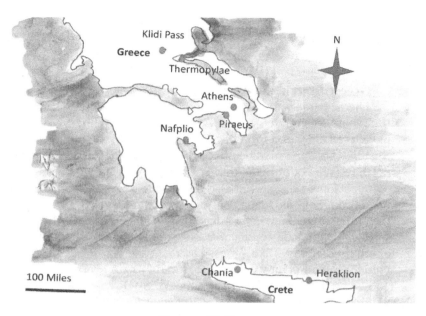

Greece 1941

Chapter 4

Greece March and April 1941

The disembarkation took as long as the embarkation had. This time there was no fleet of lorries waiting for us. They would have to be unloaded from the freighters and so we employed Shanks' pony and marched to war. We were laden as we headed north to face not only the Italians, against whom the Greeks had enjoyed some success, but also the Germans and Bulgarians. We had our kit bags as well as our weapons. Poor Harry Cunningham had the Bren gun and Geoff had to lug a rifle as well as the grenade launcher. We also had pouches filled with ammunition and Mills Bombs. The reality of war hit us. The colonel and adjutant were given a small lorry, a Morris 15 cwt, and I saw Sergeant Jones join them. We would march but they would drive, presumably so that Sergeant Jones and the rest of his team could ensure that the battalion had all it needed when we arrived at our destination. They had one route to war but ours was slightly different. We were a long snake of men all marching north to face the enemy who had managed to drive the Greek and Yugoslavian soldiers from the borders.

As we marched we sang. The song of the moment was *Roll out the Barrel*. It was a jolly song and helped us as we trudged through Greece, laden with equipment and already hotter than I could ever remember. Even their spring was warmer than some of our summers had been. Some of us were still wearing shorts and it was clear that it was the first time that most of us had done so. Our legs were white. The days since Gibraltar had tanned our faces, arms and hands but our legs marked us as Englishmen. They were in direct contrast to the other soldiers we saw. They were Australian and New Zealanders. They had the tanned skins of men who spent a lot of time outdoors. When we passed them, they hurled good natured insults at us. We responded with comments about relationships with sheep. It was all easy banter. We were warned, however, that it would get colder. We were heading to the mountains and some of them, so the rumour ran, had snow on their tops.

Conscript's Call

The Greeks we passed, as we marched north, were pleased to see us. They must have watched their wounded being brought back from the front and we were seen as hope that the enemy might not win. This was their homeland that had been invaded. I could not imagine England enduring the same. We had a sea to protect us and a navy that, whilst not as strong as it had once been, was still the most powerful in this part of the world.

We did not bother with tents but just slept wrapped in our blankets and greatcoats. We had been issued, back in England, helmet comforters which were, in effect, a woollen hat. They kept our heads warm at night. The shorts lasted one day for while the Mediterranean had been warm, once we headed closer to the mountains then the air became as cold as England, and we reverted to long trousers. Some of the hardier Anzacs who still wore shorts jeered us.

We did not have to endure their jeers for long as we were headed for the Klidi Pass where we would reinforce the soldiers there under the command of Australian Major General Mackay. We would be part of Mackay force. There were, remarkably, no complaints as we wound our way north through a land which, to all of us, was exotic. We didn't understand the language but there were smiles and cheers from the villages through which we passed. One or two even waved ancient Union Flags. It made us feel good. We were needed. Children marched next to us, sticks for guns and we gave them chocolate from our ration. We felt welcomed as we headed north to face the enemy for the first time. At night we still did not bother with tents, despite the cold, for it took time to put them up and then take them down. After the sun went down it was almost freezing, despite the month and the southerly position. We lit fires which the sentries stoked and fed all night. The best places to sleep were close to the fire. The food was predictable: corned beef was the order of the day. It was either cold between bread or cooked into a stew, Bully Beef. Sometimes we managed to get bread but at other times we had to just eat slices of it. Occasionally we were lucky enough to be given some watery stew from the villagers. It was hot food and we were grateful.

The reality of war hit us a day from the pass. We camped by a farm that had been recently bombed. We had seen the German Ju

Conscript's Call

87s in the sky ahead of us two days before. The Stuka was well known to the NCOs as they had plagued the retreat to Dunkirk. We had all taken cover in the ditches and pointed impotent guns at the sky. Now we saw the result of their devastation. It looked like there had been a column of vehicles heading for the pass and they had been attacked. The three burnt out vehicles had been pushed to the side. They were charred and blackened warnings of the war. Rubber burns easily and fuel makes fires burn hotly. I hoped that the soldiers had managed to get out before they had a horrible death by cremation. The saddest part was the farm that had been half destroyed in the attack, for it was a reminder of my home. I saw no bodies but, as we made our camp, I could not help but see the detritus of the family whose home had been taken in the sudden explosion of a handful of bombs. There was a home-made doll discarded and abandoned. It had been trampled into the mud by others, perhaps soldiers searching for survivors. I had no idea if the family had died. There was certainly no sign now that the farm was occupied. There were shards of wood that had been furniture and broken pots. They were reminders of a life in a more peaceful time. When I passed an outbuilding that was now a shell I found a small cooking pan that was whole. I picked it up and found myself seeing the farmer's wife using it. I held on to it. I saw broken pots and on the ground a red stain. It looked like blood, but I told myself that it was probably wine. My spirits dropped low and I did not sleep well that night. I was up before dawn, and I went to the fields that had been, until a few days earlier, tended by a farmer and his family. For the first time since I had become a soldier I was remembering my first life. The family had made a vegetable garden that was close to the house and, remarkably, while the buildings had been destroyed by the blast, the hardy plants had survived. I found onions and garlic. The farmer's son in me picked them. I found a stand of beans. The supports had been destroyed, and they lay flattened but they were still growing and I picked those that had survived. I put them all in the small pan I had rescued. I went back to my pack and put everything inside. I don't know why but as we set off to march the next day, I felt happier. Perhaps because I thought the farmer, wherever he was, would approve of some of his produce being used. When I had

Conscript's Call

left our farm Joe and the others had promised me that they would harvest the work we had begun. Dad would have liked that. He hated waste.

Our platoon got on well together. In many ways we had needed McGuire for it had bonded the rest of us. My beating had outraged the whole platoon and although I had suffered it was not as bad as they all seemed to think. I was tougher than I looked. While I got on with all of the others the three who were my closest friends were Wally, Geoff and Ray. I felt a little left out as I had no nickname. I had learned that Geoff was called, Weather. When I asked him why, back in Seaforth Barracks, he had pointed to the top of a nearby building and said, "Weather...Vane, get it? He had shrugged, "As nicknames goes it is not so bad. With my size I am lucky that they don't call me Frankenstein." Pie Face and Glass Man seemed happy enough with their nicknames although we still used their Christian names. As there were three Geoffs and two Wallys, not to mention two Rays, in the company then nicknames were useful. I only got John from my three friends. There were eight Johns and I usually got called Sharratt. It was like being back in school and addressed by a surname.

We always made our own little camp, and we shared the cooking. We no longer had army cooks, we were our own cooks. I was not bad as a cook and the others were good too but Pie Face had a habit of over seasoning. Geoff Vane did not like it but despite his huge size he was a gentle giant, and it was left to Glass Man to admonish his friend. In the scheme of things, it was minor and that showed how close we were.

The journey to the pass was hard but when we reached the Klidi Pass the position we were to occupy came as a shock. It was a steep and winding defile which was one hundred yards wide at its narrowest point and only six hundred yards at its widest. The peaks towered over us and it was as bleak a place as I could recall. Our company was given a section to guard. The company machine gun was at the far end of our line and we were left with Harry Cunningham and his Bren to protect us. We had the Boys anti-tank rifle too but the ground looked too rough for armoured vehicles. They would use the road we guarded. Corporal Williams, Norm Thomas and Dave Proud would have

Conscript's Call

that weapon in their slit trench. At the other side were Carrots, Fred Pratt and Smudger Smith. They just had rifles. We were lucky to have Weather with his grenade launcher. In the rocky defile it would be an effective deterrent. The lieutenant ordered Sergeant Jackson to begin the digging of slit trenches. It was easier said than done. There was barely any soil and what there was appeared to be frozen.

It was as we were digging that we heard, to the northwest of us, in the direction of Florina, the sound of an artillery barrage. One of the lads who had been in France shouted, "They are our guns, lads. Twenty-five pounders."

We kept working and when the guns stopped, we saw a column of smoke rising. Something had been hit and as our guns were firing it was to be hoped it was the enemy who had been hurt. It made us work all the harder.

Weather was a clever man. He might have looked like a lumbering bear but he had the brain of a fox. He pointed to the rocks, "Instead of fighting nature, lads, let's use it. Find rocks and rather than digging down why don't we build up?"

It seemed like a good idea and was also easier. We sought stones and like men making a dry-stone wall we fitted them together. We made faster progress than when we had been digging. When Corporal Williams saw the wall we had made he came over but shook his head, "That's not so clever, lads. It might be easier, but a machine gun fired at you will make splinters that are as deadly as bullets."

Glass Man smiled, "Then we can use soil to pile in front, Corp. I mean, we have scraped enough already. How's that?"

The corporal smiled but shook his head, "Too clever for your own good. We will see."

I think his criticism spurred us and we completely covered the stones with soil. We had a cosy nest for the four of us. Harry Cunningham and Bert Dixon were in the next slit trench with their Bren gun and they had copied what we did. The rain began to fall and, had it been England, I would have said that it was more sleet than rain. As we huddled beneath our greatcoats the sleety rain turned to snow and began to lay.

Weather lived up to his name, "I thought we were going to the tropics. This is colder than Huddersfield in the middle of winter."

Pie Face nodded, "Aye, without the benefit of a pub and a roaring fire."

Sergeant Jackson came around as darkness, along with more snow, fell, "Keep your eyes and ears open, lads. Jerry is known to be out and about. There are Waffen SS out there."

We all turned. We might be new soldiers, but the older hands had all regaled us, on the ship from Liverpool, with tales of the atrocities committed by the SS in the retreat to Dunkirk.

"SS?"

"Aye, that is what we were told." He added, "And there are tanks, but I reckon they will have to use the road. The Aussies have artillery trained on the road. The Mark III Panzer does not have thick armour." I recalled the noise of the guns before. I took some comfort from that. "One in four should be awake all the time. You lads arrange the rota. You should all be able to get six hours of sleep." He chuckled, "Soon, six hours will seem like a luxury."

Corporal Williams commanded our section and he said, "Pie Face, take the first watch. Sharratt, you next. Wake Glass Man and then I will do the last watch. The others can do stag tomorrow. I reckon we are here for some time."

It meant that Ray and I would have disturbed sleep and have to try to find that warm spot after our duty. I consoled myself with the fact that it would all even out.

The man from Wigan shook me awake, "Bloody freezing out here and there is about six inches of snow. When I was a kid I would have loved it for the snowball fights but here…"

He waited until I had risen and then he took my place. It was only fair. The place I had lain was nice and warm. I took the Lee Enfield and went to the place we had designated as the sentry post to watch. I turned and saw the white face of Bert Dixon. He had just been for a pee. He smiled and I saw he was wearing a balaclava. He was lucky. He would have warm ears. I knew that I might need my hands later on and so after placing my rifle where I could easily reach it I jammed my hands into my greatcoat pockets. It would keep them marginally warmer. I stared into the dark. My hunting of the bunnies in the dunes now came to my aid. I knew how to be patient and I knew how to watch. You did not stare at the same spot continuously; you moved your eyes to scan a different place.

I guessed that I was halfway through my two-hour watch when I heard the rifles open up but they were a mile or two, it seemed to me, to the left of us. A machine gun rattled, and it did not sound like either a Vickers or a Bren. I said, "Stand to, lads." They were rising even as I spoke, having heard the reports. The gunfire was getting louder and closer. I took my hands from my pockets and grabbed my rifle. I flicked the safety, and I was ready. I did not have a hand grenade handy for the simple reason that we had Weather Vane and his grenade launcher.

We peered in the dark. It seemed to be totally silent. The smell of smoke drifted with the snow from the north. It was an acrid smell. Vehicles had been destroyed but this time they were the enemy ones and not ours. When Sergeant Jackson's voice came from behind me I almost jumped, "Wait for the command to fire but if you see movement then let someone know. Don't waste ammo."

We all chorused a whispered, "Yes, Sergeant." It sounded like the hiss of a snake.

It was Wally whose keen eyes picked out the movement. "They are coming." As soon as he pointed I saw the shapes.

Corporal Williams said, "I see 'em. Ready your weapons."

Before dark I had estimated the distances by using particular rocks and bushes. I aimed at the rock that I had calculated was one hundred and fifty yards from me. I saw movement as a man rose from behind it and sneaked around. He was not wearing white camouflage, and the snow helped me to identify the shadow as a man and therefore an enemy. As I aimed at his chest, I suddenly realised this was a not a paper target, this was a real man. I could not see his face, but it would be a soldier just like me and if I did my job then within a few moments he would be dead. I would be taking a life. It was a sobering thought. My anger at the sight of my father's farm now seemed a thousand years ago. The man I was going to kill had not had a hand in any of that. Then I steeled myself. We had not begun this war, the Germans had. It had been the Italians who had invaded Greece. I put my finger on the trigger and listened.

"Open fire!"

Conscript's Call

It was Sergeant Jackson's voice, and I squeezed the trigger. The shadow spread his arms and fell. The sound of Lee Enfields and the crack of Harry's Bren gun stopped me from hearing any cries. I worked the bolt almost without thinking and sought another target. It was like the time I had hunted the bunnies and killed five. This time it was men I was hitting. I saw flashes from the dark. They were firing at us. I wore a steel helmet, and I hoped that it would stop a bullet. The ones around me were firing faster than I was. I heard Ray replacing a magazine. I sought targets and when I saw a hand move to command men to move forward, I moved my gun slightly and looked for the body. When it rose I fired and this time saw the face disappear as my .303 round ended his life. The first man I had shot might have survived but this one, an officer or non-commissioned officer, was definitely dead.

Next to me I heard Harry as he shouted, "Reloading."

We all knew that when the Bren fell silent the enemy would seize their chance. Sergeant Jackson shouted, "Vane, lob a grenade in the air."

"Right, Sarge." While he changed weapons I looked for targets. Four men had risen and began to move for two of our weapons had stopped firing. Some men, like Ray, had changed magazines. I fired at each man that moved. I did so slowly and methodically. I knew that some others were firing so fast that it was almost what the armourer had called a mad minute, where you just fired as fast as you could work the bolt.

I heard the sound of the grenade being fired for Geoff was next to me. He shouted, "Grenade!"

I lowered my head so that just my eyes peered over the small stone parapet we had made. When the grenade when off I saw that Geoff had sent it close to the rock I had used to estimate distances. The explosion lit up the night and I saw men scythed down by the flying shrapnel. A piece must have flown over our heads or perhaps it was a bullet sent in reply. Whatever made the zipping noise over our heads was a warning.

When Harry's Bren began to fire again, I sought more targets. The grenade, however, appeared to have ripped the heart out of the attackers. For the next hour or so they fired from the dark at our positions and we fired at their flashes. When the order came

Conscript's Call

to cease fire, I had not fired for ten minutes. When dawn came Lieutenant Hargreaves sent a patrol to check for the enemy. They came back and were smiling. The enemy had gone.

Corporal Williams came down the line, "Everyone alright here?"

Weather nodded, "Yes, Corp. Did we beat them off?"

He nodded, "Yes, that grenade of yours did the trick. The patrol found five bodies but they must have taken away their wounded. We lost none so it is one nil to us."

I asked, "Will they come again?"

He nodded, "The lieutenant heard that the Australian artillery destroyed one column coming down the road yesterday. They will come again. If they take this pass, then the road to Thermopylae is open and once they are past there then Athens is open to attack. We hold them as long as we can."

There was something in his voice that made Geoff say, "And then we pull back."

"Just wait for our betters to tell us, Vane. Get yourselves some food on the go." He pointed at the sky. "There is more snow on the way."

As they did so Harry said, "That was nice shooting last night, Hawkeye!" In that one moment my nickname was given. I was Hawkeye.

When he had gone I stood, "It is my turn to cook. Who has the corned beef?"

We took it in turns to use our rations and Wally tossed me the can, "Here, y'are." He added, "Don't forget plenty of salt."

I saw the slight shake from Weather and I smiled, "I guarantee that you will find this tasty, Pie Face."

I went down a few feet to the flattened piece of ground where we had made a fire. I took the kindling from under the piece of torn tarpaulin we had taken from the wrecked farm and found the wood beneath. The wrecked farm had yielded treasure such as partly burned wood and fresh kindling. I soon had a fire going. I used snow to fill the small cooking pot I had taken and then my bayonet to slice the vegetables and drop them into the melting snow. I made them as fine as I could to help the stew to cook quickly. There had been an aromatic bush of herbs at the farm, and I had taken a sprig. I put some leaves in and a bay leaf I had found. I did use salt but waited until the water was almost boiling. The salt set it bubbling away faster. I then added the corned beef. I had sliced that too. That done I stirred. I took the other pot we had and filled that with snow and put it next to the fire to melt. When it had melted I swapped over the pots and stirred the bully beef. Once the water was boiling I swapped the pans over and put four teaspoons of tea in the pot. We had canned milk to make it taste a little more like it was at home but we all yearned for proper milk. When I had searched the farm I had hoped to find some but failed. When the stew was heated again I went to collect the mugs from the lads and ladled some of the stock into them. It would warm them up. I gave them the cups and waited until they had sipped the liquor. It was so cold in the pass that in the time it took me to walk those few feet it was drinkable.

Weather beamed, "By, this will put hairs on your chest. Tasty enough for you, Pie Face?"

Wally nodded and then reached into his battledress pocket. He sprinkled salt into the mug, "It'll do."

We were learning that like my dad and his mates in the Great War, it was the little things you appreciated. I put the tea to stew and then took the food to the others. They held out their mess tins and I shared it all equitably.

Harry Cunningham sniffed the air, "Is there a restaurant nearby?"

I laughed, "It is just a corned beef stew. I found some herbs at that burnt out farm. They just make the corned beef smell a little better, that is all."

Glass Man called out, "Don't you listen to Hawkeye, he is being too modest. This is the tastiest food since, well, since the last one me mam cooked."

We went to make water and empty our bowels but did so in pairs. The other two stood watch as we waited for the next attack. The bodies had told us that these were Germans and not Italians. We all knew that the Germans were better soldiers and they would not let our first resistance stop them. They would come again.

It was the mid-afternoon when we saw the enemy approach and it coincided with a visit to our position from Lieutenant

Conscript's Call

Hargreaves. He had some binoculars with him and I said, "Sir, I can see movement in the distance." I had seen men moving but they were too far away to make out clearly.

He lifted his glasses and said, "You have good eyes, Sharratt. Let me see…" There was a sharp intake in breath as he added, "Well, that is a bit of a bugger."

Sergeant Jackson had joined us, "What is it, Sir."

The officer handed his glasses to the sergeant, "Take a look."

Sergeant Jackson whistled, "SS."

"Not just SS, Sergeant Jackson, but 1st SS Panzer Division Leibstandarte SS Adolf Hitler. We were briefed before we left Piraeus that they were in the area. That means they will have tanks."

Wally said, "Up here, Sir?"

The lieutenant smiled, "No, Salter, they will be coming down the road. We will probably have to deal with their panzer grenadiers. I will go and tell the captain. Take charge, Sergeant."

Wally said, quietly, "SS, Sergeant?"

"Don't you worry. They are just men. Adolf Hitler may call them supermen but a .303 will stop them. Vane, stay alert and Cunningham, not quite so wasteful with your magazines, eh?"

Both men said, "Right, Sarge."

The SS were a spectre. Back at the Seaforth Barracks we had heard stories about them. We had also read about them in newspapers but as my dad always said, the best use for newspapers was wrapping them around fish and chips. However, since speaking to the older hands the stories from the retreat to Dunkirk were seen as the truth. I made sure I had fresh magazines ready, and this time placed a Mills Bomb close to hand. It was like picking up a block of ice. If we were going to continue to fight in the cold I would need fingerless gloves.

When the order came to stand to, I was ready already. I had made water and drunk the last of the hot tea. The warmth from the mug had brought the feeling back to my hands. This time we saw the figures as they darted from rock to rock. Sergeant Jackson came to me and said, "Lieutenant Hargreaves wonders if you could hit one, Sharratt."

"I can give it a go." The nearest man was three hundred yards from me. I adjusted the sight. When hunting rabbits, you tried to

Conscript's Call

anticipate where they would move. I watched the man I had chosen as a target. He moved to my right and stopped behind a rock. I guessed when he rose he would move to my left and I aimed at the place I thought he would use. It took to the count of five for him to do so but he did and I squeezed the trigger. It was not the best shot I had ever made but I hit him and he spun around. Immediately the Germans all opened fire but as they had all dropped to the ground and the range was more than two hundred and eighty yards the bullets were largely wasted.

"Well done, son. That will make them warier." He raised his voice, "The rest of you hold fire." To me he added, "Keep sniping, Sharratt."

"Right, Sarge." I decided to make the men I was hunting into targets rather than real men. I chose the one I would hit and then tracked him. My second shot was even better than my first for I hit the man in the chest, and he fell backwards. He did not move. Each bullet I sent brought a flurry of gunfire in my direction. I just ducked below the parapet of stone and soil and when it ended raised my head. The enemy were getting closer. They were now just one hundred and eighty yards from me and approaching my rock.

When they reached the rock I used as a marker for one hundred and fifty yards, Sergeant Jackson, after the lieutenant had spoken to him, shouted, "Fire at will. Vane, grenade launcher."

I just kept on firing but now the rest of the men were firing. The staccato bursts from the Bren at my side were reassuringly regular. This time we saw the effect of the grenade that Weather sent at the enemy. We heard the cries as men were hit but then the Germans hit back. They used their mortars to bombard us. When I heard cries from our right I knew that men had been hit. The attack continued for a short while and then we heard the sound of twenty-five pounders as our artillery bombarded their position.

As darkness fell we were able to load magazines and think about food.

"Hawkeye, I know it is not your turn, and God knows you did enough this afternoon, but more of the same would be nice."

"Right, Weather. Corned beef?"

Conscript's Call

He tossed me the can. After we had eaten, I used the last of my precious finds to enrich the stew, we were told to do the same as the night before but this time it would be two hours on and two hours off. We would sleep in pairs. When Wally and I did our duty we heard, from our left to the northwest, the sound not just of small arms fire but also the sound of German tank guns and the cracks of anti-tank guns. The Germans were using their armour.

We had a night free from fighting but with a disturbed night of sleep we were all exhausted before we started. As Wally and I made water he said, "More of the same, eh, Hawkeye?"

Just then Sergeant Jackson shouted, "Pack up your gear, we are moving out."

Harry Cunningham, as he rose shouted, "Do we advance, Sarge?"

"No, we are falling back. The Aussies have taken a beating in the night and enemy tanks are on their way."

As we hurriedly packed everything we had into our packs I reflected that we had done all that was asked of us but it had not been enough. We were pulling back. We were also leaving our first casualty; Private Topp, nicknamed Carrots because of his red hair, had been hit by a bullet. Although I had not known him well I felt sad. Smudger Smith, was close to Carrots and he took it very badly and retreated into a shell which none of us could enter. Fred Pratt also appeared to be disheartened by the death.

Chapter 5

Crete May 1941

We marched south and kept marching. We marched from before dawn until after the sun had set. We had strolled north by comparison. We heard fighting to the north east and the noise followed us, getting ever closer. We were racing for the sea. We had no transport and because we had lost few men we were too great in numbers for the limited vehicles left to us. The colonel decided to keep us together. Looking back now I think it was the defeat at Dunkirk that helped us. The NCOs and most of the senior officers had learned lessons during that defeat and we, the conscripts, benefitted from them. No one deserted and no one ran. I suspect that had McGuire and the like been with us then there would have been desertions. I had seen Petersen and Harrison during the advance and the two survivors of the seven who had threatened to spoil the regiment appeared to be reformed characters. They even looked a little shame faced when I spoke to them. We had a hard ten days of marching through a land which felt more like England in late winter than a warm and pleasant Greece. Poor Smudger Smith became more and more unhappy as we headed south. We found him looking north and mumbling about his mate, Carrots. They had been close. It was a lesson not to get too attached to friends for their lives could be snuffed out like a candle. The corporal and sergeant tried to shout him from his melancholy but it did not work. The rest of us tried jokes and songs to raise his spirits. We failed.

We had nothing but corned beef to eat although when we passed anything like a farm, we tried to barter for food. We augmented our diet. We were cold, hungry and tired but since the last attack by the SS I had not needed to fire my gun. What was dispiriting was the looks on the faces of the Greeks in the villages through which we passed. The resignation on their expressions told us what they could expect from their new masters. They had greeted us with hope and now said farewell with despair. After a fortnight we reached Piraeus but kept on going. The port had been bombed by Italian and German bombers. It was not safe to embark troops from there. It was after Piraeus that we saw the devastation caused by the enemy aeroplanes. They had a shorter journey than the RAF and we passed columns of men who had been strafed and bombed. Wrecked vehicles had been pushed to the side of the road. It was most dispiriting.

We reached the port of Nafplio on the 26th of April. There were thousands of troops waiting to be evacuated. We were the only British soldiers. The rest were Australians or New Zealanders. There were many ships waiting to take us off and a few destroyers ready to act as escorts and, as Sergeant Jackson told us, to carry as many soldiers as they could. We did what the British do well. We queued and we did so patiently. I was told by Corporal Williams that at Dunkirk men had waited waist deep in the sea for hours hoping to be taken off. It made it seem a little easier for we were on dry land and we had regular mugs of tea. A British soldier can work wonders so long as he is supplied with tea and this tea had both milk and sugar. Admittedly it was goat's milk but beggars can't be choosers.

I did not see the name of the battered old freighter that took us off but she had a well-worn and battle stained yet still proud Greek flag hanging from her jackstaff. The whole of the somewhat depleted battalion managed to board but we were tightly packed. Our wounded and injured were taken below decks. One or two had what one might call war wounds. They had been injured by shrapnel and bullets but more of them were suffering from other injuries. Frostbite, sprains, diarrhoea, bleeding feet and other minor complaints. The ones who were fit were crammed on the deck. We found a nice little berth at the front. I learned it was called the foc'sle. It was as the convoy left the next day that we learned of the fall of Athens and the surrender of the Greek Army. It was the end of April and the Germans had taken Greece even quicker than they had taken France. It was depressing.

Sergeant Jackson had us clean our weapons and load magazines. He was trying to keep us busy and focussed. We had been issued with more ammunition at Piraeus. Harry Cunningham had learned his lesson in Klidi Pass. He had acquired more spare magazines. They were found discarded by

Conscript's Call

the road as we headed south and now he and Bert Dixon, his oppo, loaded as many magazines as they could. We left the port in darkness almost like someone sneaking out after a late-night and illicit liaison. We slept as the sergeant reckoned we would not be attacked until daylight. The wrecked port of Piraeus left us in no doubt that we would be attacked. The odd RAF aircraft we had seen had been more than a week ago. We would have no air cover.

When dawn broke we learned that we were heading for Crete. We had two Royal Navy destroyers, **HMS Diamond** and **HMS Wryneck**. They bristled with guns and gave us comfort. We had no guns on the old freighter and so, at dawn, orders were issued. We found some Motley mountings which were spring balanced and intended to be fitted to vehicles. When the Brens were mounted on them they could be used as anti-aircraft guns. We mounted ours close to the bow and used our knapsacks as improvised sandbags. It was not a moment too soon for, from the north, came a squadron of dive bombers. They were the Ju 87, the Stuka. I had read in the papers that Spitfires and Hurricanes found them easy to shoot down in the Battle of Britain. Sadly, we had no air cover and the Stukas would be opposed by just two destroyers and the Bren guns we had mounted.

Sergeant Jackson said, "Don't waste bullets from your rifles. Let Cunningham and the other Bren gunners use their firepower."

I was frustrated. I wanted to fight back. We gathered behind our mound of bags and held fresh magazines for Harry. Each one only fired 30 bullets and whilst short bursts might be fine against men, a dive bomber would take a wall of bullets to stop it.

The three Stukas who dived at us sounded terrifying. They had some sort of device mounted behind the propellor which seemed to scream. Harry fired at the leading one and the other Bren gunners joined in. The dive bombers flew along the length of the ship to drop their bombs from bow to stern. They also raked the ship with their twin machine guns and bullets slammed into the deck, sending splinters everywhere. The approach of the aeroplanes meant Harry had the first bite of the cherry. I do not know if it was luck or skill but I saw the bullets striking the engine cowling of the leading dive bomber. Sparks flew. The

Conscript's Call

pilot fired his machine guns too but, as Harry changed the magazine, smoke began to pour from the engine and he veered off to port. We all cheered but another two were coming. The captain and the rest of the convoy were not bystanders in all of this. The three lines of ships all turned to port at the same time. The result was that when the second bomber dropped its load we were turning. It exploded in the sea and showered us with sea water but it did not appear to have done any damage. The third aeroplane then endured the bullets from six Bren guns all of which were aimed at the single aircraft. This time we heard the small explosion that rocked the aircraft to the side and as it was jerked to the side it suddenly exploded. Splinters of metal filled the air. Wally looked up in alarm as one struck his tin hat. It had done its job and protected his head. We all cheered as the wreckage crashed into the sea. Only one bomb had come close and we had survived. At least most of us had survived. Poor Smudger lay dead. His eye and brain had been penetrated by a wooden splinter the size of a carving knife. While the rest of us had been handing magazines to Harry, he had been cowering. Our bodies had protected his but when the Stuka's bullets had hit the wooden rail the splinter had flown off at an awkward and unpredictable angle. War had truly come to the section and there was no hiding from it. I realised that you were as well to face death rather than cowering in fear. Now we had lost two men. How many more would we lose?

Others were not so lucky. The Dutch ship, **Slamat**, was attacked and this time all three bombs hit her. She was set on fire and we saw the soldiers, mainly New Zealanders, as they abandoned ship. The two destroyers went to her aid and with scrambling nets over the side they began to haul aboard the six hundred or so survivors to their already overcrowded ships. The disaster grew for as they slowed they became easy targets and every Stuka which still had bombs attacked the two ships. Despite hitting and destroying five aeroplanes, both ships were hit and sunk by multiple bombs. There were just sixty survivors from the thousand or so in the water who were pulled to safety. When the Stukas left we knew that the attack was over and, as we neared Crete we thanked God that we had survived but we had seen what could happen. I was never so glad to step on dry land as I was that day.

We landed at Heraklion which I learned was the largest place on the island. There was a garrison already there and we saw famous regiments when we were marched to the east of the port. The Black Watch and the 2nd York and Lancs. We also marched with some of the Australians who had been evacuated with us. They had lost many men and were a hollow shell of the battalions they had been. We were allocated a camp just below a pair of hills referred to as the Charlies. They overlooked the vital airfield to the east of our position.

That first night, when Sergeant Jackson came to ensure that we had done things properly, Geoff asked him what we were doing here. "Simple, lad, Jerry wants Crete. If he has this island he can use his bombers to stop convoys getting to Malta and Alexandria. This airfield is vital. We defend it."

Wally lit a cigarette, "That is it, we defend? Against whom? This isn't Greece, Sarge. They can't drive here and we have a navy."

The sergeant sighed, "You may not have noticed, Vane, that we lost two ships, destroyers, just getting here. The lieutenant said that we have lost cruisers too. We dig in and protect this side of the airfield. The 2nd York and Lancs are behind us and the Black Watch will guard the actual field. The Aussies are on the hill and the Greek regiments we evacuated are in the town."

And so we settled into a routine of preparing defences and watching for an enemy. The good news was that we were further south. We were no longer in mountains and enduring snowstorms and frostbite. It was warmer. We also had better food. Non-essential troops had been evacuated to Egypt already and we ate better than we were used to for there were supplies laid in. The watches were easier than they had been in the Klidi Pass. We did not have to watch for German SS creeping up on us.

It was easy right up to the third week in May when we heard the sound of anti-aircraft guns firing from the airfield. We had brought the Motley mounting and fixed up the Bren gun so that it could fire at aircraft. It would be easy enough to take it down and put it on its bipod. We stood to as German bombers tried to damage the airfield. We could not see the airfield but over the days leading to the bombing attack we had only seen half a dozen Hurricanes and some Blenheims using the airfield. We saw flashes from the guns and watched plumes of smoke and debris rise when the bombs were dropped. We could do nothing. We had no targets to aim at.

We caught up with sleep but we were warned that further attacks would come. It was four o'clock in the afternoon when the first of the heavy German bombers appeared. The guns around the airfield opened fire but, annoyingly, we were told not to. It was weird for the men on the Charlies and the Black Watch appeared to have been given the same orders and it was just the Bofors and Oerlikons we could hear. We did not see the results of the bombing but saw the German aeroplanes disappear and then we smelled the oily smoke. We could only speculate about the damage that had been caused.

After we had been stood down we began to cook our food. Suddenly at five thirty we heard the drone of aeroplane engines. I looked to the north. I shaded my eyes and recognised the aeroplanes. They had three engines and I shouted, "They are not bombers, they are Ju 52s."

It was an aerial armada and as they turned to head over the airfield, we saw the doors open and Corporal Williams shouted, "Paratroopers!"

Harry went to the Bren gun and cocked it, "Do we get to fire back, this time, Corp?"

"Aye, but only if they are close enough."

That made sense to me. It was now clear that we had not fired the night before to hide our positions. These aircraft were coming in so low that they could see where we were. I had a full magazine, and I waited. The anti-aircraft fire was effective, and I saw two Junkers struck by fire, and trailing flames and smoke they headed towards the ground. The aerial armada continued and as they passed closer to the Charlies I watched as the doors opened and German paratroopers dived headfirst from the aeroplanes. The Australians were closer than we were. They began to open fire and I saw men hit in the door while others were riddled with bullets as they drifted down. The sky was filled with parachutes.

Conscript's Call

Ray pointed west where parachutes flowered and blossomed over the port, "There are more attacking the town." He shook his head, "These must be mad buggers. Jumping headfirst from an aeroplane! Daft!"

I turned to Wally and said, "Well, Wally, you have your answer now. They aren't coming by sea but by air."

"Aye, Hawkeye, and we might need your sharp eyes sooner rather than later."

We heard the rattle of machine gun fire from the other side of the hill. The Black Watch were the ones defending the airfield and a gun battle was taking place. Some of the paratroopers must have landed closer to the coast for, from the east of us, we heard the 2nd York and Lancs as they opened fire. Even as Sergeant Jackson hurried to our position with new orders we heard the sound of small arms fire from the west of us. The paratroopers were fighting the Greeks for the town. The Germans were here in earnest. It was frustrating for us. We had the largest number of men and yet the fighting was too far away for us to open fire.

"Right, lads, we have to be ready to shift and support the Greeks." He pointed to the town. "Cunningham, take the Bren from its mounting. We will leave the Vickers here so your weapon will be the only automatic one we have. Dixon, make sure you have enough magazines in your pack. Salter and Jennings, take spare grenades for Vane."

"What about me, Sarge?"

"You, Sharratt, need to be able to move as quickly as you can. Your job is to shoot the officers and non-coms."

His command was chilling. I was now the platoon killer. I had not expected that when I had joined up. It was one thing to fight and fire with your comrades but I was now supposed to kill specific people and I was not sure I could do that.

As we hefted our packs and began to march towards the town, Corporal Williams sidled up to me, "Listen, John, I know Sergeant Jackson has asked a lot of you. You are a nice kid but the men we are fighting are ruthless. We have a war to win and if you shoot those giving commands then we have a better chance of doing that. Right?" I nodded, "And remember, these are paratroopers. They are tough and fearless men. They will be as good as, if not better than the SS we fought in the mountains."

Conscript's Call

"Right, Corp, I won't let you down."

He said quietly, "It's not me you would be letting down, it is England and the people at home."

"But this is Greece, Corporal. What happens if Jerry invades England while we are here?"

He smiled, "The Battle of Britain scuttled that idea. We are here because we need to protect the Suez Canal and the oil. Our ships use oil and if Adolf can cut us off from our supply..." He let me work the rest out. I would have to steel my resolve. I comforted myself with the thought that my dad would want me to do what the sergeant said.

It was dark when we reached the edge of the port and already the Greek wounded were pouring in to the makeshift hospitals. They were brave soldiers but ill equipped to fight the paratroopers. The Cretans were also defending their island, and I saw many men who had been wounded protecting their homes carried on litters. Soldier or civilian, all would be attended to.

CSM Hutton shouted, "Right, lads, we dig in here at the edge of the town. Like Klidi we sleep in pairs. We hold any who try to get through our lines and in the morning," he smiled, "well, we shall see, eh?"

It is amazing how a body can adjust to changes in sleep patterns. The four of us learned to sleep for four hours and then watch for four hours. We were tired but we knew that everyone was equally tired. Our section of eight was a happy one. Dave Proud and Norm Thomas were quiet lads who came from the same town, Blackpool. They had joined up together and, to my mind, were as close as brothers. That was their nickname from the rest of us. We called them the Brothers and differentiated by calling Brother Norm or Brother Dave. The two did not seem to mind. What we did know was that they would have our backs if things became difficult. We had also taken Fred Pratt under our wing. His two mates were both dead; one in Klidi Pass and the other on a battered Greek freighter.

We heard the Junkers again the next morning but this time they were well to the west of us. However, we could still see the flowering parachutes as they tumbled from the sky. The rumour was that the Black Watch had held on to the airfield and the Germans had been forced to the east. In the town we could hear

Conscript's Call

gunfire all through the night as the paratroopers first breached the old walls and then began to fight their way, house by house, to the port. We knew that we had to hold on to the port for if the worst should happen and we lost then that would be the only way we could escape. I dreaded another seaborne evacuation. It steeled me to do my best.

Sergeant Jackson spoke in a positive manner when he addressed us, "Right lads, B Company has been ordered to support the Greeks. There are pockets of German resistance. We have the weaponry to shift them."

We fastened our webbing and slung our packs. I made sure that my two ammunition pouches were filled with magazines and I had as many spare rounds in my battle dress pockets as I could manage. I had four grenades but mine were in my pack along with my jumper and some food. We had no idea how long we would be out and the nights, as we had found in the Klidi Pass, could be cold. Our platoon, all three sections, followed Lieutenant Hargreaves and Sergeant Jackson. I felt sorry for the mortar platoon. They had to lug their mortars while the machine gun platoon had been left to guard our camp.

We heard the firing from ahead. While Lieutenant Hargreaves and Sergeant Jackson scurried forward the corporal said, "Drop your packs. Put what you need in your haversacks."

I transferred my grenades to the haversack along with my compo rations and the pack of iron rations.

When the sergeant returned, he said, "There are some Jerries in a building a quarter of a mile away. Our platoon has been ordered to winkle them out. Vane, leave the grenade launcher here. There are still civilians, and we don't want to hurt our allies."

Weather grinned, "Thank the lord for that."

"You lead the section. Cunningham and Dixon, stay at the back."

I looked at Sergeant Jackson, "No officers with us, Sarge?"

He shook his head and smiled, "No, son, the three of us have the other sections to lead. You will be alright." I knew that we had lost sergeants during the escape from Greece and Corporal Williams was a good leader.

I suppose it was a compliment that he thought we could do it but I felt nervous as, nodding, I followed Geoff Vane. He was not afraid to lead. He was the biggest man not only in the section but the platoon and would make a good target for the Germans. He waved me forward, "Hawkeye, next to me. We might need your sharp eyes and skills with the Emily." Some of the men used the nickname of Emily for the Lee Enfield. It came from the acronym MLE.

"Right." I hefted my weapon and moved up to his shoulder. The rest of the section behind the two of us had rifles and then the Bren brought up the rear. We heard firing but I saw no sign of grey uniforms. There had not been much shelling in the port as the Germans had lighter weapons. It meant that they could use high buildings and vantage points. I happened to glance up and saw the shaft of light catch something on the church tower. Instinctively I shouted a warning, "Church tower."

We all dropped to find whatever cover we could. It was not a moment too soon as bullets were sent from the top of the tower. They were single shots but as chips flew from the wall behind which we sheltered I guessed that the man using it either had a telescopic sight or was a sharpshooter. Weather said, "Good shout, Hawkeye. Now is he alone or are there more of the buggers waiting for us?" Even as he raised his head to look there was a burst of light machine gun fire.

Wally said, "I bet that is a Schmeisser."

Sergeant Jackson had told us about the sub-machine gun the Germans used. It was a better weapon than the one used by our commandos, the Sten gun. We would need our Bren.

Weather was decisive, "Hawkeye, work your way to the left and find somewhere you can spot that sniper. Harry, set up the Bren and give the tower a burst."

"Righto. Come on, Bert."

I crawled along the wall. Ray lifted his rifle up and there was a fusillade of bullets sent in return. I heard Geoff say, "It looks like they have a section too. Norm, go and find the sergeant and tell him what we have found."

"Right, boss."

I concentrated on finding a place to raise my head. I went sixty yards to my left along a narrow passage. When I heard the

Conscript's Call

Bren gun open up I risked lifting my head above the low wall. There was a building before me. It had shuttered windows and beyond it I could see the tower. I could not see the gunner and so I slipped over the wall. When I reached the building, I went around the side where I was protected by the gable end and I slung my rifle. I began to climb. I was helped by the fact that it had large blocks of ancient masonry. When I reached the roof, I paused. I could see the barrel of the rifle and it was not aimed in my direction. I had managed to get to the side of the man in the tower. I rolled onto the pantile roof and unslung my rifle. I crabbed my way along and when I saw the sniper's body I stopped. I edged up to the ridge tiles and used them to provide a platform for the rifle. The man was two hundred yards from me. I took deep breaths to calm myself and aimed at his shoulder and head. I did not have much margin for error. I saw the flame from the rifle as he fired again. The Bren sent bullets to chip at the stonework. The Schmeisser rattled again, and I heard a cry. One of the section had been hit. I cursed myself. I had a job to do and I was wasting time. I waited until the man moved back to reload and then squeezed the trigger. The bullet must have hit his upper arm and driven up into his neck. He tumbled from the tower and a heartbeat later there was a flurry of bullets from German rifles and the Schmeisser. This time they were aimed at me. Luckily for me they could not see me because of the roof. I let myself slide down.

The Bren fired again, and this time was augmented by volleys from the rest of the section. I gambled that the Germans' attention would be elsewhere, and I slipped from the building. I saw that there was a passage between the house I had used and the next one looked more likely to afford protection. I moved along it, my rifle ready to use. I had the church tower in my line of sight and reasoned that the Germans had to be close to it. I kept moving and when I heard the sound of spent cartridges hitting the floor and adding to the gunfire, I knew I was close. The German weapons did not sound like the Lee Enfield. I had learned that in the Klidi Pass. I carefully laid down my rifle and took two Mills Bombs from my haversack. There was a sort of niche in the wall. I suppose it could have been used for a plant pot in summer. I put one grenade there and held the second. I listened. My patience was rewarded when I heard German spoken. I could not tell how far away it was but it sounded close enough for me to risk a grenade or two. I pulled the pin and after releasing the handle hurled it. I took the second and this time counted to three after I had released the handle. I threw it and then ducked down with my hands over my ears. Just before I did I heard a German voice shout, "Handgranate!"

The explosions came in rapid succession and even with my hands over my ears the concussion hurt them. I grabbed my gun. The air was filled with smoke, and I could hear moans and cries. I moved down the passage and saw a gate. There were holes torn from the gate but, for some reason, the latch still held it closed. Holding my rifle in my right hand I opened the latch with my left. I kicked it open and held my rifle ready to fire in two hands. I found a German section of four paratroopers. They were dead. I kept my rifle aimed at their bodies. It was clear that they were dead but the four had rifles and there was no MP 40, no Schmeisser.

The movement from behind made me raise my rifle. Weather and Glass Man held up their weapons, "Steady on. We are on your side."

"Some must have escaped. There is no sub-machine gun with these four."

At that moment Corporal Williams arrived with the rest of the section and number three section. He nodded to Geoff Vane, "Well done."

Weather shook his head, "Not me, Hawkeye here. He shot the sniper and took these out with two grenades."

"Right, Vane, I will lead the section." He turned to Private Hill who was in number three section. "Take the weapons back to the camp and the ID from these men. When that is done report to the lieutenant."

"Right, Corp." He turned to the rest of the section, "You heard the corporal."

I did not envy them the task. The grenades had exploded in a confined space and allied to the chips of wood and stone they had been badly cut before they died.

"Let's find the sub-machine gunner." He turned to me, "You stay at the back with Cunningham."

"Corp."

"Proud and Thomas, take the lead. Vane, you and I will follow them. Pratt, stay with Cunningham and the Bren."

Weather said, "Fred has copped a wound, Corp."

"Right, Pratt, follow Hill back to the hospital."

The streets of Heraklion where we hunted the Germans were old and narrow. A motor car would have struggled to negotiate them. The buildings to the sides of us were oppressively close. At the back Harry and Bert walked behind with the Bren and I scanned the rooftops. The sub-machine gunner and the survivors of the grenade attack were not up high. They were low down and when they opened fire the Brothers were hit. Geoff and the corporal returned fire, and I saw Wally's arm pull back as he hurled a grenade. "Grenade!" I knew better than any the effect of the grenade and I pressed myself into the wall. The smoke from the explosion filled the narrow road. Then there was silence or perhaps my hearing had gone. I stood and looked down the road. Norm and Dave lay on the ground. They were alive but wounded.

"Cunningham, up here and give the building a burst."

The two men ran forward. They set up the tripod and then Harry emptied a magazine at the doorway and house from which the ambush had been launched.

"Salter and Jennings, check it out. Vane and Sharratt, see to the wounded."

Geoff had already taken off his pack and was looking for dressings. In a way both men had been lucky. The sub-machine gun had hit them in the legs and as there was no blood gushing I assumed that no artery had been struck. They were not life-threatening wounds. Norm Thomas also had a wound to his arm. I went to Dave Proud and tied a tourniquet above the wound before dousing it with powder and fastening a bandage to it.

"All clear, Corporal. Three dead Jerries." Wally's voice was clear and there was no hint that he had seen what I had, German bodies disfigured by a hand grenade.

"Right, take their weapons and ID. Help Vane and Sharratt take these two to the First Aid station." He looked at Geoff and said, quietly, "How are they?"

"Hospital job, Corp."

Conscript's Call

He nodded, "Then that means they will be taken to Egypt. We will clear up here and then head back to camp. It seems quiet up ahead." I had not noticed before but now that I did, I realised I could not hear any firing. If there were pockets of Germans, they were not close to us.

Geoff handed his pack and rifle to Wally. He hefted Norm Thomas on his back. I was not as big as Wally but working on the farm had made me strong. I gave my pack and rifle to Ray. I smiled at Dave Proud. He was the smallest man in the section, "I will be as gentle as I can."

He gave a weak smile, "Just get me to where I can be given something for the pain. It hurts like buggery!"

Ray and Wally had taken the packs and rifles of the two men and when I hefted Dave onto my shoulder we set off back to the camp where the doctors had a sick bay. We found the body of Fred Pratt just two-hundred-yards shy of the building. Ray knelt and said, "Dead. I thought it was just a scratch to his head."

Weather said, "Head wounds can be funny. Poor sod."

When we arrived at the hospital we saw that they only had one other patient who was having his head bandaged. The doctors shouted over the orderlies who took the two men from us. Geoff handed Norm a pack of cigarettes. "We will get you some more and bring them when we visit."

The doctor said, "It will be a long time before they get visitors. We are going to patch them up and they will be on a ship heading for Alexandria. The general is getting the wounded and the noncombatants out."

As we headed back to our camp, Geoff said, "Well, the writing is on the wall, lads. We might be holding them here but that sounds like doom and gloom. I reckon we better be prepared to leave, eh?"

Chapter 6

The battle for Crete lasted a bare twelve days but our part only lasted eight. We had done all that had been asked of us but it had not been enough. We had held the airfield and the port as we had been ordered. We successfully hunted the Germans who had infiltrated the town and removed them, but it was to no avail once the German paratroopers had taken Maleme airfield and captured the port town of Chania at the other end of the island. They simply landed more paratroopers without the inherent dangers of a drop and the port allowed them to bring in more troops by sea. The Australians and New Zealanders who had been defending Maleme were heading south to be picked up by ships there. We were told that we would be evacuated from the port of Heraklion.

I knew how bad things were when, one day as we returned to the camp I saw Sergeant Jones and he had a rifle in his hands. He smiled as I passed and I risked a joke. He had been a friend of my father after all, "Have you fired it, Sergeant Jones? Are we in trouble, yet?"

He laughed, "Cheeky young thing. I have fired more bullets than you have had hot dinners." He slung his rifle and came closer to me, "I read the report about the church tower. People took notice of it. Keep it up, son. Now move along, eh?"

"Right, Sarge."

It was funny for it was just one comment and I had already been praised by the lieutenant and Captain Whittle, but coming from an old soldier from the Great War somehow meant more to me.

Our section had not suffered any more casualties after Fred died, but three men had been killed in other sections from our platoon. I was glad that the Brothers were safely in hospital in Alexandria. The hospital ships had sailed and we had not heard of any losses. The day we left we were told that we would be embarking at midnight and leaving by three am. That way it was to be hoped we could avoid the attention of the Luftwaffe. The enemy air forces controlled the skies in this part of the

Mediterranean. We were ordered to destroy any heavy equipment and supplies. We packed as many of the supplies as we could and then destroyed the rest. We took anything we could eat and anything we could use as a weapon. Everything else was either burned or blown up. The lessons of the fall of France and Dunkirk were learned. Leaving a pall of smoke over the airfield and our camp, we trooped down to the port, but we had to do so while German aircraft bombed both us and the town. That we survived, largely untouched was a miracle but the bodies we passed on our way to the port told us how narrow were the margins between life and death. Luck seemed to play an enormous part in our survival. Half an hour earlier leaving for the port might have seen us hit by a stick of bombs. As it was, the bombing lasted two hours and when it was over we reached the port over which hung an eerie silence. We queued as only the British can queue as we waited to begin to board the ships. This time they were not commandeered merchant ships but Royal Naval vessels. There were two cruisers, *Orion*, and *Dido*, and six destroyers, *Hotspur*, *Jackal*, *Decoy*, *Hereward*, *Kimberley* and *Imperial* waiting to take us off. We would be packed into them like sardines. The cruisers, however, looked reassuringly large. They had four turrets and their six-inch guns looked to be powerful.

We queued patiently and just before midnight began to board. The gangplank wobbled alarmingly as we marched aboard the cruiser. We were on *Orion* and that pleased me for she was a much bigger ship than the destroyers and we had seen what a stick of Stuka bombs could do to a destroyer. We shuffled our way along the decks. No one wanted to go below decks and we were crammed together on every available part of the main deck. When we left on time there was a cheer from the packed soldiers. We had a chance to escape Crete and to reach Alexandria. We had heard that the general there had driven the Italians back to the Libyan border. It was a hopeful sign that the disasters of Norway, France, Greece and Crete might be ending and we might just enjoy a victory. As we headed out to sea we were all too relieved to sleep and while the smokers smoked we talked of the two evacuations and what it meant. It was just the remains of the platoon, all twenty of us, who were seated just below the second six-inch gun turret just forward of the bridge. We were in the lee of the gun and there was shelter. The gun crew were closed up inside.

"It seems to me that the Germans have us beat."

Weather shook his head, "Harry, you are a pessimistic sod. We are in good spirits and Jerry didn't beat us. Every time we met him we sent him packing."

Harry held up his fingers as he went through a list, "Dunkirk, Norway, Greece and now Crete. We have lost them all. If we didn't have a navy then we would be right up that creek. They took the lads off from Norway, France and now Crete. England might be safe but we don't seem able to take on the Germans on land. I should have joined the navy."

Just then a sailor with a jug in one hand and a handful of mugs appeared from the direction of the galley, "Heads up there, matey. Kai for the lads." We moved apart and he shifted the mugs so that he was carrying them and the jug in one hand. He went to the ladder to climb into the turret. How he climbed I do not know but he was a sailor and this was his ship. He whistled when he neared the entrance and when the jug and mugs were taken from him he turned and said, "Don't you squaddies worry. The Andrew will keep taking you off beaches and making sure you have your supplies. One day you will work out how to do it." There was no rancour in his voice and we sat in silence for a while as we reflected on his words.

Ray said, "He is right. I mean look at Malta, that is only holding out because of the Royal Navy and a handful of aeroplanes."

Wally snorted, "RAF! Brylcreem boys they are. We never saw one aeroplane on the way back from Greece. Those Stukas had a field day. It is a good job we will be in Egypt before they know we have left."

Just then Sergeant Jackson came along, "Quieten down, lads, the Navy have a ship to run, and you are nattering like a bunch of old ladies."

I said, "Sarge, what do you reckon, can we beat the Germans? Harry here thinks we have been driven out of every place we tried to fight them." Sergeant Jackson would give us the truth.

Conscript's Call

The sergeant rubbed his chin. It had been a while since we had enjoyed the opportunity to shave, "Well, there are a couple of ways of looking at that. Private Cunningham is right, we have been driven out but that has never been the fault of the soldier, lads like us. It is because, well, let's speak the truth, because of politicians. They promised the French we would fight with them and they did the same with the Greeks. Until we are just fighting with British or Imperial soldiers it is hard to judge but you lads can hold your heads up. You sent the best that Jerry has to offer, the SS and the paratroopers, packing. The Aussies and New Zealanders are good lads and they did well in Greece and Crete. I am more hopeful now. We get to Egypt and after a bit of a rest we will show Jerry and his Eyetie allies what the Tommy can do. Now get some rest."

I felt a little better. Sergeant Jackson had sounded just like my dad and his mates. They never doubted themselves, just the politicians. We curled up and tried to sleep.

It seemed just like five minutes had passed before I was roused by my friends. Bert shook me, "Hawkeye, we have stopped. Summat is up."

We went to the side and saw that one of the destroyers, *Imperial*, was no longer moving. Two other destroyers were abeam of her. The same sailor who had taken the cocoa to the turret was passing. I said, "What's the problem?"

"I reckon *Imperial* has something wrong with either her steering or her engine. If it was anywhere but here they might try to fix it or tow her but this part of the Med is bomb alley. They are taking off the soldiers and her crew." He shook his head, "A shame that, the Isis class destroyers are generally good ships. I reckon your mates on the other destroyers are going to be even more crowded."

We all watched for over an hour as not only the soldiers but also the crew were taken off. When *Hereward* then sent torpedoes to sink the obviously damaged ship we were shocked. A wall of flame flew into the air and within moments the destroyer began to sink.

Harry said, "Well that does it. They will have heard that in Crete and we now have one less ship."

Conscript's Call

I nodded and pointed to the east, "Aye, and dawn is not too far away. I reckon Jerry will send his Stukas hunting us sooner rather than later."

The cruiser had a marine bugler and it was he who announced the start of the new day. The crew of the ship had been stood to all night but now they were at action stations. Every gun would be closed up and the watertight door shut. For those below decks it might seem like prison. I loaded my rifle.

Ray asked, "What are you doing that for?"

"On the last ship we were told to save ammo. If and when we do get to Egypt there will be plenty of ammo. A couple of magazines is a small price to pay to hit one Stuka. If I can do that then I am happy and the bullets will not be wasted."

Harry nodded and he and Bert prepared the Bren, laying the magazines on the deck.

It was six a.m. when we saw the distinctive wings of the Stukas as they headed towards us. I saw the pompom crews preparing their weapons. The six-inch guns of the cruiser would not be used. I had counted eight of them. It did not seem enough. The sixteen 40 mm also appeared to be an inadequate number. The destroyers opened fire first for they were like sheepdogs racing around the cruisers. The air was filled with the smell of cordite. Every time a Stuka was hit we cheered. When one bomb hit **Hereward** there was a groan across the whole ship. She was overloaded and had the survivors from **Imperial** aboard. We soon had to worry more about ourselves as six Stukas dived to attack us. I raised my rifle. The Ju 87 was a big target on the ground but in the air it was like a little bird. As the first one dived every gun on the ship and every rifle and Bren gun opened up. The sound of the guns was a crescendo of screaming, barking noise. My ears were hurting from the successive concussions. The two pounder pompoms kept up a regular thumping and puffs of smoke appeared around the wings and cowling of the Stukas. The 40 mm guns sent tracer rounds to arc at them. I just aimed at the propeller and hoped one of my rounds would hit. It was, perhaps, no surprise when a Stuka exploded above us showering the deck around the forward turret with unburnt fuel. Soldiers who were close by, aided by the crew, quickly doused it with sea water. I saw that a petty officer had organised buckets of water to

Conscript's Call

be placed close to the turrets and gun emplacements. The captain threw his enormous ship around as he tried to avoid the dive bombers. Another two Stukas were hit, one was downed and the others missed. Their bombs showered the ship with sea water. They flew off.

In the lull we saw that *Hereward* was sinking. The single bomb that had struck was enough to sink the little destroyer. The crew and the soldiers were in boats and on rafts. Others, wearing life jackets were clinging to whatever they could, rafts, boats, pieces of wreckage.

Bert asked a passing sailor, "Will the other ships pick 'em up?"

The sailor shook his head, "Not a chance, chum. Any ship that stops to do so will be an easy target for those dive bombers. The only chance for us is to keep moving and hope that we don't get hit. If any of us go down, we are on our own."

It was a sobering thought.

If we thought the attack was over, we were wrong. Even as the first aeroplanes flew off more appeared, this time Italians and Wally said, "They must have an airfield close by."

The new attack was concentrated on us and *Dido*. The Stukas and the Italian dive bombers screamed in. Their dives were incredibly steep. They were flown by enemies trying to kill us, but I knew that they were brave men. It must have been awful for the rear gunners in the two-seater dive bombers. At least the pilot could see the flak and try to avoid it. The rear gunner just waited for the hit that would end his life or send the aircraft crashing into the sea. We brought down another three but one managed a hit. The bomb hit our forward turret. I watched the bomb as it descended. It seemed to fall in slow motion. It was clear that it would hit us and we had seen what one bomb could do to a destroyer. I watched it strike and then the blast knocked all of us from our feet and a wall of flames leapt into the air. Equipment and men were flung overboard by the blast. I found myself lying on my back and I could not breathe. I could barely see anything for the air was filled with smoke, and I thought I had gone deaf. I managed to pull myself to my feet and stand, somewhat shakily. I looked at the empty hole where the turret had been. The shells in the turret must have exploded and the devastation inside

Conscript's Call

would have been complete. I could not see either the crew who had been inside or the turret itself. The fuel from the first Stuka we had hit had been ignited by the blast and flared into flames. Even as we were trying to get to our feet the fire began to spread along the deck and threatened to engulf the whole ship. As I stood, I saw that the whole enormous turret, complete with crew was gone. It must have been blasted overboard. The power to blow such a huge piece of metal overboard terrified me. The crew of the second turret began to leave their turret as damage control parties raced to put the fire out. They joined them to bring some order to the chaos that reigned.

My hearing must have returned for I heard Geoff as he shouted, "Come on, lads, I don't fancy a swim in the briny. Let's put the fire out."

We grabbed buckets and greatcoats and raced to douse the flames. We beat smaller flames with greatcoats and hurled water onto the larger fires. The crew were using hosepipes and everyone was fighting to save the ship. The horror was that the soldiers who he been sheltering close to that turret had either been blown overboard or had been set alight. None were alive but their bodies burned.

A petty officer shouted, "Everything that is on fire gets shoved overboard." He looked meaningfully at the bodies, "And I mean, everything."

I could not bring myself to simply throw the dead overboard and so I hurled sea water at the flames and then raced back to the side to draw more. Others had the grisly task of tossing burning dead bodies over the side. All the time we were doing so the bombs continued to fall. At one point I saw, not dive bombers, but high-level bombers. We were doomed. The destroyers bore charmed lives it seemed, but **Dido** had also been hit. She was not as badly damaged as we were but we were still far from Egypt. The Stukas that attacked us only had the pompoms and 40 mm to contend with. Every other man on the ship was fighting the fire. The heat was intense. It took an hour to douse the flames and as soon as we had done so we grabbed our guns and prepared to fight for the ship and ourselves once more. We hit another Stuka which peeled off and headed north trailing smoke but this time there were no cheers. For another hour we endured attack after

Conscript's Call

attack, but the ship was not hit again. When we saw the Hurricanes heading towards us, we breathed a sigh of relief. It meant we were close to an umbrella of fighters for protection but we kept our eyes to the north for another attack.

CSM Hutton and some sergeants came forward. Only the burning bodies had been hurled overboard. The corpses of the others lay littered along the deck. He looked over to us, "You lads, give us a hand. We are to take our casualties to the after deck. The colonel wants them laid by the crane so that they can be identified."

Geoff said, "There were others, Company Sergeant Major, who were tossed overboard."

The sergeant sounded very old and weary when he said, "I know, son, and this way we can work out who they were." I knew that this would be a job for Sergeant Jones and the headquarters staff. This was not counting paper clips. This was a grim duty that I would not wish to have.

It was a grisly task. Some of the bodies had been burned. Some had horrific wounds but one of the soldiers from Company C had not a scratch on him, yet he was dead. The sergeant who helped me to carry the body said, "Lucky bugger knew nothing about it. He must have been killed by the blast. Better than those who burned. You lads were lucky too. Think on that."

I was. I was reflecting that I had already used up more luck than most men. I should have been in the house at Ince Blundell, but I was not. I could have been where the Brothers walked and been shot there, in Heraklion, and we could have chosen the forward turret for shelter. I was lucky. We all moved about the ship like zombies in a cheap B Movie. This was as close to death as we had come and I for one, was frightened.

What made it all worse was that the ship now stank. Burning fuel, bodies and parts of the ship added to the smell of the cordite. Men were being sick over the side and that did not make a for an improvement. It was another reminder of the effect of a single bomb. No wonder the *Hereward* had been sunk. She had been much smaller than we were. Every time we heard an aeroplane we looked up in fear but, thankfully, it was the noise of our escorts. The Blenheims had enough armament and the

Conscript's Call

range to deal with any attacker. They had just been a couple of hours late getting to us.

It was well after six o'clock in the evening when we saw Alexandria and the coast of Africa in the distance. The umbrella of aircraft had kept us safe for the whole afternoon. We discovered that while the battalion had lost forty men in the campaigns in Greece and Crete, fifty had died or been wounded in the air attack. Once more I wished to be as far from the sea as I could. On land I felt as though I could do something about my survival. The sea seemed to be a lottery. Harry had also reconsidered and no longer thought that a life at sea was better.

We were fed on the ship. Stale bread and corned beef augmented by copious amounts of tea, but we were alive and the dead would have loved to enjoy stale bread and corned beef. No one complained. The fleet limped into port at eight o'clock at night. I knew that every ship had endured damage, but I could not help but think about the survivors from *Hereward*. Had they been picked up? If they had then they would be prisoners of war and if not…It did not bear thinking about.

The wounded were taken off first. A fleet of ambulances awaited them. Then the blanket covered bodies of the dead were moved ashore and loaded onto lorries. No one moaned at the wait for we were alive and had a life ahead of us. The dead had nothing…. We marched off in company order and were marshalled by the ships. Our numbers had shrunk.

The colonel addressed us all, as we stood in ranks that, at that moment, were shells of the men who had boarded the ships, "Men, we have done all that was asked of us and you should know that I am proud of this battalion both for its conduct in Greece and Crete as well as your action on the *Orion*. I am afraid that there is no transport for us and we will have to march." He smiled, "After that little sea voyage I am looking forward to solid ground beneath my feet. When we march keep your heads high. The Egyptian people are relying on British soldiers to save them from Fascist domination. March with pride for this battalion has yet to endure a defeat."

RSM Lawson's voice boomed out. We marched. We had slung rifles and were laden with packs. We had our greatcoats rolled for it was far hotter, even in the evening, than it had been in either Greece or Crete. We marched with swinging arms and men began whistling as they marched. I wondered if we would be reprimanded but it seemed that the sergeants and officers thought it was a good thing. The whistling seemed to help us to march and keep in step. There were few people on the streets for it was gone nine o'clock but the ones we passed smiled and waved. They did not know we had fled here and been lucky to survive the crossing. They just saw Imperial infantry coming to their aid.

When we reached our new home we found it was not a barracks but a camp. There was a wire fence, and MPs directed us to the place we would pitch our tents. Sergeant Jackson organised ours. We had lost many men from the platoon. Some were like Thomas and Proud, they had been wounded in either Greece or Crete and would be in the hospital. They would return but there were others who would not. Privates Pratt, Smith and Topp had all been conscripts but for a bare four months. As some of those who had died were corporals and sergeants there would be promotions. We had also heard a rumour that some men were to be made up to Lance Corporal. All we were bothered about was erecting our tents and getting some sleep. We had endured a long night with, perhaps, twenty minutes of sleep and it had been a fitful one at that. Here, protected by a fence and sentries we would be safe.

When the tent was erected, and we were undressed, I rolled into my blanket. It was then I said a silent prayer. I had been remiss and not prayed as much as I ought to have done in Greece, Crete and on the ship but I did that night. I had come perilously close to death. The turret and its crew that had been hurled overboard from the cruiser had been so close to me that I knew I was truly lucky. I thanked God for my survival and asked him to watch over my dead family. I felt better after the prayer and, with the picture of my smiling family in my head, I went into a deep sleep.

Conscript's Call

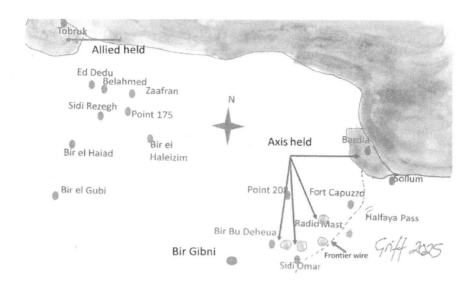

Libyan Border 1941

Chapter 7

The Egyptian Desert May 1941
Operation Brevity

When we reached Egypt any thoughts that we would be given time to rest and recover were shattered for the Germans had taken over from the Italians and, with a new general, Field Marshal Erwin Rommel, were driving our soldiers back to the Egyptian border. We heard, as we boarded lorries to take our depleted battalion to the front, that Tobruk, manned by Australians, was holding out and that was the only thing that had stopped the enemy tanks and lorries from driving on to Alexandria. It explained why we were not being given time to recover. Replacements were on their way from Britain but, as we knew, that took time and was fraught with danger. We would have to make do with what we had. We were equipped with uniforms, ammunition and weapons. I had hung onto my rifle but others had been lost when the turret had exploded. We were given a new grenade launcher and a Boys anti-tank rifle.

We drove up the dusty road that we were sharing with British armour. We had seen none in either Greece or Crete but here we did, and we soon became adept at identifying the different types. There were the old cruiser tanks but also some newer Valentines and even a few of the strange looking M3 Lee Grant tanks which had two guns. There were armoured cars and light tanks. It seemed we had come just in time. I wondered, as we camped a day from Alexandria, if I would see my first battle. If so, it would be nothing like the battles fought by my father and his friends. They had fought in muddy trenches where an advance was measured in feet not miles. Here the British army had advanced as far as Libya before being forced back by the Germans. In this arid desert we would use sand and not earth for defences. In the Great War water had never been a problem. They could always collect rainwater. Here water would be as valuable as gold. Already we were suffering from the heat. We had enjoyed some days in Greece we had called hot. We now knew what hot really meant. We learned that there was a railway

Conscript's Call

line but it had been damaged by the Luftwaffe. But for that damage we would have been at the front already.

We did not bother with tents again. It seemed too much trouble to erect them. No one reprimanded us for doing so but the officers and sergeants did have tents. We had been given new kit and our ammunition replenished. I wore shorts to try to keep a little cooler, yet at night it was as cold as it had been in the Greek mountains, without the snow, of course. We had our rations replaced and we now had army cooks. We were happy to be going to war but at the back of our minds was the thought that the Germans had managed to defeat our army at every turn. Would the desert prove any different?

It was Corporal Williams, our section leader, who put it into perspective. We were camped by the side of the road and had a fire going in an old oil drum we had found abandoned. There were many of them for tanks and lorries carried spare fuel in them and when they had refilled their tanks they simply abandoned them. The ones which had contained fuel were particularly useful. So far I had not managed to find any food to augment our rations but we had eaten our rations and our bellies were full. As the smokers smoked we listened as the corporal gave his view of the campaign, "The thing is, lads, that we all have the same problem here. Fuel. Both we and the Germans have to transport it across the Med and both sides are knocking out the other's ships. We are close to the oil fields of Persia here but once we advance then we will have longer supply lines. The Germans have pushed us back, but they have further to bring their fuel and we have more air cover. The Stukas we endured at sea and in Greece will not have such an easy time of it here. Don't get me wrong, it will be hard but from what I have seen of this section and this platoon, you are all made of the right stuff. You might be conscripts but you are good ones. Thanks to Hawkeye and his run in with McGuire, we weeded out the bad 'uns. Just do what you did in Greece and Crete and we will be alright."

I knew he was deliberately bolstering our confidence, but I believed him, and I agreed with his assessment of us. We did not yet have a full section. The three who had been killed had yet to be replaced but Dave and Norm had rejoined us. They sported scars which would impress the girls back in England as they were not on the face and when they rolled up their sleeves and trousers there would be gasps. They were keen to become part of the section again. We had lost a corporal from the company in the *Orion* and so Geoff Vane was promoted to Lance Corporal. He would be able to help Corporal Williams who now had two sections to lead. Eventually, corporals would be promoted to sergeant. I thought it was a good promotion for Geoff was a good chap. He was not cocky, and he had an attitude which seemed to belie his size for he could be gentle. As McGuire discovered, he was not a man to rile and I was happy that, in the absence of Corporal Williams, it would be Geoff who made the decisions.

We halted at Sidi Barrani just twenty-five miles from the front line which was at Sollum and Halfaya Pass. The railhead was here. Our company was chosen to be part of an armoured brigade. The rest would wait in reserve until their numbers were increased. We were reorganised and given a dozen Bedford lorries that would enable us to stay close to the tanks and armoured cars. We would be motorised infantry. The lorries were supposed to carry eleven passengers. We packed more in. There was also a Canadian Chevrolet vehicle that had been converted to carry two Bren guns on Motley mountings as well as a Boys anti-tank rifle. The captain and CSM Hutton would use that vehicle and the radio that went with it.

It was clear to all of us that the generals wanted to retake the land they had lost and to relieve Tobruk. Instead of defending or running we would be advancing and attacking. I was excited for this would be as unlike my father's war as it was possible. We would not be static but mobile. We were known, so I learned, as a Jock Column, named after the Scottish commander, General Jock Campbell. There were three such columns and our job, we were told by the captain, was to protect the left, southern flank of the main attack by the Guards Brigade. The trucks were brand new and had arrived on one of the convoys that had successfully managed to evade both submarines and bombers. The one who was really delighted was Bert. He had engines with which to tinker and even before we had set off, he had asked the RASC driver if he could look at it. He had almost purred for the engine, so he told me, later on, was the cleanest one he had ever seen. It was a brand-new lorry almost straight off the production line. In the garage where he had worked, in Leigh, they had dealt with old cars that were caked in oil and were rusty buckets, as he termed them.

We acted almost like children on a school outing. For once we were riding to war and there was a feeling of optimism. The Matilda Infantry Tank, which appeared to make up the most potent part of the column, was a solid machine, and we were told that the Italians did not have an anti-tank weapon that could penetrate its frontal armour. The only nagging doubt in my mind was the fact that the Germans were better than the Italians. They had better tanks, and I wondered if they had a better anti-tank gun.

We departed the camp at Sidi Barrani during the night and left the main road to head south across the desert. We were not driving over sand, but it was rough ground and part of me wondered if such terrain would prove too difficult for the lorries. Bert was scornful about my concerns when I voiced them. We were bumping over rocks, and he said, "These are well made. They have suspension for each wheel." He patted the body, "Tough as old boots!" I had never seen Bert as happy as he was once we rode in the lorries. He was also eager to look at the converted Chevrolet, but he was uncertain how the captain would view an inspection.

One of the lorries was also towing one of the new six pounder anti-tank guns that had replaced the quick firing two pounder. It had a much better range and the men who had been trained to use it were excited at the prospect. I was not so sure. German tank crews would target the anti-tank guns first and the small shield did not look as though it would effectively protect the crew. Weather told me not to be so pessimistic when I voiced my concerns. "Hawkeye, think about it. Think half full and not half empty. You are worried about the six pounder. If we had the two pounder, we would have a shorter range and the same lack of shield. You are right, it is not perfect, but it is better than nowt." Since his promotion Geoff had changed. It was as though he felt more responsible for all of us and yet a few weeks earlier we had all heeded the conscript's call.

Conscript's Call

We were behind the screen of cruiser tanks and the lighter Mark IV tanks. Ahead of them were the Marmon-Herrington Armoured Cars of the 11th Hussars. We could see nothing. The sides of the canvas hid us and while they protected us from the glare of the sun, we all hated the suspense for we were in the dark. The motion in the back of the lorry was similar to being on the small freighter when we had left Greece. We rolled around like shelled peas in a colander. It was when we stopped that we began to feel the tension. Until then we could have been on a charabanc trip in a bus with no windows.

"Right lads, just ammo pouches and canteens. You can leave your packs. Form up behind the lorries."

We obeyed the sergeant and jumped down to be almost blinded by the sun which glared down. I saw the other sections as they joined us. Ahead I could see the two lines of tanks and in the distance the armoured cars. Their job, so far as I could deduce, was to find the enemy and then report back. The cruiser tanks, we were told, could stop an Italian tank but the German tanks…that was another matter.

"Spread out. Corporals…"

CSM Hutton's voice seemed calmness personified. We could have been on Formby beach on manoeuvres and not about to set out across the desert to find enemy soldiers.

Corporal Williams waved us forward, "Keep pace with the tanks. Our job is to neutralise any soldiers with anti-tank weapons."

The drivers left with the lorries and the Chevrolet and would wait until they were summoned to pick us up. The tanks all had radios and would communicate with our transport. We had to move quickly to keep up with the tanks but the Valentine could only move at fifteen miles an hour at best and we were able to maintain contact. The worst part of walking behind them was the dust they threw up and I regretted not having my neck cloth tied around my mouth. As we headed into Libya, I reflected that learning to be a soldier was not all about using a rifle.

We knew when the German tanks were spotted for a head appeared from the tank before us and a voice shouted, above the roar of the noisy engine, "Jerry tanks ahead."

Conscript's Call

Lieutenant Hargreaves nodded and shouted, "Keep close to the tanks and listen for the order to take cover."

As he hurried after the tanks which had changed formation slightly, Sergeant Jackson shouted, "Make sure you have one up the spout."

Ahead I heard the sound of machine guns and the crack of a tank gun. The air was soon filled with the sound of machine guns and 37 mm tank guns as they duelled. We were now running. All I could see was the rear of the Valentine before me. I was just glad that I was close to my section, and I was happier that we would all be fighting together. We could rely on one another. When the enemy rifles and machine guns opened fire we closed up behind the tank we were following. I could hear the bullets pinging off the armour. I tried to imagine what it would be like inside but could not. I hated closed and confined spaces. The turret of the Valentine looked too small for the three men housed within.

"Take cover!" We heeded the command of Sergeant Jackson as the Valentine veered to the left. The tanks had been communicating with one another and clearly following some order.

We threw ourselves to the ground. I had already spied a rock and I chose that as my spot. It was not before time as when the Valentine moved away the machine gun bullets filled the space I had just vacated. Had they hit me I would have been sliced in two. I aimed my rifle as I sought a target. I heard Lee Enfield rifles around me as my comrades began to fire. The Bren would take some moments to set up. I was the one who the sergeant and corporal thought was the best shot and that meant I sought a target rather than just firing to keep the enemy occupied.

I used the rock for cover as I sought a target. Ahead of me I saw the flashes from the German weapons. The enemy infantry had occupied a ridge. I could ignore the armoured vehicles. They had their own battle to fight. Our job was to eliminate the infantry. All around me I heard the crack as Ray, Wally and the others fired at any glimpse of a German. I heard the spent cases as they were ejected but all the time I concentrated on looking for a target that I could hit. It had been made clear to me that I was the sharpshooter and I had decided that as the skill had been identified I would do my best to excel at it. I saw a German helmet. I could have risked a shot at the helmet, but the odds were that the helmet would protect the wearer. However, it was a target, and I aimed at it and steadied my breathing. He must have been the layer for a German machine gun as he was to the side of the barrel which spouted flames and bullets. I waited and was rewarded when he moved his head a little. I guessed that he was reaching for more ammunition and when I had a clear sight of his head I fired. As soon as his arms arched and he fell back I knew that I had hit him. The machine gun stopped. I chambered another round and sought another target. It was as though I was fighting my own private war for the others, Harry and Bert included, were sending round after round at the enemy position. Bert must have changed the magazine of the Bren gun at least twice judging by the empty magazines. I had fired just one bullet.

When the machine gun opened fire again, I was clearly the target, and the enemy rifles also sought me out. I managed to duck behind the rock as the bullets zipped towards me. If I had lifted my head, then one would have hit me. My helmet was angled and when I heard stones chipping it, I was glad I had chosen this rock and that my helmet held. I heard the sound of the explosion and I risked lifting my head. I saw to the left of me a German Mark IV Panzer on fire. I also saw, in my line of sight, a German arm. I aimed and fired. There was a huge amount of noise already, but I heard the cry. I had wounded one of them. In quick succession there were two more explosions and CSM Hutton shouted, "Up and at 'em!"

The hardest thing I had ever done was to stand up for I expected to be scythed down by machine gun fire. As I got to my feet, I saw the Germans as they too rose but, in their case, it was to run away from us. I snap fired at one of them before his head disappeared beneath the ridge. Some of the lads cheered as they charged. I saw that Dave and Norm had fitted their bayonets. I would rely on the .303 rounds in my magazines. I was the first to reach the ridge and when I found myself on the top I saw the Germans running to mount their half-tracks. I knelt to steady my arm and began to fire at the fleeing men. They were two hundred yards away but I managed to hit one who spread his arms and

Conscript's Call

fell and to wing another one who dropped his gun as he clambered aboard the vehicle. The others joined me. I saw Harry and Bert, out of the corner of my eye, as they quickly set up the Bren. The rest of the platoon were now at the ridge and firing at the fleeing Germans. Harry got off a long burst which took out the German gunner traversing the heavy machine gun.

"Cease fire!"

I changed my magazine and looked around. I saw the man I had first killed. My bullet had driven up through his arm and shoulder. The other man must have been wounded.

Sergeant Jackson's voice was reassuringly calm, as usual, "See if any of them are alive." There were four bodies in all but, like the man I had shot they were all dead. "Take any weapons and ammunition."

I searched the dead German. In the short time since he had died his blood had begun to dry and become congealed. It was sticky. I managed to search him but only by telling myself he was like a dead bunny and not a man. When his wallet fell out and lay open I saw the photograph of a pretty blond girl. Unlike me, the dead German had probably kissed a girl. Would she mourn him? His weapons were a bayonet and two stick grenades. I jammed the bayonet in my belt and attached the two grenades to my webbing. Corporal Williams led us to the place vacated by the half-tracks and we did the same for the body we found there.

Sergeant Jackson said, "The lorries are on their way. While we are waiting, bury the Germans, eh? We would want them to do that for us." He was a thoughtful man and he was right.

The Germans had left their trenching tools at the ridge when they had dug in and we buried them in the softer sand in the lee of the ridge. In time more sand would come and bury them even deeper. As we mounted the lorries, I could not help but think that we might have suffered the same fate in the Klidi Pass. We had been dug in and if the Germans had succeeded, they might have scraped a grave in the thin Greek soil. It was a sobering thought.

When the lorries came we were in an ebullient mood. One of the cruiser tanks had been hit and we had to wait while everything of value was stripped from it and then grenades were dropped inside. Had the skirmish been part of a larger battle that

Conscript's Call

we had won then it might have been repaired. Instead, it would wait with the three burnt out German tanks and their dead crews.

We put on a brew and chatted. "Did we win, Lieutenant Hargreaves?" Bert's question was one on all of our minds. We had held the field and not fallen back but we were new to this.

He shrugged, "We did our job, Dixon. We lost one tank compared to the German's three. We buried half a dozen Germans and didn't suffer a scratch but the main battle was there." He pointed north, "At Fort Capuzzo and the Halfaya Pass." These were just names. I had no idea where they were. "The only ones who really know if we are winning are the generals."

We pulled back in the middle of the night. The tanks needed fuel but, as we regrouped, at dawn, in the same place we had left for the battle, I knew then that we had not won. We had not lost but we had been forced to retreat. We held the same ground, and Tobruk was still under siege. It was only a day or so later that we discovered that while we had not taken all our objectives, men had retaken the Halfaya Pass and destroyed the enemy defences there. We made a defensive position to the south of the road and settled into a different routine from that in Greece. In Greece we had been frozen and sought heat. Here we baked and sought shade. The other difference was confidence. We no longer felt like conscripts. We had fought and killed Germans. We had driven them from the field. However, by the end of May we discovered that Halfaya Pass had been retaken by the Germans. The mood of our camp became depressed.

I had asked Sergeant Jackson if he wanted the bayonet and grenades I had taken but he shook his head, "You keep 'em, son. You might need them. Those German stick grenades make handy booby traps."

"How?"

He showed me how to rig them so that, if the cord I used was triggered, the grenade would explode. "The only thing is that when you use them as a trap, you can't throw them and if the booby trap is not triggered then the grenades are wasted. Still, they were free in the first place, eh, Sharratt."

I stored the information. We would not need them until the enemy attacked and as May became June we were reinforced by

Conscript's Call

brand new Crusader tanks sent by the most dangerous of routes, across the Med. Our new Prime Minister, it seemed, did not want us to lose again. It appeared more and more likely that the Germans would need the booby traps and not us.

If we thought we would be used again soon we were disappointed. We were pulled back to await the arrival of new tanks. The rest of the battalion arrived and it was then I saw Sergeant Jones again. Their lorries pulled in and I saw him and the clerks of the headquarters section climb down and head to the area allocated. If he was here then the colonel would not be far behind and that meant that instead of one company going to war it might be the whole battalion.

Chapter 8

June 1941 Operation Battleaxe

The name of our unit was the 7th Support Group and we were attached to the 7th Armoured Brigade and this time we knew that when we went into battle we would be one of the main attacks. More of the battalion would be going to war. One difference was that our company had earned, as they say, its stripes. We had fought in the desert and we had not lost. That was reflected in the mood around our tents. We were more confident. The three deaths in Greece and Crete had begun to fade. We had not forgotten them but they were pushed to the back of our minds. The importance of this next battle was made abundantly clear when brand new Crusader tanks, just delivered to Alexandria, began to pour into the camp at the end of the first week of June. There was a railhead from Alexandria and we always knew when men and supplies were coming.

A second company of our battalion joined us. The colonel, Sergeant Jackson told us, was ensuring that the men who were used would be the best trained. The lessons from Greece and Crete had been learned. The companies that had displayed the most skill were the ones he used. The others would be part of the next assault. We were here to stay. To be fair to the other companies that remained to train in Alexandria, they had suffered more in the two crossings of the sea and had needed more reinforcements. The rest of the battalion would be held in reserve in case they were needed. There was another difference. This time we also had Universal Carriers although we called them Bren Carriers. They arrived the day after the Crusader tanks. Each company was given four of them and to Bert's delight he and Harry, along with Norm Thomas, were designated the crew. They had a Bren gun and were supposed to have the Boys anti-tank rifle too. We just mounted the Bren gun. Bert was like a kid with a new toy. He loved the thought of having an engine with which he could tinker. Another result was more room in the lorries.

Conscript's Call

We felt like veterans as we explained to the newly arrived company how we would operate. It was strange the changes that had come over us since we had learned how to march and become soldiers at Seaforth Barracks. We had been so raw and awkward I still shivered in embarrassment at the memory. Now we wore our caps and helmets at jaunty angles. We were as familiar with our weapons as we had been with our knives and forks back in England. The sun and wind had tanned us so that we were no longer pasty-faced youths from Lancashire. We had come of age. At the back of my mind, however, was the thought that we had yet to win a battle. We knew how to fall back better than how to advance.

Lieutenant Hargreaves was keen to ensure we all knew our part in the forthcoming battle. He still kept his moustache trimmed like Errol Flynn, Ronald Coleman and David Niven and I think he still saw himself as the dashing hero from '*The Charge of the Light Brigade*'. He gathered the company around him and used his own hand drawn map to illustrate what we would be doing. "Right chaps, we are on the left of the advance again," he smiled, "they must think we did a good job the last time. That means we have to negotiate the desert. I am sure we will give a good account of ourselves. We will be, along with the Rifles and the King's Royal Rifle Corps, supporting the 2nd and the 6th RTR. We will have the Royal Horse Artillery with us and we will be a powerful force. We even have some anti-aircraft batteries in case Jerry sends Stukas." We all nodded and there were smiles. The convoy was still a painful memory. "We are to take the Hafid ridge here," he pointed to a line running east to west, "and Point 208. There are actually three ridges and our role is to ensure that the tanks are not attacked by infantry. The main attacks will be at Halfaya Pass, Point 208 and Fort Capuzzo. They will start their attack first and the brass hopes that we will be a nasty surprise for the men on the ridge. We will do as we did when last we attacked and we will follow the tanks into action but this time, we will have the Bren Carriers and the Chevrolet. We were lucky in the last encounter that we had no casualties. As we all know from Crete and Greece, we can't rely on such luck all the time."

Our section looked at each other. The three deaths rose in our midst like wraiths.

Conscript's Call

The lieutenant continued, "The Bren Carriers will be our own ambulances. I hope, Dixon, that we do not need to use them for that purpose. We will be in position at 0500. Any questions?"

It showed how much we had changed in that there were no questions. The briefing had been clear and the use of the hand drawn map had made it quite obvious what we were to do. To the south of us was nothing but desert and as we would be the last to attack it was to be hoped that the attention of the Germans, especially the Luftwaffe, would be to the north of us. The Bren Carrier was a tracked vehicle and could cope with the desert better than a lorry. If nothing else it could tow us.

"Get a good night's sleep. There are other regiments who will be sentries."

We headed to our tents and there was a buzz not least because we knew we were more mobile. The first skirmish had shown us how to fight. Pie Face said, "You know, Weather, if you had lugged the grenade launcher the last time, we could have rid ourselves of the problem of the machine gun."

Geoff shook his head, "Too bloody heavy."

Bert said, "Then stick it in the Bren Carrier. We have room and it will save you carrying it."

Harry smiled, "I plan on taking spare canteens too. I thought we might brew some tea. I don't mind cold tea and it tastes better than tepid water."

Bert shook his head as he explained, as though to a child, "Harry, we have an engine that will be hot. We can brew tea without a fire. Betty here will change our lives."

I smiled, "Betty?"

He nodded, "Betty the Bren Carrier! You have to name a vehicle. Trust me, she will respond to the affection I intend to lavish upon her."

Norm Thomas said, "See if the lieutenant will let you paint that on the side, you know like they do with bombers and tanks." We had seen some of the Crusaders with such decoration on their turrets.

Bert seemed to like the idea, "I will ask him. I used to do a bit of painting back in the garage. Good idea, Norm."

After I had eaten I disassembled and then reassembled my rifle. It was as clean as though it was brand new. I made sure that

Conscript's Call

I had enough magazines, and they would not stick. I ensured that my hand grenades had the right fuses and then, before I went to sleep I prayed. I was still self-conscious about it and did so silently, in my head. Part of it was to remember my family. It was all too easy to forget their faces. We had never been a family for photographs and, in any case, when the house was destroyed so were the only photographic memories. When I prayed, I saw my parents as well as Sarah, Kath and Tom. That night, as I lay on my blanket, I reflected that it had been eight months since the bombing but while I was getting older, their faces stayed the same. They would never age. For some reason that made me almost tearful. I would make the Germans pay. The attacks at sea and the burnt-out Greek villages had done nothing to make me feel any sympathy for the Germans.

We piled into the lorries. There was more room this time. Bert drove the carrier and we had a driver, Sid from the Royal Army Service Corps, assigned to drive. We secured our packs beneath the benches as well as our rifles. The air was chilly, but we knew that within a short time it would heat up so that by noon it would be a cauldron. We had full canteens and emergency rations. Dave Proud had a sweet tooth and he would be nibbling on his chocolate even before we reached the jumping off point. When he ran out, he would try to cadge chocolate from others. As he was a smoker, he was not like me. I could always barter the cigarettes from my ration for chocolate. I never did but it was a possibility. Any cigarettes that I was given, I gave away.

There was some chatter in the lorry. That was mainly because of nerves. Some men did not like the silence for it allowed unwelcome thoughts and premonitions of death to creep in. For others they were natural magpies. For some reason I was able to hide those thoughts from myself and I was more silent than the others. I listened more than I spoke. The noise from the tanks was a constant drumming but when the Bedford lorries started their engines then we had to shout to make ourselves heard. I remained silent. Ray held up two thumbs and grinned. I was nervous for we were going to war and facing tanks. In the first skirmish we had seen the effect of Armour Piercing rounds. The three brewed up German tanks had stunk of burnt fuel and flesh. If the Bedford was hit, then it would also go up like a Roman candle. We had plenty of fuel, and fuel, whilst we needed it to get into battle, was an enemy too. We began to move and we endured the same rocking and rolling motion when we left the road to head across the desert. Norm Thomas tried to start a sing song with *'Roll out the barrel'*, but no one joined in and his voice petered out. We drove without words but there was no silence. The noise of the engine and the gears was our constant companion.

We stopped and this time we knew what was coming. The sergeant ordered us from the lorries and we ditched our packs. The lorries would just have their drivers and the Chevrolet with its driver and radio. The rest, even the captain and CSM Hutton, would be involved in the attack. I saw that the older cruiser tanks of the 2nd RTR were at the fore. They were not as good as the new Crusader and Valentine tanks and were therefore more expendable. The new Crusader tanks would be in the second attack and we were told to follow them. The cruiser tanks would attack the first of the ridges and destroy any tanks that were there.

What I was learning about battles was that you only knew your part of it. In the Klidi Pass it had been the little rocky position we had held. In Crete it was the narrow streets close to the church tower. There had been others fighting and dying but we had no idea how they were doing. So it was here. There were three attacks and we were on the extreme flank. As we followed the tanks through the dust and sand up to the ridge we could hear, in the distance to the north, the crump of artillery and the crack of tank guns. The faint ratatat of machine guns told us that the battle was engaged but who was winning?

When the Crusaders stopped we stopped. A tanker emerged from his turret and shouted something to the captain. He was too far away to hear but when CSM Hutton shouted for us to head for the cruiser tanks we knew that we would soon be engaged. I saw that some of the company had fixed bayonets. I would keep mine in my frog. I was the one who needed the accuracy. Sergeant Jackson had great faith in me and I had no intention of letting him down.

We ran to catch up with the cruiser tanks. They began a turn to head up the valley that lay below the first ridge. As they

Conscript's Call

turned their commanders must have been overjoyed to see the lines of trenches manned by Germans and Italians. Their machine guns belched bullets and death. I had spoken to a tanker after the first battle and knew that not all the cruiser tanks had high explosive to be used against infantry. Instead the A13 cruiser tank had armour piercing rounds. Their machine guns were enough, however, and the enemy fled their trenches.

"Open Fire!" We joined in the firing. This time my accuracy was not needed and I fired as rapidly as Wally and Ray next to me. I saw Harry in the Bren Carrier as he personally emptied one trench with his Bren gun. The tanks then turned to ascend the ridge and we resumed our position. Some of those who had fled had been cut down on the slopes of the ridge. Their bodies were a stark reminder of what could happen in battle.

The A13 and A12 cruiser tanks were nearing the crest of the first ridge and they had barely crested the rise when we heard the sound of anti-tank guns. Two of the older tanks were hit immediately. The tankers used a term, '*brewed up*' and these two demonstrated why. The tanks erupted in flame as the anti-tank shells tore through their armour. Fuel or ammunition could be ignited and the best outcome for the tank crews was an explosion that would kill them all quickly. A fire promised a death by fire. When another was almost lifted into the air then it was clear, even to a novice like me, that there was a minefield and dug in anti-tank guns. Lacking HE the tanks began to withdraw and Major Hill, commanding the two companies shouted, "Queen's Rifles, forward!"

We ran. Bert, driving the Bren Carrier, did so cautiously and his caution was rewarded when another of the carriers, perhaps too eager to get into action, crested the rise and was destroyed in a single moment as the anti-tank mine lifted it into the air. Bert stopped so that he was hull down. He would not risk Betty. Harry had a good field of fire and he began to fire at the anti-tank emplacements. We threw ourselves to the ground when we reached the top. The three burning tanks and the Bren Carrier sent smoke down the ridge. That helped to disguise us. The German machine guns sprayed the top. Corporal Williams threw himself down next to me. "We have to stop the guns destroying our tanks." I knew what he meant. The surviving tanks had to get

Conscript's Call

off the ridge and that meant turning. Their sides and rear were weaker than the front. We had to discourage the German gunners.

I aimed at the nearest position. I could see how the trap had been set. The anti-tank guns were less than three hundred yards from the top of the ridge. They had a clear sight of the tanks as they exposed themselves and even as I aimed at the officer, identifiable by his raised arm, I knew that there would be more anti-tank mines within yards of where I was. I hit the officer in the shoulder. He dropped and I saw the helmeted gunners drop, too. That gun would not fire for a moment or two. I chambered another round and sought the next position. German rifles and machine guns opened up. One thing I had learned since I had come to the desert was the effect of heat haze and the sun. It was now noon and against the sky estimating range was harder. I had an easier task as I was firing down to the sand and I was not looking at the junction of the sky and the desert. Their bullets zipped over my head and I aimed at the gunner. His head was visible above the protective armour shield. The shot was one of my best and I saw his head disappear.

Sergeant Jackson shouted, "Number one Platoon, fall back!"

I knew that the tanks must have cleared the ridge. Our bullets had disrupted the gunners and bought them the time to move to safer ground. Until we called up aircraft or artillery then the ridge could not be taken. I slid backwards down the slope until I was well clear and could stand. Corporal Williams walked next to me, "Nice shooting, Sharratt. You are well named."

"Just doing my job, Corp." I nodded to the burning tanks, "I couldn't do what they do. Poor sods had no chance."

"Aye, and the Germans knew we were coming. This is going to be hard."

The lorries were summoned and when they arrived and we retrieved our packs, we began to enjoy our rations. The RAF were above and they would warn us of any imminent attack. It was two o'clock in the afternoon and we were starving. We ate close to Betty for the lorry afforded shade and Bert had brewed some tea. Norm Thomas was staring at the burnt-out Bren Carrier, "Poor lads never stood a chance. I mean the armour on these things can barely stop a bullet but anti-tank rounds and mines."

Bert said, "Joe was a good bloke," Joe had been the driver of the carrier that had been destroyed, "but he didn't use his head. Anyone with half a brain could see that if the tanks were being hit when they went over the ridge then so could we. It is why I stopped. Don't worry, Norm, Betty and I will keep you safe."

We were reliant on the radio and when at 1730 a message came in from the RAF, we were ordered to load onto the lorries and head out. As the engines started Ray asked, "What's up, Sergeant?"

"Jerry is abandoning their position and heading out. The Crusaders are going to show the Panzers that we have a new tank."

There was an air of optimism in the lorries. The Crusaders were good tanks and faster than the Matildas. This time we would only leave the lorries when there were infantry to clear. Those good feelings vanished when the German tanks sprang their ambush, for it was soon obvious that the battle was lost. We saw nothing for we were in the lorries but we heard the sound of tanks as they were hit. We had learned to differentiate between the sound of a round hitting a tank and doing no damage and the noise of one exploding. When the lorries turned to flee east we saw the fires burning all along the ridge. The Crusader was a good tank but the Germans had known what we were doing. They had sprung an ambush and the brand-new tanks were hit by tanks and anti-tank guns.

By the time darkness fell we were to the east of Hafid Ridge. Gossip was rife about the scale of the disaster but Sergeant Jackson gave us the right information. "We have been hurt. I heard that we have lost fifty tanks, twenty-two of them the new jobs." He saw the looks on our faces when we were given the bald and painful facts. "Don't get disheartened. We managed to account for most of their defences on Hafid Ridge. When dawn breaks we shall have another crack. We won't bother with tents. Sleep under the lorries. Section 1, you have first stag."

Corporal Williams said, "Right, Sarge."

It meant we would have a shorter night of sleep but one that was uninterrupted. We would wake Section 2 at 2300 and

Section 3 would be woken for the dawn shift at 0300. If we were out for a second night then we would have the midnight watch.

This would be the first watch in the desert at night and it was not what I expected. Firstly, we had to wear our greatcoats for it was cold. Secondly, there were more noises than I had expected. In Greece it had been silent in the Klidi Pass. Any noise meant danger. Here there were noises. We could hear the crackling of the fires from vehicles that were still burning. There must have been some Germans left on the battlefield for we heard cries in the distance. We had been the only allied infantry and all of our men were accounted for. There were also the noises of the animals of the desert feasting on bodies. Rats and foxes, hidden during the day, both from sun and man, emerged at night. We patrolled the perimeter in pairs. There was another section from the other company and we stopped to nod at our counterparts but no words were spoken. We were all conscripts but we had learned that noises at night showed the enemy where you were. By the time our watch was over I was exhausted. We had been awake for almost eighteen hours and the nervous tension of a night watch merely added to it. I kept my greatcoat on and rolled into my blanket taking the warmed spot of my relief. I was so tired that there were no prayers that night.

The next day we moved but this time we were not advancing but following a parallel course to a German armoured column that was trying to outflank us. We would stay in the lorries. We had all been refuelled, both tanks and lorries at night and that meant the tanks had another ninety miles of range. As we moved, Sergeant Jackson asked Lieutenant Hargreaves if we could raise the canvas on the sides. He agreed. It meant we had shade overhead from the sun but we also enjoyed the breeze a little more and, vitally, we could see what was happening. We were to the right of the tanks as they shadowed the German column that was headed south and east. They were trying to outflank us. It was that day when I saw the difference between the German and the British tanks. They were both well armoured but the guns of the German Mark IV tanks had a far greater range than the Crusaders and cruiser tanks. Both sides sent shells at the trailers that were being towed and the vehicles containing the infantry. Our tanks had success at first and so the Germans merely moved

Conscript's Call

their vehicles beyond the range of the two pounders. We tried to move away too but for one slower reacting Bedford it was too late. A 75 mm round hit the Bedford containing two sections from C Company. The lorry had a full load of fuel. It exploded like a fireball and the lorries around were showered with burning debris. They were lucky not to be set on fire themselves. The Chevrolet truck and Bren Carriers went to its assistance but it was a vain attempt for there were no survivors.

As we set off again we all looked at each other in silence. It could have been us.

It was as dusk fell that the Germans launched their attack at us. They concentrated all their tanks in one place and knocked out another two Crusaders. It was clear that we were outgunned and we were ordered to head for the Frontier Wire. The Frontier Wire was the old border between Libya and Egypt. There was barbed wire there but it was not continuous. Some had been cut and some destroyed in battle. It was a marker that, when we crossed it, told us we had lost. It was another retreat and clear to us all that we had been beaten, again. The tanks stopped on the Egyptian side of the wire but we pushed on to Sidi Suleiman. There the rest of the battalion had built a camp and it was defended. It was midnight when we pulled in. The colonel had food ready for us and we ate it but I did not taste the food. Defeat was in my mouth.

I had just finished the corned beef sandwiches when Sergeant Jones walked up, "Alright, son?"

I shook my head, "It is hopeless, Sergeant. All we do is to keep running from the Germans. Even our best and newest tanks are no good against them."

He sat next to me and spoke quietly, "In the Great War we had the same problem. We were doing our best but thanks to some poor decisions by senior officers we lost good men. It leaves a sour taste, I know, but the battalion is doing well. We lost men in the Bedford but we are still in good shape and I am confident that old Winnie will intervene. Our Prime Minister knows how to fight and sooner or later he will appoint someone who knows how to beat this Desert Fox as men are calling him." He stood, "You just keep your chin up and do what you are doing. Trust to these lads. You are a good bunch. It looks black now but believe me, it will get better."

I know he was just trying to cheer us up and he knew little more than we did but he was a link to my father. I trusted that generation and I had to believe that the sergeant was right.

Conscript's Call

Chapter 9

It was clear that changes had been made to our command structure. This time it was not just gossip but orders now signed by a new commanding general. The most senior officer, General Wavell, was sent to India. I was a lowly private but even I could see that mistakes had been made. I am not sure it was all the general's fault but someone had to be blamed and it was him. The new commanding officer, General Auchinleck, would need time to reorganise and, fortunately, the Germans gave him time to do so. I say the Germans but the real heroes were the Australians in Tobruk who resolutely defied Rommel. Until Tobruk was taken then the Germans did not have a port that they could use. Bardia had proved to be inadequate and Benghazi was too far away. Their supply lines were under constant attack by the reinforced aeroplanes of the RAF. Now that Greece and Crete had fallen and with the Battle of Britain over, then the Egyptian Desert became a priority.

We settled into life in the desert. We took cover when the Luftwaffe came and we all stood watches but apart from that, life was relatively easy. We had no drilling and we learned how to cope with the sun. We wore shorts when we could and tied cloths about our necks and head. We foraged for wood and camel dung for our fires and we became more like the creatures that lived in this oven of a land. It was the sergeants and corporals who gave us orders. We did not mind those orders for there was always some reason to them. What we did not know was that Captain Whittle and Lieutenant Hargreaves were planning. We only learned it after the event but when they disappeared for days at a time and we were left under the command of CSM Hutton and Sergeant Jackson we began to suspect something. There was speculation that they had been granted leave but that was soon dismissed; neither officer seemed the type to want to enjoy leisure time in Cairo or Alexandria. I raised the question and I speculated about what they were doing. I think, however, that I was the only one so preoccupied with their absence for we had a delivery of letters and parcels from home. Birthdays and

Conscript's Call

anniversaries had come and gone, almost unnoticed, but the families at home had sent cards and presents. They had followed us around. Thanks to Greece and Crete the battalion had been bereft of mail. Luckily for the recipients, they had not been lost or sunk with a bombed ship. They arrived in Egypt. I had no one who wrote to me but everyone else had a letter either from family or in one or two cases, sweethearts. The others were engrossed in the letters and that allowed my fertile mind to conjure up all sorts of explanations for the missing officers.

However everyone became more interested when all the officers in the battalion were summoned to a meeting at Headquarters. They returned and next day the sergeants and NCOs were all gathered. We were eager for news as it was clear that something was up. The next day the lieutenant and Sergeant Jackson gathered the platoon together. It was the lieutenant who spoke, "Now I know that some of you have been more than a little depressed at our lack of success thus far in the war. We seem to run backwards more than we go forward. You should know that some of your officers feel the same. I can't give more details away but there is a big push coming. However there is something which will happen sooner." We were all on tenterhooks. "Captain Whittle and I went to Cairo to present a little idea we had and the powers that be, have sanctioned it. They have given us the opportunity to demonstrate if it might work." We were all intrigued and I for one just wanted him to get on with it. He smiled, "This will be a time for volunteers. What I am about to tell you is, obviously secret but I think we can trust each other. This platoon has the finest record in the regiment." He paused.

Sergeant Jackson said, quietly, "I think you have both their attention, Sir, and their interest."

"Quite. Well, chaps, Captain Whittle and I have permission to launch a raid into Axis held land. We intend to sabotage the German airfield at Sidi Azeiz." We were all excited. I tried to picture where the airfield lay and thought back to the hand drawn map he had shown us before the last battle. "It is forty miles away and twenty miles behind the Frontier Wire. We intend to take one Bedford lorry and the Chevrolet. We will need one

Conscript's Call

sergeant and fourteen men. The captain and I will, naturally, lead. Now, who would like to volunteer?"

More than half of the hands went up, including the sergeant's.

The lieutenant smiled, "Excellent, I knew I could count on you. Sergeant Jackson, take the names and bring the list to the captain and me. We will pare it down. The whole company is being offered the opportunity so many of you will be disappointed but if this is successful who knows what might transpire?"

When the sergeant and the lieutenant left there was a buzz of excitement I had not known before. Some were confident that they would be picked. I was not sure. What skills would they need? I tried to envisage what it would be like. We would have to drive across the desert at night. That would be a problem as both vehicles were far from silent. Then we would have to leave them some way from the airfield. That meant some men would have to guard the vehicles. At least two men would have to stay behind. The men who went would need skills with explosives and my heart sank. That was not me. I looked at the others and tried to work out which ones would be chosen. I kept coming up with the problem of lack of experience with explosives. So far as I knew none of our section had those skills. We had other qualities. If they needed a Bren gunner then there was no one better than Harry. As for a driver then Bert had shown that he not only had the skills but the ability to repair one if it broke down.

It was the next day when the lieutenant and captain appeared. They had a clipboard with them.

Sergeant Jackson did not look happy and I guessed that he had not gained a place. It was the captain who spoke, "We have made our selections and it was not easy. I know that there will be many of you left disappointed. However, if we are successful then this will be the first of many such," he smiled, "raids. I think that Lieutenant Hargreaves has had a splendid idea and I am honoured that this company has been chosen to carry out the raid." He paused. I could picture him in the classroom holding the attention of a class of pupils. "From this platoon Corporal Williams, Private Dixon, Lance Corporal Vane and Private Sharratt will take part."

Conscript's Call

I was not surprised about the others but shocked that I had been chosen and not Sergeant Jackson.

The lieutenant said, "The four named, get your gear and report to Sergeant Baxter. He will be the NCO in charge of the raiding party."

Sergeant Baxter was from number 2 Platoon. Ray and Wally followed me to my tent, "Who is the blue-eyed boy then?"

I turned to Ray, "What do you mean?"

"Well, obviously someone at Headquarters likes you. Must be your mate, Sergeant Jones."

I shook my head, "I honestly don't know why I was picked. You two are eminently better qualified."

Geoff smiled, "I knew you would be picked before anyone else. You are such a good shot and as you showed in Greece, you can be quiet as. Yes, I knew it would be you who was chosen. I mean Bert is a whizz with engines and not a bad driver but why take me? I am just muscle."

Corporal Williams poked his head in the tent, "And that might be what they need on this raid. Come on you pair of nattering Norahs. Tempus fugit."

Part of me wondered if this was guilt on Lieutenant Hargreaves' part. I knew that he and the captain thought that he had been remiss at Seaforth and his mistake had led to my beating. Was he trying to put that right and give me a chance for a medal? I hoped not for I needed no medals. I had my pack on the cot and three things I put in which the others did not have were the bayonets and two German grenades. I also put in some cord. I had found the cord when we had found a parachute from a downed flier. The others had wanted the parachute itself which was cut up to make headdresses and neck cloths but I wanted some of the cord as well. I thought they would all be useful things to take. "Bye lads."

We hurried out and followed Corporal Williams. Bert shouted, "Norm, look after Betty for me will you?"

Norm shouted back, "Aye, I will kiss her goodnight and tuck her in for you." I heard the laughter from the others.

Bert mumbled, "Not such a daft idea."

We headed across the camp and saw Sergeant Baxter waiting. The sergeant was like Geoff Vane, a big man. He had worked on

Conscript's Call

an iron gang in a factory in Manchester and was one of the strongest men I had ever met. I wondered at his inclusion. What skills did he bring? I saw the others waiting. I knew their faces and even a couple of their names. Five of them were from the mortar platoon: Peter Davis, Rob Allen, Graham Cowley, Harry Robinson and Ifan Evans who was known as Taff. Their inclusion was more understandable. They were used to handling explosives.

The officers were not there but Regimental Sergeant Major Lawson was with his swagger stick tucked under his arm. We were the last four to arrive and he snapped, "Move yourselves! Who do you think you are? The Household Cavalry." I had not had many dealings with the sergeant major but he had also served in the Great War and from what Sergeant Jackson had told me was not a man to mess with. No one said a word. Anything, even an apology, would have been a mistake. "Attention!" We all stood to attention but laden as we were with packs, rifles and, in Weather's case, a grenade launcher, we looked anything but smart. "Now, you ladies have made the cardinal error, you have volunteered." He shook his head, "Why, I have not the foggiest. There is no extra pay involved and from what I have been told little likelihood of you getting back. However, you are the Queen's Rifles and so you will conduct yourselves as such, at all times. Sergeant Baxter, I rely on you to maintain discipline."

"Yes, Regimental Sergeant Major."

"Now, you shower have all be allocated new quarters. Follow me and I will take you there. Step smartly for we will be passing not only locals but the Royal Tank Regiment. Let us show the tankers how smart riflemen can be."

The RSM clearly had pride in the regiment. The sentries at the barrier saluted as we left and we were marched through the tiny settlement. We passed the parked and camouflaged tanks and the camp of the Royal Tank Regiment. I saw that we were headed to a half-wrecked building. I suspected it had been damaged in one of the advances or retreats from the armies who had fought over this particular piece of land. I saw the two vehicles there. The Bedford was not one of the new ones but an older, rather beat up one. The Chevrolet was the same one we had seen before.

Conscript's Call

The sergeant major pointed at the roofless building. "Here are your quarters. Your officers will be here shortly, I suggest you make yourselves at home, eh?" He scanned us all. I noticed that one eye appeared bigger than the other as he squinted at us. I think he did that deliberately. Then the hint of a smile crept upon his lips, "Good luck!" He turned on his heel and smartly marched away.

The building had no roof but the floor had been swept and was empty. Sergeant Baxter had the flat vowels of a Mancunian. "Choose your own spot to sleep. I don't think we will be here that long."

As we all moved to our own places I realised this would not be like the section. I was not sure that I would be getting close to any of these men in the same way that I viewed Ray. Geoff and Wally as brothers. The other three from our section all moved close to me so that the four of us had one corner.

Bert said, "Sarge, I am, I assume, the driver and the mechanic." Corporal Williams nodded. "Can I go and look at the bus?"

"Aye," he glanced at his clipboard, "Dixon. Good idea. Shows initiative."

Bert nodded to me, "Sort my bed out, eh?"

"Sure thing."

I laid my blanket down with the pack as a sort of pillow and then placed the greatcoat on the top. I had just finished Bert's when the officers came in. "Good, you are here." Captain Whittle frowned, "Where is Dixon?"

"Tinkering, Sir."

The captain smiled, "Good. He was well chosen then. Come, let us go outside and join him."

The glare of the sun hit us. None of us wore our helmets. I had my comforter on my head and some of the others wore their caps. I saw that Lieutenant Hargreaves had adopted a slouch hat such as the Australians wore. I wondered if he had picked it up on the two retreats from Greece and Crete.

The captain led us to the shade of the truck, "Dixon, fiddle on when the briefing is over."

"Sir." Bert hurried around the lorry wiping oil and grease from his hands.

118

Conscript's Call

"Now, you have all been chosen for this operation because of your skills or because we think you have the aptitude for the job. Dixon is both driver and mechanic. Sergeant Baxter and Private Cowley have experience in explosives. Private Featherstone is an expert with the Bren gun. When we trained in England Lance Corporal Vane showed skill in hand-to-hand combat. The rest of you have also shown skills that we will need." He turned, "Lieutenant." Lieutenant Hargreaves had drawn another of his maps. He placed it on an easel. I was learning that he was a skilled map maker and artist. The advantage of his hand drawn maps was that they showed just what we needed and all extraneous material was ignored. It made it easier to visualise. The captain pointed, "Tonight we leave here at dusk and drive to the Frontier Wire. We will cross here." He tapped the map with his pointer, "RAF reconnaissance aircraft report that it is remote enough from the enemy listening posts to allow us to cross. Thanks to our little retreat the wire is broken in many places and the Italians guarding that section have not had the time to repair it. We drive to within three miles of Sidi Azeiz. Dixon, Davis and McIntire will guard the vehicles and the rest of us will go to the airfield. We will cut a large hole in the wire. Vane and Evans you will take the wire cutters and make a hole big enough for all of us to use easily. We don't want to get snagged making a quick escape." They both nodded. "We eliminate the sentries. When that is done we go back to the wire and guard our escape route. While the lieutenant, Sergeant Baxter and Private Cowley set the charges we will watch for the enemy. The targets are the fuel tanks, hangars and aeroplanes." He looked at Sergeant Baxter. "Sergeant."

Sergeant Baxter continued, "It will take some time for the three of us to set the charges. We will have someone with us to carry the charges. There will be timers on the explosives. The charges will have a thirty-minute fuse on them. As it takes time to set them and we have twenty of them then the first ones might go up twenty minutes or more before the last one is set."

The lieutenant pointed, "Lang, Robinson and McKay, you will carry the explosives." The three men nodded. "As you will have realised that means we will have to run back to the vehicles."

119

I could see Corporal Williams working things out. "So, Sir, that means we will still be on the other side of the Frontier Wire when the explosives go up."

"That is correct. It will be a race to get back to our own lines. The RAF will have a couple of fighters up to give us cover."

The Welshman, Taff Evans, said, "Sir, I am quite happy to go on this little jaunt but why can't the RAF simply bomb it?"

"They have tried but there is strong anti-aircraft surrounding it and we need to ensure that their storage tanks for fuel are destroyed." He looked at us. "Any questions."

Rob Allen asked, "You said eliminate the sentries, Sir, what did you mean?"

The lieutenant went to his bag and took out a small leather bag and after handing one to the captain said, "You will all be given one of these, a sap. You give them a smack on the back of the head. When they are out then you will tie their hands and feet with cord."

Corporal Williams said, "And if they are wearing a helmet?"

The silence was a long one. The two officers looked at each other and, finally, the captain took out his bayonet and said, "You use this."

Ifan Evans said, "Murder."

The captain sighed, "This is war, Evans, but if you are unhappy with the thought then let us know. We have reserves on our list."

Ifan must have been aware that every eye was on him. He eventually shook his head, "No, Sir. I will go along with it."

The captain smacked his sap into the palm of his hand. It sounded like a slap. "We need silence. If the garrison wakes while we are there then the best we can hope for is a prisoner of war camp but in all likelihood we would be killed in the firefight."

The lieutenant tossed us the saps. I caught mine. It was surprisingly heavy.

The captain pointed to some crosses on the map of the airfield, "There are two machine gun emplacements, here and here. They may or may not be manned at night. We only know for certain how they operate during the day. There will probably be a section on duty. That means a non-com and seven men or more. The Italians operate similar systems to us. We think that they will be here, here and here." He tapped the map. "Now, you are all bright lads and will have worked out who is doing what. With three men watching the vehicles and six men setting the charges that leaves me, Corporal Williams, Lance Corporal Vane, Privates Allen, Featherstone, Evans and Sharratt to eliminate the sentries."

I said, "That means one of us will have to get rid of two sentries." He nodded.

The lieutenant said, "We have the rest of the day to get some sleep. We eat at 1600 and then black up our faces and hands. We don't take packs when we leave the lorries. Your rifles will be left in the lorries."

"Sir, what if we are fired on. These saps and knives will be neither use nor ornament then."

"I know, Featherstone. Lieutenant."

Lieutenant Hargreaves opened the packing case that lay next to the lorry. He took out three Sten guns. "From your records we know that Featherstone, Allen and Evans can use these." The three men nodded. The lieutenant went to each one and handed them a weapon and ammunition. "Now you should know that if you have to fire them then disaster has struck." They nodded, "They are to be used in an emergency. He went back to the case and took out three belts with holsters and pistols. He handed one to Corporal Williams, one to Weather and one to me, "This is the Beretta M1935. These were taken from Italians captured at Halfaya Pass. They are a single-action, semi-automatic blowback pistol that fires a 7.65 Browning cartridge. We have plenty of that ammunition. Like the Stens, they are for emergency use only." He handed us the guns and I took the little Beretta out of its holster. It felt light. "Sergeant Armourer Daley will be along shortly to give you three lessons in the firing of them."

The captain said, "That is it. This is bold, daring and risky. It is why we asked for volunteers. The lieutenant and I think that this is a way to hit the enemy between the operations like Battleaxe and…" He paused, "Whatever is coming next. The Queen's Rifles are going to hit the enemy back. We have run enough."

It was the right thing to say and we all nodded.

Conscript's Call

The lieutenant said, "Those designated to carry explosives, come with me."

I stood with the other two and we looked at the pistols. "Are they loaded?" I asked.

A voice behind me said, "Not yet, Sharratt." I turned and saw Sergeant Armourer Daley. He had the magazines in his hand. "Come with me and I will give you a little lesson." He smiled, "I was listening and I know that if you have to use these then you will be well and truly up that creek without a paddle."

He led us away from the buildings and beyond the sentries. He took my pistol from me and demonstrated, "The small magazine capacity of eight rounds and short effective range means that the M1935 is a weapon to be used at close range. The slide is not of the self-catching type. When the magazine is removed the action returns forward on an empty chamber. It is a drawback as it slows down reloading of the pistol. However, if the safety is thumbed into the safe position it also acts as a slide catch, the magazine can then be released and a full magazine can be inserted. The slide release and safety can then be released, loading a round, then the pistol can now be fired in single action." He loaded the magazine and took a stance with the pistol in two hands. He fired and chambered a second round. It made just a crack but at night that would sound like thunder. He handed my pistol to me. "Right, Sharratt, let us see if you are as accurate with this as a Lee Enfield." He took an empty corned beef can from his pack and tossed it as far as he could throw. It landed forty feet from us, rolling a little on the slope.

I took the pistol and aimed. The sight appeared tiny. I aimed and fired. After the Lee Enfield the recoil was minimal. I hit the can. I fired all six remaining bullets and Sergeant Daley took it from me and said, "Clear." He took out the empty magazine and handed me a fresh one. "Nice shooting for the first time. Reload and then holster your weapon." I did as I was told. "Next." When the other two only hit the can with half of their bullets I knew that I had skill. Sergeant Daley handed us two spare magazines. "You shouldn't need these but better to have them and not need them than to need them and not have them. Good luck lads." He shook his head, "Volunteers."

Conscript's Call

I fitted the belt and the weight was not that bad. I saw that there was a frog attached to my Italian belt and deduced it must have belonged to a non-com. I would fit the German bayonet I had taken. Geoff Vane grinned, "I feel like Tom Mix with this."

The corporal said, "It is just for show. The lieutenant and captain are right. We need silence if we are to pull this off. I am not sure we have enough men."

Weather took out a cigarette and lit it with his lighter, "You know sentries, Corp, some will be useless."

I said, "I know, but what if two of them are chatting? That happens too."

"I am guessing that is why they chose us. They must believe that we can think on our feet. I know you two can." Corporal Williams shrugged, "I can't speak for the others but you two will do for me."

Back at the new camp I disassembled and reassembled the gun. It was easy enough to do and I was happier knowing that I could do so. I also cleaned my rifle. The sand and the dirt from the desert made it a daily occurrence. That done I slid the German bayonet into the frog and then practised with the sap. A chill ran down my spine when I realised that a blow that was too hard might end up cracking a sentry's skull. Ifan Evans was right, that would be murder. I hoped that I would judge it right.

Bert fiddled on with the two vehicles until three and then he came indoors with the smile of a child who has had all his Christmas wishes fulfilled. "Well, the Bedford looks like a challenge but that Chevrolet, what a lovely machine that is. I know which one I would rather drive." The rest of us were all silent. In my case it was wrestling with the thought of taking a life. It was one thing to send a bullet at a man who was trying to kill you but these men were just standing watch. Bert must have realised as he said, "Tell you what, lads, we will try and have a brew ready for you when you get back, eh?"

Corporal Williams shook his head, "You can't light a fire, Dixon, we will be behind enemy lines."

Bert smiled and tapped his nose, "After a drive through the desert the engine will be hot enough to fry an egg. I can boil water and stewed tea will have to do."

Conscript's Call

I knew why Bert suggested the tea. He and the others would need something to do. Just waiting and watching was the hardest thing in the world. It was always easier if you had something else to occupy your mind.

We all ate together under an awning that was rigged over the front of the burnt-out building. I happened to be seated across from the lieutenant. I said, "Sir, do you mind me asking why I was included. I mean, I know I am a good shot but it seems to me that you don't need that skill."

He smiled, "No, Sharratt, we don't. It was Sergeant Jones who suggested you. He said that any man who could stalk rabbits in Formby Forest could easily sneak up on Italians. When we head across the desert tonight you will be what the Americans call *'point'*. Along with the captain and me you will be the eyes and ears of the raid. You and I will have to navigate and find a way across the desert at night and do so silently."

I nodded for now I understood. I was not being taken because they felt sorry for me but because they needed me. My mates had been right. Sergeant Jones had recommended me; not out of sympathy but because he thought I had skills. I smiled. It was almost as though the hardships of pre-war Britain had prepared me for this raid. The food tasted better after that.

Chapter 10

With blackened faces and hands and soft headgear we took our canteens and rifles and headed to the lorry. I had my haversack attached to the webbing. The two officers along with Featherstone, Lang and Evans were in the Chevrolet and the rest of us were in the Bedford. The sergeant sat in the front with Bert and we had plenty of room in the back. We knew we should not need our rifles until our return and I fastened mine beneath the bench. I jammed my haversack there. I had pared my webbing down so that I just had one pouch with the magazines for the Beretta, the second with chocolate as well as some lengths of cord. I thought they might be useful if I had to improvise a booby trap. I had two Mills Bombs in my battle dress pockets and the two German grenades hung from the straps. My canteen was on my belt. I had seen that the lieutenant had a commando dagger. I knew that would be a better weapon to use rather than the bayonet. I wondered how he had acquired one. He seemed a resourceful officer. We set off and this time there was no noise in the lorry. This was not the platoon or company going to war, this was a handful of men sneaking around behind enemy lines. We were all nervous and, if they were like me, a little scared. It if went wrong then the best we could hope for was to be taken to a POW camp but at worst, death was the option.

When Sergeant Baxter poked his head through to speak to us we knew where we were and his words confirmed it, "Just crossing the Frontier Wire. It all looks quiet but be ready to grab your weapons."

The three of us with pistols took them out and the one with a Sten gun cocked it. Bert was driving as quietly as he could. He was not over revving the engine and using the downhill slope, when he could, to coast. It was as though the lorry was tip toeing over the border. It was when we began to move a little more quickly that we knew Bert had passed one obstacle that necessitated slow manoeuvring. I slipped on the safety and holstered the pistol. I drank some water. Little and often was the rule and we did not know when we might get a chance later on.

The lieutenant was the navigator and he and the captain had chosen the place we would hide the vehicles from the aerial photographs he had studied. We knew we had arrived when we first stopped and then reversed. When the engine was shut off it was clear that we had reached our destination. Bert had done his part and now we had to do ours.

Sergeant Baxter opened the back, "Right lads, sharpish."

We jumped down. I saw that we were in what I had learned was called a Wadi, a dried-up river bed. We would be hidden from the ground but an aeroplane would spot us easily. That should not be a problem as we needed to be over the border by the time the sun came up. Compared with how we normally went to war we were remarkably unladen. The three mules who would carry the explosives had large packs but that was all. I felt sorry for the three of them. They had just a bayonet for protection and would have to wait while the explosive charges were set. I had grenades, a gun and a bayonet. I hurried forward to join the two officers.

Captain Whittle said, quietly, "From now on hand signals only." We all nodded. Lieutenant Hargreaves pumped his right arm and pointed forward. I wondered if he had seen the cavalry do that in the cowboy films we had seen at the pictures. Errol Flynn had done the same thing in 'They Died With Their Boots On'. The lieutenant pointed to the right of the captain and I went where directed. We moved off.

There was no road close by. The lieutenant's map had shown one running east to west and we would head from the south. I fell into a familiar routine. I had not hunted rabbits for more than a year but it all came back to me. I glanced at the ground and then ahead. I sniffed the air and I sought movement. Alarmingly a snake slithered along the ground not more than six feet from me. I held my hand up and we all stopped. We must have disturbed it but it did not bother us and after a short pause we continued. As I went I looked for landmarks to help me on my return. They were little things but in the pine trees at Formby I had learned to use small things to guide me. I spotted strangely shaped rocks which I named in my head. They would be my markers on the way back to the two vehicles.

Conscript's Call

There were no lights around the airfield but the wire and buildings, even though they were camouflaged, stood out at ground level from the rocks and desert. We stopped just short of the wire. It was very dark and I doubted that we would be seen, not yet anyway. Two of the men with Sten guns pointed them at the fence and the lieutenant led Vane and Evans forward to cut the hole. I saw that we were at the furthest side of the airfield from the buildings and, presumably, the garrison. There was no moon but I could just make out buildings. They looked to be more than three hundred yards away. I saw a dozen aircraft. They looked to be covered with netting and were spread out. While the wire was being cut I sought the sentries. I identified one from the glow of a cigarette held in a cupped hand as he lifted it to take a surreptitious drag. He was close to an aircraft. Having seen one I sought others. I saw two who were by a sandbagged gun position. When the voice of the Italian sergeant barked I jumped for I was sure that we had been seen. I realised when the two men stood to attention, saluted and then scurried off in opposite directions that they had been reprimanded. In that brief encounter I saw that the sentries were not wearing helmets but had, instead, soft caps. I did not seek other sentries but tracked, instead, the sergeant. I had decided that I would take him out. He walked to the man who had been smoking but, having heard the sergeant's voice, the man must have stubbed it out. The sergeant then walked down the line of aeroplanes. He stopped twice more and each time the halt allowed me to identify the sentries. Keeping my eye on the sergeant I crept towards the captain. I tapped his arm and pointed with two fingers at my eyes. I then pointed out the four sentries by the aircraft. I tapped him again and pointed to the sandbags and the fifth. I tapped three fingers on my arm and then pointed to the sergeant who, obligingly, had just moved. Finally, I held up seven fingers and waved a vague hand in the direction I thought the reprimanded sentry had taken. The captain nodded and I saw his teeth as he smiled in the dark. I took out my sap and after tapping it in my hand put three fingers on my arm. He nodded again. He turned and went to tell the others their targets. Having identified them it would ensure that two men did not go for the same sentry. I never took my eyes from the sergeant. He walked back down the line of aircraft. At

Conscript's Call

one point he stopped to talk to a sentry. I realised it was the one who had been smoking. The smell of tobacco smoke would linger. He was being reprimanded but silently.

The captain tapped me on my shoulder and pointed, the wire was cut. I slipped through and made my way down to the far end of the row of aeroplanes. I guessed where the sergeant would go. He would head for the sandbags and the sentry who was there. I hoped that his attention would be on the sentries. I moved as fast as I could without making sudden movements. My rabbit hunting experience came to my aid. The sergeant did not do as I had expected. Instead he headed towards the wire at the eastern end of the airfield. I don't know if he saw something or it was part of his routine but I changed direction. There were four metal drums at the end of the concrete and he passed them. I thought they might have been filled with fuel. When I reached them I used them for cover and saw the sergeant walk closer to the wire. I sniffed the metal drums but it was not fuel that was in them. I gave one a slight shake and it did not move. It was too heavy and it did not contain a liquid. When he stopped I wondered why but then the hiss of urine told me that this was a call of nature. It gave me my chance. I knew that he would have to come back the same way he went. It was dark and the four drums would act as a guide for him.

He was a smoker and I smelled the smoke on him. I could also smell garlic. He was oblivious to my presence for he was whistling as he approached. I knew I would find what I was about to do hard and so I imagined that this man was McGuire. I worked out which side of the drums he would come and positioned myself close to the ground. When he passed me I rose like a wraith and I had my hand around his mouth in an instant. I smacked him on the back of the head and raised my sap in case I needed a second strike. It was clear that he was out. I lowered him to the ground and lay him face down. If he vomited then he would not choke himself. I took some cord from my pocket and tied his hands behind him. I then attached the cord to his feet which I also bound. I took his pistol, holster and ammunition. It was the same one as I had and I slung it over my head and under my arm. I made sure that his body was both hidden by the drums

Conscript's Call

and that they would afford him some protection when the airfield exploded. I had decided that they must have contained sand.

I made my way towards the sandbags. I could see Taff Evans heading for them too. Knowing that he would reach them first allowed me to see if any other sentries were close by. I saw Weather by the wheel of the Messerschmidt 110 trussing up one sentry. I knew where to look but if anyone had been in the watch tower they would have seen them. No alarm sounded and that alone told me that it was unoccupied. It was as I neared the sandbags that I heard the sound of a tussle. Taff was having trouble. I still had my sap but I also drew the Italian pistol I had been given. The fight was on the other side of the sandbags. I saw why no one had shouted for Taff had his hand over the Italian's mouth. Even as I watched I saw the stiletto appear in the Italian's hand and slash at Taff. Blood gushed and his hand fell. Even as the Italian's mouth opened I pointed the pistol and shook my head. I would never have fired but he did not know that. I gestured for him to drop the knife and he did. I made a circling motion with the gun barrel and he obeyed that command too. He turned and presented his back to me. This time I hit the man hard. He had hurt Taff and I needed to see to the Welshman's wound.

I tore the scarf from the unconscious Italian's neck and made a tourniquet. It was as we did so that I knew we needed someone with medical skills. We had all been given the briefest of training and I felt inadequate. When I had finished Taff gave me the thumbs up with his good hand. I took his cords and tied up the Italian. After picking up the Italian rifle I rose and peered over the sandbags. All was quiet. I put my pistol and sap away. I slid the stiletto into my boot and then helped Taff to his feet. He was obviously a tough man but he had lost blood. I grabbed his Sten gun too. Keeping my arm around his waist to stop him falling I retraced my steps and we passed Cowley and Davis as they fixed explosives to the first aeroplane. They looked up as we passed. We headed for the wire and the captain was there. I pointed to the wound and he tapped Corporal Williams on the shoulder. He nodded and took out the first aid kit. He would make sure that the wound was sealed. The captain gave me the thumbs up.

Conscript's Call

I turned and drew my pistol. The airfield looked quiet. One nagging doubt I had was that they might change the guard while we were still at the field. I had no watch but it seemed to be taking far longer than we had expected. The captain must have thought so too for he signalled Featherstone to take the wounded Welshman back to the lorry when the corporal had tended to him. It made sense. They both left and we waited.

Dawn in the desert was a strange affair and when the sky grew a little lighter I saw the captain chewing his lip. I think he was debating fetching the demolition teams back but before he had to make that decision the six men hurried towards us. Questions were in the captain's eyes but they would have to wait. He pointed to me and I headed off towards the lorry and truck. This time I led and the others followed. I used the signs I had spotted on the way out. I navigated by rocks and bushes I had memorised and when I saw the top of the Bedford lorry I gave myself a silent, well done.

Bert had done as he had promised and he pressed a mug of lukewarm tea in my hand, "You lads were cutting it fine. It is almost dawn."

I swallowed half of the tea and nodded, "It was the demolition teams. How is Taff?"

"Alright."

Just then the sky was lit up as the first of the explosives went off. Sergeant Baxter said, "That's torn it."

The captain and the others were just seconds behind me and the captain said, urgently, "In the lorries and put your foot down, Dixon. McIntire, get in the Chevrolet."

"Righto, Sir." McIntire took the position previously occupied by Taff.

Bert nodded, "Will do. See you lads." It made sense for Taff would be more comfortable in the lorry.

We had no time to waste and we hurled ourselves in the back of the lorry. The first thing I did was to retrieve my rifle and chamber a round. That done I ate a chocolate bar. I would need energy soon and even with the alarm given I had time to gobble down the chocolate. We kept the back of the lorry open. We tied the canvas back and we all held a weapon. All that is, except Taff. His right hand and arm were heavily bandaged. As we

Conscript's Call

looked to the airfield we saw the flames rising in the sky and heard the other, successive explosions. Clearly the last ones had been set some time after the first ones.

Weather said, "Keep an eye out for aeroplanes."

Corporal Williams said, "Too early for them and besides, they will have to come from another field. This one is wrecked. At least we did a good job with it."

Graham Cowley shook his head, "It was my fault. I couldn't attach one of the charges and I spent too long on it. I should just have left it by the wheel. It would have had the same effect."

Corporal Williams said, "Water under the bridge. Our job was to wreck aeroplanes and looking at the inferno we have done that."

Jack Williams was a good NCO. He would make a good sergeant. I could tell that Cowley felt bad about his mistake but we could do nothing about it. Next time he would be better. Even as I thought about it I knew that there might not be another time.

Sergeant Baxter poked his head through the canvas that separated the cab from the back of the lorry. "Coming up to the Frontier Wire. Keep your eyes peeled. Pass me Evans' Sten gun. We might need it." Corporal Williams passed the gun through.

The sky behind was lit by the fires we could see and spirals of smoke told us that we had done a good job but it was also becoming apparent that the sun was rapidly rising and we were not yet over the border. The RAF would not be overhead and the men guarding the Frontier Wire would be alert.

Sergeant Baxter cocked the Sten as he said, "Heads up! There are Eyeties ahead."

We heard the chatter of the Italian machine gun and I recognised the Bren as it fired in return. The Italian weapon was a heavier calibre. I knew that Sergeant Baxter would hold his fire with the Sten gun which was, essentially, a close-range weapon. When he did fire it would be a warning that the enemy were almost in touching distance. I heard the sound of Italian mortars too and their familiar whump and then the crack of their explosion was like the crack of doom. Once they had us ranged in then it would only be a matter of time before we were hit. The bullets that tore through the canvas came as a terrifying shock. When I had fought in Greece, Crete and even during Operation

Battleaxe, I had been able to see my enemies. Here I could not. Weather and I were lying on the floor of the lorry and using the tailgate to rest our rifles. We were watching for aeroplanes and any pursuit from the direction of the airfield. Thus far there was none but the attacks from the front and side were worrying. How would we get past them?

Sergeant Baxter began to fire. Bert shouted above the sound of Sergeant Baxter's Sten gun, "Frontier Wire ahead." The next bullets that hit us were lower. They did not strike the top of the canvas but tore through at head height. I heard screams and shouts as men were hit. We did not turn and so I trusted and hoped that Bert was still in control.

When I did glance behind I saw that Taff had no head and Graham Cowley was lying in a pool of his own blood. Jack Williams was trying to stem the bleeding from a wound to his shoulder and another to his leg. Private Robinson was looking at the pool of blood that was coming from his stomach and pooling on the floor and said, "That is a bit of a bugger." His eyes closed and he pitched forward.

Bert shouted, "Sergeant Baxter has bought it. I need someone up here."

Davis shouted, "I am closest and I will go." He began to climb through over the back of the seat when there was a sudden explosion on the passenger side of the lorry. Shrapnel tore through the back of the lorry and I heard a dying scream from Peter Davis as he died.

Just then I saw an aeroplane in the distance. It was silhouetted against the flames. That there was only one was hopeful but I saw that it was a Stuka. I shouted, "Stuka!"

Bert said, "Lovely!"

Jack Williams said, pointing to the dead bodies, "These lads bought it in that last attack. You pair are our only defence now."

I aimed my rifle at the approaching aeroplane. It would have to climb to drop its bomb but it had machine guns and it was clear that he intended to strafe us first. There would be two forward firing machine guns and they could shred the lorry in moments.

There were still the sounds of firing from the Italians but we seemed to have outrun the mortar. The Stuka opened fire before I did. I saw the tracer as it arced towards us. I began to fire. I did not know where it was vulnerable. I just hoped to damage it in some way. If I could hit an oil pipe or the windscreen…I was looking for a miracle. The bullets that struck us hit dead men and as the dive bomber screamed over us I heard Bert say, "McIntire has been hit." It was almost like a commentary on a football match on the radio except I knew from the bodies in the lorry, exactly what was happening. He was watching the Chevvy ahead. McIntire was there with the officers.

Geoff Vane stood, "This canvas is not helping. His powerful arms tore the shredded canvas to reveal the sky. He was right. The two of us now had a better chance of hitting them. Geoff picked up Rob Allen's unfired Sten gun and cocked it. It had not been fired yet. We saw the Stuka climb. It was going to come in for a bombing run.

I shouted, "Zig zag, Bert, the Stuka is diving."

"Aye, alright." There was a pause. "The Chevrolet is leaving us." He said it without acrimony. They had a wounded man on board and they had to look out for themselves. They had the Bren gun, though, and their firepower was greater than ours. The two of us rested our backs on the cab and watched the dive bomber as it screamed towards us. The **Orion** had shown me what they could do. If I was going to die then this German would die too. It had been the Luftwaffe that had killed my family. Perhaps the bomb that had killed them was the same type as the one that would soon descend to end my life too. I had a better range than Weather and more ammunition. I began to fire and I used the cowling as my target. I emptied two magazines before Geoff opened fire. I don't know which one hit the German but even as he released his bomb I saw his wings shudder.

I shouted, "Bomb!" It was for Bert's benefit. He was a good driver and as I shouted he must have put the wheel over. I could feel the lorry as Bert fought to keep it upright. It was ironic that the bomb that exploded to the side saved us from toppling over. It sent rocks and stones into the air as it struck the ground and the force of the explosion righted us. Shrapnel flew through the shredded sides of the canvas but mercifully missed us. I saw the Stuka peel away, pouring smoke. We had survived. Suddenly we

Conscript's Call

stopped and Bert's voice was flat as he said, "That's it, lads. The tyres are shredded. All ashore that's going ashore."

Geoff said, "Right, Corp, let's get you out."

"Leave me. I will only slow you up. The Italians will have a doctor." I saw that he had collected the ID tags from the dead and had put them in his battle dress.

In answer Geoff bodily picked him up and said, "Hawkeye, give us a hand and I will carry him."

I jumped down and helped the wounded corporal to the ground. Geoff Vane grabbed his rifle, the corporal's and the Sten gun. When he jumped down he slung his rifle and hefted the corporal over his other shoulder. He said, "You take his rifle. Bert, bring the other Sten."

I ran around to the front of the lorry. Bert was right; all the tyres on the driver's side were beyond repair. Bert had the Sten, he said. "We got through their lines but you can bet they will be after us."

Jack Williams said, "What happened to the Chevrolet?"

Bert shook his head, "He lost sight of us. When the bomb went off he must have thought we bought it. We are on our own." He pointed east, "Home is that way and as near as I can make out it is more than a fourteen-mile trek."

I nodded, "You three set off. This is a good position and I will try to hold up the pursuit."

Jack shook his head, "We stay together."

I looked at Weather who nodded, "Hawkeye is right and he is a clever chap. He has more chance of evading them than we do."

I said, urgently, "Go, or we will all be in the bag."

"Take care, son. I owe you." The corporal sounded weary.

I knew what I had to do. I took the German grenades out of my bag and I booby trapped the back of the lorry. It would make a mess of the dead bodies but they were beyond caring. That done I ran and made myself a defensive position in the rocks that lay just seventy feet from the lorry. A path led there and there was a drop. It could be climbed easily by a man on foot but Bert would have had to take a detour if we had not been stopped by the dive bomber. I knew that the Stuka would have reported our position and the Italians would soon come. I would be ready. I had two rifles and that meant I could fire one after the other and

Conscript's Call

make them think they were fighting a whole section. When I had settled down I took out two Mills Bombs. I had found myself a little niche and ahead I saw two rocks. I had used them to guide me to the path and now, after slithering forward like a snake, I strung the Mills Bombs between them and tied a piece of thin cord to the two pins. I disguised the cord with sand taking care that I did not trigger the device. I then moved back and levelled my rifle.

I heard the vehicle as it drove up. The Bedford hid most of it but I could see, in the increasingly bright sun, that it was painted in camouflage. I heard boots as men descended and I waited. Every moment that I could hold them up gave the other three more chance to escape. I heard the men speaking as they approached the lorry. It was Italian. One must have a had a sub-machine gun for he sprayed the back of the lorry. There was more shouting. The German grenade booby trap was on the passenger side of the lorry. When two Italians came around the driver's side I squeezed off five bullets. I hit one for certain and I might have even wounded the other. I heard orders rattled out and then men came around both sides. I fired at those on the driver's side and then I heard the double whump as the two German grenades exploded. My distraction had made them careless and they had paid with their lives. I had emptied the magazine of one gun and then I took out the Beretta I had taken from the Italian sergeant. As shadows appeared through the smoke on the passenger side, I emptied all eight shots and after ramming it in its holster hung around my neck, I picked up the rifle with the loaded magazine and readied it. There was a great deal of shouting and cries. I had hurt some of them and I guessed from the uproar that I had hit one of those giving the orders. Suddenly the sub-machine gun opened fire. It was around the side of the lorry and I had no target. I had bought some time and I would have to leave soon. When the sub-machine gun stopped I aimed at the barrel and when the face appeared above the gun I hit the man.

I had done enough and taking both rifles I slid down the slope. Bullets zipped at the place I had just occupied. I was able to stand at the bottom of the slope. I saw that it was a shallow wadi. I turned and ran along it. I had gone just four feet when I heard a single explosion and a wall of smoke and shrapnel flew over my head. They had used a grenade. I ran, the rifles slung over each shoulder. The wadi turned to the right and as I ran along it I heard the sound of the two Mills Bombs exploding. The two booby traps would make them cautious and as they could not follow me in the vehicle down the slope that, too, bought me time. I ran because I wanted to catch up with my comrades. I knew that Geoff would struggle to move quickly with the corporal slung over his back. When I had run for perhaps a mile I saw the three of them ahead. Geoff was no longer carrying the corporal. He and Bert were supporting him.

I was just five yards from them when they heard me and their heads whipped around. "I thought you lads would be back at the camp by now and enjoying a nice cuppa."

Jack Williams shook his head, "My fault. I insisted I could walk."

"They will be behind us soon and," I pointed ahead, "the wadi ends up there. Once we leave its safety then they will be on to us."

Bert said, "Maybe the captain will come back for us."

"This is not the terrain for a truck, Bert, you should know that better than any. I think this is the shortest way back to the camp but not for a vehicle."

Jack shook his head, "I can't go much further. I reckon I have lost to much blood and I am ..." With that his head slumped forward.

Geoff put his hand to his neck and said, "He is still alive."

I looked ahead and saw a place we could use. There were rocks and it looked like we could make the top of the wadi if we lost the battle. I pointed, "Then let's get up there and make a defensive position. Perhaps if we get some chocolate in him and check his dressings…"

Bert nodded, "It's better than nowt."

Geoff lifted him on his shoulder and I faced back down the wadi. One of the rifles still had bullets and I pointed it down the wadi. I could still see smoke drifting from the last grenades. Perhaps I had discouraged them. I had to have hurt some of them.

Geoff shouted, "In position."

Conscript's Call

I walked backwards down the wadi. The other three were nestled behind some rocks about six feet above the wadi floor. It had a good field of fire and the rocks afforded some protection. There was a sort of shelf and they had laid down the corporal. I saw that we could climb the few feet to the top. Bert held up his oily fingers, "One of you lads should be the nurse."

Geoff nodded and as he began to remove the hastily applied dressings said, "Bert, I forgot to take the spare clips from the dead lads." He handed him the two Sten guns.

"They will do."

I gave Geoff my spare chocolate bar and reloaded the Beretta and the two rifles. That done I drank some water and listened. My ears picked up the rumble and drone of a tracked vehicle. Had they sent a tank after us? I laid my weapons down and began to climb up the side of the wadi. Even in the desert vegetation struggled for life and I peered through thin and straggly grass at the dust that looked to be more than a mile away. I could not make out what it was at first and then it stopped. I caught the glint of light on binoculars as someone scanned the desert for us. When the dust settled I saw that it was a half-track with German soldiers on board and two machine guns. I checked to see that it was alone before I moved.

I slithered back down and said, "Well, there is a Jerry half-track up top."

"That's it then, we are done for."

I shook my head, "Not necessarily, Bert. We are below the surface of the desert. If we keep quiet they might miss us."

Geoff nodded, "And I do not fancy spending the rest of this war in a POW camp." He smiled, "The corporal woke while you were taking a shufti and I got a bit of chocolate and some cold tea down him. If he saves his strength then when the Germans have passed he might be able to make the last few miles to the camp."

Bert said, hopefully, "Perhaps the colonel will send out men to look for us."

Geoff shook his head, "And risk losing more men? They will have written us off. The raid must have been a success. We destroyed aeroplanes and an airfield. We took out a Stuka and Hawkeye here accounted for half a dozen of the enemy. The

Conscript's Call

accountants who measure success will say that the loss of one lorry load of conscripts is a small price to pay."

"Weather is right but we are not yet done and dusted." I was not willing to simply give up. It was not in my nature.

We listened as the half-track's rumble drew ever closer. I still prayed that it would pass us and, camouflaged as we were, it might not spot us. Even my hopes faded when the Italian infantry appeared down the wadi. I had my rifles ready, as did Weather, and Bert had the Sten. I looked at Geoff, "You have the stripe, when do we fire?"

He sighed and said, grimly, "When they are so close that we can't miss. Then we take off and try to avoid the half-track." He gently shook Corporal William's shoulder, "Corporal, we have company."

Corporal Williams woke. He looked a little better. I handed him the captured Beretta. He smiled and said, "Like Custer's last stand, eh?"

Geoff said, "There is a Jerry half-track yonder, too. Once we open fire then…"

The Italians drew closer. From the way they were looking to the side I didn't think that they had seen us, yet. It looked to be two sections and they were led by an officer and a sergeant. The officer held a Beretta like the one I had given to the corporal. I saw the sharp-eyed sergeant point when they were eighty yards from us and said, "They have seen us."

Geoff shouted, "Fire!"

I emptied my magazine as fast as I could and then picked up the second rifle. The Sten rattled and barked and the corporal fired into the dust and smoke with his pistol. I emptied my second rifle as I heard voices shouting in the distance and they were in German.

I said, "I will risk a look see." The Italians who had survived our ambush had raced for cover. With a Beretta in my hand I ascended the side of the wadi and saw the half-track turning and heading directly for us. I turned and said, "Half-track coming for us."

The rest must have done the corporal some good. He took command, "Right lads, let's join Hawkeye. We all have grenades. Who knows, we might be lucky." He reached into his

Conscript's Call

pocket and took out the IDs he had taken. "Here, Hawkeye, look after these. You are the lucky one. If I don't make it then see that they get to the officers."

As Bert handed me my rifles and the others joined me to peer over the top of the wadi, Weather said, "I never thought I would miss the grenade launcher but here, for once, it might do us some good."

Bert chuckled, "Always moaning about what you haven't got. We might as well hope for a squadron of tanks to appear over the horizon."

As the two heavy German machine guns began to fire we ducked down. We had no helmets for protection.

Behind us I heard the sound of the Italian rifles as they fired at the position we had just abandoned. Soon they would discover we had gone and then it would be all over. The German gunners stopped firing and I risked a peek over the top. It was then I saw the most welcome of sights. Three Hurricanes were heading for the half-track. They were low down and the Germans had not seen them through the haze of the sun in the east. I dropped down and said, "The RAF are here but so are the Italians." We turned with our backs to the top of the wadi. I thought that we should be safe from the Hurricanes' armament. I reloaded and aimed through the clearing smoke and dust. I fired at the movement and while that halted the Italians, it also told them our position.

When the machine guns and 20 mm cannons from the three aircraft opened up it was the most wonderful and terrifying sound. The bullets and shells tore into the half-track. It was not a tank and there was no armour to protect the gunners and crew. I heard the screams and then the explosion as shells exploded the fuel and ammunition. A fireball rose in the sky and the air was filled with the stink of exploding fuel and ammunition.

Corporal Williams shouted, "Get down! The Hurries are turning." We threw ourselves to hide behind whatever rocks we could find. The bullets tore too close for comfort but when I heard Italian screams then I knew the RAF had done their job. They had saved us.

Conscript's Call

We stayed crouched for a long time and when the three aeroplanes disappeared back to their field we risked rising. The corporal said, "Vane and Sharratt, go and take a look see."

When I clambered over the top of the wadi I saw that the half-track was written off. Flames were still licking it. I saw that one of the crew must have been set on fire and tried to escape the inferno. His blackened body lay ten feet from the wrecked half-track. I hurried beyond the vehicle and peered into the distance. I saw the dust thrown up by approaching vehicles. This time they were neither German nor Italian, they had to be British. I turned, "The cavalry is here, lads. We are saved." I dropped to my knees and said a silent prayer of thanks. We had come to within a few moments of death or capture but we had survived.

As the others joined me Corporal Williams tossed me the Beretta, "Thanks for that, Hawkeye. You better keep it, eh?"

Chapter 11

Corporal Williams was taken directly to the hospital. A medical orderly checked us out and then passed us as fit. We three were driven to Headquarters where Major Hill waited for us. RSM Lawson and CSM Hutton were there too. We had taken off our caps and were stood to attention. The major said, "Stand easy." He looked up at us after a few moments, "So you three and Corporal Williams are the only ones left from the lorry?"

Geoff was the Lance Corporal and he said, "Yes, Sir."

I reached into my battle dress pocket and took out the IDs, "Corporal Williams took the tags from the dead, Sir." I handed them to him, and he placed them on his desk. I saw that there was one there already.

He shook his head as he laid them out, "Half of the men on the mission failed to return, a heavy price to pay."

CSM Hutton, trying to defend the officers, said, "To be fair, Major Hill, the raid has to be considered a success. From the captain's report more than a dozen aircraft were destroyed as well as the fuel for the aircraft and the means to repair them."

The major nodded and gave the CSM a sad look, "All well and good, CSM Hutton, but how do we replace the eight good men who died?" He turned his attention to us, "And these men could have joined them."

RSM Lawson nodded, "But they showed that they represented the spirit of the Queen's Rifles, Sir. Three men with a wounded non-com held off a determined attack by an Italian platoon and were willing to take on a German half-track. Quite remarkable in my view."

The major smiled, "That it was and I will not denigrate the efforts of these brave men. If you would go next door and write out your own accounts of the raid they will be passed on for evaluation and then you can rejoin your platoon." He stood and smiled, "The sergeant major is quite right and while you were conscripts a few months ago, your recent actions show that you are now veterans."

Conscript's Call

Next door was a small room with tables and chairs. A corporal handed us some paper and pencils. I sat and began to write. I had never been particularly academic at school. Never naughty, I had struggled with both reading and writing. I had to concentrate to put down on paper what had happened. I started at the beginning and wrote it as I saw it. I couldn't write about the Chevrolet or the demolition teams because I had not experienced them. I did write down what Graham Cowley had told me. The truth was not always pleasant. I was the last to finish and I went to the door. CSM Hutton and the others were waiting. There was a Morris truck and he said, "Hop in. I shall be your chauffeur."

I had mixed feelings as we drove the half mile or so to our camp. I had not expected praise to be heaped upon us but the major had implied that it had been a failure. Geoff asked, "Did the lads in the Chevvy all make it?"

CSM Hutton shook his head, "McIntire was dead by the time they reached safety. The captain had a wound but the others are all well." He paused, "They thought that you were all dead. They saw that you stopped after the Stuka attack and...understandable."

We said nothing. It was, and had they come back for us then they might have been taken. It had been the wadi that had saved us.

Bert said, "Nice little motor this, Company Sergeant Major."

He nodded, "And the Chevvy has proved popular. This way we can arm them and have some protection when we go into action the next time."

"And will that be soon, CSM?"

"No, Lance Corporal. We have a new Commanding General and as we lost more than a hundred tanks in the last battle we aren't in a position to do much in terms of an advance. We hold what we have and the ones with red collars will make the decisions." He stopped the Morris and pulled on the handbrake. Turning he said, "The regiment can hold its head up and that is down, in many ways, to you lads. We are all proud of what you did. We lost men but that happens in war. I reckon you three know that better than most. There will be others who will all look up to you, now. You have all come a long way but now I

Conscript's Call

think you have found your feet. Until Corporal Williams returns, Vane, you will take charge of the section."

"Yes, CSM."

We got out and he held out his hand, "The Stens and the Berettas, lads." We handed over the ones issued to us but I kept the one I had taken at the airfield and the ammunition as well as the stiletto. The major had been right, we were no longer conscripts and I had learned to look after number one when I could. The Italian pistol that lay in my pack gave me an edge, especially at close quarters. I would hang on to it.

We were welcomed by the rest of the platoon as though we were returning heroes. Sergeant Jackson beamed like a proud father whose son has just passed his scholarship exam. There was the inevitable banter too but that just showed the camaraderie in the platoon. We had not lost any men. Corporal Williams would, in the fullness of time, return and as we had been told we were just to hold the position we held. That we had not retreated, for me, was a first.

The first thing we did, after we had been treated to a pot of tea and bacon sandwiches, was to have a shower. We would be at this camp for the foreseeable future and we had shower facilities. The burnt cork we had used to blacken our faces came off as did the sweat, dirt and blood. All of us had uniforms and bodies that had dried blood on them. We had not noticed being sprayed with it during the attack on the Bedford but Ray gently pointed it out to us. The blood was a reminder of the deaths we had suffered. The back of the lorry had been a charnel house when the Stuka had strafed us. It had been a miracle that three of us had avoided being hit. As I scrubbed my naked body clean I reflected that while I had not known the dead well, the action had drawn us closer. I knew that I had saved Taff's life and he had been grateful. That he had died anyway was another matter. We had bonded on the raid. The deaths of the eight, especially the ones from the Bedford, would never leave me. They would be my private thoughts. I couldn't and I wouldn't share them. As I dressed myself in my spare uniform I knew that should I survive the war and marry then I would still keep those thoughts to myself. It would not be fair to anyone else to have to endure the nightmares that I knew I would have. We then went to dhobi our

Conscript's Call

dirty clothes. It was a necessary chore but, thankfully, here in the desert they would be dry by the evening and we would all have clean, spare clothes.

That night we ate well. The RSM sent over some lamb. There were local herders and sometimes they sold us a kid or a lamb. It was a measure of the feelings for the survivors that our section was given a whole leg. It was July but it felt like Christmas. CSM Hutton sent over some beer too. We had just finished gorging when the lieutenant came in. He had not been in the camp. The rumour was that he had either gone to the hospital with the captain or he had gone to Headquarters to report. I thought that the lieutenant was ambitious and it would be the latter.

He came in and put his arms on my shoulders and Weather's, "Well done, lads. I am so proud of you. You did not let anyone down and your escape shows the grit you all have." His face became serious, "You should know that we wanted to come back for you but McIntire was still alive then and..." he shook his head, "hindsight is a wonderful thing."

We had spoken about this on the way back to the camp and Weather spoke for all of us, "Sir, it wouldn't have made any odds. Hawkeye found the wadi and held off the Eyeties." He chuckled, "We should call him '*booby trap*' from now on, Sir, he set two of them. The RAF saved us, Sir. They came in the nick as they say. Don't reproach yourself. You were trying to save McIntire just as we were trying to save Jack Williams. We were luckier than you."

"Well, you should know that the powers that be are more than happy with what we achieved. They want us to repeat it." He smiled, "Not yet, of course, but we have shown what can be done by a determined group of men."

I had been right. He had been to Headquarters. I was not sure that the regiment would agree with his assessment of the situation but if he had the backing of HQ then, if he planned another raid, it would go ahead.

"Anyway, have the next few days off. You have earned it. The captain will be away for a week and until then I am in temporary command of the company. In light of our experiences I have some engineers coming at the end of the week to give lessons to

Conscript's Call

us all in the use of demolition charges." He took his hands from our shoulders, "Enjoy yourselves and carry on, chaps."

We had lost our two experts and we might need training but I wondered at the wisdom of using a rifle regiment for a task which would be better carried out by commandos. His words did not inspire us and, if anything, ended the good humour. The party came to a natural close soon after. The ones who had survived exchanged looks and I knew that the others, like me, would be wary of volunteering a second time.

I slept the sleep of the dead. It was not just the night without sleep that had exhausted me but also the long twenty hours of action. We had eaten little and, as I had already learned in Greece and Crete, action tired a man even if he was just sitting in a trench. Dad had never spoken of it but I think I now understood a little more of his life and his comrades. If I ever got the chance to sit again in the pub and talk to them I would understand them far better than I had before. I had walked a little way in their shoes but I still had a long journey ahead of me. The next day the three of us were bombarded by the others about the raid. I knew that some of them would want to volunteer despite the fact that the three of us told the truth. The horror of a dive-bombing Stuka was bad enough on a ship but when the bomb was coming directly for you it seemed more personal. The attack from the guns and mortars had also been something that was terrifying.

Bert said, "I reckon we ought to roll up the sides of the canvas on the lorries. It gives the lads in the back no protection and if you can see then it isn't as scary. I know that it must have been easier for me and Sergeant Baxter in the front because we knew what was coming." He gestured at Weather and me with his thumb, "These lads had no idea."

"What was the Sten like?"

"I never used one, Ray, ask Bert. He was the only one who used one."

"Noisy but it was good to send a shed load of bullets at the enemy. Hawkeye here can fire almost as fast with an Emily as I could but for the likes of us a sub-machine is what you need."

Wally said, "My cousin is in the Marine Commandos and he told me they use Tommy guns, you know Thompson machine guns like Jimmy Cagney used in the gangster films."

Weather nodded, "Aye, and they have Colt pistols too. What was the Beretta like?"

I had been the one to fire it and I said, "Handy but from what I hear a Colt is a fully automatic and so would be even faster."

Harry sniffed, "What we need is the Yanks in this war, not just their guns and tanks."

Norm Thomas shook his head, "My dad was in the Great War and he said they will only start to fight when it is almost over."

That began a debate and opinions were divided. My dad reckoned that as the last war was a European war we couldn't expect the Americans to join in. On the other hand this was a wider war. We were fighting in Africa too. I kept my opinions to myself. I was not well versed enough to join in.

When the captain returned he sent for the three of us. His arm was in a sling and he had a couple of scars on his face. He let us sit down and allowed the others to smoke. "I wanted to speak to you three alone. I spoke to Jack Williams in the hospital and cleared the air. I want to do so with you. You have to know that if I had thought for one minute that you were all alive we would have come back. Private Featherstone mistakenly said that you had brewed up."

Bert nodded, "To be fair to him, Sir, it must have looked that way and even if you had come back you would have been captured. Sharratt here found us a way out."

I added, hurriedly, for I did not want the captain to think I was a hero, "And if it had not been for the Hurricanes, Sir, we would have been dead and not just in the bag. It all worked out."

He smiled, "I am not sure that in your position I would be quite as forgiving. Anyway there will be rewards. Corporal Williams is to be promoted to sergeant and will take over Sergeant Baxter's platoon. You, Lance Corporal will be made up to Corporal."

"Thank you, Sir."

"And you two, well, I can see promotion just on the horizon. You both did very well. We have more men coming from England to replace those lost already. I know that Lieutenant Hargreaves wants another raid but for the rest of us we just do our jobs and wait for the next battle. We are not commandos, we

Conscript's Call

are riflemen." That conversation told me the captain's true feelings about the raid.

The promotions were immediate and it meant that Jack Williams would go directly to his new platoon when he returned from hospital. We celebrated with Weather and enjoyed a few bottles of beer. No one resented the promotion which we all felt was well deserved. Neither Bert nor I were bothered at the thought of promotion. So long as Bert had Betty he was happy and I did not want the responsibility. I liked being low man on the totem pole.

The commandos who came to train us were from Number 11 Commando and they had worked in the desert. That we had done what we did impressed them and they seemed quite happy to share their skills. It was just our company who enjoyed the training. I think that Lieutenant Hargreaves intended asking for volunteers for the next raid from the men he knew best. Nothing had been said but I did not think that the captain would be part of the next raid. We were introduced to Gun Cotton TNT, primers, Cordtex and safety fuses. By the end of the day I felt that I could help someone to set a charge and blow a bridge or a railway line but I would not like to do so unsupervised. Ray and Wally seemed to enjoy the training more than I did and when the commandos left us they were animated in their discussions about the chance to blow something up.

Geoff and I tried to introduce some caution into the discussion, "Graham Cowley had worked in a quarry and he was used to explosives. It was his delay that meant we left late. Think about that." Neither of us said that the delay had cost not only Graham his life but another seven men.

Pie Face was eminently confident, "I can see what you are saying but I reckon that if you are careful then it would not be a problem."

I said, "So you are thinking of volunteering then?"

He grinned, "Of course and Glass Man is too, aren't you?"

Ray nodded, "Yeah. You lads had all the fun last time and we missed out. Surely you two will volunteer again."

I looked at the newly promoted corporal, and said, "I am not sure. When that Stuka began to strafe us," I shuddered, "it was all down to luck. Weather and I were lucky, that was all. If our

Conscript's Call

heads had been six inches higher…only Bert would have survived."

Bert stubbed out his cigarette, "And I would be in a POW camp. It is not something to be undertaken lightly, lads."

I could see they were not convinced but as there was no prospect of another raid for a while anyway it was a moot point. However, over the next days I felt the excitement from the two of them as they pictured themselves blacked up and raiding behind the lines. It sounded romantic and heroic. I knew it was not.

The newly promoted Sergeant Williams returned to the battalion at the same time as the fresh-faced replacements. The voyage from England had given them a skin tanned like ours but there the similarity ended. Their uniforms still looked crisp. They wore their caps differently and they stood almost awkwardly. I felt sorry for them from the off. We had come to the war as a section, a platoon and a company. They were coming to fill gaps by men who had been killed or invalided back to Blighty. There were forty of them. We knew we had at least one coming to us as Geoff Vane was now the corporal. As most sections had ten men it was likely that there would be two or even three. They arrived on Sunday and had missed Church Parade. The rest of the day was earmarked for dhobying. The next day, we had been told, we would be taken out in lorries to escort men detailed to shift some mines that had been laid in the night. That was a job none of us relished.

We watched with interest as the lorries pulled up and the men disgorged. There were two other wounded men returning with Sergeant Williams and they were greeted by the MO and the major. I saw them all hand over a chit of paper, salute and then head to the waiting battalion.

Jack Williams came to us. He had a new platoon to command but we all knew he would come to say goodbye to our section first. He grinned as he walked over and tapped his three stripes. Geoff Vane apart we bowed. Jack feigned a back hand slap, "Cheeky…"

"How are you, Sergeant?" Geoff emphasised the rank.

"The wounds are itchy and that is a good sign but I was fed up with being in the hospital anyway." His face became serious,

Conscript's Call

"No more volunteering for me. I know how close I came to meeting my maker the last time." He looked at the others, "Take my advice, don't volunteer."

I saw the looks on the faces of Wally and Ray. It was one thing for me to advise them not to volunteer but Jack Williams was well respected. Their minds were changing. I nodded to where his new platoon were watching, "And your chicks await their mother hen and wonder, no doubt, if you bark."

He nodded and then said, "Hawkeye, I just wanted to thank you. I know that Bert and Weather carried me but if you hadn't risked your life then we would all be in the bag." He shook his head, "Who am I kidding, I might have been dead. I owe you. Anything you ever need, just ask."

I shrugged. I was uncomfortable with the attention, "Don't be daft, Sarge. Anyone else would have done the same."

"No they wouldn't, so thank you."

Geoff said, quietly, "Lieutenant Hargreaves is planning another raid."

Jack's face became serious, "Bucking for a promotion, that one. Well, here is one who will not be volunteering. I am beginning to see what the RSM meant. Anyway, I had better be off. See you around."

As he headed to his new platoon I saw Sergeant Jackson come over, shake his hand and then speak to him. While we had been talking the replacements had met the adjutant and CSM Hutton was allocating them. As soon as Jack had left us Weather gave all his attention to the CSM. We saw men, in ones and twos, head off to join their platoons. When we heard our name we all looked over and saw two men. One was almost as big as Geoff and Ray said, "It looks like we have someone else to lug the grenade launcher around."

Norm Thomas said, "Aye, but what use is the other one? He looks like a stiff breeze would knock him over."

He was right. There could not have been a bigger contrast in the two men. The second one was tall enough but he looked almost emaciated in contrast with his burly companion. Sergeant Jackson had joined us. As well as the two men obviously joining our section there were half a dozen others who would make the platoon up to regulation. He had a clipboard and read off their names. They all said "Yes, Sergeant."

"Corporal Vane, Privates Poulter and Brown are in your section."

"Right, Sarge. Pick up your necessaries and follow me." Now that we had full numbers the tents would be more crowded. Geoff pointed to the two tents, "One in this one and the other in the next one. Your choice."

The bigger one of the two looked in and said, "I'll have his one." He went into the one occupied by what we called Harry's crew. Bert, Harry, Norm and Dave. "Roly, you can have the other."

I looked at the thin young man and said, "Roly?"

He nodded, "My name is Roland but because I am on the thin side the others thought that Roly, as in Roly Poly, was a good nickname." I noticed that he sounded like the lieutenant. He was what we called posh.

"And do you like the name?"

He sighed, "I don't have much choice in the matter, do I?"

He sounded sad and I decided to take him under my wing. I knew what it was like to be alone and Private Poulter seemed to be lonely, "Then I will call you Roland." I held out my hand and when he shook it he smiled. "My name is John but the lads all call me Hawkeye."

He smiled for the first time and looked a different person, "Because you are a good shot!"

"I am not bad."

He looked in the tent, "Where do I sleep?"

"Wherever you like. The lads here are a good bunch. The corporal sleeps in here and then there is Pie Face, Wally Salter and Glass Man, Ray Jennings." Just then the two of them came in. "This is Roland." I pointed, "Ray and Wally."

Wally frowned, "I thought you were Roly."

Before the young man could speak I said, "It is a nickname he was given out of spite. Roland will do, eh lads?"

I had changed since I had been in fear of my life when McGuire and his gang had intimidated me. I felt more confident now and the two lads from St Helens and Wigan nodded, Ray said, "Whatever you say. Welcome, Roland."

Conscript's Call

That evening as we ate in the mess I sat with Roland, and my other three close companions. Geoff might be a corporal now but we were all still close. The other new man sat on the opposite side of the table. He was Sandy Brown and his nickname was an obvious one. He had been given it when he had worked in ICI at Widnes and it had stuck.

We learned about Roland. I suspect no one had bothered to talk to him. He did sound different and some people can be intimidated by such things. Once he began to talk he became more confident and as we neither mocked nor disapproved when he spoke, he grew in confidence. "My family come from Poulton le Fylde."

Wally grinned, "Near Blackpool! My dad took us there one Whit Sunday. We went on the bus. Nice place, by the seaside." He nodded to Ray, "A lot posher than Blackpool. No rock!"

Roland smiled, "Yes, it is a little posh." He gave a shy smile, "I know I sound posh." He shook his head, "I can't help the way I speak. It is the way I was brought up."

Geoff was a good man and he said, "You are what you are, son, and you shouldn't have to change but how come you aren't an officer? I bet you went to a good school."

He nodded, "I did and my father had connections but…" he sighed, "I am not sure I could be a leader. I would hate for men to die because I made a mistake. My father was more than a little cross when I refused his offer."

"His offer?"

"Yes, Corporal, he is the Lieutenant Colonel of a regiment. An honorary title but…I refused and when I was called up he said he disowned me." He sighed, "My brother is a lieutenant in the Grenadier Guards and one of my cousins is a fighter pilot. I think my father is a little ashamed of me."

I understood better than anyone else what Roland meant. I did not want the responsibility of rank. I was happy just to follow orders.

"Anyway, I always wanted to be a doctor. I had a place at University, Edinburgh. I dare say when this war is over I shall take up the place." He suddenly stopped, "What a fool I am. If my father disowns me then I shall never be able to afford to go."

Conscript's Call

He was different to us. None of the rest of us would ever have had the chance to go to university. That was for those who went to public school and whose parents could afford to support them. Although we could never aspire to university I think that the four of us understood what his disappointment meant. There was silence on our side of the table. On the other side they were talking football. We were ignored.

Roland smiled, "Anyway, I found that I had skills with First Aid and I am the section's First Aider."

That made us all smile, "And not before time. Well, Bones, welcome to the section."

Geoff Vane changed the young man's nickname in that instant. Sandy Brown continued to try to call him Roly but as Geoff and the rest of us gave him the name, Bones, it was a lost battle and he, eventually, took to the new nickname. We made Roland one of our own. He might have lost his family, as I had done, but, like me, he had found a new one in the section.

The next day the company was marched out to the desert where engineers with detectors were waiting to clear mines recently laid during the night. I think both sides did it to annoy the other. We were there in case it was an ambush and men were hiding in the rocks to kill the skilled men who would clear the mines. For me the worst part was when they found one and then had to dig it up and defuse it. They knew their job but I could not have done that. If a mine went off then not only the man disarming it but any within a thirty-foot radius would be hit. They had to have the greatest trust in each other to do what they did. I was glad when the area was declared safe and we could head back to the camp.

Chapter 12

Taking Roland under my wing meant giving him the benefit of all that I had learned. He seemed to like me and heeded all that I said. I was not sure he would ever be a good rifleman. He seemed to flinch when we fired our weapons but he was a hard worker and never shirked any of the duties assigned to us. He was also the cleverest person I had ever met. He could speak not only French but understood and spoke a little German and Italian. That made him invaluable. It showed the total difference in our backgrounds. He had a family with wealth, foreign holidays and servants. I had never even enjoyed, as the others had, a day trip to Blackpool. It had just been something we could not afford. I loved listening to Roland when he spoke of holidays in his family's French home, of travelling in expensive cars and eating food which was exotic. His clothes, at home, were tailored. His father had a title and he knew others with titles.

"Do you have a title?"

He shook his head, "My brother will inherit the title. Besides, as my father wants nothing more to do with me it is irrelevant."

"What about your mother? What did she say about all this?"

He gave a sad smile, "I think it broke her heart. She writes to me. I eagerly anticipate the next letters from home for the last one I had was before we embarked. She says she is working on my father but I think it is a lost cause, you know? He is stubborn."

In the month we had with the new men we all became closer. Even Sandy changed a little. I think that was Bert's doing. Since he had been put in charge of Betty, Bert had become more assertive. We had no Lance Corporal but Bert was the unofficial one and he was the one who modified the big gruff man who tended to speak before he thought. When Sandy tried to throw his weight around or to disparage Roland, Bert took him down a peg or two. The chemical worker from Widnes began to change. He was not a lost cause as McGuire had been. He had merely picked up some bad habits and rough edges. We sanded them smooth.

Conscript's Call

When Lieutenant Hargreaves asked for volunteers for another raid behind enemy lines, none of the three of us who had been on the first one volunteered. That influenced the others who also did not volunteer. Sergeant Jackson did. The day after the request had gone out the lieutenant and sergeant came to our tents. That was unusual. We stood to attention. "Stand easy." The lieutenant looked ill at ease as he said, "None of the men in this section volunteered. I wondered why."

None of us could meet his gaze. Corporal Vane said, "Sir, we were lucky to make it back alive the last time. A man has only so much luck. There are others who can take a chance."

Sergeant Jackson said, "I told you, Sir."

The lieutenant said, "Salter, Jennings, Cunningham, you volunteered the last time and you didn't go on the raid." They looked at each other. I saw doubt on their faces. The lieutenant saw the weakening of resolve and said, "I need chaps like you." In that moment I saw that the lieutenant did not want volunteers this time. He wanted to hand pick his team. "You have shown in Greece, Crete and now North Africa that you are a credit to England and your families."

The blatant flattery worked. Any lingering doubts harboured by my two friends disappeared when the lieutenant's eyes lit upon them. Ray and Wally looked at one another and nodded. Ray said, "If that is the case, Sir, then we are your men." Harry had not been taken in.

My view was confirmed when the officer turned to Bert, "And you, Dixon, I need someone who can fix motors. We were lucky last time and you are the best driver we have. I really wanted you to drive the Chevvy."

That offer and the flattery convinced Bert who nodded.

He cast his gaze on me, "Sharratt, these are your friends and the whole battalion knows of your skill with weapons. I have managed to acquire a silencer and a Colt. They are yours if you volunteer."

When I had attended Sunday School I had been told of the devil tempting Jesus on the side of the mountain and to me that sounded just like the lieutenant now. I shook my head, "Sorry, Sir. Let someone else have the glory. I shall stay here." I saw in the faces of the others that I had shocked them, perhaps even

154

disappointed them. I did not worry about that for I knew I was no coward.

The lieutenant shook his head and then his eyes fixed on Roland, "Private Poulter, you have unique skills that would be useful. I have read your training report and you have skills that we need. I need someone with medical experience. How about it?" The slight glance the officer gave me told me why he had made the offer. He wanted me to be forced into volunteering. I prayed for Roland to refuse.

Roland, too, was flattered, "Of course, Sir, I would be honoured."

When Lieutenant Hargreaves' hawklike eyes fixed on me and he said, "Well, Sharratt..." I knew I had no choice.

In that instant my view of the lieutenant changed. I had been manipulated and I did not like it. "Yes, Sir, I would love to volunteer." I imbued my voice with as much irony as I could but it was like water off a duck's back. The lieutenant had won and he had the men he had wanted all along.

He smiled, "You have tonight here and then tomorrow we will gather at the camp we used last time. We raid tomorrow night."

When they had gone every eye looked at me. Roland had a quizzical look and he said, "Why did you change your mind, John?"

I saw in their faces that the others knew the reason. I would not let the raw conscript go off and get himself killed. I did not want Roland to know the real reason, that I was looking out for him. The others could look after themselves on the raid but not Roland. Geoff just said, "He did not want his mates to go without him. We look after our own. Isn't that right, Hawkeye?"

I forced a smile, "Aye, Corporal, that is about it."

What we learned was that one reason the Commandos could not do as much raiding here in the desert was because of a series of disasters. The last one had seen the enigmatic Colonel Laycock attempt to capture Rommel. It had ended in disaster with many men, including Colonel Laycock, being killed. There were rumours of soldiers who were based in the desert raiding but their identity and their units were a mystery. The commandos were busy training both themselves and men like us. Until more

Conscript's Call

commandos arrived it would be up to small units like our raiding party to annoy the enemy. I had already worked out that was all we were doing. The aeroplanes that had been destroyed by us at Sidi Azeiz had not stopped the enemy attacks from the air. The raids were more for morale. They showed that we were hitting back.

This time I was the expert. Bert and I were the only two from our section who had been on the first raid. We both knew what to expect and we made sure that we warned the others of the dangers that I knew the lieutenant would skirt around. Even Sergeant Jackson listened to what we said. When I explained why, they heeded my advice about lengths of cord and Mills Bombs, I saw them listening as though their lives depended upon it. They would all know what to pack regardless of orders from the lieutenant. I showed them my stiletto and when I told them that meant I was able to leave the heavier bayonet in my tent they resolved to acquire a similar weapon. They were also envious of my Beretta. I had been promised a Colt. Perhaps that was just a lure but I told Ray that he could borrow my Beretta if it was replaced. Bones had the heaviest pack as he was required to carry the medical equipment and spare chocolate. He had been promised, like the sergeant, a Sten gun. The rest of us would have rifles.

Our goodbyes were heartfelt. Half of the first raiders had failed to return. The looks we exchanged were meaningful. We were British and we did not open up. Our eyes could not hide the regret of this being a last meeting.

When we reached the camp we saw that we had the Morris but it had now had a pair of twin Lewis guns on a Motley mount. Bert, of course, ignored that and lifted the bonnet to examine the engine. I assumed that we would have the small truck. The canvas only covered the top. Our advice had been heeded and the sides were open. I also saw that sandbags had been placed along the side, beneath the bench. They would not stop a tank shell or a cannon from an aeroplane but they would be better than just the wooden side walls. The Chevvy also had a Lewis gun as well as the Bren gun.

Sergeant Jackson said, "Get your gear inside. Dixon."

Conscript's Call

"I won't be a mo', Sarge." He continued to inspect the Morris. We knew they were good desert vehicles because some had been armoured to make the Morris CS9 Armoured car.

We were the first ones there and we each chose our own spot in the back of the truck but we were all close to one another. We heard the others arrive and Lieutenant Hargreaves said, "Right, lads, outside. Meet the others."

There was a corporal and four privates. They were from C Company. It looked like the lieutenant had gone beyond his own company. Perhaps others had been put off because of the deaths. We were introduced. He introduced us first and then said, "Corporal Jenkins, Private Grant, Private Taylor, Private Jones and Private Swift." We nodded to each other and were then led into a small building with a table and, pinned to the wall, a map.

The lieutenant pointed to Bert and me, "These two have been on a raid before. For the rest of you it is all new but all of you have a good record." I glanced at Roland and saw that he had his head down and was blushing. He was here for different reasons and had yet to prove anything to any anybody. "We are smaller in number because our target is not as big. It will be defended but there should not be as many sentries." I was intrigued. If it was not an airfield, what was it?

There was a map pinned to the wall and this time it was not a hand drawn one. I recognised some of the places on it. We had fought there during the Operation Battleaxe. The lieutenant took out his commando dagger and tapped a dot. "Point 208. Some of you may remember it. We took it and then lost it. We do not need to take it in this raid but we have to destroy what is there. The Germans, not the Italians this time, have a well defended position with a radio transmitter as well as an artillery observation post. There will be a new offensive soon and we need to knock out the transmitter in addition to the two 88 mm anti-aircraft guns which are there. As you know the 88 can be used, with the right ammunition, as an anti-tank or anti-personnel weapon." He smiled, "Before you ask, the RAF has been trying to damage it for some time but the enemy are defending it with their own aeroplanes. Many have been lost already and, well, it is too expensive. We do not have enough aircraft."

The unwelcome thought crept into my mind, aeroplanes and pilots were expensive but riflemen were ten a penny and expendable.

"This time we need to eliminate the sentries and take the garrison prisoner. Then we set charges and blow up the transmitter and the guns."

"And the garrison?"

"We take their boots and set them off to march west."

Sergeant Jackson frowned, "Isn't that contrary to the Geneva Convention, Sir?"

The lieutenant's eyes narrowed, "This is war, Sergeant, and we are not harming the men. If this was the SS then whoever they took would be shot. They would not worry about the prospect of killing prisoners and I promise you that we won't do that."

"Sir?"

"Yes, Sharratt?"

"What is to stop the Germans from simply returning and disarming the demolitions?"

He smiled, "Private Poulter can speak some German. He will explain that we will be leaving booby traps and if they return then they risk death." He nodded to me, "I read the reports, Sharratt, and your clever use of booby traps did not go unnoticed. We will booby trap the demolition charges so that if they attempt to tamper with them…Boom!" He was grinning and I realised that he was enjoying this. "We will use just fifteen-minute fuses. I do not wish to risk an air attack this time. There will be just three or four charges on this and I will ensure that they are all set. One on the transmitter and one each on the two guns. We will have a spare in case there is a target we had not yet identified from the aerial photographs. Sergeant Jackson, you showed aptitude when the commandos trained us. You will help me to set the charges."

"Sir."

"We will head back by the most direct route we can. As Point 208 is close to the Frontier Wire we will not have to risk passing through it. We can simply head for the broken parts. There may be pursuit but we have two fast vehicles and their half-tracks, whilst sturdy, are not as fast." He paused, "Any questions?"

Conscript's Call

This time there were none. The only two with experience were Bert and me. I thought that the plan had more chance of success than the first one. The only fly in the ointment, in my view, was the lieutenant. He seemed to crave the danger and excitement. To him it appeared to be a game. Would he take unnecessary risks just to gain the glory or, perhaps, the promotion?

"Right, the QM should be outside with the equipment. Sergeant Jackson, your section will man the Morris and I will command the Chevrolet. Both teams will have the same explosives so that if something happens to one the other can still finish the job. You decide who mans the gun."

There was a table outside and the TNT, primers, Cordtex and fuses were in two piles. They looked identical. There were four drums for the Lewis guns in each pile and one had Bren magazines. There were .303 magazines and two Sten guns in each pile. I saw the Colt automatic and silencer. The lieutenant came up behind me, "I promised you this." He sounded pleased as though I was being rewarded.

"Sir, if I use this I will be trying to kill someone."

He nodded as though I had said the most obvious thing in the world, "Of course. It goes without saying but you will be doing so, silently."

"Sir, that is murder."

"No, Sharratt, it is war. Besides, you will only have to use it if we are about to be discovered. Remember Taff."

I did and that was the only reason I would take the gun. Had I had such a weapon at the airfield I could have shot the Italian, Taff would not have been wounded and if he had not been wounded he might have been in the Chevvy and not died. There were a lot of ifs and maybes but it eased my conscience slightly.

"There is plenty of ammunition. Go and practise. Apparently the gun's range is affected by the silencer; you had better find out how." He then turned to speak to Sergeant Jackson who would be in charge of our demolitions.

I saw Roland looking at his Sten gun. I smiled, "Come with me. We might as well practise together, eh?"

I saw the relief on his face, "Thank you."

Conscript's Call

I decided to try the new handgun first. It was, I had been told, fully automatic. I ensured it had a magazine and the safety was off. I aimed at a rock where there was no chance of a ricochet of stone hitting anyone and then squeezed off two shots. The action was easy and the recoil not as bad as I had expected. I had hit the rock but as it was only fifty yards from me I did not impress myself. I screwed the silencer into the end and took a twohanded stance. This time I took careful aim and squeezed off three shots. Two of them were direct hits and the third clipped the top. It was barely a whispered trio of pops I heard. I did not waste any more ammunition. I did not think that the range I would use would exceed twenty yards. It would be in the dark.

It took longer to make sure that Roland could use the Sten. "Hold it so that the stock is pressed into your shoulder. That rock I aimed at is about the best range for you to use. Now pull the trigger and fire of a couple of bullets."

He did as I asked but out of the ten bullets he sent only one hit. The rest sprayed up into the air. "Sorry."

"Don't worry. The rock is low down and you hit that with one. At least two of the other bullets might have hit a man but keep the stock pressed into your shoulder. Feel it. Now try again."

This time he fired six bullets and most of them went close to the target.

"Good. Now empty the magazine and then I will show you how to reload it."

By the time we returned to the others he was smiling. "I am not sure I could fire at a man, though, John."

"When the time comes, Roland, self-preservation will take over. Besides, if you have to open fire then we are in trouble. We need to sneak in and sneak out. Any gunfire will draw the bad guys to us straightaway and we will have to run."

When we went back inside the others were packing their bags. As the last time, we would leave the packs in the vehicles when we went to raid but the first raid had shown us the importance of taking more than we thought we needed. Sergeant Jackson was packing the explosives in his pack and Ray's. He said, "You and Wally can man the Lewis gun. One loader and one firing."

Conscript's Call

I said, to Wally, "Which job do you want?"

He grinned, "As much as I would love to use the machine gun you aren't named Hawkeye for nothing."

Bert came in wiping his hands, "That Morris is a nice little truck. I have asked the boss if I can take her out for a spin this afternoon. Anyone fancy a trip?"

We all shook our heads. Any spare time this afternoon would be spent in getting some shut eye. We had food and then prepared to get some rest while Bert and Paul Grant took out the two vehicles. I was to be denied that for the lieutenant summoned the sergeant and me, "I need to speak to you two." We joined him outside and we walked in a circle while he went through his thoughts, "We leave just the drivers with the vehicles. There is no wire and so we don't need cutters. We will leave the two vehicles a mile from the hill. I have spoken to the two drivers. They will try to coast the last two hundred yards as it is downhill."

Sergeant Jackson said, "We need to climb over rough ground I assume."

"Yes, Sergeant, it is the highest point around and it is steep. As the enemy approach it from the west there is neither road nor track from the east." He handed me a packet of aerial photographs, "You and I will be leading, Sharratt. Spend the afternoon studying these."

"Sir."

"The two of us will be at the fore. I, too, have a silenced weapon." He smiled, "The general was so pleased with our first effort that he acceded to every request. We will eliminate any sentries. Corporal Jenkins and Private Poulter will enter the barracks but they will follow you, Sharratt. The sergeant and I will be busy with our teams setting the charges. When the garrison has surrendered then take their boots and set them off. Follow them until they reach the bottom of the hill."

"How many men in the garrison, Sir?"

"We know that there will be twenty men to man the guns. There will be at least three, perhaps four radio operators and there could be up to half a dozen others."

"That seems a lot, Sir, shouldn't we have more men?"

Conscript's Call

"The more men we have the more chance there is of this all going wrong." He spread his hands, "If it does go pear shaped, Sergeant, then we use grenades as well as the charges and use the grenades to set off the TNT. We have plenty of grenades."

"That seems messy, Sir."

"It is but, as I said, Sergeant, that will only happen if we have a disaster and I hope we don't. These troops are gunners. They aren't the SS and they aren't paratroopers."

I glanced at the sergeant. The lieutenant seemed determined to be optimistic. "What if they have vehicles, Sir? It seems likely that they will."

"Good point. Slash the tyres and booby trap them." I nodded. That I could do. "Now we should be able to set the four charges in less than ten minutes. When we leave, you and Corporal Jenkins will be the rearguard."

I asked, "Four charges, Sir?"

"I have decided to make sure we do the job properly. One for each of the AA guns, one for the mast and one for the radio. We are hoping that the exploding ammunition will add collateral damage but so long as we put the hill out of operation, the RAF can then make sure that Jerry does not put more AA there."

They went back inside and I studied the photographs. I had not envisaged doing this back at Seaforth Barracks. I looked at the photograph and saw that there were two vehicles there. That did not mean they would be there when we attacked but at least I had their position in my head. I saw that while there was no actual path from the east there was a line of least resistance. We could zig zag our way up. I frowned for I could not see the sentries. That was, perhaps, not surprising. They would take cover when the reconnaissance aircraft flew over. I tried to imagine where they would be and after studying them I decided that they would be inside the gun emplacements. They would be slightly warmer and have sandbags to lean against. They would simply pop their heads up now and then or perhaps wander to take a leak. I had seen enough. I returned them to the lieutenant and then made a bed and tried to sleep.

I didn't manage to sleep but I had my eyes closed and I rested. I opened my eyes when I could smell the food being cooked. I went outside to make water and then went to my pack

162

Conscript's Call

to check it one last time. I had three clips for the Colt and a small box of the .45 ammo it used. I had my magazines for the rifle and four grenades. I might have wanted more but there was a limit to what I could carry. I had given my Beretta to Ray with the proviso that he returned it to me after the raid.

"Come and get it while it is hot." I had come to realise that the cooks, despite the sometimes unkind comments about their cooking, were proud of what they did. They wanted the food to be eaten while it was still edible. It was not their fault that they had to use tinned food all the time.

I took my mess tin and mug of tea and went to sit between Ray and Wally. Roland was still checking over his medical kit and I shouted, "Come on, Bones."

I used his nickname when others were around as he wanted the new nickname rather than Roly. There were still men who had come over on the ship with him who called him Roly. It would take time but the more I used Bones the better it would be. When we had eaten, the lieutenant, who had eaten with us, said, "Right lads, time to darken our faces and hands."

Only Bert and I were familiar with the process and others watched us as we turned our tanned skin into something almost black that would not reflect the light. I donned my comforter and then helped Ray, Wally and Roland to do the same.

By the time we went out it was pitch black. Sentries had been set and we went to the vehicles. As last time the lieutenant would lead. He was a good navigator. I had heard he was a bit of an amateur yachtsman and it must have helped.

Conscript's Call

Chapter 13

It was still light when we ate. We waited until darkness fell before we went out to our vehicles. The lieutenant waited until eleven o'clock before we left for he wanted to strike in the early hours. We would be close enough to our own lines, so he hoped, to make it back before dawn. This time the journey was less than fifteen miles and even at the steady speed we would use it would just take half an hour. We could see the vantage point from our new camp. It was slightly silhouetted against the sky. Had we tried to move in daylight then the spotters would have called in either aeroplanes or artillery. The route there was flat; there were no wadis in which to hide. The desert was scrubby and rocky but there was not much cover. Darkness would be our only friend. The lieutenant had to time our arrival to perfection. We had to ensure that the garrison was not on duty and just had sentries. It had to be well before dawn to allow us to escape without the aircraft dogging us. I could see why he had chosen that particular night. It would be moonless again.

I stood at the Lewis. I realised I should have test fired earlier but the lieutenant had distracted me with the aerial maps. I had fired a Lewis gun but not since Seaforth Barracks. If this had been a normal operation I would test fire the weapon but we were too close to the enemy. They would hear the Lewis and use their binoculars to spy us out. I hoped that we would not need the gun. Machine guns in the night would only alert the rest of the German and Italian strongpoints strung out on the escarpment. Ray had placed the grenade launcher in the well of the lorry. It was unlikely that we would need it but better to take it and not need it than need it and not have it. The Chevvy set off and I remained standing, holding on to the gun. I found it better than sitting as I could see the terrain ahead. I liked to know where I was going. Grant and Bert were not driving fast. Their relative slow speed kept the noise down and as we only had a few miles to go there was no rush. Driving fast at night over a rocky desert risked damage to the vehicles. It made for a more comfortable journey. The land rose towards the high ground that was Point

164

Conscript's Call

208. During Battleaxe there had been serious fighting around the hill and many Indian soldiers had died trying to take it. Their bodies had long since been removed but I couldn't help wondering about their spirits.

I glanced down into the lorry. All the faces were pensive. For them all this was new. Even the normally ebullient Ray and Wally had serious looks on their faces. Poor Roland looked as though he was going to throw up. I knew why. He would not be able to hide. His job was to follow me into a barracks full of Germans. If it turned into the gunfight at the OK Corral he would die and he knew it. I realised then that my father had prepared me to be a conscript. I had been brought up knowing how to shoot and how to take orders. Roland might have been able to shoot a shotgun and he would have obeyed his father's orders but they were not the same thing. My father had given me a preparation for life in the army. Even the times in the pub playing dominoes had been preparation. McGuire apart there had been no great surprises.

I heard the gears change as we began to ascend to the jumping off point. The engine laboured but the two drivers slowed to minimise the noise. Then the engines were cut as we coasted down the slight slope the lieutenant had identified from the aerial photographs. I saw the Chevvy silently stop. There was no squealing of brakes. I let go of the Lewis and grabbed my haversack. Despite the orders to the contrary I slipped it on and then drew the Colt with the silencer attached. We jumped from the back. There would be just two men left with the vehicles and this time there was no helpful wadi in which to hide. Even worse, the two drivers would have to perform a three-point turn to head back to base and that might be while we were under fire.

I smiled at Roland who nodded nervously. I hurried to join the lieutenant and Sergeant Jackson while Corporal Jenkins formed the men up. I led when the lieutenant waved his hand forward. Like me he had the silenced Colt in his hand. I zigzagged up the hill. The photographs had given me a rough idea what to expect from the ground. The mast stood out as did the sinister barrels of the two guns. They were pointing skyward. I did not rush. We passed the empty slit trenches. They were deep and would enable the defenders to rake any attacker

165

struggling up the steep slope. I placed each foot carefully to avoid sending stones skittering down the slope. Such a noise would alert a sentry. This was bunny hunting time again and I did not want to make a noise. The silence helped me for I heard the Germans behind the sandbags. It sounded from their voices as though there were three of them. It was lucky I had studied the aerial photographs for I had identified the danger of the slit trenches close to the sandbags and I skirted them. We had reached the top and I could now hear the three voices clearly. Not only that, but I could also smell the smoke from their cigarettes and even detected the aroma of ersatz coffee. Those smells told me that their hands would be occupied. I did not wait for the lieutenant but headed to the entrance of the emplacement. Roland had taught me a couple of German words and as I stepped into the entrance I hissed, "Hands Hoch!" I am not sure that I said them right but the Colt in my hand did the trick. The lieutenant appeared next to me and the three men raised their hands. They still held the mugs of coffee.

The lieutenant smiled and whispered, "Well done, Sharratt." He turned, "Poulter, tell them to take off their boots." As Roland gave his order the lieutenant waved to the next men, "Taylor, Jones, and Salter, tie their hands and watch them. Jennings and Swift you go with the corporal and his men. Sergeant, let us go to work."

Corporal Jenkins nodded to me. I could see that he was a little nervous. He had a Sten gun as did the other two but if they opened fire then all hell would be let loose. I went to the door and listened. Inside there was some noise but it was a whispered conversation. Men were awake. I saw, from the slight glow, that there was a light on inside the barracks building. I had seen from the aerial photographs that there was a rear entrance and I pictured where it was as I put my left hand on the doorknob. I turned it, pushed and silently stepped in. I made sure that I went far enough in to allow the others with their Sten guns to enter.

There was a dim light on the table. I saw a table and two men were seated there playing cards. The rest were in their beds. As I opened the door the two card players turned around and began to rise. I waggled the silenced Colt at them and waved with my left

Conscript's Call

hand. They resumed their seats. The corporal and the others were behind me and their Sten guns added to the menace.

Corporal Jenkins said, "Poulter." His command woke the rest of the Germans and they all stared at the blackened faces of the British soldiers. We must have been their worst nightmare. We looked like commandos and they inspired the same fear in the enemy as the SS did for us.

There was the slightest of pauses and then Roland, in a firm commanding voice, told the Germans to stand and put their hands in the air. I noticed that none of them had footwear on. It would make the next command easier. I began to think that this might work but I kept my eye on them all. I think it was a feldwebel, a German non-commissioned officer, who made a dart for the rear door. I had located it already and the Colt came up and a bullet fizzed into the door sending splinters of wood into the man's hand before he could reach it. He stopped and held his injured hand. Roland said something in German and the man came back.

"What did you say to him?"

"I said that you were a dead shot and the next bullet would be in his head."

Just then a door to the side opened and I swivelled my Colt around. The young German officer who emerged in his underwear from the room adjoining the sleeping quarters, stared in disbelief. I nodded to Roland who spoke to the officer. He raised his hands and joined his men. I saw that he was a very young officer. The feldwebel looked much older. I guessed which one was the real leader. It was the feldwebel we would need to watch.

Corporal Jenkins said, "Tell them to get their greatcoats and put them on." As Roland told them that the corporal added, "Jennings, open the door and cover them as they come out." He smiled, "I think they are all worried about Dead Eyed Dick here." I saw that every German eye was on my Colt. It must have looked like a cannon to them. The sound of the silenced bullet hitting the door had unnerved them. I glanced at Roland and saw his Sten was shaking. He was even more nervous now but as the Germans were looking at me it mattered not. When we stepped outside, the demolition crews were busy at the guns and radio

Conscript's Call

mast. The corporal nodded at Roland who told the Germans to begin marching. The three dressed Germans were standing outside with their hands on their heads and the three Sten guns in their backs prodded them into action. They began to march. We passed the four vehicles at the back of the barracks. The road wound down the slope and I saw, just behind the vehicles, what looked like an ammunition store and a petrol tank. The two were camouflaged with netting and that explained why they had not been visible in the aerial photographs. They were good targets and I decided that I would tell the lieutenant as soon as I was able. We would need to destroy them too. We walked all the way down the slope to the level ground close to the road and then Roland told the Germans, his voice firmer when he spoke, to go home and not to return. I heard him say '*versteckte Bombe*', which I knew meant booby trap. The feldwebel looked a little truculent as did the officer. The feldwebel clenched his fists and I feared that they might do something. They outnumbered us and I wanted them to move. I had to cow the two men. I pointed the barrel of the Colt at a rock next to the officer and fired. Splinters of stone struck his leg and he shouted a command and they all began to march.

We watched them disappear and when their heads reappeared on the rise to the west, Corporal Jenkins said, "Right lads, let's get back up the hill and then we can disable the vehicles."

I said, as we ascended, "Roland, run ahead and tell the lieutenant that there is a petrol tank and a cache of ammo near to the vehicles."

"Right."

He ran.

The corporal said, without rancour, "I should have given that order."

"Sorry, Corp, but I wasn't sure you had seen the fuel tank."

"I hadn't." He would make a good NCO for he was honest.

When we reached the vehicles we slashed the tyres quite happily. It was childish but gave us pleasure. There was a satisfying hiss as they deflated. I fixed a pair of hand grenades to the half-track's door and then closed it. The first thing they would do was open the door and when they did the grenades would go off. The tyres were slashed but the caterpillar tracks

Conscript's Call

could still move it. I climbed up and removed the MG 34 machine gun. The lieutenant arrived. I pointed to the tank. "Sir, a petrol tank and I think that is ammo for the 88."

"You have sharp eyes, Sharratt. Right, Private Swift, put that charge there and I will use this last one on the ammunition." He glanced at his watch. "A slight delay but worth it. You chaps get back to the sergeant and be ready to move as soon as we return."

As we neared Sergeant Jackson, working next to Roland and just finishing off the last demolition charge, I saw a figure emerge from the barracks. He was dressed in a uniform. He had a machine pistol in his hand and I watched in horror as he raised it. I dropped the MG 34 and raised the Colt almost without thinking. I fired four bullets at the German. I hit him but even as he fell, dying, his finger tightened on the trigger and a burst of bullets rent the air. Everything had been silent until that moment. It was as though we had pushed an alarm bell. We had alerted the Germans to our presence.

The sergeant turned in horror and I ran into the barracks. I cursed myself. I had not checked the officer's room. There had been another man within. I ran into the room from which the officer had emerged and saw that there were two beds in the room. It was empty now. I checked the far side of the bed. Had I checked earlier then we would have taken him too. Instead we had missed him and the whole raid could be jeopardised because of one mistake.

The lieutenant and Private Swift raced up. He looked at the dead man and Corporal Jenkins said, "We forgot to check all the rooms, Sir. Sorry." He was a good non-com. He didn't try to blame anyone.

"Spilt milk, Corporal. Back to the vehicles lickety-split. They could have heard those bullets in Benghazi."

I picked up the MG 34 and as we hurried down the slope, said to Sergeant Jackson, "How long on the fuses, Sarge?"

"The first ones will go up in ten minutes. About the same time we reach the vehicles. The rest…" I nodded. "Thanks, Hawkeye, Poulter and I would be dead men but for your quick reactions."

I said nothing. I had killed a man again but at least it had not been murder. As we reached half way down the steep slope I saw

Conscript's Call

that the two vehicles were facing in the right direction. At the bottom I heard the sound of the vehicles and their engines as they moved towards the slope. Good old Bert. He must have realised that when the gun was fired he could move the two vehicles. He and Grant had done their three-point turns. The tailgates were down and the two vehicles were facing in the right direction. It gave us a fighting chance. Just so long as there were no enemy units between us and the camp we had half an hour to get back to the safety of our lines. I hurled the MG 34 in the back and climbed aboard. I cocked the Lewis gun and turned the twin barrels to face west. To the north I could hear a siren. It was an alarm from another defensive position and it sounded close. It meant that they would send men and vehicles after us. Suddenly the sky lit up as the first of the explosives went off. The skyline was lit by bright flames and the air filled with smoke and noise. It must have been one of the gun emplacements that exploded for we heard a succession of smaller explosions as the shells inside the sandbags exploded. The rest of our men threw in their packs and jumped aboard. Wally banged the cab roof. "Go! Go! Go!"

The Chevvy moved off first as the two drivers headed up the slight slope down which we had coasted just a couple of hours ago. If we were caught this time there would be no Hurricane to come to our aid like an avenging angel. We would be on our own. Our hope was that we were close enough to our lines to reach them before the Germans or Italians reached us. I heard the other explosions as the charges took out the tower and radio. We had achieved what we needed to. The question was, would we escape as we had done the last time?

The lieutenant was directing Grant and the officer did not follow the same route we had on our way west. He headed slightly further north to aim for the road which would allow us to drive faster for the last twelve miles. It made sense but it would bring us closer to the men who would be coming from the position the siren had sounded. I saw a little flash on the skyline and knew that the Germans had not heeded Roland's warning and they had returned to the hill. I heard the sound of the booby traps exploding. They were a dull, almost muted crump. Suddenly I saw the sky light up and there was the loudest explosion we had heard up to now. The fuel tank and the

Conscript's Call

ammunition charges had exploded. The German soldiers who had returned to the post would all be dead. I was looking at the fire as it burned and it was Ray who spotted the German motorcycles coming from the north. He tapped me on the shoulder and pointed. We had seen them in Greece. The Germans had units made up of motorcycles with a side car. Armed with a light machine gun they were fast and manoeuvrable. More importantly they could go across the desert faster than we could and they would be able to bring all their machine guns to bear at once.

He shouted, for the benefit of those in the cab, "Germans, to the north."

We were on a converging course with them. I swung the Lewis gun's barrels around as the Bren gun on the Chevvy opened up. I counted eight motorcycles and, in the distance, I heard the sound of a half-track. It would be much slower than the motorcycles but if the machine guns in the side cars could slow us then we would be in the bag. My hope lay in Captain Whittle. More than anyone he would know what the gunfire meant. I prayed that he would bring men to our aid. The Bren missed but its bullets made the motorcycles swerve. I opened fire with the Lewis gun. I had two magazines and each one held ninety-seven .303 bullets. My elevated position was a better one than on the Chevvy and I fired two short bursts. The first missed as we went over a bump which sent the bullets into the night sky then as the leading motorcycle took avoiding action, I had the opportunity to rake its side. It crashed and burst into flames. I aimed at the next motorcycle. The German gunners were now firing back at us. I heard bullets striking the side of the Morris. The others were firing Sten guns. The range was too great but a lucky bullet could always strike something vital. When a second and a third motorcycle was hit, by whom I knew not, I grew hopeful especially when Bert shouted, "Road ahead!"

It was then that disaster struck. Some of the motorcycles had raced down the road to cut us off. Three of them opened fire at the Chevvy and it slewed around as its tyres were shredded. It slammed into a rock. Bert jammed on the brakes and we swerved to avoid hitting it. I saw the lieutenant stand. He was bleeding. He waved his Colt, "Go, get out of here!"

Conscript's Call

I fired a long burst at the three motorcycles heading down the road as Sergeant Jackson said, "We look after our own. Get aboard, Sir, but be a bit sharpish."

We were now more vulnerable than ever. Stopped, we made a good target and I could see, coming down the road, the German half-track. My Lewis gun accounted for two of the three motorcycles and the Stens hit another but having switched our targets the ones who were following us had caught up. Corporal Jenkins was cut in two as he tried to clamber aboard. There were just three survivors from the Chevvy crash, the lieutenant, Jones and Swift and all three were wounded. Ray went to help Roland lift them aboard.

I emptied the Lewis gun and then shouted, "Ray, the grenade launcher." I clicked on empty, "Empty!" Wally dropped his Sten and as I took off the two magazines he replaced them. The couple of Sten guns that were still firing were not enough to hold off the motorcycles and when I heard the heavy machine gun on the half-track begin to fire then I knew we were in trouble. We had reloaded in seconds but it was not fast enough. Bullets slammed into the little Morris. Luckily they were from the lighter machine guns. The half-track had still to range in.

Roland, who was tending to the wounded, shouted, "All aboard!"

Sergeant Jackson shouted, "Go! Go! Go!" His Sten gun chattered away.

Just then the grenade sent by Ray exploded and took out the last of the motorcycles. The half-track's machine gun sent tracer to the space we had just occupied. The grenade had helped. The half-track was partly blinded by the smoke and dust from the exploding grenade. Ray continued to reload and send grenades into the air. Even if he did not hit anything he was making a smoke screen and damaging the ground. Once we were on the road Bert put his foot down. The tyres had better traction on the road and the Morris was faster than the half-track. I found that I was having to cling on to the Lewis gun for dear life as the little Morris bounced along the dust covered road. The dust sprayed up behind us and helped to mask us. I had to fire in short bursts and even then half of the bullets were wasted as we bounced

Conscript's Call

along the road. The MG 34 on the half-track fired one last burst and then when it stopped we knew that the pursuit had ended.

Sergeant Jackson shouted, "Front line ahead. I can see sandbags!" That meant we were within a couple of miles of our camp and the firefight had to have alerted them. The Germans might be angry but they were not stupid. We guarded the front line with troops who were alert and well-armed with anti-tank guns and heavy machine guns. The half-track would stand no chance against the six pounder anti-tank guns that awaited them. Bert did not slow down until we reached the first of our defences. Men were in trenches and there were two cruiser tanks on the side of the road. There was a barrier crudely made of barrels mounted on wheels. A platoon had stood to and we saw a six pounder and manned Vickers machine guns awaiting us.

Sergeant Jackson leaned from the cab and shouted, "We have wounded on board."

The officer nodded, "Move the barrier." The barrier was rolled to the side and we were waved through. As we passed the officer he said to Sergeant Jackson. "We were told that you had two trucks."

"Aye, we did and more men."

I looked down at the three survivors. The lieutenant looked to have the least serious injuries and he was sitting up. Roland was still working on the other two. They were in for a lengthy spell in the hospital. The others had taken their chance for glory and it had all ended in the desert.

173

Chapter 14

It was only when the three wounded had been taken away that Ray revealed he had been hurt too. Although superficial, a piece of flying rock had scored his cheek. Roland tended to it as though Ray's life depended on it. If nothing else the value of our medical orderly had been clearly seen in his first action. Once again we did not see our officer for he was at the hospital but Captain Whittle and Major Hill, along with an officer from Intelligence, came along to debrief us. This time we had only lost a couple of men but as only half of us had avoided death or wounds that did not sound so good.

The captain from Intelligence, Captain Miller, was po faced. He just needed the facts and he had no interest in our state of mind. Captain Whittle and Major Hill were more concerned about us. I saw it in their faces. Sergeant Jackson did most of the talking but as he had been busy setting the charges he had not been in either the barracks or where we sabotaged the vehicles. The others looked at me as I had been the most involved and it was I who had the better picture. I tried to be calm when I spoke. This had been a better planned attack and there was no way we could have anticipated the unit of motorcycles and side cars.

When we had finished and given our opinion about the results Captain Miller stood and nodded to our two officers. "A good mission and if what these chaps say is true then it will help us strategically. We shall send a Spit up later on to photograph the damage. There are things coming up that hinge on the raid. Lieutenant Hargreaves did well. Headquarters and the general will be delighted."

I could see Captain Whittle becoming annoyed but he could say nothing. It had to be the major, as senior officer, who spoke and he did, "Captain Miller, all the men did well. These are just riflemen and yet they achieved more today than many commandos who are trained for such things."

The officer suddenly turned and saw us not as men who had given him the report but soldiers who had done their duty, "I apologise, Gentlemen, Major Hill is quite right and what you

Conscript's Call

have achieved in two raids is quite remarkable. You should know that your efforts have not gone unnoticed and I will bring your conduct to the attention of my superiors."

When the officer had gone Captain Whittle took out his pipe and tobacco pouch and said, "Intelligence Corps, now there is a contradiction in terms. They wouldn't know a Schmeisser from a broomstick."

Major Hill smiled and sighed, "Quite, but I think that instead of criticising the Intelligence Corps we should give praise where it is due." He tapped the reports, "From what you have all told me every single one of you can hold your heads up for you have shown exemplary courage under fire. The Queen's Rifles are lucky to have you. This was an operation carried out with courage and determination. Well done. Now cut along back to your tents. Rest for the remainder of the day. We shall send a suitable reward to you later on today." He tapped his nose, "A little more welcome than just a pat on the back, eh?"

Sergeant Jackson stood, "Thank you, Sir. Right lads, get your gear and back to the Morris."

We picked up our packs and headed back to the Morris. We would be driven back to our camp and as no one had asked for the Morris back we would keep it. Ray said, "I shan't complain about the grenade launcher again. It saved our bacon and that's no error."

I sat in the back next to Roland, "Well, how was it? You know, going on your first raid and having close contact with the enemy."

"So scary but, you know, once I started speaking German I lost my nerves. I was too busy thinking about the words I was going to use and if they would obey me. It helped having you there."

I laughed, "I had a gun with one magazine and there were more than twenty men in the room. If they had rushed me I could have done little about it. I might have hit one or two but…"

"But they didn't know that."

Ray nodded, "You did all right, Bones. I watched you with the lads. You were as good as a doctor."

Conscript's Call

When we reached our camp the whole platoon came out to greet us. Weather was grinning, "No one hurt then." A frown appeared on his face, "The lieutenant?"

"Flesh wounds. He'll be back." Sergeant Jackson lifted his pack down. "Any problems while we were away?"

"No, we had a make do and mend day. The lads were all like nettled hens, Sarge. They were glad when we saw the Morris. Is that it, then? No more derring-do?"

I said, "I only went to save these soft lumps from getting into trouble."

Ray and Wally put their arms around each other. Wally said, "Never knew you cared, Hawkeye."

I laughed. Sergeant Jackson said, "Shower time and get these Al Jolson faces put away."

We were still close enough to Point 208 to see the spiralling smoke from the burning vehicles. Rubber always sends clouds of black smoke. The sergeant major had been right, it did not do to volunteer although I was intrigued by the comments from the Intelligence Officer. It had been some time since Operation Battleaxe. My father had said that in the Great War as soon as one operation finished they were planning another. I knew that this was not as bad as either Greece or Crete for we had not had to leave the country, but we had still to achieve a victory. The Australians were still besieged in Tobruk and the word was that the German armour had lost far less in the last battle than we had. His words suggested that our raid had been part of some plans for another operation.

As I walked back from the shower I felt much better. I liked to be clean. I had washed my uniform in the shower and walked back to the tent with a towel wrapped around my waist. Some of those from other companies wolf whistled. I merely smiled. I could take it. I had learned that you need a sense of humour in the army. Back at our camp there was tea on the go. I think that Corporal Vane had felt a little guilty about not being on the raid and it was he and not Sergeant Jackson who was the mother hen. He had Sandy Brown, Dave and Norm fuss around us. I saw the other new man looking at Roland with new eyes. They had come together and the bigger man had thought that he would be the one we would all wish as a friend. Now it was Roland who was

Conscript's Call

attracting smiles and friendly banter. He had shown what he could do under fire. His calmness in the back of the Morris had saved the two wounded men. That the two were not from our platoon was immaterial. We knew that he could do something that no one else could. Firing a rifle was easy but knowing how to stop bleeding and save a life, well, that was almost like magic.

The reward from the major came just as we were eating. CSM Hutton brought two bottles of whisky. He rarely smiled but I had learned that the twinkle in his eye was always a good sign, "Now don't abuse Major Hill's generosity. Sergeant Jackson will want some of this so don't sup it all at once."

He cocked an eyebrow and we chorused, "No, Sergeant Major."

He nodded, "You did alright."

That was fulsome praise indeed. When he had gone I took one of the bottles, "Look lads, I don't drink much. I think we should give one of these to Sergeant Jackson."

Roland said, "I think that is a good idea."

The other three who had been on the raid nodded. Bert said, "Good idea."

I walked over to the tents used by the sergeants from the company. It was as close to a mess as we had in the desert. They were all seated outside the tent talking and smoking. I said, "Sergeant Jackson, the major sent over a couple of bottles of whisky. The lads thought you should have one."

I was aware, as Sergeant Jackson stood and walked over to me, of the scrutiny of the other sergeants. I had seen them, of course, in Greece, in Crete, on the boat and in the battles but Sergeant Jackson was our sergeant and we always looked to him.

Sergeant Wilson threw his cigarette butt into the fire in the oil drum and said, "Bill told us that you are something of a dead shot, Sharratt."

I knew that modesty was always the right attitude to adopt and I shrugged, "I can hit most things I aim at, Sergeant."

He nodded, "Aye, but you have the coolness to keep your head and react quickly. We were all saying as how we could all do with a Hawkeye in our platoons."

Sergeant Jackson took the bottle and said, "Are you lads sure about this?"

Conscript's Call

I nodded, "Bones and I don't drink much and besides, you brought us back."

He smiled, "You are a good lad. Tell them thanks." He became serious and held up the bottle, "This doesn't get you any favours, though."

"I know, Sarge, we never thought it would."

As I walked away I was aware of eyes boring into my back. I knew that I did not look particularly impressive. Sandy Brown and Geoff Vane were better examples of what a good soldier should look like. I was lean and lanky, some would say almost awkward but I felt like a soldier. I looked at the skies. The stars were out and I looked up at them, "I hope that you would be proud of me, Dad. I am what you made me."

By the time I reached the camp half the bottle had been consumed. The others had shared it with the rest of the section for we shared what we had. Roland handed me a mug. He had one too. He smiled, "They had a couple of toasts while you were gone, I saved mine for your return." He handed me my mug which had just a finger's width of whisky in it. He stood, "Hawkeye," he grinned, "our own Dead Eyed Dick!"

The others stood and toasted me. "Dead Eyed Dick!"

I sipped the whisky. It burned. I wondered if I would ever get used to it. "Thank you. Sergeant Jackson thanked us but he said it would not get us any favours."

Geoff Vane said, "Wouldn't expect it but I think we are lucky in our sergeant. He is a good bloke."

Sandy Brown said, "A sergeant, a good bloke?"

Harry said, "You will learn. He shouts at us but he makes sure we survive. Other sections and platoons have had wholesale losses. Not us. You and Bones are the only two replacements. I am happy with that. The more we work together the better chance we have of surviving this war."

His words made everyone silent. I broke it, "If we survive, will we win?"

Sandy scoffed, "Of course we will win! We are British."

Ray sighed, "You have a lot to learn. There is no bigger patriot than me but Hawkeye is right to ask the question. We might have beaten the Eyeties but Jerry has sent us packing every time. It came as a real shock in Greece to be chased out in

Conscript's Call

a couple of weeks and we had even less time in Crete. We are holding them here but when we left England we had driven the Italians all the way back to the Tunisian border. By the time we got here we had lost it all and why? Jerry. Don't underestimate them, Sandy."

Wally said, "They are brave men. We warned them about the booby traps and yet they still came back."

The new man snorted, "That's just plain stupid."

Ray said, "We would have done the same." He smiled, "Of course we would have checked for booby traps but we would not have simply run away. I like this regiment but I like this section and our platoon more."

Geoff stood and drained his whisky, "And while we had an easy time of it, these five lads had no sleep last night. Off to bed and no noise tonight."

Norm Thomas gave a Stan Laurel curtsy and said, "Yes, Mother dear." He had clearly had more than one whisky. He did a good Stan Laurel impression. His long lugubrious face helped.

The corporal smiled, "Be off with you!"

I went to sleep quickly. I think the whisky helped but I was exhausted. However, I woke with a start. I had a dream that the man I had shot rushed at me with a gun. I sat up in bed and stared around. I knew it was a dream but it had seemed so real. The others were all asleep. I got up and went outside. The sentries were a hundred yards from us. I went to find a quiet place and I made water. I calmed myself. It was just a dream. If I had not shot the man then two others would have died. As I rolled into my blanket I saw his face again. I had shot many men but none had been as close to me as he had been. I know I must have killed some of those on motorcycles but their faces had been hidden by helmets and goggles. They were anonymous. I had seen the eyes of the young soldier who had tried to take on almost a dozen raiders. He had been truly brave. I managed to get to sleep again but I was not as rested when I woke as I had hoped.

The armourer came mid-morning to collect the weapons. Surprisingly he did not ask for the Colt. It was only at that moment I realised it had been given to me by Lieutenant Hargreaves. It told me it had not come through official sources. I knew that because the armourer checked off the Sten guns against a list. The question was, would I need it again? I resolved to leave it, with the Beretta, in my pack. I was not a fortune teller and I did not know if and when I would need it again. When the corporal from transport arrived to take the Morris, Bert adopted an innocent look, "Sorry, Corp, but there is something up with it. I tried to move it this morning but it wouldn't start."

The corporal frowned, "I will get a tow truck to take it to the repair yard."

Bert smiled, "No need. I was a mechanic in civvy street. We have a day or so before we resume normal duties. I feel guilty that it doesn't work. Let me fix it."

I knew that he was lying but he did it so well that I was not surprised when the corporal, deciding that it meant less work for him, agreed, "Thanks, I will be back at the end of the week."

We gathered around him when the corporal had gone. Ray grinned, "You lying little...there's nowt wrong with it."

Bert said, "I know. I am hoping that they forget about it."

I asked, "But I thought Betty was the love of your life?"

"She is but I like little Morris too."

Weather said, "They won't let us keep it you know."

"Listen, Corporal, we will have to go into action again and they will provide a Bedford. Now a Bedford is all very well but this one has teeth. We have the twin Lewis and Hawkeye found an MG 34. If we can get ammunition then if the Luftwaffe attacks us again we will have more than Lee Enfields to fire at him." I could not fault his logic. "And besides, I can tinker with it. I think I can make it shift a little faster."

I used the day to clean all the weapons I had used and store them. Then I took apart the MG 34. While a similar gun to the Bren, it had a bigger drum magazine and could be belt fed. As we intended to use it on a vehicle, if we could get hold of ammunition, we could use it belt fed. As I put it back together I reflected that to get more ammunition we needed to win.

Captain Whittle came to our section a few days after we had returned. He spoke to us and to Sergeant Jackson, "I thought you should be the first to know, Lieutenant Hargreaves has been promoted to captain and he has now transferred to another unit."

Sergeant Jackson said, "Another regiment, Sir?"

Conscript's Call

The captain said, enigmatically, "Another unit that, shall we say, suits Captain Hargreaves' ambitions. It is one which is not so rigid nor regular army. Your new officer, Sergeant Jackson, will be here by the end of the week. His name is Lieutenant Fowler. Until then you are in charge. There will be some Bedford trucks arriving before then. Have the men practise getting out of them as fast as they can."

"Another offensive, Sir?"

He smiled, "Corporal Vane, you know that if there was it would be secret. Loose lips and all that. Just practise, eh?"

He turned and left. Sandy Brown sniffed, "Before we joined you lads we heard some chaps talking and they were saying as how the last offensive failed because the Germans knew what we planned."

Sergeant Jackson said, "That just proves the point then, doesn't it?"

The new man grinned, "We heard as how it was our radio transmissions that were intercepted. Isn't that right?" He looked at Roland for confirmation.

Roland nodded, "Someone said that we only avoided a disaster when the Indian Division realised it and started speaking on the radio in Hindustani."

Sandy said, triumphantly, "See."

Ray said, "It makes no odds anyway. Who would we tell? The rats and foxes are the only ones we see. I haven't seen a single local since we set up camp."

That something was going to happen became obvious when more men and tanks arrived at the railhead. We heard rumours that the New Zealanders were being moved into forward positions close to the Bardia enclave and the Halfaya Pass. More ammunition and replacements arrived for us and with them came Lieutenant Fowler. We saw him as he walked to the headquarters building. We had been collecting more ammunition and saw him and the replacements for those lost in the recent attacks as they came from the lorries that had brough them from the railhead. He looked older than Lieutenant Hargreaves and, well, a little plainer. Lieutenant Hargreaves had always appeared like the dashing hero from a film. Lieutenant Fowler looked almost anonymous. We had the Bren Carrier with us and the three of us

181

Conscript's Call

were nosey. We hung around hoping to get a closer look at the new platoon commander. That he was Lieutenant Fowler was clear. There had been no promotions and the only officer to have left the company was Lieutenant Hargreaves.

We leaned on the Bren Carrier. We had attached a trailer and on it were stacked boxes of .303 ammunition and Mills Bombs. I said, "You know, Corporal, I am disappointed that he never came to say goodbye."

"Who? Lieutenant Hargreaves?" I nodded. "He might not have had the chance. He might have gone directly from the sick bay to… well, wherever he went."

Bert said, "I reckon the Commandos."

I shook my head, "I don't think so. They raid but the lieutenant had different ideas. Look at our two raids. We used a small number of men and vehicles. The commandos tend to go in mob handed."

One of the sentries had been listening and he leaned in, "You might be right, chum. When I was on duty at the wire I saw some rough looking types, no uniform and wearing those Arab headdress things. They were in a truck that was loaded with more guns than I have seen anywhere. They headed into the desert. I think that is where Lieutenant Hargreaves has gone."

I remembered seeing a truck and driver like that when we brought Lieutenant Hargreaves back to Headquarters.

Geoff sighed, "It makes no odds, does it? Wherever he is it has nowt to do with us."

Just then Company Sergeant Major Hutton came out, "Ah, you are still here." He glared at the sentry who stiffened, "Gossiping with Gobby Gibson here. He has a mouth like the Mersey Tunnel. Anyway, you can give Lieutenant Fowler a lift back to your camp. Drive steady and the replacements can trot on behind."

Geoff nodded, "Righto, Sergeant Major."

The CSM went back inside and brought out the lieutenant and the replacements, "If you would like to put your gear in the Bren Carrier, Sir, the corporal will take you to the platoon." His voice changed when he addressed the replacements, "And, you shower, try to keep up with the vehicle."

Conscript's Call

The lieutenant put his bag in the Bren Carrier and then climbed next to Bert. The officer was tall and he struggled to get his legs in, "A little tight, eh?"

Geoff smiled, "Made for other ranks, Sir, and not officers. Still it is only a hop and skip." He climbed in the back.

With the ammo on the trailer and the lieutenant's bag in the back of the Bren I had to clamber aboard and squat on the ammo. I shouted, "You can let Betty have her head whenever you are ready, Bert."

"Righto."

I heard, before the engine started, the question, "Betty?"

The answer from either Geoff or Bert was lost as the little carrier roared into life and puffing smoke headed back to our tents. I saw the replacements as they followed. One or two tried to appear casual and walk but Betty had a fair turn of speed when needed and soon they were all doubling as they ran to keep up. I could not help but smile.

They were huffing and puffing by the time we stopped. They were new to the desert and with all their gear with them it was more exercise since they had left the barracks. The PE on the ship would hardly have stretched them.

Geoff had waved over to the sergeant as we had approached to attract his attention and he hurried over with the other corporals from the platoon. I jumped down and said, "These are the replacements, Sergeant Jackson." I said his name for the benefit of the officer and replacements. I lifted out the lieutenant's bags and Geoff climbed out.

He held out his hand, "Need a hand, Sir?"

The grateful officer smiled, "Thank you, Corporal...?"

"Vane, Sir."

When he was out of the vehicle he patted the carrier, "And thank you...Betty." I knew in that moment we would get on. He turned and as Sergeant Jackson saluted he returned the salute and said, "I am Lieutenant Fowler, Sergeant, here to take command of 2nd Platoon, B Company."

"I am Sergeant Jackson, Platoon Sergeant. Welcome. Private Sharratt, pick up the officer's bag and take it to his tent."

We had cleared Lieutenant Hargreaves' tent and, so we had been told, CSM Hutton had loaded it on to a Chevvy truck. The

Conscript's Call

driver of the truck had worn an Arab headdress. I learned they were called a keffiyeh and it seemed to confirm the view that he had gone to a slightly more irregular unit.

I picked up the bag which was much heavier than Lieutenant Hargreaves'. I wondered what it contained. I headed for the tent aware that the sergeant and the lieutenant were walking behind me. I heard their conversation.

"I hear, Sergeant, that some of the men in this platoon have seen a great deal of action. Captain Whittle talked of raids behind enemy lines."

"Yes, Sir. They have done well considering that a year ago they weren't even conscripts and now they have fought in Greece, Crete and North Africa."

"I am envious, Sergeant. I was still lecturing at university a year ago. I hope to learn much from you all."

I could not see the sergeant's face but I guessed that he was not happy. A University lecturer did not sound like a man of action. He said nothing. I halted at the tent and waited.

"Your quarters, Sir. Would you like Private Sharratt to help you unpack?"

"That is a good idea and then I should like to meet the Platoon."

"Of course, Sir. Sharratt, bring the officer along as soon as you have finished up here."

"Righto, Sarge." I put the bag on the cot and opened it. "If I pass the clothes to you then you can put them away, eh Sir?"

He looked around the tent seeking a wardrobe, "And where might I do that?"

I reached up and tugged at the rope that ran the length of the tent, "If you look down yon end, Sir, you will see hangers."

"Ah! Very practical."

I handed him the items of uniform and then his boots and shoes. When I lifted up his socks and underwear, I found books. Not just one or two paperbacks but thick, heavy, hardback tomes. I chuckled, "Something amusing you, Private?"

"Yes, Sir, I wondered why the bag was so heavy. You have a lot of books."

"I am afraid that I cannot be parted from my books."

"Are they story books, Sir? Like Zane Grey?"

Conscript's Call

"Good heavens no, these are academic books about history. They are mainly about the Romans and Carthaginians. That is my field of study."

I looked around the tent. We did not have many books in my home but those we had were well cared for. It did not seem right to put them on the ground. I had an idea, "Sir, I think I can get you a bookcase."

He gave me a quizzical smile, "Really? Out here in the desert? You are a most resourceful soldier."

I placed the books I had in my hand on the cot and hurried back to the Bren Carrier. The boxes with the ammunition had been unloaded and one box had been emptied already. I picked it up. Ray said, "What do you want that for?"

"The lieutenant has books. I am going to make him a book case." I grabbed the box and the lid. The lieutenant was still emptying his bag. He turned and watched me as I entered. I placed the box so that one side was open and it was on its end. I placed the bigger books on the bottom. I ensured that the two at the ends were larger than the others and then I took the lid. There was a strip of wood that ran around the edge. I took my bayonet and prised it off. Then I carefully slid it into place on top of the books. I placed the rest on top and then stood back.

"A little crude, Sir, but they are off the floor and you can use the top for your pipe. It will be a sort of bedside table, eh Sir?"

He laughed, "I can see that I am going to have to be creative out here in the desert, Private..."

"Sharratt, Sir, the lads call me Hawkeye."

"As in James Fenimore Cooper, eh?"

I shrugged, "I thought it was because I was a good shot, Sir, but you are an educated man. I stand corrected."

He smiled, "Hawkeye is the hero in the book *'The Last of the Mohicans.'*"

Weather shouted, "You done, Hawkeye? We have work to do!"

"If that is all, Sir?"

"Of course and thank you. You have made me feel more than welcome."

"Right then, Sir, if you would follow me."

Conscript's Call

I think that those not in our section thought I was sucking up to the officer but I was not. However, as he knew not only my name but nickname he tended to use my name and me more often than others in the platoon so it was understandable. We just seemed to get on. I had liked Lieutenant Hargreaves, at Seaforth, in Greece and in Crete, but after the last mission I had realised that if he had not joined the mysterious group of raiders then my life span would have been shorter. He was reckless. I had barely met Lieutenant Fowler but I had the impression that, if anything, he would be cautious rather than reckless.

Conscript's Call

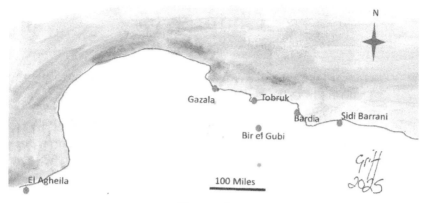

Cyrenaica

Chapter 15

Operation Crusader November 1941

That first time the new lieutenant came to meet all the company he went out of his way to speak to as many as he could. He was a quietly spoken man. I did not think that mattered for Sergeant Jackson could roar like a bull when he chose and we did not need two foghorns. When he came to our section he spent longer than he had with the others. He asked the others about their nicknames and seemed quite amused by their origins.

"You know the Romans did that. General Gnaeus Pompeius Strabo, the father of the Pompey who fought Caesar, was called Strabo which means cross eyed. His son was called Magnus which means great. You chaps are following an ancient tradition."

I said, "Sir, if he was a general, didn't he object to the name?"

The lieutenant shrugged, "Apparently not but who knows. Perhaps that is just what history records. I know that the Duke of Wellington was called Nosey by his troops. Whilst it was an affectionate nickname I doubt that any of his soldiers let him hear them use it."

Norm Thomas said, "You know a lot, Sir. Shouldn't you be back in Britain telling them how to fight the war?"

"Why, do you think they are making a bad job of it?"

There was silence, especially from those of us who had been in Greece and Crete. Eventually Geoff said, "The thing is, Sir, we have been in Greece and Crete as well as the desert. So far we haven't won a battle. When we don't lose we treat it as a victory but it isn't and the word is that we lost a lot more tanks than the Germans, last time. So you can see why we wonder who is running this war."

The new officer took out his pipe and began to fill it. I could imagine him back at his university wearing a tweed jacket with leather patches at the elbow and talking to other academics. He looked to be a thoughtful man. When he had it going he threw away the match and said, "Mr Churchill seems to know his business but he is fighting a war that is far more global than the

Conscript's Call

Great War. He has men fighting in East Africa too as well as here in the Middle East but from what Captain Whittle has told me you have had a couple of victories yourselves. You raided an airfield and destroyed guns and a radio mast. They are achievements to be proud of."

Sergeant Jackson was with the officer and he was keeping silent. That meant he was happy for us to talk. If we said anything inappropriate he would let us know in no uncertain terms. They all looked at Bert and me for we had been on both of them. Bert took a last drag on his cigarette and threw it to the ground, "What you should know, Sir, is that, in that first raid we lost half of our men and four of us almost didn't make it back. But for Hawkeye here we would now be in the bag. The second one was a little better but there are three lads whose bodies we left in the desert. You are right we did our bit but, like the corporal says, we want the Germans to be on the run for a change."

He nodded, "I see." He looked in his pipe and then said, "Well, thank you for your honesty. I appreciate your candour." He chuckled, "You know I feel like Henry the Fifth on the eve of Agincourt discovering what his men really think. I shall see you all again, I daresay."

He and Sergeant Jackson wandered off. Dave Proud said, "He is a strange one. Agincourt? Isn't that near Bolton."

Ray snorted, "That is Accrington, you dope."

Geoff said, "Agincourt was a battle fought against the French."

Dave Proud said, "I thought they were on our side."

We all laughed and I said, "It was a war fought hundreds of years ago, Dave, even I know that!"

We did not see much of the new lieutenant after his first day, for the next day Sergeant Jackson told us that the lieutenant and the other officers would be away for a day or so. There was something big in the offing. That he offered so much information was revealing. It had been the same in the days before Battleaxe. When we saw more Crusader, Valentine and Matilda tanks as well as lighter Stuart tanks being unloaded from the trains, it confirmed that there would be an offensive. We were getting to the time of year that in England we would call autumn. In

Conscript's Call

peacetime we would have been clearing hedgerows and making bonfires. Leaves would be collected and preparations made for winter. Here the sun still shone and there was, unlike England, little variation in the length of days but it would be Christmas in a few short weeks and then a new year. I worked out it was just about a year since my life had changed. That meant a year since a bomb had taken my family and I had begun a new life as a conscript. I would not commemorate the actual date for I could not celebrate their deaths but I would remember them with a prayer.

We were issued new uniforms. These had a shoulder flash that was a red animal. We were told, by Sergeant Jackson, that it was a Jerboa, a desert rat. It was distinctive and we quite liked it. Our Bedford lorries arrived. There were strange looks cast at Morris but no one tried to take the vehicle from us. Perhaps the corporal from transport had been transferred or simply forgotten about the Morris. Bert had been working with Dave Proud who had shown skills as a driver. He would drive the Morris. We would use the MG 34 on the top of the cab so that the Morris was the best armed vehicle in the whole company. There was limited ammunition for the German gun but the fitting of the extra gun created a mood of optimism amongst the section. It was strange but the quietly spoken new officer, who had been with us for a short time, seemed to inspire confidence. I was not the only one who was reminded of a good teacher from our school days. Perhaps it was the voice or the pipe. I know that he reminded me of my teacher from school. Bill Campbell had been a Scotsman but he had been quietly spoken too. However, if you crossed him you knew you were in trouble. I used to love last lesson on a Friday when he would sit, smoking his pipe and reading passages to us from '*The White Company*' by Sir Arthur Conan Doyle. Some of the other lads would have a nap while he was reading but I was mesmerised. Lieutenant Fowler reminded me of him.

We had to make adjustments to the Morris which was smaller than the Bedford. Bert was handy and he managed to make fixings for under the bench to hold our packs there safely. During the two flights from the enemy the bags had flown around on the floor and had been a hazard. We also rolled up the canvas so that

Conscript's Call

we could see from the sides. The need for the grenade launcher had manifested itself on the last raid and that was also secured behind the cab. The MG 34 was fixed on the cab of the lorry and the twin Lewis guns were at the rear. It meant the only place with cover from the sun was the middle. As there were three of us on the guns and with Geoff in the cab with Dave that only left Bones and Sandy to need shelter. We were happy.

When the officers returned from the conference the lieutenant gathered us together. He chose the Morris and Bren Carrier as his lecture theatre. He sat on the back of the Morris and we were like school children squatting to hear his story. When Lieutenant Hargreaves had briefed us his voice had been filled with excitement. Lieutenant Fowler did not use notes but he spoke in a calm and measured manner. There was no hand drawn map, instead he had an official one.

"Now I know that I am new to the desert. The men who came with me are also new but I know that we are joining a battalion that has shown the Germans and Italians that they know how to fight." He paused and I saw that men were nodding. I was on his side already but his words were making the other older hands like him. If you like a leader then you fought for him. Sergeant Jackson was just such a leader. "I also know that some of you think we should be winning. Well, I am here to tell you that Operation Crusader has the potential to deliver such a victory." He paused again. I liked his style for it allowed those who, like Dave Proud, were slower on the uptake, to process the information. "I say potential because in war there are many events that can conspire to turn victory into defeat. The Emperor Napoleon thought he had the British and Dutch defeated at Waterloo and we all know how that ended." I looked around at some of the faces and saw that clearly they did not. "Now, this operation is a big one and while I know most of the elements I intend to tell you just about our part." He tapped the stem of his pipe at the coast, "This is Tobruk and the New Zealanders are going to try to break though and relieve their antipodean comrades."

I heard a grunt of confusion and Sergeant Jackson growled, "The antipodes, Garthwaite, are Australia and New Zealand. Did you learn nothing at school?"

"I was always sat at the back, Sarge."

Everyone laughed.

The lieutenant smiled, "Well, at least you have heard me. The Indian Brigade will support the New Zealanders. The Guards and the South African Brigades will sweep through the desert. We have a new unit, the Long Range Desert Group, and these chaps know the desert. They will scout ahead of the columns heading across the desert." He paused again, "So that is what the rest of the army will be doing but what will the 7th Support Group of the 7th Armoured Division be doing?" He paused again and every eye was on him and every ear listening. He was a good speaker. "Our job is to drive here between the Guards and the Indians. Our target is Bir-El Gubi."

I said nothing but I recognised the escarpment we had failed to take in the last campaign. I also saw that we would be close to both the radio mast we had destroyed and then the airfield we had raided. It would, at least, be more familiar to some of us.

"Now, we are there to support the tanks. We are designated as motorised infantry and we will do as you did in Battleaxe. We leave our vehicles and attack the enemy infantry. We will be taking out their anti-tank weapons. To that end I have decided that my command vehicle will be the one that this platoon has somehow acquired, Morris, I believe you call him."

Every eye shifted to us and Bert grinned, "Aye, Sir, Morris." He tapped his new shoulder flash, "And in light of this, Sir, I thought Morris the Mouse might be appropriate."

The officer laughed, "Jolly good. I hope that I will not inconvenience you, Corporal."

Geoff would have been the one in charge of the lorry had the officer not decided to use it. Geoff shook his head, "Honoured, Sir, honoured."

"Good. The main attack will begin on the night of the 18th of November. We will head north west and then west. I think this is a good plan for the Germans will think that three divisions are heading for Tobruk when, in fact there will only be two. The powers that be think that we might steal a march on them. Don't get me wrong, there will be strong points, especially on the escarpment, but as men from this platoon have already fought there we have their experience and expertise to help us." He was

Conscript's Call

looking at Bert and me. I knew then why he had chosen to travel with us. "We need to practise as much as we can. I hope to learn all that I can from those who are more experienced in desert warfare."

In the week leading up to the start of the operation we worked non-stop. Sergeant Jackson wanted to ensure that the replacements, not to mention the officer, were as well prepared as they could be. I had decided that while I would take my tin helmet I was quite happy wearing the helmet comforter on the journey to the front. When shells began to fall I would don the tin lid but I found that the rim obscured my vision a little. It was a risk but, in my view, outweighed by the advantages it would bring. We made sure that we had plenty of ammo and grenades in Morris the Mouse as well as water. The four jerricans of fuel attached to the rear were a little worrying for if we were strafed then it would be like having an incendiary device fastened to our rear. Bert was adamant that we would need them. He could not carry them in the Bren Carrier as he was the one carrying the radio. Lieutenant Fowler would need access to that. The Bren Carrier would drive next to Morris the Mouse. Bert made a joke, "Morris and Betty, such a lovely couple, eh?"

On the morning of the 17th Captain Whittle and Major Hill toured the camp. They made a point of speaking to Bert and to me, as well as the others who had raided the radio mast, "Thought you lads should know that your attack on the observation point was a great success. The RAF have been able to harass their attempts to repair it. The enemy has placed men there again but no AA and the lack of a radio means that when we begin our attack they will be less likely to be able to report our presence." Major Hill added, "Thought you should know that the men who died did not die in vain."

Although it was good to know, the fact remained that those men were dead. They would never see a Britain free from war. They would never have families to watch grow. Their lives had been cut short. The idea of a family had been growing of late. Perhaps it was the anniversary of the bombing of my home or may have been the looks of joy on the faces of men when they had letters from home, I honestly do not know. The idea just appeared in my head and once there it grew. It seemed

Conscript's Call

ridiculous. I was in the desert with more likelihood of death than meeting a young woman and I knew, from Sergeant Jackson, that until we had cleared the desert of the Axis forces then there would be no home leave. It made me all the more determined to stay alive so that if and when this horrible war ended I had something to look forward to.

I blacked up that night. Some of the others were surprised. Sandy Brown scoffed, "We aren't raiding, Hawkeye. The whole army is moving forward."

I shrugged, "And we are going at night. If putting a little burnt cork on my face means that I am less of a target then I am well happy."

Some of the others decided that they would do the same. Bones, Ray and Wally all emulated me. I had my Colt in my pack. I could not think of a reason that would mean I might need a silencer and a Colt but as we had a lorry I decided to take them. I fastened the Beretta around my waist. If we had to take a building then that was a better weapon than the rifle. I had not used my rifle for a while but I still kept it in perfect condition and I knew that this time I would need it. The MG 34 was part of the lorry's defences. We took our emergency rations and brewed up a pot of tea. Someone had procured a Thermos. I had no idea where from but we filled it with hot tea. It meant we could have a hot drink on the journey.

We had rested during the afternoon and so we ate later than we normally did. The general had ensured that we all had plenty of food. Until this operation was over we would be on short rations and have to eat cold food. We were marshalled to the vehicles by the NCOs. Lieutenant Fowler hung from the door. I saw that he had a Sten gun in the cab. Perhaps he had listened closely to our stories of the raids and saw the advantage of a quick firing, short range weapon. I was the first to board and after stowing my pack stood next to the captured German machine gun. Geoff followed me and he arranged the others. Ray and Wally would man the Lewis gun and the others just sat on the benches. Bones had checked his medical kit so many times that I was sure he could find anything blindfolded.

We headed out to the area we would begin the attack. We were supporting the 11th Hussars in their new tanks, the Stuarts.

These vehicles were not the sort of tank that was able to take on other tanks. They were light and fast. We were to support them when we assaulted the strong points on the ridge close to Sidi Omar. We followed the light tanks and I wondered at the wisdom of such a noisy attack. You could have heard the sound of our tanks and lorries far behind the enemy lines. I mentioned my fears to Geoff as we bounced along the desert.

He was a thoughtful man and while he had not enjoyed a great education, he liked reading and had a mind that could organise thoughts and plans, "A nighttime attack means no enemy aeroplanes and they won't be able to see us. It is one thing to hear an enemy but sound can be misleading. The good news is that we have armour in front of us."

We stopped half a mile from the escarpment. Perhaps Geoff was right for no one opened fire. If they enjoyed 88 mm anti-tank guns then we would have known about it. We jumped down and stood with Geoff while the rest of the platoon joined us. I knew that the lieutenant was nervous. He licked his lips and had a funny half smile on his face. He nodded to Sergeant Jackson as though afraid his voice might fail him.

The sergeant's voice was reassuringly familiar, "Right lads, spread out. Five-yard intervals and try to keep up with the Stuarts. They are fast but I reckon their drivers will want infantry support. Corporals, make sure you have a good man on the grenade launcher. They might be worth their weight in gold."

Sandy Brown had the grenade launcher. It was not necessarily because he knew how to use it well but he was a big man and could carry the launcher and his rifle. We had still to be issued a new Boys Rifle. The one we had begun the war with had been lost on the *Orion*.

"Right, Sarge."

"Bren Carriers, keep as close to the Stuarts as you can."

An officer waved from the leading Stuart and Lieutenant Fowler waved us forward. He walked next to the Bren Carrier. Harry had the Bren traversing already as he sought an enemy. Over the last nights we had discussed what might happen in this attack. One thing that had worried us was the thought of enemy soldiers hiding in slit trenches below the strong points. We had seen them in our last attacks and at the radio mast. Such trenches

Conscript's Call

could allow men to use grenades as we advanced. The noise of the Stuarts, their crews called them Honeys, as they drove up the escarpment, seemed deafening. Engineers had been out the previous night clearing mines but that did not mean that there were none left. They might have laid a few. The first we would know would be as it was in Operation Battleaxe when a tank suddenly exploded.

The enemy machine guns and the cracks of the German anti-tank guns were the first sign that the enemy defences had been alerted. I heard the 37 mm Stuart guns crack and their machine guns rattled. Lieutenant Fowler shouted, "Keep up with the tanks." He ran forward.

The Stuarts had one machine gun in a ball turret, a second in the hull and a third, normally for anti-aircraft, by the hatch. The commander normally fired the AA machine gun and I saw one raking the enemy positions with it. He was brave and paid for it with his life as a machine gun scythed through his body. Suddenly two Stuarts erupted in flames as they were hit by anti-tank shells.

Major Hill roared, "Queen's Rifles, forward."

This was not like Greece or Crete. Here we had the steel bodies of American made tanks that we could use for shelter. Our job was to eliminate the infantry and we followed Geoff as he led us forward. We were in a platoon but we would fight as a section. Harry and the Bren would not be needed yet, he needed to find shelter first. This would be a job for the grenade launcher and rifles.

We crouched close to a Stuart whose machine guns were sending a wall of bullets at the hidden defenders. We could see the flashes from their guns and knew where the machine guns were to be found. Geoff said, "Right, Brown, lob a grenade to hit the top of the escarpment. Hawkeye, find a gunner."

"Right." I used the tank to support my left arm as I sought a target. Brown's grenade could hurt the machine gunners but I sought the Pak gunners. The flash from the barrel of the Pak 38 as it sent a shell at a Stuart tank showed me where one was. There was a shield protecting the gunners but I had a slight angle that allowed me to see a helmet. I heard the first crump as Sandy Brown sent a grenade to explode behind the lines.

Conscript's Call

"Long, Brown, but a good effort."

"Right, Sarge." He would adjust his aim for the next grenade he sent.

I aimed at the helmet and waited. I heard another grenade as it was launched but I did not take my eyes from the helmet. This time, when the gun fired I saw the helmet rise and the German's face appeared. I fired in that instant. The head disappeared and I chambered another bullet. Another of the gun's crew made the cardinal error of peering over the shield to see where the bullet had come from. He was hit full in the face by my next bullet. When we had been briefed about the weapons we would face we had been told that the Pak 38 needed five crew. Forty percent had been hit by me and the gun did not fire for some minutes. That delay allowed two Stuarts to get closer and their shells did what my Lee Enfield could not do, they blasted the Pak and its crew. Brown had dropped four grenades and as the tanks moved forward Lieutenant Fowler shouted, "Up and at 'em." He fired a short burst from his Sten gun. I suspect the bullets were wasted but it encouraged us. We cheered as we charged.

The tanks sprayed the ground ahead before they moved off. A battle is a strange thing. You could only gauge what was happening in your eye line. We were near to the top of the escarpment and, it seemed to me, that we had taken it. Some of the others had fitted bayonets and they screamed like banshees as they ran at the defenders. The enemy had been hurt already and our screams, not to mention the tanks' weapons, made many lift their hands in surrender.

Captain Whittle shouted, "Disarm them and make sure they can't be a nuisance." He paused at a Bren Carrier and said, "Have the lorries move up."

With a Sten gun, the machine guns of the light tanks not to mention the rifles that were pointed at them made sure that the ones who had surrendered were cowed. I saw that these were a mixture of German and Italian soldiers. While Harry covered them with the Bren gun the rest of us went to collect their weapons. I saw that the Pak's crew were all dead. The 37 mm shells had finished what I had started.

"Sharratt, check out the bunker at the back."

"Right, Sarge."

Conscript's Call

The sandbagged bunker looked empty but, after the incident at the radio mast, I was not taking any chances. I moved around the side and kept my rifle levelled. The officer who jumped up and pointed a pistol at me was less than ten feet from me. I just reacted and fired. He fired too but my reactions were quicker and my bullet tore a hole in him. I cursed myself. The rifle was the wrong weapon, especially when I had a pistol in my belt.

Roland and Geoff came racing towards me with levelled weapons. "I got him before he got me."

Geoff nodded, "You give him a hand, Bones."

After first checking that he was alone I slung my rifle and drew my Beretta. It looked like a grenade had killed the men manning the machine. The officer I had shot had a Beretta too and I put the pistol in his holster and handed it to Bones. "Keep hold of this. It is yours if you want it."

He shook his head, "The rifle is enough for me."

I took the dead man's ammunition and put it in my pouches. I saw that there was an MG 34 with a box of ammunition. I picked up the box of ammo. "Take this and when the Morris arrives put it in the back." He left me. I saw that the machine gun itself was useless. Sandy's grenade had wrecked it. The shrapnel had devastated the machine gun nest. It looked to have exploded in the air and that was always lethal. I could have searched the dead bodies but they were too messy. I had enough with the pistol and the ammo. As I headed back to the others I could hear gunfire to the north and south of us. We must have been lucky. We had taken the strongpoint.

I heard the Bedford lorries as they ground up the slope. Sergeant Jackson was speaking to Geoff Vane, "We are sending the prisoners back in the lorries. We are going to make camp here for the night. It will be a four-hour watch for each section. Your section has the first watch."

Lieutenant Fowler came over, "You chaps did really well. The Hussars were delighted with the close protection. They wanted to thank whoever hit the Pak gunners."

Geoff pointed to me, "Hawkeye, Sir. Two bullets, two dead Jerries. He never misses."

"Remarkable. Perhaps we ought to get you a sniper rifle."

I shook my head, "My Emily will do for me, Sir."

Conscript's Call

The Bren Carrier and Morris the Mouse came up the hill. We secured the ammunition and then, as we were on first watch, we foraged for food and ammunition. Those who smoked sought cigarettes but were disappointed with what they found amongst the dead Germans and Italians. Bert shook his head, "These stink. I'd rather smoke Woodbines than this."

We did, however, eat some of the German and Italian food. The salami was popular but the sauerkraut was not. I liked both. Mum had often pickled our surplus vegetables. I know that other families had made piccalilli but we were quite happy with simple pickled cauliflower, onions and carrot. The pickled cabbage was little different. After we had eaten we relieved the five who had watched while we ate. Poor Roland was nervous. Geoff placed him between us and we both made a point of talking to him at the end of each patrol. Geoff had the watch and it was he who sent me to wake Corporal Higgins and his section. By the end of the watch the gunfire had dwindled. There were still men fighting but the escarpment was quiet. Lieutenant Fowler and Sergeant Jackson were by the oil drum in which we had lit a fire. They nodded as we passed, "All quiet, Corporal Vane?"

"It is now. What is the score, Sir?"

"Score?"

"Yes, Sir, it is like half time. What is the score? Are we winning?"

He smiled, "Oh, you mean like a football match?" We all nodded. "We lost just two men from the company and a couple were wounded. I heard that some tanks were lost. We lost three altogether so I suppose you could say a goalless draw. Tomorrow will be more difficult. The weather chaps say it will be clear skies and that means the Luftwaffe."

We nodded again and Sergeant Jackson said, "Aye, Sir, but the RAF are here. That was what was missing in Greece, Crete and in the Med."

I said, "And you, Sir, how did you find your first action?"

He scrutinised my face, "A thoughtful question, Private Sharratt. I did not as I was told I might by some chaps, *'piss my pants'.*" We all smiled for the vulgarity sounded out of place coming from a university lecturer but it also made me realise that a fellow officer must have made the comment. That told me a great deal. "I found that I had no time to be afraid. I was just concerned that I would give the right orders and, you know, I was quite worried about you chaps. I mean, I had a Sten gun. You just had rifles."

Sergeant Jackson said, "Never underestimate a Tommy with a Lee Enfield, Sir. You give us a good position and we can hold off anybody. Ask the SS at Klidi Pass. They thought they would simply bowl us over. They found different."

The lieutenant smiled, "I can see I have much to learn."

The sergeant said, "You lads get to bed. It will be a big day tomorrow."

"Right, Sarge."

We got our stuff from the Morris. I was happy to sleep underneath but some, Roland and Sandy Brown, were worried about creepy crawlies and snakes. They slept in the Morris. I had long ago lost my fear of such creatures. We all made so much noise that they moved away before we ever got around to sleeping.

Chapter 16

The sergeant was right. Morning came around too quickly. We were roused before dawn and stood to. While half of the section cooked, the rest of us watched dawn break in case the Luftwaffe chose to make an early morning appearance. They did not and when our lorries arrived, not long after the sun had risen, we were ready to move. We had taken our strongpoint relatively quickly but others had not. They would have enjoyed even less sleep than us.

As the sun rose higher in the eastern sky I scanned the horizon. Standing atop Morris the Mouse gave me a good view. I could see columns of smoke well to the north and some thinner smoke to the south but ahead was devoid of any signs of combat. The Germans now knew we were coming. We had taken them unawares the previous day but now they would muster their armour, and as we had discovered, their tanks had a greater range than ours. What I had realised was that while the German tanks could not destroy our tanks at extreme range, they could demolish an unarmoured lorry with ease. I remembered Battleaxe and how the Germans had lured our tanks into a trap. We had seen the trap and it was to be hoped that those with red along their collars had too.

We heard the Honeys start up and we were ordered into our lorries. I had not needed the MG 34 the previous night but I would now. However, I had more than enough ammunition and I did not need to be sparing. As I looked towards the coast I saw that there were armoured units moving along the coast road. We had no such luxury. There was a road ahead but it ran north east to south west. Our target lay fifty miles to the east. Although our armour support was provided by the lighter Stuart tanks I knew that the bulk of our armour were the new Crusader tanks and the older cruisers. The one thing they all lacked were powerful guns that could knock out a German tank. The Royal Horse Artillery were with us to give mobile artillery support.

Lieutenant Fowler had decided that he wished to see more and so he swapped places with Geoff Vane. I saw that he had

Conscript's Call

acquired a keffiyeh and he looked less like an academic and more like a rogue. He smiled when he saw my scrutiny, "When in Rome, eh, Sharratt? The locals have the best idea and besides, I don't need a cap. This is more comfortable."

He scanned the tanks ahead with his binoculars as they moved across the desert. It was hard to see much even with glasses. The tracks threw up dust and as we had quickly learned the heat haze made things shimmer. I could understand how tanks could miss their targets when they fired.

"You know, Sharratt, in ancient times armies fought here. You can see why the Egyptians used chariots. That is what we are fighting with, modern chariots."

Just then, from the leading tanks, we heard the crack of the guns and saw in the distance the muzzle flashes of enemy tanks as they opened fire. Norm Thomas, in the Bren Carrier, was manning the radio and he shouted, "Orders from HQ, Sir, we are to close up with the tanks and give them close support."

"Righto. Dixon, put your foot down." As we moved ahead of the line of lorries he put his arm forward.

Other platoons in the company had received the same order and the whole line leapt forward. I was seeking, not tanks or infantry but instead I had my eyes on the sky. I saw the German aeroplanes in the distance. They were like little dots but they would close with us rapidly. I pointed and shouted, "Aeroplanes!"

I heard the twin Lewis guns as they swung around on the Motley mount. The lieutenant lifted his glasses and said, "It looks like Stukas and fighters, probably the Messerschmitt 109." He lowered his glasses and said to no one in particular, "They will be going after the tanks."

I cocked the MG 34 and shook my head, "No, Sir, we are a softer target. Those fighters will strafe us. All we can hope is that the RAF are on their toes."

In the time it had taken to have a brief conversation the aeroplanes had closed up and my predictions came true. The Stukas screamed down to strike at the tanks but the fighters roared in towards us.

Roland, in the rear, shouted, "Hurricanes!"

Conscript's Call

It would be a race. Would the Hurries reach us before the German fighters could send their shells to rip through unarmoured lorries? I saw the Stuart tanks using their anti-aircraft machine guns to send a hail of bullets towards the Stukas. The only defence we had were the Bren guns and our Morris with not only its two machine guns but the open sides that allowed the Lee Enfields to fire.

I did not wait for an order. I aimed the German machine gun slightly above the leading aeroplane as it screamed in and then squeezed the trigger. There were tracer rounds in the drum I had loaded and I saw the flight of my bullets. I did not hit the leading aeroplane but my bullets went close enough to make him jerk up his nose and his bullets missed us. I heard the Lewis behind me and they had better luck as they tracked the belly of the fighter above us.

There was a cheer and Sandy shouted, "Well done, lads, you hit the bugger." There was no explosion and the Lewis must have just damaged it.

I neither cheered nor looked, for the next aircraft were coming. I used the same technique but this time used a longer burst and lowered the barrel slightly. This was a brave German and he held his nerve. I saw the muzzle flashes from his guns but Bert had swerved a little to the left and the bullets missed. The swerving made my arms jerk and a last short burst hit the German's tail. I steadied myself and heard the Hurricanes as they tore into the fighters. It was then I saw the smoking lorry. It was not our company but it was one of ours, the men of the Queen's Rifles. One of the fighters had scored a hit. The column of smoke was rising high and I knew that there would be no survivors. Even if there were they would have such burns as to render them ineffective. Eight Crusaders were also burning. I saw some Italian tanks burning too but not German ones. The Italian tankers fought bravely enough, the Hussars had told us at our camp, but they had inferior machines. Their armour was too thin even for the Stuarts' 37 mm.

As soon as we reached the first of the burning tanks we saw Captain Whittle jump from his Chevvy truck and wave us forward. I grabbed my rifle and pack and leapt down. Before I

Conscript's Call

put my pack on my back I took out two Mills Bombs and put them in my battle dress.

The lieutenant waved us forward. We went in a long line. Roland was close to me. He had the heaviest pack for he carried the medical supplies. Ray and Wally were to his right. They had taken to the young soldier and I knew they would protect him too. It was hard to hear commands and Lieutenant Fowler used his hands to signal us. It was Sergeant Jackson's voice we heard. "Keep moving and zig zag."

There was so much smoke from burning tanks and lorries that it was hard to see. That lack of vision was compounded by the dust thrown up by the tracks from the vehicles. The Italian soldiers who loomed up before us were as surprised as we were. Lieutenant Fowler might have had the appearance of an academic but he had the reactions of a cat. Even as I brought up my rifle he was spraying them with his Sten gun. His inexperience with the weapon meant he emptied the magazine but it bought the rest of us time to bring our weapons to bear. Harry cocked his Bren in the carrier and even as I chambered and fired my rifle his Bren was chattering. The eight Italians had no opportunity to surrender for between us we accounted for them all. Norm and Dave checked them and we moved on.

We barely made another fifty yards when we were stopped. There was a burning Crusader ahead of us with a charred body hanging from the turret. Ahead were sandbags. It was a defensive position. The Hurricanes had chased the fighters and dive bombers back to Libya otherwise the position could have been strafed. The machine guns from behind the sandbags kept us down but it was the anti-tank guns that were causing the problem. I saw a Stuart tank brewed up as it drove closer to the sandbags to fire with its machine guns and 37 mm.

"Take cover." It was Sergeant Jackson who issued the command. I threw myself to the ground. The fire in the Crusader was almost out but the Stuart that had been hit was still burning. I used the smoke to wriggle my way forward. I heard Geoff shout, "Brown, start lobbing grenades in the air. Harry, see what you can do."

Harry had a slight advantage in that he was in the Bren Carrier and there was metal to protect him.

Conscript's Call

Their answers were lost in the noise of battle and the sound of explosions and bullets. I felt oddly detached. I was the one who could shoot with the most accuracy and I snaked my way as close as I could get to the enemy. One of the Stukas must have been hit and crashed. I saw part of its tailplane before me. It must have come loose and fallen from the rest of the fuselage. I did not know where the rest of the aircraft lay but the tailplane was a gift from heaven, quite literally. I made my way to it and used it for cover. I was two hundred yards from the enemy positions. Even as I sought a target the first of Sandy's grenades exploded. Daylight was easier when using the launcher. You could track the flight of the grenade and then adjust your aim. I knew that he would be behind the Crusader where he was safe from enemy machine guns. I, on the other hand, was close enough to risk being hit by one of his grenades. I sought the machine gunners first. The tanks would not advance until the anti-tank guns were eliminated but infantry had to destroy their machine guns before the anti-tank guns could be taken out. I had an angle and I used it. I fired five bullets at the Italian machine gun crew. It was not a mad minute. I just aimed and fired at the three men huddled around the gun. When two of them fell the attention of the Italians switched to me. The advantage I had was that they could not see where I was. The angle I had used meant that the only ones who knew where I was were dead. However, as soon as I fired then my position would be seen. If the Italians had a grenade launcher then the Stuka's tail plane would afford me no protection at all. I changed my position marginally and sought another angle. I did not see a machine gun but I did see an anti-tank gun manned by Italians. The shield hid three of the crew but there were two I could hit. I fired and emptied my magazine. Even as one fell clutching his arm I heard and saw the grenade explode just forty yards from me. Brown had managed to make it explode in the air. Shrapnel whizzed towards me and hit, not my unprotected head, but the tail plane. I resolved to wear my tin lid next time. I knew just how close I had come to death. I reloaded.

I heard the lieutenant shout, "Up and at 'em." I jumped up and ran. I had a better idea of where the danger lay. The machine gun to my right was gone and the Pak to my left had no crew left to man it. The grenade had taken care of them. That meant there

Conscript's Call

were men ahead of me. I screamed as I ran. It would put fear into the Italians for to them it would have appeared as though I had risen like a wraith from the ground. I was just a hundred yards from them. I fired from the hip as I ran. Sergeant Armourer Daley would not approve but if I stopped to aim then I would be a dead man. My only hope lay in zig zagging and spraying the enemy with bullets. I saw them duck behind the sandbags. Two lay slumped over it. I had hit them. As I neared it I realised I had an empty gun. I held my rifle in my left hand and, as I reached the sandbags, drew and then aimed my Beretta. There were four soldiers there and when they saw me with the pistol they dropped their weapons. I saw that the two men I had killed were both non-commissioned officers.

Roland had taught me a couple of phrases in Italian and German. I used one and told them to raise their arms. They obeyed and I found myself smiling. Who knew that the lad from Ince Blundell could speak Italian?

Sergeant Jackson and the section arrived behind me, "Well done, Sharratt. You shifted fast enough."

"Aye, Sergeant." I pointed to my right, "Machine gun over there. I think the crew are all dead."

He nodded, "Proud, Brown, take these prisoners back to the others."

Just then we heard the Stuarts as, the danger gone, they moved forward.

The Bren Carrier arrived and Bert shouted, "Lieutenant Fowler, HQ."

This time it was not a message to be passed on. As the lieutenant put on the headphones I put my pistol in my holster and reloaded my Lee Enfield. I saw some stick grenades and picked them up. I put them in my pack. This being an Italian position they also had salami sausages amongst their rations and I grabbed two. They went into my pack. We would share them later on. Some of the men liked the taste but we had discovered that putting some in a stew with corned beef made a much tastier meal. We had all become better at cooking since joining the army.

We looked up as a flight of Blenheims, escorted by Hurricanes, flew overhead. We were hitting the enemy. The

Conscript's Call

thought crept into my head that, perhaps, we were winning. It was hard to tell. The tanks that had been knocked out looked to be the same number for both sides but then again we had only destroyed Italian tanks. Where were the German ones?

The lieutenant shouted, "We are to hold here and bring up the lorries. Well done, all of you."

As the rest of our section joined me I smiled at Roland, "Looks like we have not needed your skills today."

"No," he held up his rifle, "I emptied three magazines but I am not sure I hit anything." I saw that he had the bayonet fitted and I nodded at it. He said, "Sandy told me to fit it. I don't know why. In basic training I found it hard enough to stab a bag filled with straw. I don't think I could do that to a man."

"Next time leave it off. If you can't use it then it just adds extra weight."

I thought back to the first raid and Taff Evans. That had been the only time when I might have needed to use a blade to stab someone. Luckily I had used a pistol to cow the Italian. Had I been forced to use a blade then, like Roland, I was not sure I could have done it.

By the time the lorries arrived we had piled the dead bodies to one side. I knew we would have to bury them, unless we moved on, but I put the thought of having to bury men whose bodies had been shredded and slashed by shrapnel, from my mind. With the bodies out of the way Sergeant Jackson said that we could eat. The Italians had fires and so it meant hot tea and food. Back in England they would have seemed commonplace but here the tea and food were a treat.

It was at about two in the afternoon when we were ordered to advance again. As Lieutenant Fowler climbed next to me I loaded a fresh magazine into the German machine gun. He banged on the roof of the cab and I said, "Still off to take Bir el Gubi, Sir?"

"We are to support the 22nd Armoured Brigade who are set to assault it. We are to guard the right flank. The good news is that we get to drive on the road. The 22nd are relatively fresh and we have taken casualties. Our job is to ensure that they are not attacked in the flank while they do so."

I shook my head, "I have no idea how anyone knows what is going on, Sir. Who has the big picture?"

"That is the problem, Private, the generals only have what we tell them. They know that we have taken strong points but we have suffered casualties. The 22nd appear to be in better shape than we are and so they will attack." He shook his head, "When we were at OTC training this all looked to be so simple. They were little blocks being moved on a map. A does this and B will do that. I am rapidly learning that the reality is somewhat different."

"And we have not come up against German opposition, yet, Sir."

He lowered his binoculars and said, "Greece and Crete did something to you, didn't they, Private?"

"Yes, Sir, they shook my confidence. I realised it was not enough to be as good a soldier as the enemy because it is about more than that. It is about aeroplanes, tanks, and a whole host of things that we can do nothing about."

"You lads have done alright."

"Yes, Sir, but we have still to make Jerry fall back. The day that happens will see me smile, Sir. Until then I will carry on being worried."

As we drove we saw, ahead, the tank battle unfolding. We saw the smoke from the guns and the dust. We could hear the sound of the guns as the armoured cars, light tanks and Crusaders attacked the Italian positions. The lieutenant had his glasses trained to the north for if 22nd Armoured were to be attacked it would be from that direction. Our Crusader and cruiser tanks were to the south of us and we knew that the battle was not going well when they were ordered to leave us and head to Bir el Gubi. We were left with C Troop of the 11th Hussars for protection. They had sixteen Stuart tanks but they seemed an inadequate number to face German tanks. There was also a troop of Horse Artillery with three 6 pounder anti-tank guns.

The road was a better surface and we made better time. However when Norm Thomas signalled to the lieutenant that we had a message from HQ, we stopped. The same radio message must have gone to the tanks too for the Stuarts stopped. The lieutenant put on the cans and when he returned he said,

Conscript's Call

"Everyone, except for Sharratt and the Lewis gunners out of the lorry. We have to make a defensive position here."

"Sir, can I have Poulter as a loader?"

"Of course."

Roland came to stand next to me. I heard Geoff say, as he stepped onto the ground, "Problem, Sir?"

He nodded, "Afraid so, Corporal. The Italians have held Bir el Gubi and the 22nd are falling back. If the Germans try to exploit the retreat then we will be the front line."

I saw why he had left the guns manned. We would both have a good field of fire. To facilitate that he had Dave Proud turn the Morris so that our section could make the lorry into a small fort.

I said to Roland, "The magazines are there, next to my pack. When I shout reload I will take off one magazine and you load a new one, right?"

He said, nervously, "Right."

"There are four spares and ammo but I am not sure you will have time to reload the magazines." He nodded and licked his lips. He held onto the magazine as though his life depended on it.

The rest of the company emulated us and I thought of the western movies we had watched at the cinema. We were like a wagon train but the Indians who attacked us would have tanks, armoured cars and aeroplanes.

It was aeroplanes from Sidi Rezegh who attacked first. We were not the primary target but as the surviving tanks were heading back to the road for a retreat back to Sidi Azeiz, we were inevitably fired on. The fighters were going for the softer targets that were the lorries and trucks. I knew from bitter experience that firing from the back of a lorry bouncing along a road involved more luck than judgment or skill. We, on the other hand, had a solid platform. The fighters were using a north to south route. It enabled them to hit the lorries in the side. However, as they banked it brought them into the line of fire of Bren guns and our machine guns. Our three weapons made a cone of fire that was deadly. We hit one and it began to emit smoke and headed back to the airfield. The second one was even more spectacular. One of our bullets must have hit the fuel tank. As the airfield was so close it meant it had a full tank and it exploded in spectacular fashion. It was like poking a wasps' nest.

Conscript's Call

The other five fighters saw us as a target. While it meant it left the other lorries alone, it put us in harm's way.

Lieutenant Fowler saw it too, "Every rifle, fire at the fighters as they come in."

I had not felt such fear since I had been on the **Orion**. The Me 109 fighter had four machine guns. Two fired through the propellor and as the Me 109 had a bright yellow nose it made the aeroplane seem larger and, as it was spitting fire, I felt sure that the bullets would hit me. I steeled myself. If I ran I might be shot in the back. This way I had the chance to inflict damage on the Germans and they were the Luftwaffe. They had killed my family. I aimed directly at the propellor. I emptied the magazine and as Roland reloaded I saw that we had damaged the first aeroplane. The second and third were heading towards us at great speed. I had not begun to fire when the Lewis, manned by Ray and Wally, hit the Messerschmitt. I saw pieces of the propellor struck. It obviously affected the interrupter gear on the aircraft and its own bullets finished the job, tearing through the propellors. The fighter plunged to the ground and crashed precariously close to another of our lorries. Luckily the impact drove it into the ground and the explosion and debris were not as bad as we might have expected. I began to fire and hit the wing of the next aeroplane. The flight had been hurt and when some Hurricanes appeared they headed, not back to the airfield, but west. That in itself felt like a victory.

The horse artillery had been able to prepare their defences and, with the Stuarts using AP, when the Italian armour approached from the west they received a hot welcome. The lorries and tanks of the 22nd were able to withdraw but it left us as the front line. As darkness fell we prepared our defences. The sandbags we used to protect the side of the Morris were taken out to make a short wall linking the Morris to the Bren Carrier. While food was being cooked we sought rocks to make another barrier between us and the rest of the platoon. We knew that it would be a sleep deprived night. It was ten o'clock before the first of the platoon was able to go to sleep and as we would only have four hours no one would be rested. Our section had the three am until dawn watch. We wore our greatcoats for it was cold and we saw the glows of vehicles that were still burning.

Conscript's Call

We had counted at least twenty-five of the new Crusader tanks hit. They had been hurt by the inferior Italian tanks. How would they fare against the superior German ones?

Chapter 17

The Germans did not come. We were relieved for the Stuart tanks did not have the guns to penetrate the German armour at any distance. We were ordered to board our lorries and, with the rest of the 7th Support Group, head to the German airfield at Sidi Rezegh. It was bold, and it was unexpected. We had failed to take Bir el Gubi and had lost tanks. Was this a face-saving operation?

Once again I enjoyed the wisdom of the lieutenant. When I expressed my doubts he said, "The thing is, Private Sharratt, that the battles, especially in this land, are always determined by supply. In the ancient world, the one I studied, it was water and missiles. In this modern war it is supplies of ammunition and, increasingly, fuel. Until Rommel takes Tobruk, he has a three-hundred-mile supply route. The Germans will be waiting to get all their ducks lined up before they attack. This attack makes sense although I am not sure that we can hold it. Still, we shall do our best, eh?"

I liked the lieutenant. I think that I would have learned a great deal if he had been my teacher.

What worried me most was that we appeared to be isolated. We had artillery and we had tanks but neither were in great numbers. We had three battalions of infantry. Like us the others were rifle battalions but we seemed to lack anti-tank guns. As we headed to the airfield I wondered about fuel. There were still German strongpoints behind us and getting petrol and food to us might be hard.

There were enemy positions between us and the airfield. There were Italians at Bir el Haleizim and they were dug in. They were there to protect the airfield. They had anti-tank guns and when they knocked out two Stuarts it was decided to send in the Queen's Rifles. The other two battalions in the group were the 1st Battalion, King's Royal Rifle Corps and the 2nd Battalion, Rifle Brigade. Both battalions had both been knocked about a bit and had fewer Bren Carriers than our battalion. We left our vehicles and prepared to advance. This would be a platoon

Conscript's Call

action. Lieutenant Fowler would lead our platoon to attack the small, defended outpost from the south. The other platoons in our company would be on our flanks. Like all battles we had one small part and we had to take our objective. I did not envy A Company's task. They would make a frontal attack and the anti-tank guns could easily take out their Bren Carriers. We, at least, had some cover from a wadi and we made our way down it to get into position. When the lieutenant held up his hand we prepared ourselves. This would be like the battles my father had fought on the Somme. We would rise from the wadi and use weight of numbers to overpower the defenders. They would have sub-machine guns and, as I had discovered, they could be deadly.

Ray said to Roland, "You stay behind Hawkeye, me and Pie Face. I know Hawkeye is skinny as a lat but Pie Face is built like a brick..."

"Cheeky bugger. I used to be a big lad but..."

"Shut the chatter." There was no rancour in Geoff's voice. He knew we needed the banter to ease our nerves, especially Roland's.

"Yes, Corporal."

The Bren Carriers took time to get into a position where they could use their tracks to emerge from the wadi. When they were ready Captain Whittle blew his whistle and we all rose. The Bren Carriers made a huge noise as they roared up the slope. Harry and the other Bren gunners would not be able to fire as they climbed the sides of the dried-up riverbed and even an anti-tank rifle could hurt them as they revealed their softer bellies. I ran, flanked by Ray and Wally. The Italians opened fire with their rifles. Some of our men slowed to stand and fire. I just fired from the hip as did Ray and Wally. We probably didn't hit anything but we just hoped to keep the heads of the defenders down. When Harry's Bren opened up we took heart for the Italian gunfire slowed. The others had fitted bayonets but I had not. As we neared the enemy lines I saw an officer rallying his men. I stopped and aimed. The others ran on but I squeezed two bullets off and saw him fall. I ran to catch up with the others. They had reached the defenders and two maniacs leapt the sandbags and screamed. I saw their bayonets plunge down. This time the enemy did not surrender but they ran. They had vehicles and they intended to flee. As we followed them I saw one turn. He had a sub-machine gun, the kind the Germans called a machine pistol. I dropped to one knee and, as the Italian raised it to fire, emptied the clip into him. I knew that a dying finger on a trigger could continue to send bullets from the weapon and I wanted him dead.

The last minutes of the battle were frenetic as the Italians tried to escape with as much as they could. That was their undoing and A Company, perhaps angry at their losses, took the anti-tank guns before they could be hitched to the trucks and removed from the battlefield. We took another forty prisoners but if we thought we were done we were in for a shock. We were ordered back onto our vehicles and we raced to get to the airfield. Lieutenant Fowler was in an ebullient mood. He banged the roof of the cab and ordered Private Proud to go even faster. We began to pull ahead of the Bren Carriers and the slower Bedford lorries. The Stuart was a fast tank and we found ourselves behind C Troop as they raced to the wire surrounding the airfield. I saw aeroplanes parked and heard the siren as the alarm was given. In hindsight I think that the intention was for us to leave our vehicles and to make the assault on foot.

"Open fire!" Lieutenant Fowler was using the offensive capabilities of Morris the Mouse.

I cocked the gun and shouted, "Bones!"

Roland stood and prepared to hand me another magazine. I opened fire and used the tracer rounds to hit the first of the aeroplanes that were parked there.

"Not the aeroplanes, the defenders."

"Sorry, Sir!" He was right and I had been caught up in the excitement of the moment. The airfield had a similar layout to Sidi Azeiz and I switched direction to aim at the sandbags at the end of the runway. The twin Lewis chattered too as Ray and Wally sent their bullets at the sandbags. I added my firepower. Even though they had sandbags the bullets tore through the canvas and as the sand poured out the integrity of the position was lost. The machine gun that was firing at us was also an MG 34 and I heard the bullets as they struck our lorry. We bore a charmed life. There would be holes but nothing important was hit. One of our bullets hit the gunner and as he fell backward he

Conscript's Call

pulled the gun with him. The 37 mm of a Stuart tank sent some high explosive at the control tower and when that was destroyed the garrison began to surrender. The ten tanks had enough machine guns to wipe out the whole garrison if they chose. By the time Brigadier Jock Campbell arrived the airfield was in our possession. He wasted no time in preparing the defences. This was now the most forward position of any of the Allied forces. Even I, a lowly private, a conscript, knew that Rommel would want it back.

We were allocated a section on the road side of the airfield to camp and defend. We used the vehicles again. It made sense to me. If we had to leave quickly then we wanted the lorry and the Bren Carrier as close to us as we could manage. It also meant we had somewhere to sleep and would not have to put up tents. We moved the machine guns and scavenged what we could to make gun emplacements. We also made slit trenches. They would be used when the Luftwaffe came or if the Germans and Italians used artillery to bombard us. A couple of the tanks were dug in too. The tankers called it hull down and it added extra protection for them. The 51st (Westmorland and Cumberland) Field Regiment, Royal Artillery, would be our main artillery. We liked them for they were, like us, northerners. By dark we had empty oil cans we had found filled with wood and were using them to cook our food. Later they would warm us. The officers had a mess; they took over the one in the building used by the air crews. It meant we didn't see Lieutenant Fowler. Instead, the NCOs took charge and they always ran a tighter ship. We were lucky. We didn't have to do a duty. That was partly because we had done one the night before but also Lieutenant Fowler's crazy dash had garnered us praise.

As we ate and after the sergeant had left us we spoke of the attack. Harry was not happy. "Has the man got a death wish or what? We could have all been killed."

Geoff shook his head, "What are you going on about? We were the ones charging. You were tagging along behind in an armoured Bren Carrier. If anyone was going to get hit it would have been us and you don't see any of us complaining." He glared at Dave Proud who looked as though he might say something. Geoff was a very loyal man.

Conscript's Call

I smiled, "Anyway, Harry, doing something unexpected sometimes pays off. I wouldn't want to do it too often but now and again, well, I felt quite heroic. I know it wasn't but I liked the way the major and even the general spoke to us after we took the airfield. Jock Campbell is a legend out here. If he thought it was a daft thing to do he would have said so."

Harry wouldn't let it go, "This new man is a glory hunter."

I shook my head, "No, he is not. I have spoken to him many times and a glory hunter he is not. Lieutenant Hargreaves was a nice bloke but it is clear now that he was looking for advancement and he got it. I tell you something, Lieutenant Fowler would not have left us like Lieutenant Hargreaves did."

It was the first time I had mentioned it and it made an uncomfortable silence. Eventually Bert nodded, "I reckon you are right, Hawkeye. You and I were on the two raids and, well, I felt let down by the lieutenant."

Geoff said, "Look, we now have an officer who seems to me to be made of the right stuff. The orders were to race to the wire and that is what we did. If anything, Harry, he made it easier for you lads in the Bren Carrier. I don't think he will do it again."

Silence fell until Ray said, "And there will be no charging now. I reckon the Germans will throw the kitchen sink at us. We are a salient protruding deep into their land. They have lost two airfields and Tobruk could be relieved at any time. We haven't seen German tanks yet. I think we will see some tomorrow." He stood, "So, with that, I bid you all a fond goodnight." He gave a mock bow, "And whoever is on breakfast duty, bacon and eggs with a nice sausage and black pudding would not go amiss."

We all laughed for we dreamed of such fare.

The Germans made their intentions clear the next day. We were awoken early and stood to. Any thoughts of a hot breakfast soon disappeared. We ate cold rations behind our sandbags. We could hear the attack from the Tobruk garrison although it was too far away for us to see. When the lieutenant came to inspect our position I asked him about the battle to the north of us.

"The Australian garrison is trying to break out and that is why we are here, Private Sharratt. We are the anvil and the Australians and Poles are the hammer. There will be pressure on us but we must be resolute and do as the Spartans did at

216

Conscript's Call

Thermopylae. They held the pass as we hold the northern edge of the airfield and this road."

It was only then that I saw where we had been placed; I had known we were beyond the airfield but now I saw that we stopped any reinforcements heading from Libya. Rommel would have to use the desert. We had a chance.

We heard the tank battle to the south of us. We, of course, could see nothing for our attention was to the north. One thing we had learned was to discriminate between the sounds of the different tank guns. The 37 mm sounded like a pop gun compared with the 50 mm and 75 mm of the German tanks. We could hear the six pounders as they duelled with the tanks and the barrage laid down by the twenty-five pounders. Above us there was also a duel between the two air forces as they fought for supremacy of the air. We would know if the RAF lost for we would have to endure the attacks of the dive bombers. We had a morning to improve our defences with anything we could find: stones, rocks pieces of wood and even corned beef tins filled with sand. It was noon before we were attacked. It was almost a relief when the enemy rifles began to fire for the tension of waiting was unbearable.

The attack was not a wave of men recklessly charging. It was the attack of men who used cover and half-tracks to advance. General Campbell had allocated one six pounder to the northern sector. It proved a godsend for it knocked out two half-tracks quickly and their crews took shelter behind them. We were given the order to fire when the Germans launched an attack on the six pounder. I think the sound of the MG 34 came as a shock to the Germans. It had a different sound to the Bren gun and the Vickers that defended the six pounder. I fired in regular short bursts. I had no idea if I had hit anyone or not. I fired and Ray and Wally joined in with the Lewis gun. The Bren barked as well and we held their first attack. They used half-tracks and one of them came to within a hundred and forty yards of us. The machine guns at the front made us take shelter but a Boys anti-tank rifle, fired at an angle, hit it on the side and exploded the fuel. It was a short and spectacular explosion. We had to duck to avoid flying debris but when we looked up we saw that the attack had been beaten back. The other half-track retreated to

Conscript's Call

where it could not be hit. It lay beyond the range of our Boys anti-tank rifles.

The second attack was a different one. They used mortars. As they ranged in they began to enjoy success. We had a mortar platoon and they sent our own shells back at theirs. The mortar that hit our six pounder was a disaster. It left us with just the Boys anti-tank rifle against their armoured vehicles. However, the mortar barrage ceased. We didn't know if it was as a result of our success or a lack of ammunition. We were just grateful that it stopped. Roland joined the other medical orderlies to see to the wounded.

The next attack was just before darkness fell. Alarmingly, the tank battle seemed to be much closer and some men kept glancing over their shoulders. Sergeant Jackson snapped their attention back to the north as the Germans came again with armoured half-tracks. Their machine guns scythed through the air. The tracer they used showed the tracks of their bullets. Geoff Vane shouted, "Brown, start lobbing grenades in the air."

I heard the launcher and the crack of the anti-tank rifles used in other sections. When one machine gun stopped we cheered. I kept firing. By the time darkness had fallen the attacks had ceased and Roland scurried off to help the wounded once more. Before he left he handed me a magazine. "The last one." We had found four when we had taken the field but the long day of firing had eaten into the supply. Most of the bullets had missed their target but they had done their job and kept the enemy at bay.

We would be getting little sleep that night for the enemy seemed determined to recover the airfield and remove the salient. We were the meat in a German/Italian sandwich. We ate but it was at our guns. We drank just water and dreamed of hot tea. The Germans came as soon as the darkness of the desert descended. Captain Whittle ordered a Very flare to be sent up and we saw the Germans sneaking forward. I emptied my magazine and barely replaced it in time with the last one. With the Lewis and Bren guns we held them but only just.

Geoff Vane ordered Sandy to launch another grenade. There was silence. "Come on, Brown, get a move on."

"Corp, the thing is jammed."

Conscript's Call

"Give it here." We kept our eyes on the darkness. I heard Geoff as he tried to make it work. We had heard of this problem before but so far our launcher had proved to be reliable. Perhaps the dust of the desert had been the problem. "That is it then. We have no grenade launcher."

I had an idea, "Cover me. I will make some booby traps. I have some German grenades."

Weather looked at me, "Are you sure? You want to go out there?"

I nodded, "I don't want to but now is the best time. They will attack again but not yet. The longer we delay the more chance I have of being taken."

"Right lads, cover him and the password is Hawkeye, reply, Weather." He took charge of the MG 34.

I reached into my bag and made sure I still had the four grenades and the cord. I slipped on the pack. I had a Beretta and plenty of ammunition. If I was attacked I would be able to defend myself. The worst part was slipping over the sandbags. I steeled myself for the rattle of bullets that would end my life. Once safely over I crawled across the no man's land between our lines. Before night had fallen we had seen the German positions. They were a hundred yards away. Once I had moved twenty yards I stopped. I needed to assess where they would come and place the booby traps there. I spotted one obvious place. It was ten yards to my right and forty yards closer to their lines. There were two dead Germans there. They were about four feet apart and anyone sneaking towards us would use the passage between them rather than stepping on the bodies. After crawling towards them I took two of the German grenades and broke the ends. I jammed one under one body and tied some cord to the pull cord and then did the same on the other side under the dead German who lay there. The trick was to hide the cord but make it so that anyone passing it would set if off. I found a piece of rubble and passed the cord over it so that it was taut. I then grabbed a handful of dust to cover the cord.

I slithered back to look for another place. This time it was not dead Germans I saw but a wrecked half-track. It was the one we had destroyed in the first attack. It could not be driven as the explosion had wrecked the tracks. It still had one machine gun

Conscript's Call

and, I assumed, inside would be the dead crew. It lay twenty yards nearer to the German lines. Anyone attacking us would use the vehicle for cover but they would have to pass on one side or the other. I chose the driver's side and I jammed a grenade under the wheel arch. I fastened the cord to the pull cord and then placed the other grenade on the ground. Once again I used a rock to disguise it. This time the cord was at an angle but I doubted that anyone would look at the wheel arch.

I slipped the pack on my back and drew my Beretta. I would have to slither backwards to our lines. I had only gone four feet when I smelled something. It was the smell of cigarettes. The slight breeze came from the north and the smell had not been there before. It was the smell of tobacco and cigarettes on a uniform. When you did not smoke you noticed such things. Once I had identified the smell I sought the source. When I heard the scraping of a boot on metal I knew that whoever it was had climbed up on the wrecked half-track. The curse in German confirmed it. When a second voice hissed a command to be silent I knew that there were two men there. I aimed the gun at the half-track's cab. If I moved I might be seen and I had some distance to run to reach safety. There was a chance I might make it but, equally, just as much chance that I would be cut down in a hail of bullets. The half-track still had a machine gun.

I saw the helmeted face peer over the shattered windscreen and I waited. The whispered conversation was too low for me to hear but when the head disappeared I risked sliding back a few more yards. I was undone by the small pile of stones that my boot disturbed. The two heads came up and when I heard the sound of the MG 34 being cocked I knew I had been spotted. I rose and held the pistol in two hands. I fired six bullets, three at each head. There was a cry and the heads disappeared. I stood and ran. As I neared our lines I shouted, "Hawkeye."

Geoff shouted, "Weather."

Suddenly the MG 34 on the half-track opened fire. Our three machine guns as well as the rest of the rifles from the platoon all fired. I had just dived over the sandbags when the two German grenades I had left by the half-track's wheel went off. The air was filled with shrapnel and screams. The MG 34 fell silent and

220

Conscript's Call

Sergeant Jackson shouted, "Cease Fire!" He made his way over to us, "What's going on?"

Geoff said, "Private Sharratt went to place some booby traps in no man's land. It looks like one worked."

I pointed to where I had laid the other two grenades. "There is another over there."

"Well done. Now save your ammo. The major has just had word. The Germans destroyed most of our tanks. We just have four left and we are going to head back to Point 175 and the escarpment. The New Zealanders have taken the ridge."

I nodded but I felt despondent. We were retreating again.

However, the night was not yet over. Geoff had used the last of the MG 34 magazines and so we put the now redundant gun in Morris the Mouse. I took my rifle. It was close to dawn and we had been warned that we would be leaving soon when the next attack began. First there were mortar shells. There were not as many as before and they were less accurate as it was nighttime.

Lieutenant Fowler came around, "I think this is a prelude to an attack, boys, be ready." I saw that he had a pistol in his hand. He must have run out of Sten ammunition or perhaps, like the grenade launcher, it had given up the ghost.

It was the first booby trap I had set which was the start of the assault. The Germans must have crept closer under the barrage from the mortars and they were close enough for us to see their helmets. The grenades exploded and sent their deadly shrapnel left and right. They cut through what I assumed was a German section. We opened fire. This was no time for me to measure each shot. I had to fire as fast as I could. What I did do, however, was aim at anyone who looked to be in command. I hit an officer in the arm and he spun around. The feldwebel I hit died instantly for the bullet smacked into his screaming mouth. They kept coming for they were desperate to retake the airfield. Perhaps they had been told that their tanks had won the battle. When the Bren fell silent and Harry shouted, "Ammo!" I knew we were in trouble.

I took one of the Mills Bombs from my pouch and I stood.

Roland shouted, "Get down!"

I had to take the risk. I pulled the pin and then threw the grenade as high and far as I could, "Grenade!" I dived to the

Conscript's Call

ground and covered my ears. I was trying to achieve what the grenade launcher would. I wanted an airburst. The grenade only went forty or so yards but it exploded in the air and the screams told me that it had worked. The sun was just rising in the east and as I lifted my head I saw the carnage caused by the grenade.

Captain Whittle blew his whistle and CSM Hutton shouted, "Get in the lorries and head east."

My heart sank. The Germans were still attacking and a man cannot run and fire accurately. I grabbed my pack and rifle and ran for Morris the Mouse. Dave was already at the wheel but disaster struck when he was hit in the arm by a bullet. Worse was to follow. A mortar shell hit Betty. Bert had yet to get into it and Harry still had the Bren gun but the carrier was wrecked.

Geoff shouted, "Bones, get Dave in the back. Bert. Get the wheel."

Our mechanic had no time to mourn his Betty. As Dave was manhandled into the back by Sandy and Norm and while Ray and Wally set up the Lewis I emptied my rifle at the Germans who were now slightly more than shadows. Bullets whizzed and zipped around me but I ignored them. If I was hit then so be it. When Morris roared into life we saw the difference in our drivers. Bert knew how to drive and we sped off in a cloud of dust. Geoff was firing his rifle as fast as he could. I suddenly realised the lieutenant was not with us. Had he been hit? I had no time to look for him. The enemy were hot on our trail. One slight advantage we had was that we were a smaller vehicle than the Bedford lorry and as we had removed most of our canvas we were not only a smaller target but we could fire from the side. When the Lewis opened up it took the Germans by surprise. Ray raked the line of rifles and machine pistols as we passed. They had to take cover and it bought us enough time to be free from the attackers.

There were vehicles ahead of us. I saw an armoured car from the Hussars. It was a Morris CS9. The engine was the same as ours but with the armour it was slower. We were better armed too for it only had a Bren gun and a Boys anti-tank rifle but it was armoured and the German bullets bounced from it. They would have been better to have aimed at the softer Bedford lorries. The

Conscript's Call

armoured car cleared the way and when the bullets ceased to be fired at us I knew we had escaped but we had yet to reach safety.

I looked down at Roland, "How is Dave?"

Dave shook his head, "Last bloody time it was my left arm and now it is my right."

Roland smiled, "It is a clean wound. The bullet went through the flesh and missed the bone. I have given him pain killer so he should be alright." He stood and held on to the metal struts that were used to attach the canvas, "Any other wounds?" We all shook our heads.

I asked, "What happened to the lieutenant?"

Harry was busy loading bullets into a magazine for the Bren and he nodded back to the airfield. "I saw him and Sergeant Jackson jump in number three section's Bedford. He looked to be alright."

Just then I looked up and saw, from the east, a flight of Blenheims escorted by three Hurricanes. We all cheered as they passed over. We had a chance now. We had won the airfield and now lost it but we were alive. We had been battered but we had survived.

Chapter 18

The ridge showed that the New Zealanders had fought hard to take it from the Italians. The battlefield was littered with discarded equipment and spent bullet cases as well as wrecked vehicles. Potholes marked where artillery had smashed those fighting for the vital escarpment. MPs marshalled us to new positions. The sun was well up when we arrived and we had a good view of the battlefield as well as the coast. As we could see men moving from Tobruk, we wondered if it had been relieved.

Once again our company was placed on the Tobruk side of the ridge. The rest of the battalion was spread out. I took that as a sign that those who made such decisions felt we were good soldiers. We were put where we would face the enemy and help bolster the men who had fought so hard to take the ridge. We made our camp and dug our trenches. The New Zealanders were tough men but they were also friendly. I was sent to ask if they had any oil drums we could use for a fire. The corporal from the 24th Machine Gun company waved me towards a wrecked building, "There are some in there, mate."

"Thanks."

He came with me, "Were you lads at the airfield?" I nodded. "We hear you lost a lot of tanks."

"Aye, so we were told. We didn't see the tank battle. We held the road. You know how it is, you see the battle before you and the rest is all gossip and rumour." We had reached the building and I chose an oil drum that had been peppered with machine gun bullets. It would make a good one to cook with as the holes would allow it to draw. "Have we relieved Tobruk yet?" I thought that as the Australians were holding the port the New Zealander might know.

"Nah, there are still Germans there and they are keeping the road to Bardia open. They have strongly defended the Halfaya Pass and they hold Sollum." He patted me on the back, "I reckon, mate, that they will soon try to shift us and unless we get more tanks we are in bother."

Conscript's Call

I manhandled the drum and said, "Another retreat then. I am sick of it."

"Don't be so down in the mouth, young 'un. Some of our lads captured some senior officers. They will be back in Egypt by now. That has to hurt Jerry. Our General Freyberg is a good officer. We will be alright." I liked his confident attitude and it made me feel better. Perhaps I was being too pessimistic.

The fact that we could cook food and make tea seemed to lift our spirits. The doctor who checked over Bones' work was well pleased and, in light of our precarious position, allowed Dave Proud to stay with us. We would need every man we could. We also found more ammunition for the MG 34 amongst the discarded materiel left by the enemy. As we made our new camp we were able to reflect that we had been luckier than most. We learned that the New Zealanders had taken heavy losses in their attack on Point 175 and that the South African Division had been just as badly handled. In comparison we were in good shape. That night, when we hoped that we might get some sleep, Lieutenant Fowler came to check up on us. It was from him that we gained more information.

"Most of the rest of the 7th Support Group are further south and they have joined up with the remains of the 22nd Armour and the South Africans. I am afraid we don't have many tanks left but from what Major Hill told me the Germans have lost a great deal too. Those Blenheims this morning managed to hit a column of tanks. If we can hold this ridge…"

Geoff asked, "And can we, Sir?"

He took out his pipe and began to fill it, "You know there were many who said we couldn't take the airfield and that if we took it we couldn't keep hold of it but we did. They retook it but by then we had damaged it so much as to render it useless and they lost more men than we did in trying to retake it. I call that a victory."

I stared into the oil drum fire. If this was a victory then I couldn't see it. We had new tanks and the enemy had simply gobbled them up. What were we doing wrong?

When the lieutenant spoke again it made me jump. I must have been staring into the fire for longer than I had realised. The

Conscript's Call

others were smoking and chatting and I was alone. Even Roland was joking with Ray and Wally. "Still brooding, Sharratt?"

I gave him a shaky smile, "Oh, I am just a pessimist, I guess."

He blew out some smoke and said, "From what I have learned from Sergeant Jackson and Sergeant Jones, you have been dealt a hand which would make any man pessimistic but, you know, I don't see a pessimist before me. You didn't just sit on your backside back at the airfield, you went out and did something. It was not only brave, but it was also vital. Your booby traps alerted the whole company. Had they managed to attack us then we might not have got away as easily as we did."

"Easily, Sir?"

He chuckled, "Relatively easily. We only lost one Bedford."

"But we lost all our Bren Carriers."

"True, but we win wars with men and not Bren Carriers. I am optimistic," he smiled, "Hawkeye, and these New Zealanders give me hope that we can win."

We did manage to get sleep. It was interrupted by a watch but it was just a two-hour watch and I felt much better when we rose, before dawn, to see what Fate would bring our way.

When two hundred and fifty lorries arrived from the railhead bringing supplies, ammunition and more anti-tank guns our spirits rose. We divided the ammunition and food between the whole company. We were given a new Boys anti-tank rifle. We would have preferred a grenade launcher but the rifle would have to do. Geoff gave the weapon to Ray and Wally. If nothing else the war thus far had shown us that we needed to be able to act as independently as we could. The anti-tank rifle helped us to do that. I shared a slit trench with Roland. We used the natural rocks to help us build a defensive position and I was confident in our ability to both fight and protect ourselves. We had learned much since Klidi Pass. The lieutenant came to tell us that the South Africans had been ordered to join us. The smiles it brought made it seem like a party was taking place.

Once again disaster struck. This time it was the New Zealanders who were fated to be cruelly treated. It was late afternoon and we had enjoyed a day without any attacks. Suddenly, from the south and the top of Point 175 we heard firing and we stood to. It was Sergeant Jackson who raced in.

Conscript's Call

The normally calm sergeant was as animated as I had ever seen. "Get your weapons, the Italians have broken through."

It seemed inconceivable that the New Zealanders had been defeated so quickly. Grabbing our rifles we ran up the slope. Once we neared the summit we saw New Zealanders streaming towards us.

Lieutenant Fowler shouted, "Skirmish line."

Sergeant Jackson shouted, "The Italians have armour. You lads with the Boys, be ready!"

The New Zealanders were turning to fire at the pursuing Italians before running towards the sanctuary that was the Queen's Rifles. Roland and I were lying in a cleft in the rocks. Next to us was the Boys Rifle. Harry and Bert were at the far end with our Bren gun. I saw one New Zealander turn to fire his rifle and then, as he ran towards us, his arms spread as he was hit by a burst from a machine pistol. I aimed my rifle. If the Italians were close enough to use machine pistols then they were well within the range of us and our Lee Enfields. I saw an Italian officer. He was two hundred yards away and exhorting his men to charge. I aimed at his middle and squeezed the trigger. He spun around, and clutching his arm, dropped to the ground. The other Italians dropped to one knee and opened fire at us. It allowed the last of the New Zealanders to reach us and form their own skirmish line.

Another Italian officer, more circumspect than the one I had hit and who was being treated, knelt and I saw him talking into a radio. The reason became clear a moment or two later as two Italian tanks appeared. They were the Italian M11 and looked like a heavier armoured version of the armoured cars used by the Hussars and South Africans. While they were not much good against tanks they were perfect against infantry, and when they rose like prehistoric beasts, they lumbered a few yards and then stopped. The turrets turned and opened fire with their machine guns. They did not use their 37 mm for they did not need to. I fired at the officer with the radio and he fell. I sent another two bullets and the radio began to spark. I had hit it too.

Sergeant Jackson shouted, "The ones with the anti-tank rifles, your Boys Rifles can hit them at five hundred yards but it is better to wait until they are closer."

Conscript's Call

Waiting was easier said than done but as the two tanks were more than four hundred yards away their own bullets were not as effective as they might have been. Someone in command of the tanks must have thought so too for they began to lumber towards us, the infantry lurking menacingly behind the two of them. I saw that one of the commanders was out of the turret and using glasses. He wore a black beret and looked just like one of our tankers. It was too good an opportunity and I aimed at him. The bullet missed him but hit the rim of the hatch and something must have ricocheted and he dived into cover.

Ray and Wally held their nerve. One of the other platoons fired their weapon at three hundred yards. It hit the armour but the tank came on. A second and a third fired when they were two hundred yards from us. One of the rounds must have hit the tracks because the tank stopped. Other Boys rifles began to pepper the stricken tank and when smoke came from it the crew baled out. Ray waited until the second tank was just one hundred yards away. His projectile slammed into the tank and it must have struck ammunition or fuel for the tank exploded in a spectacular fashion. It was lucky we were lying down or we might have been scythed down. The Italians following the two tanks stood no chance and they retreated.

Captain Whittle shouted, "Fall back!"

Once more we retreated. It was clear to us all that Point 175, captured at such a great cost, was, like the airfield, now lost.

We hurtled towards our transport. If nothing else the November offensive had taught us how to get aboard our vehicles efficiently and smoothly. I cocked the MG 34 which lay on the cab as Roland stowed our packs and rifles. It took longer for the Lewis to be mounted but Ray and Wally managed. Now that we had no Betty, Harry laid the Bren across the cab roof too. We had doubled our forward firepower. I knew the other men in the platoon looked enviously at us for we were the only transport which was armed. This time Lieutenant Fowler joined us but it was at the last minute as we were just setting off.

He leaned over and shouted, "Dixon, your vehicle is to lead the company out, Captain Whittle's orders."

"Sir. Where to?" Geoff Vane was in the cab.

Conscript's Call

"Head for El Duda. It is to the west of us on the other side of the coast road."

Geoff must have peered ahead for he shouted, "You mean through that lot, Sir?"

I looked ahead. I had been fiddling with the gun during the interchange. Ahead of us were Italian infantry. They had clearly thought we would be heading either north to Tobruk or east back to Egypt.

I heard the lieutenant mutter, "Bugger." Then in a more confident and louder voice he said, "Yes, just the ticket, eh? Put your foot down, Dixon."

"Right, Sir. Hold on to your hats, lads."

"Open fire."

Had we enjoyed any armour, even an armoured car or a Bren Carrier it might not have been so hard but we were just a Morris 15 cwt lorry that happened to have three machine guns. As the alternative was surrender we just got on with it.

I aimed at the startled Italians who turned to face us and tried to bring their weapons to bear. They had rifles and their machine guns were slung over their backs. That was our advantage and when the Bren and the MG 34 opened fire and cut down the leading element, the rest dived to take cover. The remainder of the section and Lieutenant Fowler lined the side of the lorry and they sprayed the Italians with Sten guns, rifles and pistols. The other lorries of the battalion emulated us. Some of the lorries had copied us and taken down their canvas. As some lorries had been destroyed already it meant that there were many lorries with twice the number of men they were intended to carry. The result was that we destroyed the Italian company and broke through.

The lieutenant was laughing as he clapped Harry and me on the back, "Well, that was exciting."

Geoff's voice came from the cab, "Sir, I am not sure where to direct Bert."

It was a plea for help and I understood it. Geoff was leading the battalion and that needed an officer. The lieutenant said, "Quite right. Budge over and I will slip through." Bert had taken off the panel that normally separated the cab from the back when he had realised we could supply the driver with food and drink while he was driving if it was removed. Now it proved a

Conscript's Call

godsend. The lieutenant would be able to read the map and make crucial decisions.

He handed his Sten to Norm Thomas and manoeuvred himself through the back of the cab and into the front seat. It would be a tight fit.

Ray said, "Well, it looks like the New Zealanders are heading east."

I turned and looked behind the line of lorries back to the ridge were I could see the 2nd New Zealand Division. Ray was right, they were not following us. I saw other lorries belonging to the Queen's Rifles joining them. They were heading back to the railhead. Roland looked back too. "What does it mean, John? Why are we heading towards the enemy and the others are going away from them?"

I knew why he was asking me for, to him, I was a veteran but if truth be told I was as much in the dark as he was. However, I felt obliged to look after the young man who was ill suited to the role of soldier. "We don't have the big picture, Roland. There is a battle going on to the south. The ones who know best have aeroplanes to tell them what it is like on the ground. We just have to trust that they know what they are doing."

Roland said, quietly, "And do they?"

I didn't answer him, immediately, for I was remembering a conversation in the pub one Armistice Day. My father and his friends had marched to the memorial to the Great War wearing their medals and were in the pub toasting the dead. Old Joe had said, bitterly, "And how many of the lads would be drinking with us now and not lying in a field in the Somme if the generals had had any idea of what they were doing?" The silence from the others had told me how much they agreed with him. At the time I had not understood. The men who made the decisions were officers and had been promoted. Surely they knew what they were doing. Now I was the one being ordered hither and thither, back and forth and I was not sure that anyone had any idea of what was going on.

Eventually I said, "We just do our best. We are a good platoon and company. We haven't lost a man in this section since Crete and I reckon we have a good officer. Captain Whittle knows his

Conscript's Call

business. If he was in command of this army then I don't think that it would be the shambles it appears."

There was a village ahead but we did not stop there. It was occupied by Australians and we were waved on. Wally shouted, "What is this place called, mate?"

An Australian shouted, "Zaafran. Why, do you want by a house here?"

His mates laughed and Wally called "No thanks, we are looking for something a little classier."

I liked the Australians. They were tough men and did not like all the spit and polish of the British army but they were, like the New Zealanders, the most dependable of men in a fight and I was glad that they were with us.

Norm Thomas pointed ahead. In the distance we could see the battle for Tobruk. From the top of Point 175 it had looked as though we were about to relieve it. Now we could see that it was not close to being relieved. A battle raged there. The Australians were holding a perimeter and we would, in effect, be just as beleaguered as the garrison. When we stopped it was dark and we had reached a village called Belhamed. We were close to the Tobruk bypass and the front line of the Australians trying to break through to Tobruk was at Ed Dedu.

As we jumped down from the lorry Major Hill, Captain Whittle, CSM Hutton and the other lieutenants from the company joined Lieutenant Fowler. CSM Hutton said, "This is our new camp. You know what to do."

We nodded for we did. As we began to make this our new home we heard drifts of conversation from the officers. It was clear that Major Hill had been in radio contact with Headquarters. "It looks like we have just two companies from the battalion. The rest went east with the New Zealander 2nd Division. I am in command of what is left. We are to work with the 70th Division and hold this line. Our orders are to ensure that the road to Bardia and Sollum is held and that the Germans do not relieve their garrisons nor do they break out to the bypass. If they take the Tobruk bypass then Tobruk will be cut off again. We believe there is still armour to the east of us."

Lieutenant Wilkinson said, "Sir, do we have armour?"

Conscript's Call

He shook his head. "We have the Boys anti-tank rifles and that is all. We shall just have to be creative." As I took the MG 34 to the sandbagged area I heard the major add, "We have to husband our ammunition and food. There is a well here but we have to hold on to the last man and the last bullet."

Captain Whittle said, "We will do it, Sir. We have good men and I do not intend to let them end their lives here."

"Right, Gentlemen, the HQ will be over there in that building that still has a roof. CSM Hutton, arrange the duty roster."

"Sir." Dave Proud, his arm in a sling, was staring at the officers. We had excused him duty and he had made the mistake of standing and listening. CSM Hutton snapped, "Proud, you have one good arm, use it, do something useful and stop being a nebby little man!"

"Sorry, Company Sergeant Major." He rushed off.

We began to make a fort. We used whatever we could to make a barrier behind which we could fight. We took broken pieces of building and they formed the foundations. Any pieces of wood were added to strengthen it and then we used sand, there was plenty of it, to fill in gaps. We had learned that if you peed on the sand it sometimes dried a little harder. We would do that. There was no convenient oil drum and the one given to us on Point 175 was probably being used by the enemy now. Instead we made a hearth and gathered wood that was too small to be used in our wall.

Sergeant Jackson came along and said, "The fire will need to be doused after dark. The enemy have artillery spotters and we don't want to invite a barrage."

Geoff said, "Right, Sarge. Get the food and tea on the go now, lads."

Ray said, "There is only enough wood for a short time anyway. Make the most of it tonight, eh lads?"

It was Roland and me who were on cooking duty. We left the building of the fort and I lit the fire. We were adept at this now. We used a little petrol to get it going. By the time the food was put on to cook, the stink of petrol would have gone and would not taint the food. We took out the corned beef tin and while Roland opened it I took out the dried veg and soaked them in some water. They were never completely soft by the time we ate

Conscript's Call

them but that could not be helped. I sliced some of the Italian sausage I had taken and dropped that into the soaking liquor. Dave Proud had been foraging. He could do that onehanded and he emerged from a half-wrecked building. He held a bag in his hand. "Can you use this, Hawkeye?"

I opened it. It was a bag of dates. "I don't see why not."

Norm Thomas was passing and he said, incredulously, "Dates? With beef? Are you trying to make us sick?"

I smiled, "It will work and I don't think it will make you sick," I paused, "It might make you need to go to the toilet a little more but that is all."

Roland and I lifted the pot with the vegetables, water and sausage and put it on the fire which had taken quite nicely. He had emptied the corned beef tin and after we had sliced the corned beef into the stew we put more water in the tin to wash it out. Even after the tin would still be used as a cooking utensil. We filled it with water to make the tea. I then chopped the dates and added those too.

Roland said, "Won't the tea taste of corned beef?"

I shrugged, "It might do but that will do no harm and when we have finished with the tin as a tea pot we fill it with sand and it goes into the wall. We waste nothing. We are like these," I tapped the red shoulder flash, "we are desert rats who make do with whatever is to hand."

Half of the section was allocated the first watch and our half ate our share of the feast first. That done we went to relieve the others. Norm Thomas had eaten with us and I said, "Well, did the dates make you sick?"

He smiled, "You were right. I didn't taste them but the stew was tasty. I am not sure me mam would approve."

Ray laughed, "I am not sure our mothers would approve of anything that we do. Best that they never find out, eh? It must be hard enough for them worrying about us being shot or wounded without worrying about what we eat or how we go to the toilet."

The lieutenant came to taste our stew and I filled his mess tin with it. It was from him we learned the full extent of the disaster at the ridge. The New Zealanders had mistaken the Italian tanks for South Africans and had allowed them to get close. It was the designs of the tank and the fact that they wore black berets like our tankers that had done it. It was an accident but it had lost us the escarpment.

We had watch on and watch off for the rest of that first night. I like to think that the ones with red collars were reorganising and planning what to do but I was not certain. I was no military strategist but even I knew that the fact that we had pulled out a whole division and lost so many tanks had to have made the enemy more confident and the next day we saw the result of that confidence. We found ourselves facing the German tanks of the 21st Panzer Division.

The first we knew of the attack was when artillery from self-propelled guns began to open fire. The shells were coming from the south and east. The enemy spotters on Point 175 were doing a good job and at least four Bedford lorries were hit. We were lucky in that most men either had a trench where they could hide or they had wrecked buildings for cover. Certainly when the shelling stopped and we heard the distant rumble of armoured vehicles, we saw that most of the defenders were still alive. The artillery had been almost indiscriminate but when the tanks and half-tracks arrived they would target the flashes from our weapons. Then we would have to battle in earnest. The platoon was down to twenty-one men and the two companies who defended our part of the defences numbered less than one hundred and fifty men. We had begun the campaign with two hundred and fifty. It meant that Lieutenant Fowler and Sergeant Jackson were with us rather than being further away from us. The lieutenant still had his Sten gun and Sergeant Jackson had managed to acquire an Italian machine pistol. The capture of the airfield had yielded ammunition and so we were better prepared than some other platoons. Roland and I had the captured MG 34 poking through a hole in our little wall. I could still traverse it and I had a good field of fire but we both had some protection from enemy bullets. We had six grenades in a little nest next to us. I had no more German grenades and that was disappointing. I had seen that they could be thrown further than a Mills Bomb.

The Germans liked to attack with panzer grenadiers in half-tracks supporting their tanks. We had heard that when the 22nd Armoured Brigade attacked the Italians at Bir el Gubi it had lost twenty-five tanks because they had no infantry with them. We no

Conscript's Call

longer had tanks to support but when we had we had provided good support. Our tanks had been lost to a tank battle and not to anti-tank guns. The Australians still had a couple of anti-tank guns as well as the Boys rifle. The panzer grenadiers would seek to destroy those rather than risking their tanks.

We had been forced to reorganise. Ray would fire the Boys rifle and Sandy Brown would assist him. Wally would have Norm Thomas as his loader on the Lewis. Bert would load for Harry and Dave Proud would be a runner fetching ammunition and assisting where he could.

"Mark IIIs and a couple of Mark IVs."

Lieutenant Fowler was using his binoculars. Geoff asked, "How can you tell the difference, Sir?"

"You count the wheels. The Mark III has six road wheels and the Mark IV has eight and two of these Mark IVs have the 50 mm gun. This could be interesting, eh chaps?"

I know he was trying to cheer us up with his understatement but the sight of the twenty odd tanks filling the horizon not to mention the panzer grenadiers had me wishing I was somewhere else, anywhere. I turned to see if there were any reserves but I saw no one.

CSM Hutton saw me turn and ran crouching from the headquarters building, "What's up, son? Do you need something?"

I was aware that Roland had turned too and was also looking at the sergeant major as I shook my head, "No, Company Sergeant Major, it's just, well, I am scared. These are German tanks and…"

He put his hand on my shoulder, "Son, we are doing just what your dad did in the Great War. We face our front and do our best."

"Can we win?"

He smiled, "For us, winning is just about surviving. We get through this and we will be stronger for it. Now turn around because I think it is going to get a bit warm."

Almost as though he had ordered it the first of the German tanks opened fire. They belched flame and their shells screamed towards us. The air was filled with such a noise that all I wanted to do was to run away but the sensible side of my brain kicked in

Conscript's Call

and told me that if I did so and left the little nest that Roland and I inhabited then I would be dead. We endured the barrage. I have no idea how long it lasted but it was telling that the Panzers did not move while they fired and sprayed the defences with machine gun shells. As the lieutenant had once explained, the Germans had an even more acute petrol shortage than we did. They would drive only the bare minimum. When they had finished their shelling there was a brief silence or that might have been that because we were temporarily deaf. However, we saw the tanks when they began to move. They must have reloaded their machine guns for they began to fire once more.

Our Boys rifles were only any good when the tanks were close enough to smell their fumes. The Australian guns, however, had no such restrictions and within a short time three of the Mark III tanks were ablaze. The others stopped. The Germans had already lost tanks in Operation Crusader. That we had lost far more was irrelevant. They could not afford to lose tanks and so they sent in their panzer grenadiers and infantry. This time we knew how to fight them for when we had attacked the escarpment we had done what they were doing. Now with more experience we held the advantage for we had machine guns and outranged the machine pistols and Schmeissers.

The Germans came as we had done on the ridge. They ran in pairs and used whatever cover they could get. There was precious little. They were helped for a while by the tanks' machine guns but once they ventured closer the machine guns had to cease. The infantry were heading for the Australian anti-tank guns which had not stopped firing and when a Mark IV brewed up our hope rose with the rising smoke from the stricken tank. The German infantry ran and it was only when they were two hundred yards from us that Captain Whittle shouted, "Queen's Rifles, open fire."

I squeezed the trigger of the captured German weapon. I was now familiar with the buck of the weapon and knew how to use short bursts and traverse. I could hear the twin Lewis gun and the Bren but my battle was with the enemy in my sights. Men fell but that could have been any of our bullets. I just knew I had to stop them getting to the Aussies. I did not see them as men. The attack failed and so the tanks were forced to come once more.

Conscript's Call

Sergeant Jackson shouted, "Ready the Boys rifle. Wait for my order." He was giving orders to more than our platoon. At least two platoon sergeants had been killed and he was not a man to shirk his duty.

Once more the shells flew and the screaming noise returned. The bullets from the German tanks, once they had passed their infantry, began to rattle against our defences and, as they closed, did more damage. I heard the cries of men who were hit and the call for medics.

Roland said, "Should I go?"

"Magazine." As he handed me a magazine I said, "Bones, Dave will let us know if any of our lads are hit. The other sections have their own men. We have to hold here."

He tapped me on the shoulder to let me know he had reloaded and said, quietly, "John, I am scared."

"So am I. There's nowt we can do about that, is there? Get another one ready."

The German infantry were now at the side of their tanks and adding their firepower. Roland and I were lucky that we had made such a good position. While bullets struck the rubble we had used to build our little fort, none ricocheted to end our lives.

"Boys, fire!" Sergeant Jackson had waited until the tanks were less than one hundred and fifty yards from us. It was terrifying but the wait was worth it.

Two Mark III tanks were hit. It was not as spectacular as the ones hit by the Aussies but they were stopped and as more of the anti-tank shells were slammed into what were becoming hulks, the crews abandoned them. When a shell ignited the ammunition in one of them and it blew up before us the blast and fire almost singed our hair. We cheered. I stopped firing because there were no enemies before us. When the tanks that had survived withdrew I could not believe that we were still alive. In all we had damaged and stopped eight tanks. In the scheme of things it might not have been a great number but we had stopped the Germans from breaking through to Tobruk and held the line. It felt like a victory.

Chapter 19

It was, I suppose, a victory but it had come at a cost. The Australians had lost one of their anti-tank guns and we had taken another twelve casualties. Our section seemed to bear a charmed life. We were now the biggest one in the platoon. Men began to call us lucky. Soldiers are never disparaging about luck in the same way that few soldiers are atheists. We were all so close to death that the thought of a benevolent God who would give a promise of eternal life was necessary. Luck was something else we valued. We waited with some trepidation for the next attack for we were now much weakened by the first one. We watched and listened for the sound of enemy aeroplanes or the rumble of armoured vehicles. By late afternoon, however, there was no sign of the German Division and we wondered if they would return or if we had beaten them off.

Lieutenant Fowler was tasked with taking out a patrol to find out where they had gone. Aeroplanes had reported no sign of Germans or Italians in the area but we knew that there were many places where the Germans could hide. He chose our section. Our job was to see if they had gone. We took just rifles but I had my Beretta strapped on my waist. Sergeant Jackson must have told the lieutenant of the way we had operated with Lieutenant Hargreaves for I was commanded to take what the lieutenant called, *'the point'*. It meant I led and he followed behind. Weather was the rearguard and we left Dave Proud to watch the camp and cook our food. Harry would carry the Bren gun but that was our only quick firing weapon.

The bodies we passed were not yet stinking, but they soon would. I did not envy the men who had to shift the dead. Inside the tanks we could smell the burnt bodies. It turned a man's stomach. There were no wounded. They had left with the Germans. When we found a half-track I was waved forward to inspect it. The others covered me. The first thing I did was to check for booby traps. Having set them myself I knew how to spot them. There were none but there was a belt of ammunition for an MG 34 and I hung it from my neck. I waved all clear and

Conscript's Call

stepped from the back of the half-track. We searched as far as the last of the bodies and we stopped.

"Looks like they are gone, Lieutenant."

"It does indeed and the Luftwaffe is no longer with us."

Geoff pointed towards the south east, "Yes, Sir, but aren't there still strong points in the ridge where we took out the radio mast?" The New Zealanders had told us that there were still strong pockets of Germans and Italians at Bardia, Sollum, Halfaya Pass and the ridge.

"I know, but they have no tanks there and we can starve them into submission." He smiled, "You know, Corporal Vane, I feel quite hopeful. I didn't this morning when they attacked but we survived and now I think…" he shook his head, "better not to jinx it. Back to base and report to the major."

We had a day of just waiting for an attack that didn't materialise. At dusk, when lorries arrived from the east with supplies of food and ammunition then we became more optimistic. We even managed to get, that night, six hours of sleep. It felt like a luxury.

The next day was momentous for many reasons. During the day we heard a tank battle. It was to the south of us and we were all on tenterhooks as we heard the now distinctive sounds of British and German tanks duelling. We were not attacked and we stayed in our little fort which now seemed like a home from home. The other news began as a rumour. There was a radio in the Headquarters and any who had business near there always tried to listen. The news that the Japanese had attacked Malaya and were having success came as a shock. The Germans were one thing but the Japanese? The Australian who told us was almost in disbelief. "What are me and my cobbers doing here in the desert when we should be back home? The Japanese won't stop in Malaya. They will want Oz."

That set the rumours flying. It was after dark when Lieutenant Fowler visited us. He gathered the remnants of the platoon around him. "Now, as you all know there are rumours circulating about Malaya." He paused, "I have to tell you that they are true. There is more news. The Japanese have attacked an American naval base in the Hawaiian Islands. The first reports are that they sank more than twenty ships, some of them battleships."

Conscript's Call

There was disbelief, although the Australians' news had partly warned us, but for battleships to have been sunk was unthinkable. He had said ships in the plural. We had lost **HMS Hood** and that had made a major impact. The Germans had lost **Bismarck** and that had seemed incredible, but for the Americans to have lost battleships in the plural was almost unthinkable.

Roland was thoughtful and he asked, "Sir, what does it mean for us?"

"Good question, Poulter, and the honest answer is that I don't know. I am guessing that we and the Americans will fight the Japanese."

I said, "Won't the Australians and New Zealanders be sent home to defend against them?"

"Perhaps, but we still have a war of our own and the other news is that we think the Germans are in the process of withdrawing. Tomorrow we rejoin the remnants of 7th Support Group and the 7th Armoured Division. Together with what is left of the New Zealand Divisions we are to advance." He smiled at me, "Who knows, Sharratt, we might actually have a victory soon."

I shook my head, "Baby steps, Sir. So long as we are not heading east I will be happy."

"I hope to make you more optimistic, Private. I think that by Christmas we shall be celebrating."

We were up early the next day and mounted Morris. The replacement lorries had also brought the rest of the battalion and we had the colonel in command again. I suspected that it would be Major Hill who would make the important decisions. He had to have more experience. We also found that we had armour once more. There were ten Valentine tanks. We learned that while they were not particularly fast they were reliable and had a better gun. The 40 mm was a much better weapon than the 37 mm. Their slower speed would not hurt us overmuch as it meant that when we left our lorries to support them we could keep up with them. They moved at a pace that a runner could maintain.

It took a few days to reach the new German positions at Gazala. Our opponents had prepared the defensive position well and they were dug in. Luckily for us we had more aeroplanes now and they spotted the defences. We did not stumble upon

Conscript's Call

them but would wait until our artillery and the air force had softened them up before we risked armour and men.

Our battalion was closer to the coast road. We waited for the order to attack. At night, far to the south, we saw the flashes of light that told us other elements of our army were trying to outflank the Germans and Italians. I reflected that such words as outflank were unknown to me a little more than a year earlier. I now used it just as familiarly as I might have discussed the drainage at the family farm with my father. Now I spoke with the rest of the section as we champed at the bit. The mere presence of new tanks, the first since we had lost the airfield, had made us optimistic. The tanks' crews themselves were hopeful although, as Weather pointed out, they had not yet come up against German tanks.

We were ordered to prepare for a dawn attack on the coast road. The officers were well briefed and when Lieutenant Fowler came to tell us the plans he was in a good mood. "We leave before dawn and we will follow the Valentines. They have armour piercing rounds and if we meet armour they will give a good account of themselves. We leave the lorries at the jumping off point. This time the drivers will stay with the vehicles. A radio will be left with them so that they can be brought up when we are successful."

I was not alone in noticing the use of the word '*when*'.

"Our job is to threaten to outflank the enemy along the coast. The Royal Navy will be on hand to shell the enemy if we need to call them in. The Indians and the Poles in the south have made the Germans nervous. They do not want to be outflanked."

Sergeant Jackson asked, "Sir, do we have any more anti-tank guns?"

The officer shook his head, "Just the Boys, Sergeant, but they worked well the last time."

He was right but we had been in a well-made defensive position. This time we would be exposed. Panzer grenadiers would be on hand and we would have a real battle on our hands.

That night it was decided that Dave would be the driver. His arm had healed enough to allow him to do it and Bert was adamant that he would not be left behind. He offered him the chance to drive. Bert would make, sometime in the future, a

Conscript's Call

good NCO. Dave happily accepted the task rather than being left behind. In our tent I packed my ammunition and food in my pack. I had six hand grenades. I would have two attached to my webbing. I had spare magazines for my Lee Enfield. When we had been at our fort I had scavenged magazines from the detritus of battle. I had my Beretta and plenty of ammunition. I would leave the German bayonet but take the two German grenades I had taken when searching for Germans after the battle.

My preparations for the battle made, I said my silent prayer. It was then that I realised that my families' faces were fading. I had no photographs to remind me what they looked like and time was playing tricks with me. It struck me that I had not invoked their memory since the attack with Lieutenant Hargreaves. Events had meant I had no time for such reflection. That night I did. I forced myself to picture my mother and remember her pinnies, her hair, the touch of her hand and her smile. As soon as I focussed in on the memories then all their faces came flooding back to me. I could hear my sister's laughter. I could picture my little brother's wild hair. I could even smell the bread baking in the range. They were back. When the bomb had taken everything from me I had felt such despair but now, a year later and having grown to like the men I was fighting with, I felt more hopeful. I might have a life when this war was over. Roland had a future planned. He would take up his university place and become a doctor. Bert was going to open a garage of his own. The others all had hopes and dreams. The end of the war was just as far off as it had ever been but the advance made us more hopeful that we might actually win.

We ate a cold breakfast and then boarded the lorries. When we reached our destination the MG 34 and the Lewis would stay with the vehicle. Harry would have to lug the Bren gun while Ray and Wally would have the Boys. They took it in turns to carry it.

Dawn had barely broken when we left the lorry. We formed up behind one of the Valentines. There were also four armoured cars. They had brave crews for their only hope lay in their speed. Even the 37 mm shells of the Italian tanks could easily penetrate their armour. They were only protected from light machine gunfire and rifles. Roland was the only one who did not carry his

Conscript's Call

rifle in his hands. He always slung it over his shoulder. We had accepted this for he was skilled in all matters medically related. When we came under fire he would hold the weapon but the rest of us would advance with rifles at the ready and with a chambered round. When Roland fired his rifle it was more to annoy the enemy. We waited behind the comforting armour of the Valentines. The whole platoon was there. We now mustered just twenty men. The platoon had a couple of replacements and they were marked by almost pristine uniforms and Lee Enfields that had barely had the grease removed. The rifles had yet to be fired in anger. Sergeant Jackson made sure that the new men were at the rear of our skirmish line.

The Germans along the Gazala line were well dug in. While we had waited for another attack Rommel had been preparing his defences. There were anti-tank pits guarding the tanks. Luckily the commander of the Valentines, alerted by the armoured car, stopped beyond the effective range of the guns and we were waved forward. The German tanks waited just behind the anti-tank pits. There were machine guns too. Captain Whittle had the Bren gunners set up as soon as we took fire and we found whatever cover we could. To help us the Valentines sent HE at the enemy. The pits were protected but not the slit trenches. The mortar companies were summoned. The two-inch mortar had a range of four to five hundred yards. Without a spotter much luck was needed to hit a target but as soon as they began to drop their shells close to the pits we noticed that the machine gun fire diminished. Our Bren guns were largely ineffective too and so Captain Whittle ordered the mortars to send smoke and as soon as the ground was filled with smoke he led us forward.

The machine gunners knew that we would be coming but they had no visual target and the chances of being hit were diminished by the billowing smoke, but men still fell. When I saw the flash from the end of the MG 34 I took out one of the German grenades. Their design facilitated a longer throw and after arming it I hurled it as high and far as I could.

"Grenade!"

Everyone dropped thinking that it was a Mills Bomb. I levelled my rifle and as the explosion shifted the smoke a little, I fired half a magazine at the German machine gun post. Without

Conscript's Call

waiting for orders I ran on. I knew from the last battle that after an explosion men are disorientated and I took advantage of that. I made it to within forty yards of the enemy positions before I heard the Germans order their men to open fire. In my prone position I raised my rifle. The barrel of the MG 34 swung ominously in my direction. I fired at the barrel. I had fired one and knew that the gunner would have his head close to it. When the barrel fell back, firing through the actions of a dying man, I rose to my feet and ran on. As I neared the position I dropped my rifle, armed a Mills Bomb and after shouting, "Grenade!" threw myself to the ground. The sandbags of the machine gun emplacement took some of the force of the explosion but most of it was taken by the crew and riflemen. I picked up my rifle and peered over the top. They were all dead or dying.

The next machine gun began to open fire but by then I was sheltered behind the sandbags. The rest of the section arrived. They had used the two explosions to follow me through the smoke. My two grenades had added smoke and dust.

Ray laughed, "You mad bugger!

Corporal Vane said, "It was brave, I'll say that. Anyone hurt?" When there was no reply he said, "Right, Bones, pick up your rifle. You have soldier work to do. Harry, set the Bren up here. We will be able to enfilade the next machine gun."

"Right, Corp."

"Brown, Salter and Jennings, let's see if you can throw as far as Hawkeye did. Send some grenades to the next machine gun." The three would enjoy the competition.

The Germans had made sandbagged defences and the machine guns were there to protect the anti-tank guns from infantry. Having taken one such post we had weakened the integrity of the line of defences. There were four or five machine gun posts and four anti-tank ones. Until the machine guns were neutralised we could do nothing about the anti-tank guns. The German gunners were firing at their own position but the dead men within and the sandbags meant that even the heavier machine guns that they were using could not reach us.

Geoff Vane had grown into a confident and competent corporal, "The rest of you, on my command, a mad minute." A mad minute was where you fired and chambered until your

Conscript's Call

magazines were empty. It took a brave man to stand and endure that. "Now!"

Our five rifles, not to mention the Bren gun, sent a hailstorm of .303 bullets at the nearest German gun. All I saw were the helmets behind sandbags and the barrels of their weapons. After the first few shots the three with the grenades stood and hurled them high. The fact that the three men were different heights, builds and had different strengths meant that the three Mills Bombs would not explode in the same place. It was what we wanted.

We needed no warning and we all ducked down. The three grenades did not go off simultaneously. It was a rapid ripple of explosions but one of them must have ignited some ammunition or perhaps the Germans had petrol to accelerate a fire as we did. Whatever it was caused the whole pit to erupt in fire and flames.

As with my attack, speed was of the essence. Geoff roared, "Harry and Bert, cover us. Charge!"

The Bren gun chattered and we raced to the next gun pit. It was carnage within. The three grenades had killed them all and, even better was the fact that we were now in a position where we could enfilade the nearest anti-tank gun.

"Harry! Shift yourself. The rest of you, open fire." Harry picked up the Bren and raced to join us.

The German anti-tank gun had protection from the front but not the side. The gunners reached for their rifles but they were too late. Even without Harry and Bert we still had enough rifles to pour bullets into them. Two survived and raised their hands and began to walk away from the scene of carnage towards us. It was at that moment that three Mk IIIs opened up with their machine guns. We were luckier than the Germans. The opening shower of bullets cut them down as the gun traversed to try to kill us. We all lay on the ground and the bullets passed over us. Suddenly there were six distinctive cracks. The Valentines, seeing the threat of an anti-tank gun eliminated, moved forward. The three German tanks were all hit and as the Valentines hit their side armour they were able to penetrate. Two brewed up immediately. The third tried to traverse its turret and couldn't. The Boys rifle held by Ray sent a shell into the track and that enabled another Valentine to end its threat. The other German tanks, now outnumbered and lacking protection, began to move away. The enemy machine guns opened fire but the gap we had created meant that there was a clear passage for our armour. The machine guns in the Valentine scythed through the gunners both anti-tank and machine gun. Even the armoured cars were able to move safely. The column poured through the middle and Germans began to surrender.

"Poulter, over to you!" Weather was grinning. Roland stood and commanded the Germans to lay down their weapons and head towards us. We all levelled our guns at them.

Weather took out a cigarette, "Nice shot, Ray."

Glass Man also took out a cigarette, "I thought there is no point trying to punch a hole in it and the tracks stop it moving." We were all in a good mood. This felt like a victory.

"Having a nice time are we, lads? Put those cigarettes out! This was a nice piece of work but the battle is not over, yet."

The smokers immediately obeyed as CSM Hutton and more men moved up to join us. We were the most advanced section in the battalion. "Sorry, Sergeant Major."

"Escort your prisoners to the rear and then rejoin us." A rare smile creased his face, "Smartly done. All of you."

We had twenty prisoners to escort. Roland was a different man when he spoke German. He seemed far less diffident and was far more confident. As we walked he asked, "John, did you not think you might be killed when you attacked the first gun position?"

I shrugged, "I didn't have time to think about it. If you think too much you hesitate and hesitation, in my experience, is fatal. Better to do something rather than wait for it to happen to you. Besides, I knew that the chances of being hit were slimmer thanks to the smoke the mortars laid down and I ran fast."

"I am scared that I will be killed."

"Me too but worrying about things won't keep you alive." I sighed, "It must be something inside me I got from my dad, I don't know, but I think I was meant to be a soldier. I don't want to die but I would rather do something than await my fate."

Once we reached the lorries we saw that Dave and the other drivers had a brew going on. Weather said to the corporal in

Conscript's Call

charge of the lorries, "We were told to bring them here and then get back to the front."

He nodded, "Half a mo' and I will get on the radio to get some escorts for Jerry. We broke through then?"

"We did but CSM Hutton reckons it is not over yet."

He sniffed and shook his head, "Never satisfied."

Half of us had a mug of tea while the others watched the prisoners and then, when the corporal returned, swapped over.

"Some Redcaps coming to take over."

Wally grinned, "Then we can't rush back, can we?"

An hour had passed by the time the MPs arrived to take charge of our prisoners. By then we had not only managed a brew but Dave had made us some sandwiches. Our mad attack had paid dividends and we headed back to the battle a little fuller than the rest of our comrades.

When we reached the rest of the company we saw that they had advanced just half a mile from where we had taken the prisoners. I saw a brewed up armoured car almost five hundred yards ahead of us and I was aware that everyone was waiting. Weather said, "What is it, Sarge?"

Sergeant Jackson said, "A minefield. Luckily we only lost one armoured car. We are waiting for the engineers to come and clear it."

Just then there was a single shot and Corporal Best spun round. He had been hit by a bullet. We all took cover. I sheltered behind a Valentine. Lieutenant Fowler raced up. He pointed, "There is a sort of tower ahead. It is half a mile away and they must have a sniper there. We have to shift him before the engineers get here." He looked at me, "I think this is a job for Hawkeye."

Sergeant Jackson said, "But the minefield, Sir."

"I think, Sergeant, that they are meant for armoured vehicles and not infantry."

Wally pointed, "Then why don't the Valentines follow the tracks of the German armour. They should be safe."

Lieutenant Fowler said, "And we can't afford to lose these tanks. We have precious few of them as it is."

247

Conscript's Call

Just then the artillery brought up a twenty-five pounder. Sergeant Jackson said, confidently, "These lads will soon have that tower down, Sir."

Even as the gun crew swung the gun around there was not only a single shot from the sniper but a burst from a machine gun. They had more than one man in the tower. Three of the gunners fell. The officer in charge of the gun said, "Sorry, no can do." They began to hitch up the gun as quickly as they could and even as the machine gun rattled more rounds at them they were driving to a safe distance from the threat, the wounded men in their vehicle.

"Sir, can't we ask the air force…?"

"They are busy in the south. This is a minor engagement. The real battle is to the south." He smiled at me, "Look, Private, we will lay down a smokescreen and you and I will follow the tracks to that broken down armoured car. We can use that for shelter." I heard the truck with the engineers pull up and even before they had disembarked there was a rattle and a crack as the windscreen was hit and the driver shouted in pain. That decided me. The men in the tower had a clear field of fire and their elevation gave them a dramatic advantage. All that we had achieved in our attack so far would be rendered useless if we couldn't clear the minefield. The longer we waited the more chance there was of the Germans bringing up more tanks or sending the Luftwaffe to finish us off.

"Right, Sir."

"Good lad. I will go first, okay?"

"Okay." I took off my pack and my helmet. I donned my comforter and picked up some mud to smear on my face.

Sergeant Jackson shouted to the others who were still sheltering behind the other armoured cars and the tanks. "Get Lieutenant Foster to send smoke."

The Valentine behind which we were sheltering was the closest vehicle to the tower. It fired a round and hit the tower but it appeared to do no damage. The tower had buildings before it and they would absorb any damage before the tower became unsafe. I heard another round going into the breach but they had to have had a spotter in the tower. A moment or two later German artillery began sending rounds at the tank. Although

Conscript's Call

they did not hit the target, they came perilously close. The commander rose from the turret, "Sorry, lads, too hot for us. We will move back where we can be hull down." The shells continued for a few moments as the Valentine reversed to the safety of the hollow where the other tanks waited.

We moved out of the way as he reversed. Lieutenant Fowler had picked up a rifle. "It is now or never, Sharratt."

We heard the whump of the mortars and as soon as the smoke began billowing I nodded and as he ran I followed him. The sniper would not send bullets blindly and the machine gun did not have the accuracy. It had hit the gunners and the lorry because it had sprayed. I heard it chatter and bark. We had a chance, a slim one but a chance, nonetheless. I kept my eyes on the tyre tracks made by the armoured car. I did not run between them but followed the actual track.

We managed to make the relative safety of the CS9. The armoured car was still hot although the fire had burned out. The tower was just three hundred yards away. We stayed behind the armoured car without moving. The machine gun opened fire again as the smoke thinned but the bullets were sent blindly at the smoke. The dead crew were still inside. I would not risk going within. I moved to the right-hand side of the armoured car and peered over the bonnet. Had I been wearing my helmet then I might have been seen. As it was I knew that I would be barely visible until I raised my rifle.

I saw the lieutenant reaching for his binoculars and I shouted, "Don't!" He looked at me. I softened my tone, "The light might reflect off them, Sir. He doesn't know where we are yet. As soon as I open fire he will and then the machine gun will open fire. When I know where he is I will try to get him and if I succeed, then I will move to somewhere I can hit the machine gunner."

"Right, sorry, Sharratt, I wasn't thinking."

I moved my head imperceptibly as I had done when hunting rabbits. I peered at the tower. I saw the machine gun first. It was not at the top of the tower but slightly lower down. There were sandbags protecting it. I moved my eyes and saw the sniper. He was at the top of the tower and was peering through his telescopic sight. I saw the light reflecting from it. He did not know where we were and the barrel moved in an arc as he sought

Conscript's Call

us. I estimated the range at between two hundred and eighty and three hundred yards. I slowly moved my head down and then adjusted the sights. I had to be quick. I would need to work the bolt quickly while keeping the barrel as still as I could. I needed a distraction.

"Sir, could you lob a grenade as far as you can to the far side of our position, the side away from me. I want his attention there. He might think we have stepped on a mine."

"Good idea." He laid down his rifle and took a grenade. Smiling he said, "Takes me back to my cricketing days. Ready."

I had to trust that he could throw it a long way and that I would be protected from the blast by the armour of the Morris. "Now." I heard the handle as it flew off. I counted to three and then slowly raised the rifle. The explosion was a good forty yards away. The lieutenant had a good arm. I sighted the sniper who was looking for us where the explosion had taken place. I squeezed the trigger, pulled back the bolt and sent three shots at the head. The first one hit him as did the second. I saw him tumble from the tower like a puppet whose strings have been cut. The machine gun's barrel swung in my direction and I ducked and then rolled beneath the Morris armoured car. I heard the machine gun bullets striking the bonnet. There was a hiss as one bullet hit the radiator and steam poured out but I was safe. I rolled to the other side. It was not as good a position but I had the body of the car above to protect me. I also had the steam from the radiator which helped to obscure me. I slowly raised the rifle. I could not see the whole of the two men operating the machine gun but I could see their heads. I also gambled, as I chambered another round, that any bullets which missed would strike rock and ricochets could cause as much damage as the actual bullets. I took a breath and then emptied my magazine at the tower. I hit something because a cloud of dust could be seen, as I loaded another magazine. Then I saw one of the men and the gun tumble from the tower. I heard a cheer and then the Valentines moved up. They formed a line close to the starting point for our attack and they all opened fire. Their collective shells brought down the tower. The German artillery had lost their spotter.

Conscript's Call

I pulled myself from beneath the Morris. Lieutenant Fowler held his hand to help me to my feet. "Outstanding, Sharratt, you are well named as Hawkeye. You should have a medal for this."

"I will be happy just to wake up in the morning, Sir. That could have gone badly wrong. If they had sent artillery shells at us..."

"Quite. Come on, let's go back and then the engineers can do their job."

There were smiles from the rest of the platoon and Captain Whittle came over to say, "Well done, to both of you."

I just nodded and endured the slaps on my back. Sergeant Jones, however, made my day. I had not seen him since the attack on the airfield. He came over and just said, "Your dad would have been proud of you, well done...Hawkeye."

Conscript's Call

Epilogue

With the minefield cleared we moved forward and that was the first of the enemy dominoes to fall. The Germans feared being outflanked on two sides and they retreated, not just a couple of miles but a couple of hundred to El Agheila. They were seen and pursued by the RAF. We did not chase them but others did. Instead we made a camp by the sea at Gazala. With Tobruk relieved we had achieved what we had intended to when Crusader began. The general sent food for us to enjoy a war time Christmas. We had all lost track of time. The only date that had stuck in our heads was December 7th the day, we now learned, when America had joined our war and Britain had declared war on Japan. This war had truly become global. We consolidated our position in the positions previously occupied by the Germans and it was while we were there after enjoying a Christmas that was warm rather than snowy that we heard more snippets of news, all of it good. Bardia fell on the 2nd of January and the fortified Halfaya Pass and the escarpment fell a week later.

For me the action at Gazala felt like a victory and I felt like a soldier. We were two hundred miles behind the new front line which had moved all the way across Libya. We had played a major part in that victory. We had begun life a year ago as conscripts. We had learned to fight and now we knew how to make war. We thought of ourselves as veterans. More importantly, so did the men I respected most, the NCOs of the regiment. We had good officers but we all believed that it was the sergeants and corporals who kept us alive. I was considered a hero but I did not feel like one. The action that was most talked about was the elimination of the tower with its sniper and machine gun. The riskiest part of the taking out of the sniper had been getting to the armoured car and Lieutenant Fowler had been a walking shield. If they had blanketed the area with shells I might have died but that would have meant they destroyed their own minefield. I had just done my job but as Sergeant Jones had said, my father would have been proud of me and that was enough. The war was not over and Rommel had not finished

252

with us but now I knew we could beat the Germans and there was hope where before there had been only despair.

The End

Glossary

AP – armour piercing
BD - Battle Dress
bully beef - beef and water to make a soup and cook meat
cobber - (slang - Australian) friend
compo - (slang) composite rations
conchies - (slang) conscientious objectors
CSM - Company Sergeant Major
dhobi - (slang) washing
HE – high explosive
kai - (slang) cocoa- Royal Navy
KD - Khaki Drill
Nebby - (slang) nosey
Redcaps - MPs
RTR - Royal Tank Regiment
RSM - Regimental Sergeant Major
sparrow's fart - (slang) early morning
stag - (slang) duty/watch
tankers - men in tanks

Conscript's Call

Historical Note

As far as I know there was never a regiment called the Queen's Rifles. There is a Canadian regiment called the Queen's Own Rifles and a British regiment called the Queen's Westminster. I have made up the regiment but the structure and the training reflect the time. I have used the regiment to illustrate the war in Greece, Crete and North Africa.

The Frontier Wire was a 168-mile obstacle in Italian Libya, along the length of the border of British-held Egypt, running from El Ramleh, in the Gulf of Sollum (between Bardia and Sollum) south to Jaghbub parallel to the 25th meridian east, the Libya–Egypt and Libya–Sudan borders. The Italians had built forts along it.

The information about the explosives comes from a lecture given at Lochailort Fieldcraft Course in March 1941. It comes from a great book, ***The Commando Pocket Manual***.

The three operations I mention in the book were Brevity, Battleaxe and Crusader. Brevity was in May, Battleaxe in June and Crusader in November.

Losses: (Dead, wounded, missing and captured)

Brevity: the allies lost 5 tanks and 208 men. The Axis Forces lost 3 tanks and 605 men.

Battleaxe: The allies lost 98 tanks, 36 Aircraft and 969 men. The Axis Forces lost 12 tanks, 19 aircraft ad 1270 men.

Crusader: The allies lost 800 tanks, 300 aircraft and 17,700 men. The Axis forces lost 340 tanks, 560 aircraft (destroyed or abandoned) and 38,200 men.

The losses in Crusader for both sides were eye watering.

It was only when I was on my second edit that I remembered where most of the information in my head came from. While much of it came for the books listed below, more came from men I knew who had served in the desert. I worked at Fiberglass in the late 60s and many of the older men who worked there had served in the war. Two who had served in the desert were my Uncle Bill and Arthur Cartledge who, coincidentally, published a book of poetry. The stories they told me stayed in my head. Then there was the Sprayhurst Club in St Helens. It was also called the United Services Club and many of those who drank there had been in the war. They represented men who had served in the Army, Navy, Royal Air Force and even Combined operations, my dad. They told me stories, normally, as they played dominoes. It was from them that I learned of the camaraderie and the banter that existed during the war. They still bantered and joked with each other in the club. Navy and Army would happily insult each other and then join ranks to lambast the Air Force. It was their way. I never heard stories about firing weapons and killing the enemy. I heard stories about cooking with whatever was to hand. When I moved to the north east a pub landlord, a mad little Scotsman called Alec, told me how, when serving it Italy, he had taken a Sten gun to hunt chickens. Those were the stories men brought home from the war. They were not stories about battles or fighting. They were tales like that. They were stories of how a drunk stoker coming back to a ship dropped his hat in the drink, dived in, retrieved and marched aboard, soaking wet but knowing he would not be before the captain for losing his cap. These stories stuck with me and while they are not the meat and potatoes of my stories, I hope they are the gravy that makes them pertinent and real.

Books used in the research
Military Slang - Lee Pemberton
Historical Atlas of World War 2 - Swanston and Swanston
World War 2 - Ivor Mantale
Desert Rats - Tim Moreman
The British Army 1939-45 (1) - Brayley and Chappell
The British Army 1939-45 (2) - Brayley and Chappell
The Lond Range Desert Group - Charles Rivers Editors
The Special Air Service - Shortt and McBride
German Tanks of WW2 - Moore and Bocquelet
World War II Tanks: Western Allies - Porter
Jane's Fighting Ships of World War 2
World War II aircraft - Robert Jackson
Army Commandos 1940-45 - Mike Chappell
The Commando Pocket Manual 1940-45
Military Small Arms of the 20th Century - Hogg and Weeks

Conscript's Call

The German Army 1939-45 (1) - Thomas and Andrew
The Second World War- a Miscellany - Ferguson

Griff Hosker
January 2025

Other books by Griff Hosker

If you enjoyed reading this book, then why not read another one by the author?

Ancient History

Roman Rebellion
(The Roman Republic 100 BC-60 BC)
Legionary

The Sword of Cartimandua Series
(Germania and Britannia 50 A.D. – 128 A.D.)
Ulpius Felix- Roman Warrior (prequel)
The Sword of Cartimandua
The Horse Warriors
Invasion Caledonia
Roman Retreat
Revolt of the Red Witch
Druid's Gold
Trajan's Hunters
The Last Frontier
Hero of Rome
Roman Hawk
Roman Treachery
Roman Wall
Roman Courage

The Wolf Brethren series
(Britain in the late 6th Century)
Saxon Dawn
Saxon Revenge
Saxon England
Saxon Blood
Saxon Slayer
Saxon Slaughter
Saxon Bane

Conscript's Call

Saxon Fall: Rise of the Warlord
Saxon Throne
Saxon Sword

Medieval History

The Dragon Heart Series
Viking Slave *
Viking Warrior *
Viking Jarl *
Viking Kingdom *
Viking Wolf *
Viking War*
Viking Sword
Viking Wrath
Viking Raid
Viking Legend
Viking Vengeance
Viking Dragon
Viking Treasure
Viking Enemy
Viking Witch
Viking Blood
Viking Weregeld
Viking Storm
Viking Warband
Viking Shadow
Viking Legacy
Viking Clan
Viking Bravery

Norseman
Norse Warrior*

The Norman Genesis Series
Hrolf the Viking *
Horseman *
The Battle for a Home *
Revenge of the Franks *

Conscript's Call

The Land of the Northmen
Ragnvald Hrolfsson
Brothers in Blood
Lord of Rouen
Drekar in the Seine
Duke of Normandy
The Duke and the King

Danelaw
(England and Denmark in the 11th Century)
Dragon Sword *
Oathsword *
Bloodsword *
Danish Sword*
The Sword of Cnut*

New World Series
Blood on the Blade *
Across the Seas *
The Savage Wilderness *
The Bear and the Wolf *
Erik The Navigator *
Erik's Clan *
The Last Viking*
The Vengeance Trail *

The Conquest Series
(Normandy and England 1050-1100)
Hastings*
Conquest*
Rebellion

The Aelfraed Series
(Britain and Byzantium 1050 A.D. - 1085 A.D.)
Housecarl *
Outlaw *
Varangian *

The Reconquista Chronicles

Conscript's Call

(Spain in the 11ᵗʰ Century)
Castilian Knight *
El Campeador *
The Lord of Valencia *

The Anarchy Series
(England 1120-1180)
English Knight *
Knight of the Empress *
Northern Knight *
Baron of the North *
Earl *
King Henry's Champion *
The King is Dead *
Warlord of the North*
Enemy at the Gate*
The Fallen Crown*
Warlord's War*
Kingmaker*
Henry II
Crusader
The Welsh Marches
Irish War
Poisonous Plots
The Princes' Revolt
Earl Marshal
The Perfect Knight

Border Knight
(1182-1300)
Sword for Hire *
Return of the Knight *
Baron's War *
Magna Carta *
Welsh Wars *
Henry III *
The Bloody Border *
Baron's Crusade*
Sentinel of the North*

261

Conscript's Call

War in the West*
Debt of Honour*
The Blood of the Warlord
The Fettered King
de Montfort's Crown
The Ripples of Rebellion

Sir John Hawkwood Series
(France and Italy 1339- 1387)
Crécy: The Age of the Archer *
Man At Arms *
The White Company *
Leader of Men *
Tuscan Warlord *
Condottiere*
Legacy*

Lord Edward's Archer
Lord Edward's Archer *
King in Waiting *
An Archer's Crusade *
Targets of Treachery *
The Great Cause *
Wallace's War *
The Hunt*
The Prince and the Archer*

Struggle for a Crown
(1360- 1485)
Blood on the Crown *
To Murder a King *
The Throne *
King Henry IV *
The Road to Agincourt *
St Crispin's Day *
The Battle for France *
The Last Knight *
Queen's Knight *
The Knight's Tale *

Conscript's Call

Tales from the Sword I
(*Short stories from the Medieval period*)

Tudor Warrior series
(*England and Scotland in the late 15th and early 16th century*)
Tudor Warrior *
Tudor Spy *
Flodden*

Conquistador
(*England and America in the 16th Century*)
Conquistador *
The English Adventurer *

English Mercenary
(*The 30 Years War and the English Civil War*)
Horse and Pistol*
Captain of Horse

Modern History

East Indiaman Saga
East Indiaman*
The Tiger and the Thief

The Napoleonic Horseman Series
Chasseur à Cheval
Napoleon's Guard
British Light Dragoon
Soldier Spy
1808: The Road to Coruña
Talavera
The Lines of Torres Vedras
Bloody Badajoz
The Road to France
Waterloo

The Lucky Jack American Civil War series

Conscript's Call

Rebel Raiders
Confederate Rangers
The Road to Gettysburg

Soldier of the Queen series
Soldier of the Queen*
Redcoat's Rifle*
Omdurman*
Desert War*
An Officer and a Gentleman

The British Ace Series
(World War 1)
1914
1915 Fokker Scourge
1916 Angels over the Somme
1917 Eagles Fall
1918 We will remember them
From Arctic Snow to Desert Sand
Wings over Persia

Combined Operations series
(1940-1951)
Commando *
Raider *
Behind Enemy Lines*
Dieppe
Toehold in Europe
Sword Beach
Breakout
The Battle for Antwerp
King Tiger
Beyond the Rhine
Korea
Korean Winter

Rifleman Series
(WW2 1940-45)
Conscript's Call

Conscript's Call

Tales from the Sword II
(Short stories from the Modern period)

Books marked thus *, are also available in the audio format.
For more information on all of the books then please visit the
author's website at www.griffhosker.com where there is a link to
contact him or visit his Facebook page: Griff Hosker at Sword
Books or follow him on Twitter: @HoskerGriff or follow Sword
Books @swordbooksltd
If you wish to be on the mailing list then contact the author
through his website.

Printed in Dunstable, United Kingdom